Watching her gaze, he took that very finger, drew it into his mouth, and licked it. "Aye."

"There's more lying under the surface with you, whether you realize it or not. I saw it in your eyes the first time we met."

"But you're who I desire now," he whispered. Indeed, this woman was too perceptive. But two could play her game. He slid his hand around the back of her neck and captured her lips. And this time he didn't toy about. Taking command, he devoured her mouth and showed her exactly how passionate a kiss could be.

"See, lass?" he growled, forcing himself to ease away.

Her lips parted as she leaned toward him as if asking for more.

He raised her fingers upward. Watching her, he kissed each knuckle, slowly, seductively, showing her just how much he looked forward to their wedding night.

PRAISE FOR AMY JARECKI

THE HIGHLAND RENEGADE

"Flirtatious, sensuous romance and adventure fill the pages of this mesmerizing historical, and the undercurrent of Jacobite rebellion raises the tension."
—Publishers Weekly

THE HIGHLAND CHIEFTAIN

A "fast-paced, expertly crafted romance."
—Publishers Weekly

"*The Highland Chieftain* was a smoking romance that was both endearing and sexy!"
—The Genre Minx

THE HIGHLAND GUARDIAN

"Magnetic, sexy romance is at the heart of this novel, made complete with a cast of richly depicted characters, authentic historical detail, and a fast-moving plot."
—Publishers Weekly

"A true gem when it comes to compelling, dynamic characters.... With clever, enchanting writing, elements of life-or-death danger and a romance that takes both Reid and Audrey completely by surprise, *The Highland Guardian* is an historical romance so on point it'll leave readers awestruck."

—*BookPage*

THE HIGHLAND COMMANDER

"Readers craving history entwined with their romance (a la *Outlander*) will find everything they desire in Jarecki's latest. Scottish romance fans rejoice."

—*RT Book Reviews*

"Sizzles with romance . . . Jarecki brings the novel to life with vivid historical detail."

—*Publishers Weekly*

THE HIGHLAND DUKE

"Readers will admire plucky Akira, who, despite her poverty, is fiercely independent and is determined to be no man's mistress. The romance is scintillating and moving, enhanced by fast-paced suspense."

—*Publishers Weekly*

"This story was so much more than a romance, it was full of intrigue, excitement and drama. . . . a fantastic read that I fully recommend."

—*Buried Under Romance*

THE
HIGHLAND
EARL

THE
HIGHLAND
EARL

A Lords of the Highlands Novel

AMY JARECKI

FOREVER
New York Boston

Copyright © 2019 by Amy Jarecki

Cover design by Elizabeth Turner Stokes
Cover illustration by Craig White
Cover copyright © 2019 by Hachette Book Group, Inc.

Forever
Hachette Book Group
1290 Avenue of the Americas, New York, NY 10104
read-forever.com
twitter.com/readforeverpub

First Edition: June 2019

Forever is an imprint of Grand Central Publishing. The Forever name and logo are trademarks of Hachette Book Group, Inc.

The publisher is not responsible for websites (or their content) that are not owned by the publisher.

The Hachette Speakers Bureau provides a wide range of authors for speaking events. To find out more, go to www.hachettespeakersbureau.com or call (866) 376-6591.

ISBNs: 978-1-5387-1602-1 (mass market), 978-1-5387-1601-4 (ebook)

Printed in the United States of America

OPM

10 9 8 7 6 5 4 3 2 1

ATTENTION CORPORATIONS AND ORGANIZATIONS:
Most Hachette Book Group books are available at quantity discounts with bulk purchase for educational, business, or sales promotional use. For information, please call or write:

Special Markets Department, Hachette Book Group
1290 Avenue of the Americas, New York, NY 10104
Telephone: 1-800-222-6747 Fax: 1-800-477-5925

To the best parents in the world.

They gave me every opportunity they could afford and encouraged me to step outside the norm and stretch my boundaries. Mom wanted me to be an oboist. Dad wanted me to be a professional golfer. Neither wanted me to be an author, but they love me anyway. Both of my parents enjoyed enriching lives and Mom was given the Lifetime Achievement Award by her alma mater, Whitman College, in 2016. Dad was an aerial photographer in the Korean War and an elementary school principal. He was diagnosed with Alzheimer's in 2004, yet by strength of mind, his decline has been very slow. Mom fell twice in the past two years, first breaking her hip, then her pelvis. She now has dementia. It is difficult to see one's parents go into decline, but important to remember and respect their achievements, their strength of character, their support and love. I'll never forget Dad singing with me at the top of his lungs in the car or Mom taking me to the theater where she was directing a Pirates of Penzance *(and I had every word memorized). Thank you, Mom and Dad. You are treasured in my heart always.*

Acknowledgments

I can hardly believe this is my sixth novel with Forever. Writing for a New York publisher comes with challenges all its own, but each one is a step toward creating a better book. Heartfelt thanks to all the hardworking and dedicated people who have helped with this novel. I am truly grateful. To my tenacious agent, Elaine Spencer. To Kim Rozzell, a brilliant new addition to my marketing team. To my wonderful editor Leah Hultenschmidt, who gave me a well-deserved thrashing with my first draft, only to make this story better. I truly appreciate her hard work and dedication to making every scene meaningful. To the Grand Central Publishing art department, especially Craig White and Elizabeth Turner Stokes—the cover of *The Highland Earl* reaches a new height of smoldering, especially with the hot pink title! To Estelle Hallick— how she juggles the marketing for so many books is mind boggling; and to Mari Okuda and Karen P. Thompson for their fastidious and diligent copyediting. Thank you, all!

Chapter One

*E*velyn hesitated before she accepted the glass of honeyed lemon juice from the Frenchman. A royal ball was no place to demonstrate malcontent, so she held her drink aloft in a halfhearted toast while turning her head away from the crowd. "I wonder how many people suffered to bring us the queen's latest fancy."

Mr. Claude Dubois took a drink for himself and returned her gesture with an arch of a wiry eyebrow. "You grow bold, my lady."

"I am impatient."

"The bane of youth." As Dubois spoke, his keen gaze scanned the ballroom. "Tell me, what news from Nottingham?" In truth, the French emissary inquired as to the present status of her father's corrupt dealings.

Evelyn sipped her drink, the tartness tickling the recesses of her jaw. "Nothing of late. Though I expect mail in a fortnight." With these words she confirmed a shipment arriving from one of the Duke of Kingston-upon-Hull's many vessels.

"Are you anticipating anything of particular interest?" he asked, not surprisingly. The Frenchman's influence in the past year had been instrumental in raising support for the Jacobite cause, which included Evelyn's particular passion: to end the aristocracy's misuse of power. She herself had witnessed the devastating effects of her very father's treachery.

Checking over her shoulder, Evelyn confirmed no eavesdroppers lurked nearby. "Silk."

"Hmm." Mr. Dubois snatched a savory pastry from a passing footman's tray and popped it into his mouth. "At least it is not wool. And thank heavens for your fine work, my lady. If those two ships laden with wool had been smuggled into England without paying import duties, Scottish crofters would have gone hungry for an entire year."

Buoyed by a sense of achievement, Evelyn followed the emissary's line of sight to her father—Hull, as his peers called him. Beside Papa stood a well-dressed courtier with whom the duke was deep in conversation. Finding her father's companion to be an *unusually* attractive gentleman, she drew in a sharp breath. Truly, he might possibly be the most striking man she'd ever seen. A head taller than Papa, he wore a fashionable blond periwig and an expertly tailored suit of blue silk. And by the breadth of his shoulders, he appeared as if he could challenge any man in the hall to a duel of swords and win. Obviously a peer, the courtier had neither hair nor thread out of place.

"My," she said, the admiration in her tone unmasked. "Perhaps the ball will not be dull after all."

Mr. Dubois turned his back to the object of her admiration. "Do you have any clue who that is having a word with your father?"

Evelyn licked the sweet tartness from her lips. "I cannot say I do."

"*Alors*, he has been away since your arrival in London. Though now he has returned, I imagine your path will cross with the Secretary of State for Scotland now and again."

She nearly choked on her next sip. "That is the Earl of Mar?" Yes, John Erskine was oft in the papers—but not in a good way. The Highlander sat on Queen Anne's cabinet and had to be one of the absolute last men Evelyn would ever trust.

"Bobbin' John, the Scots call him. I'm surprised to see the man so soon. His wife's death was a shocking loss."

"He's a widower?" Unable to help herself, Evelyn stole another glance at Mar. In fact, it was all she could do not to openly gawk. No, she'd never met a man such as he. Beautiful, yet masculine. His face youthful, yet sophisticated and wise. The inability to put her finger on what made the earl more alluring caused her to stare more. "Poor man."

"Poor boys."

"He has children?"

"Two young sons."

"It must be devastating for them all. And the boys left without a mother." Attempting to mask her overt staring, Evelyn took another sip of lemon juice and watched the man from behind her glass. "I quite expected the Earl of

Mar to be a short, gaunt man of advanced age, but he is rather imposing, is he not?"

Mr. Dubois's stout stature better reflected her imaginings. "I have no doubt he will soon be the most eligible widower in Britain if he is not already. 'Tis a shame no one knows for certain where his loyalties lie."

"Hmm." Evelyn forced herself to look at the French emissary, who now appeared far more wizened than he had two minutes ago. "I was merely appreciating the workmanship of Mar's tailor. A man with the earl's vacillating politics could never be of interest to me."

"I would think no less, though you'd be hard-pressed to find a husband with more influence over the crown." Mr. Dubois grinned and deviously waggled his gray brows. "Imagine the mischief in which you might embroil yourself under his roof."

If only they weren't at a ball with dozens of nobles surrounding them in courtly finery, she might have thwacked the Frenchman with her fan. "Is my father's roof not enough?"

"Pray, what is your age, my lady? You will have no choice but to marry soon." Dubois knew her age.

"I'm in no hurry," she said as Papa nodded at her, his gray periwig shifting with the movement.

"See there, the duke is coming this way. Oh my, that is interesting. Mar is on his heels. I'll bid you *bonsoir*." Mr. Dubois bowed. "My lady."

She curtsied. "Monsieur."

"There you are, my dear." Father approached, grinning as if he had embarked upon a profitable scheme with the nobleman. "Allow me to introduce the Earl of Mar."

Evelyn's gaze shifted to the man. With a sharp squeeze

of her stomach, a gasp slipped through her lips before she had a chance to suppress her reaction.

Beneath a striking slash of brows, hawkish blue eyes stared at her with the intensity of a pointer homing in on his prey, yet his gaze was guarded, tormented, or wounded by something devastating. That such a tall and braw man might be cut to the quick by *anyone* was beyond Evelyn's imagination. He must have truly loved his wife. And yet, if her intuition was right, there appeared to be more underlying this man's grief. Something layered and complex.

After a pause, which for all Evelyn knew may have lasted ten minutes while she pondered the possibilities of her assessment, the corners of Mar's lips turned upward—a polite smile but still guarded. He stepped forward, grasped her hand, and applied a well-practiced kiss. A bit of a breeze must have wafted through the air, because she was suddenly bathed in a delicious fragrance. Clean. Masculine. A hint of the sea. Warm lips whispered over the back of her hand, sending tingles up her arm.

And when he straightened, Evelyn leaned forward just to sample his scent once again. "M'lady, 'tis a pleasure to make your acquaintance," he said with a deep, rolling burr. He might be dressed as an Englishman, but there was no questioning this man's Scottish pedigree.

Evelyn drew her hand from his grasp and quickly snapped open her fan to cool the sudden blast of heat beneath her stomacher. "And yours, my lord. May I be so bold as to express my sympathy for your loss."

After giving a nod, the earl winced and shifted his gaze aside.

Father rubbed his signet ring on his lapel—a habit

which oft expressed his unease. "Mar has returned to London at the queen's request."

"I'm sorry to hear it," Evelyn said.

"The queen's business rests for no one." With his next breath, Mar assumed an air of unreadable pleasantry. "Ah, the orchestra has returned. Would you do me the honor of a dance, m'lady?"

The speed at which she fluttered her fan grew more vigorous. "Dance?" Evelyn didn't want to dance with the earl. As a queen's man, he represented everything she despised. Moreover, he must be in his midthirties, perhaps fourteen years her senior. And, bless it, he made her too self-aware.

"Her Ladyship would be delighted," her father answered, curse him.

Mar slid his fingers down the meticulously embroidered filigree along his doublet. "I wouldn't want to supplant someone else."

"This dance is presently not promised to any other gentleman." Snapping her fan shut, Evelyn tucked it into the hidden pocket designed by her modiste. If nothing else, she might gain a tidbit of useful knowledge. Mr. Dubois said one must draw near those with opposing views and come to know them well. "Shall we?"

"M'lady."

Reluctantly, she placed her fingers atop Mar's forearm while he led her to the center of the ballroom. Good Lord, his muscles were like steel beneath his silk doublet. Worse, the silence between them stretched uncomfortably.

She watched him out of the corner of her eye—a wolf in sheep's clothing. What had he been thinking when he'd signed his name to the Act of Union to subjugate his native Scotland to England? Was he completely oblivious to the needs of the common man? Most likely, he was. Could there be a man more politically flawed? Her father suffered from the same highbrow affliction, after all.

"Are you enjoying the All Fools' Day Ball?" Mar asked, stepping across from her and joining the men's line.

She almost laughed aloud at the irony. "I am." Though *enjoy* mightn't be the right word. *Amused* was more apropos.

An accursed minuet began, one that would ensure they danced hand in hand throughout.

Poised like a man who'd spent the greater part of the past decade at court, he seemed oblivious to her discontent. "Your father tells me this is your first season in London."

"It is, though Father has brought me to Town many times before." The eldest of three girls with no living mother, Evelyn had avoided making her debut. But having reached her majority, Papa had insisted this was the year for her to come out. Though expected to marry well, she was in no hurry whatsoever, especially now she was in the employ of Mr. Dubois.

"Do you like Town?" Mar asked.

"I suppose, though if I had to choose, the countryside is more pleasant."

"How so?"

Goodness, the earl was full of questions. Why couldn't he simply enjoy the dance or the music or the hall, or do anything aside from make idle chat?

"For starters," she said, "a woman can breathe deeply in a pastoral setting without enduring the disagreeable odors that come with humanity living in close proximity."

"I agree with you there." Together they executed a half turn. "Though I'd think a young lady such as yourself would enjoy the access to the shopping one finds only in London."

Evelyn touched her palm to his as they promenaded. His hand was a great deal larger than hers. Quite warm as well. "Nottingham has most everything I need. And I prefer my modiste there."

He glanced at her out of the corner of his eye—not a glance, precisely. It was more like an examination. "A practical woman. I commend you."

If she'd known he'd reply favorably to her response, Evelyn would have sworn she adored to shop endlessly.

"What is it you enjoy doing most of all?" he asked.

Spying on people like you. A sly grin played on her lips. Aside from her talent at snooping, one of Evelyn's favorite pastimes was gardening. She loved to dig in the earth and make beautiful flowers grow. "Horticulture."

"Another surprise." Mar led her around in a circle. "What is your favorite flower?"

"The dog rose." Without hesitation, she stared straight ahead and spoke aloud a secret Jacobite symbol. Prolific in the Highlands of Scotland, the dog rose was far from the most beautiful, but it carried with it great meaning. Pinned to a man's lapel, the flower told those committed to the Jacobite cause the wearer supported Prince James as the first in the succession and the rightful heir to the throne.

If Mar was aware of the dog rose's significance, he didn't let on. "Pink or white?"

She smirked. "White, of course."

By the grace of God, the minuet came to an end and, hopefully, Mar's interrogation with it. She curtsied while

His Lordship bowed. "Thank you, my lord. Your dancing is truly as polished as your mien."

* * *

John awoke the next morning with a minuet humming in his head, accompanying visions of Lady Evelyn Pierrepont. Though she'd not been what he expected, the memory of the young woman was a pleasant respite from his persistent woes. She seemed such a level-headed lass and her father quite keen to see her wed.

Eleven years ago, John had followed his heart and married a woman with whom he'd fallen deeply and irrevocably in love. Even though his father had left him saddled with debt, John had proposed to Margaret because he couldn't imagine himself with any other woman. Regrettably, he still could not.

And now she was gone...their two young boys left without a mother.

John sighed and looked to the bed-curtains above.

Lady Evelyn was a handsome woman. Not the beauty Margaret had been, but well proportioned and stately. The daughter of a duke, she would be more than acceptable as a candidate to assume the role of stepmother and countess. A woman who preferred a pastoral life, who was practical and even-tempered, would suit his needs ideally. And Her Ladyship came with a generous dowry. If all went as planned, at last John would be free of his father's creditors and loosen the chains Queen Anne had around his neck. How he longed to lessen his courtly duties in London and spend more time at his Scottish estate in Alloa. Invest some real capital into his coal mine and improve conditions for clan and kin.

Aye, Lady Evelyn's brunette locks had shimmered beneath the chandeliers like polished mahogany—quite a change from Margaret's blonde. Thank heavens. John could never bear to marry anyone who looked like his bonny lass. Her Ladyship posed a picture of everything Margaret was not—full-figured, English, shocking turquoise eyes, a heart-shaped face, and, most importantly, she was the daughter of a wealthy duke.

John stretched. Nay, 'twas not a decision to be made in haste. Yet, on the other hand, his creditors would see things differently. What was the purpose of waiting? To continue to draw out his misery? Hell, his misery would linger forever no matter the decisions he made.

Nonetheless, to be shed of Da's debts would bring a peace of mind John had never known. *I cannot and will not leave such a burden to my sons.*

John's father had died at the age of eight and thirty. And one year from now, John would be the same age. It was nigh time to ensure his estate was set to rights and be rid of the debt that had plagued him for so many years.

With his thought, the door burst open. Squealing with laughter, Thomas, aged nine, shoved past his younger brother, dashed into the chamber, and took a flying leap onto the mattress.

"Da! Why are you still abed?"

John wrapped his arm around the lad's shoulders and scrubbed his knuckles into his mop of unruly blond locks—the same color Margaret's had been. "Because I like to sleep, ye wee whelp."

Squealing with glee, Thomas scrambled aside while John hefted Oliver onto the bed. At the age of five, the youngest was a tad undersized but otherwise healthy and as sharp as the blade on John's dirk. "And how are you, son?"

The splay of freckles on Oliver's nose stretched with the lad's grin—not as wide as it once was before the death of his mother, but the boys were proving more resilient every day. "Ready to sail boats in Hyde Park."

"Och aye?" John looked between the two, both staring at him with hopeful faces bearing painful resemblance to their mother. "You've broken your fast? You've washed? You've completed your lessons?"

Thomas sat upright and batted a pillow. "'Tis Saturday, Da."

"Och, there's no better time to review what you learned during the week than Saturday morn before an outing." John pulled himself up and leaned against the headboard. "First I've an errand to run. That will give you plenty of time to eat, wash your faces, and review your lessons. We'll take luncheon here and then spend the entire afternoon with our wee boats."

Oliver's bottom lip jutted out. "But Da, I want to go now."

"Work before play. You'd best learn such discipline directly, else you'll not succeed when you grow older."

"Forgive me, m'lord." MacVie, the valet, cleared his throat from the servants' entrance. "Mrs. Kerr said the lads got away afore she woke."

John wrapped an arm around each of his boys' shoulders. "Not to worry. There's no better way to greet the morn than with the laughter of my sons." He gave them a squeeze. "Now off with you. I'll return by the noon hour."

Chapter Two

*F*rances waltzed across the floor while Evelyn watched her sister from the reflection in the looking glass. "I'm *fifteen*. Papa should have let me attend the ball. It just isn't fair for you to have all the fun."

"You think *you* are excluded from everything?" Phoebe complained from her position lying on her side across the bed. "Try being the youngest. I'm never invited to do anything."

"Mind you, royal balls are full of pompous old men who are only in attendance to impress the queen." Evelyn cringed as her lady's maid dragged a comb through the tangle remaining from last night's coiffure. "Ow."

Lucinda withdrew the comb and began at the ends. "Forgive me, my lady. But you should have let me brush this out last eve."

Frances twirled up to the toilette, shoving her face in the mirror and twisting her brown locks atop her head. "I think I'd look divine with a pile of curls entwined with yellow ribbon."

"I think you'd look ridiculous," said Phoebe.

Evelyn glanced over her shoulder at her youngest sister, who had recently enjoyed her twelfth birthday. "Oh, really? You should have told me I looked ridiculous before I left for the ball and was presented to the queen."

Phoebe pushed up on her elbow. "I didn't say *you* looked ridiculous, but Frances has a thinner face and—"

"Beg your pardon, my lady," a footman's voice rumbled through the timbers. "You have a caller."

Brutus, the old Corgi, didn't quite raise his head from the mat in front of the hearth, but he managed an unconvincing growl.

"A caller?" Frances dashed across the floor and opened the door wide, regardless that Evelyn was still wearing her robe. "Is it a lady caller or a gentleman caller?"

The footman cleared his throat. "His Grace requests Lady Evelyn's presence in the parlor straightaway."

"But who is here?" asked Phoebe and Frances in tandem.

"'Tis the Earl of Mar."

Thank heavens her sisters' eyes were turned toward the messenger, because Evelyn nearly fell off her stool.

As the footman turned away, Frances shut the door, whipped around, and gave an accusing snort. "You said the ball was dull and pallid."

Quickly averting her gaze to the mirror, Evelyn casually pulled the stopper from a bottle of perfume and sniffed. "And I still say so."

"Then why is an earl calling, and at this hour?" asked Frances.

"I have absolutely no idea." Evelyn hastily dabbed the fragrance on her neck. "I need a moment to breathe before I face the likes of Mar. Both of you, go busy yourselves elsewhere."

Phoebe slid off the bed. "But—"

The bottle nearly tipped over as she replaced the stopper. "Go, I said. With the pair of you twittering like finches, I can scarcely think."

Lucinda stepped back, brandishing her comb. "What would you have me do with your hair, my lady?"

"Twist it into a chignon and put a few pins in it. I am by no means worried about impressing the man."

"No?" asked the lady's maid, setting to work. "Is the earl old and crusty?"

If Mar were old and crusty, Evelyn's stomach wouldn't be entertaining a dozen leaping lords. "He's a widower," she replied, as if that explained everything.

"Well, I'll have you set to rights in no time, not to worry, and the blue day dress ought to suit."

Usually Lucinda's efficiency was a boon, but today her deft fingers were maddening. If only the maid would have dropped the hairpins or broken the laces on Evelyn's stays or ripped a hole in her skirts or spilled the ewer of water down the front of her gown, she might have an excuse to send her apologies to the earl.

But in no time, she was presentable and walking out her chamber door.

Whyever was the earl here? There were all manner of lovely and marriageable gentlewomen at the ball, why in heaven's name had Mar come to see her? Surely he didn't have a mind to court her. They were utterly, unquestionably, unimaginably incompatible.

While she proceeded to the parlor, Evelyn considered

his every plausible excuse. Had he seen her speaking with Mr. Dubois? Was he suspicious of her ties with the Jacobites—had she been too bold mentioning the dog rose? Did he know that a fortnight past she had informed the French emissary to the exiled Stuart prince about her father's shipments from the Orient—cargo which in turn would lower the prices of British goods, thus putting in jeopardy the incomes of local laborers?

How could he? Even though he is the Secretary of State for Scotland, Mar has only recently returned to London.

Perhaps he had come to see Father, and the duke had contrived some silly reason to send for her. Moreover, by the time she reached the bottom of the stairs, she was convinced Mar wasn't as tall as she had remembered or as handsome or as well mannered.

Remember his politics.

"Ah, here she is, my lovely eldest," said Papa, opening his arms and smiling as brightly as he had done last night. "Do you remember His Lordship, my dear?"

How could she forget? Mar not only had danced with her once, he'd persuaded her to the floor five times. Unheard of! And every time they'd danced he asked so many questions, Evelyn hadn't managed to inquire about a single of his interests. Not that she cared a fig about whatever amused him.

Every bit as tall and far handsomer than he'd been last eve, Mar stepped from behind a chair and bowed. "'Tis delightful to see you again, m'lady." Adding to his allure, the Highlander wore a kilt and had clubbed his hair back rather than wear a periwig. Bare knees with scarlet garters held his stockings in place. How on earth was she to resist such masculinity when he donned red-and-black plaid?

Before Evelyn managed to look away, His Lordship produced a bouquet of white roses from behind his back. "Regrettably, no street vendor in London was selling dog roses. I hope these blooms will suffice until I can procure your favorite. They tell me these are called Great Maiden's Blush, which I find quite uncharacteristic since they're white without a single trace of pink."

Oh dear, what was the swaying feeling in the pit of her stomach? A dozen beautiful, heavenly blooms presented by a man with the deepest brogue she'd ever heard. "This variety comes in white and pink." In truth, Evelyn far preferred these full blossoms to plain, five-petaled dog roses. But she couldn't admit to it now. "These are magnificent," she said, her voice full of sincerity as she accepted the gift and breathed in their rich fragrance.

"I say, dear, do you not grow these very blooms in Thoresby Hall's gardens?" asked Papa.

"I do." Deciding it best to concede on one point, she added, "Truly, I enjoy roses of all sorts."

"That's right, Mar," said the duke, "and you should see the wisteria trellises Lady Evelyn has nurtured. My master gardener has had quite an invested student over the years."

At the mention of the former gardener at Thoresby Hall, Evelyn's pulse pounded at her temples. Throughout his life, Mr. Wilson had been a faithful servant to the Pierreponts. Under the tenure of three dukes, he'd lovingly cared for the expansive gardens at Thoresby Hall. He'd taken Evelyn under his wing and taught her everything from soil to flowers to herbs and pruning. But when he'd fallen ill and a few weeds had sprouted in the flower beds, her father had dismissed him without a pension and no way to support himself.

The earl slid his foot forward and bowed again, distracting Evelyn from her thoughts and drawing notice to the sgian dubh peeking above his garter. "I'm glad not to disappoint."

"I've ordered tea and cakes. Please, sit and enjoy each other's company." Papa gestured to the settee. "Regrettably, I have some urgent correspondence I must attend."

Drawing her hand to her chest, Evelyn took a step back. "But—"

"Perhaps one cup of tea." Mar gave the duke a nod, then faced her with a smile warm enough to melt butter in a snowstorm. "I'm afraid I cannot stay long."

Feeling cornered, she had no choice but to sit on the blasted couch, from where she always poured the tea. And there was no opportunity to shift the table over to the chair because the housemaid promptly walked into the parlor carrying the tea service. What was Evelyn's father thinking, leaving her alone in the parlor with a man? Mar might be a trusted friend, but heaven forbid someone outside the house learn of this little chat.

She gave the maid the flowers before she took her seat. "Would you please replace the lilies on the mantel with these lovely roses?"

"Straightaway, my lady."

Mar slid onto the settee beside her. "I hope I'm not intruding. I meant to leave the roses with my card and a note, but your father invited me in."

"Not at all." What else could she say? Yes, your presence in my house is awkward and disconcerting and I want you to leave. *Now, please!* She picked up the teapot with such vigor, a bit of liquid spilled from the spout.

The earl seemed not to notice as he sat very erect, his

feet firmly planted on the floor. Out of the corner of her eye, it was impossible for Evelyn to keep from staring at the way his kilt hiked up his leg—a very muscular thigh, strewn with tawny hair that looked softer than silk.

"Did you enjoy the ball last eve?" he asked.

With a jolt, her gaze snapped to the task at hand while the teacup clanked in the saucer. "It was quite a stately affair."

"Aye." He leaned nearer, his blue eyes focusing on her face as if she were the most diverting person in London. "Stately it was, but that's not what I asked."

How did a man manage to smell like sea breeze? It simply wasn't natural. Evelyn poured the second cup, managing not to spill or clank anything. For the love of Moses, she'd been pouring tea for years without a single slip. The Earl of Mar had no business making her so self-aware. She vowed to stop her silly nervousness this instant.

Clearing her throat, Evelyn set the teapot down with perfect control. "It was my first royal ball. I have nothing with which to compare." She picked up the sugar bowl. "A spoon to sweeten your palate?"

"Please." He tapped his foot, making the muscle on his thigh flex. "Is it safe to assume you prefer not to attend balls?"

Pretending to contemplate his question, she stared at his disconcerting bare knee. If only she could touch his skin to see if it was as hard as it looked. "I-I'd say yes. I am particularly disinterested in attending balls that cater only to the nobility." After preparing the earl's tea, she handed him the cup and saucer, their fingers brushing slightly.

Mar took in a sharp breath—or had it been her own inhalation? Evelyn shifted her gaze to his eyes—they grew darker.

"Ah, yes." He sipped and set the cup on the table. "You prefer a pastoral life—flowers, and, shall we say, country dances?"

"If you'd like."

"Well, then I'd reckon you'd be quite comfortable at a Highland ceilidh."

"A *kay-lee*?" she asked, phonetically pronouncing the Gaelic word.

"'Tis the Scottish equivalent of a country dance, except it is with clan and kin, and outdoors, weather permitting." He brushed a hand down his kilt.

Her gaze slipped to those garters, Scottish daggers tucked in each, but far more distracting were his bare knees. *Scandalous*. "Does the weather ever cooperate in Scotland?" she asked.

"On occasion, but never when it is important."

Drawing her fingers to her mouth, Evelyn covered a sudden urge to laugh. In no way should she encourage him. She inclined her head to the windows, through which beamed rays of sunlight. "'Tis a shame you're not in Scotland, my lord. Today appears to be ideal for a Highland gathering."

"It is a fine day. And London is abloom with flowers at the moment."

"It certainly is. Hyde Park is awash in a carpet of bluebells and enormous plots of daffodils."

"Hyde Park?" He reached for a tiny cake and popped it into his mouth. "Why, I'm sailing boats with my lads there this very afternoon. You ought to come along and enjoy the flowers."

"Oh, I couldn't."

"Why not?" Phoebe's rather loud voice came from the corridor.

Ready to melt into a puddle of mortification, Evelyn met the earl's amused gaze. "I must apologize for my sister." She stood, marched across the floor, and flung open the door. "Lady Phoebe, it is *very* impolite to eavesdrop!"

"But Frances told me to—"

Evelyn threw up her hands. "You've never done anything your sister has asked you to do before. Why start now?"

"I-I..." Phoebe shot a panicked glance to the earl. "But going to the park today and sailing boats would be fantastically diverting."

"That settles it." Mar stood and met them at the door. "My sons and I will bring the carriage around for both of you bonny lassies at half past one." He bowed to Evelyn's sister. "Lady Phoebe, it is lovely to make your acquaintance."

The vixen curtsied and blushed scarlet. "Thank you, my lord."

"I truly am sorry for my sister's impolite behavior, Your Lordship." Evelyn shot the holy terror a heated glare. "By no means should you feel obligated to escort us to the park today or any day, for that matter."

"Och, the lads will welcome the company." He gave a hasty bow. "And I will look forward to it as well."

Evelyn curtsied and watched the Earl of Mar take his leave. Her day had just gone from bad to worse. She focused her ire on Phoebe. "Exactly what were you thinking, first listening in and, secondly, blurting out 'why not' loud enough to wake the dead? If you're going to eavesdrop, you must be able to exercise a modicum of control over your person."

The shrew toyed with the bauble hanging from her necklace. "I'm sorry."

"Sorry? You sound as sincere as a traveling peddler. Now we have to go to the park and sail toy boats with a pair of juvenile lads whom we've never met."

"But we've played with our cousins at Thoresby Hall. They're boys."

Evelyn paced. She'd wanted to discourage the earl and have him leave posthaste. "It's not Mar's children I'm worried about."

"Oh...you do not think the earl wants to marry you, does he?"

"Most certainly not." The vase of Great Maiden's Blush roses on the mantel caught her eye. "You cornered him into extending an invitation this afternoon. Otherwise, I'm certain he would have finished his tea and that would have been the last we'd see of him."

"But it's not."

"No."

"And the outing will be fun."

"Perhaps for you. And I do not want to ever hear you complain about not being invited along again."

Phoebe danced over to the vase and made a show of sniffing the roses—all dozen of them. "There are flowers at the park, aaaaand..."

Evelyn dropped onto the settee and looked to the ceiling. "And what?"

"Weeeeell...did you see him?"

"Of course I saw His Lordship. He was the only other person in the parlor."

Phoebe fluttered her eyelashes, the tart. "Yes, well, he is rather pleasant to look upon, is he not?"

Chapter Three

$\mathcal{J}$ohn's town coach had been in the family for at least twenty years, and he'd had the undercarriage of the creaking pile of rusty bolts restored twice. The red velvet upholstery had faded to pink, but it was functional and well cared for by his coachman. The carriage had always served his needs, but then he'd never endeavored to court the daughter of a duke.

Initially, he'd thought inviting Evelyn and her sister to the park was a splendid idea. It would give him a chance to observe the lady's interactions with his sons as well as help to move along the negotiations with her father. But John may have acted a bit hastily. At the moment, the air inside the carriage was nothing short of stifling and tense. Oliver had welcomed the guests to their outing in stride, but Thomas sat with his arms folded and his face scrunched like an angry prune while he tried his best not to come in contact with Lady Phoebe, who perched between the two lads.

On the other side of the lass, Oliver had been told twice not to make flatulating noises by snapping his armpit closed against his hand. Poor Lady Phoebe, who had initially chattered happily, after being snubbed by Thomas and repulsed by Oliver, sat like a statue between the two lads, her hands primly folded, her lips pursed as if she didn't know what to make of the pair of kilted, barbarian Scottish boys.

To John's left, Lady Evelyn seemed to be captivated by the passing scenery beyond the window and hadn't said a word since they'd set out. For a young lady being primed for marriage, she seemed rather reserved, even for an Englishwoman. But then, John wasn't looking for a hellion. A quiet lady who enjoyed spending her time in the garden ought to suit his needs.

"Mother always loved the park," said Thomas, none too cordially.

John's heart twisted. It had been three months since Margaret's death. After two, he'd lifted the requirement for mourning dress for himself and the lads, though nothing but time would serve to heal their loss. And no matter how much John wanted to sit in his library with a bottle of whisky, draperies drawn, he had no alternative but to set the example for his sons and conceal his grief.

"Aye," he agreed, but changed the subject before Tom added something even more melancholy. "Lady Phoebe, how long have you been in London?"

"Merely a fortnight, my lord."

"And have you found it invigorating?"

"I suppose."

"Och, you do not sound convincing."

The young lass gave her sister an evil eye. "Honestly, there's been so much ado about Lady Evelyn's fittings and appearances, I haven't done much else but read."

Lady Evelyn's gaze finally shifted from the window as she regarded her sister. "Oh please, Phoebe, you've had fittings as well."

"But nothing like yours."

It seemed they all needed respite. John pulled open the curtain on his side and glanced out, relieved to see the park's towering oak trees as the coach rolled to a stop. "I'm certain when you come of age, you will be equally as busy, Lady Phoebe." Not waiting for the footman to open the door, he pulled on the latch. "Are you ready for some good sport?"

"Aye!" Oliver said while Thomas clambered down the steps.

John followed his eldest and gripped the boy's shoulder. "I ken you're eager, but I expect you to assist Lady Phoebe."

"Must I?" the lad asked under his breath.

Evidently, Thomas was in sore need of an adjustment to his priorities. Bending down until his lips were even with his son's ear, John whispered, "Do it now and erase the scowl from your face, else I shall toss you back inside and order the coachman to take you home."

He then took in a deep breath as he straightened and smiled, offering his hand to Lady Evelyn. "I hope you do not mind playing referee, m'lady."

"Not at all."

Thomas avoided a miserable trip home when he helped Phoebe alight. "We only have three boats."

"I'm the privateer!" hollered Oliver, hopping to the ground and running around to the rear of the coach, where the footman had opened the trunk.

"It is the gentlemanly thing to do to allow Lady Phoebe first choice." John gestured inside the chest. "We have the *Francis Drake*, a privateer; the *Tortuga*, a pirate ship; and the HMS *Thistle*, which patrols the high seas." During the long days of mourning, he and the boys had made the schooners all with the same two-masted design.

As the lass looked over the options, Oliver came up beside her. "You ought to take Her Majesty's *Thistle* because it's for lassies."

"Do you prefer the *Francis Drake*?" Lady Phoebe asked.

"Aye, 'tis my favorite."

"And I'm in a mood to be a pirate," said Thomas, picking up the *Tortuga*.

Evelyn looked over Phoebe's shoulder. "The *Thistle* is lovely. I'm sure my sister will be happy with any of them."

"'Tis settled, then." John led the crew to the Serpentine, the park's loch—or lake, as the English preferred.

"What are the rules?" asked Lady Phoebe.

Thomas ran ahead with his brother on his heels. "You move your boat along with a stick and try to beat the others."

"Stay well away from the water," John added. "No pushing or shoving of the enemy's captain—"

"We are the captains," Oliver explained, gesturing to himself with his thumb.

"You'll need to stop your boats before you reach the grove." John peered down the length of the loch. "What landmark can we use for the finish line?"

Lady Evelyn pointed. "Is that white post down the way a mooring cleat?"

"Indeed it is." John gave her an appreciative nod,

relieved that the dreary overtones in the coach seemed to disappear with a bit of fresh air. "Sail your boats to the cleat. And be careful not to push them too far from the bank or else they'll be lost at sea."

"Not mine," said Oliver as if he'd mastered the art of toy boat sailing.

"I'll go down and watch the finish line." Her Ladyship retreated practically at a run.

After a hasty look to ensure the children were being assisted by the footmen, John started after Evelyn. "I'll accompany you."

By the sudden rigid bent of her shoulders, he sensed she wasn't enamored with his idea.

Why would she be averse? Was it their difference in age? That shouldn't matter. It wasn't uncommon for a maid to marry a man sixteen years her senior. However, after the lads' behavior, she might be worried about becoming a stepmother...or marrying a recent widower. Was she fearful? Or did she already have her sights on another?

But she has only been in London for a fortnight.

Before John took things further, he needed to find out.

When he fell in beside her, she glanced up. The sun caught the turquoise of her eyes, making them shimmer as brightly as a peacock. "I believe Lord Thomas would have preferred an afternoon alone with you and Lord Oliver."

With the brim of her bonnet upturned, John took the opportunity to study her face more closely. Though she looked nothing like Margaret, the lass had a sultry, perceptive countenance—defined eyebrows, high cheekbones, and sensual lips made striking by the sunlight. Her dark lashes framed her astonishing eyes, making them more vivid. Odd, Margaret's eyes had never appeared as bright.

"Lord Tom mightn't be aware, but in truth, the three of us have had far too much time alone together," John replied.

"I know how difficult it is to lose one's mother. I'm sure you are aware I lost mine to childbed fever. I was the same age as Lord Thomas at the time."

Hmm. "I knew she'd passed. I didn't realize when."

"Phoebe's birth proved too much for Mama. After, I resented my sister until she was two years of age."

John knew too well about resentment, except he resented his bloody self. "What happened to change your mind?"

"Lung sickness. When I realized my infant sister might die, it suddenly became the most important thing in the world to save her. I felt as if I'd brought on her ailment because of my deep-seated animosity. No one could convince me to leave Lady Phoebe's bedside until she made a full recovery."

"I commend your tenacity."

"Grief is a complicated emotion. Perhaps Lord Thomas needs more time."

A tic twitched in John's jaw. He didn't like that Lady Evelyn provided her opinion about his son as if she had any clue what was best. But then again, that was exactly why John needed a wife—to be a stepmother. Rather than argue, he turned the conversation toward Her Ladyship. "Tell me, m'lady, are you apprehensive about the prospect of being courted?"

Arriving at the post, she stopped and faced him. "Whatever do you mean?"

"You've expressed to me the depth of your attachment

to your sister. When you marry, you will no longer be living under the same roof. Eventually Lady Phoebe will find her match as well. To think of such changes must be unnerving for you."

"Unnerving?" she asked slowly, as though the idea had crossed her mind for the first time. "Why, yes. I would hate to marry someone who would take me away from my family—all the way to Scotland, perchance."

"I see. I would think a Scottish husband would be sensitive to his wife's need to see her family. And now that the queen has combined English and Scottish parliaments, from November to May all peers must generally reside in London, where you would be sure to see your father and sisters whenever you'd like."

"I suppose you're right. But Scotland is so remote— such a wild place." As her gaze drifted to his kilt, her lips parted slightly.

John nearly berated himself for welcoming the lady's attention. Nearly. Though he would blame himself for Margaret's death and mourn her loss until he took his last breath, it still made him feel like a man to receive a woman's notice. "I think you'd be surprised. Edinburgh, in particular, is modern, cultured, and quite diverting."

"Do you have lands near Edinburgh?"

"Not far from. There is easy access from my main residence in Alloa if we sail a galley down the River Forth and into the Firth. We moor at Leith and take a coach or sedan chairs up to the Royal Mile. There's never a loss for amusements—theater, shopping, whatever you fancy."

Her Ladyship chuckled, the sound as sultry as her lips. "Surprising. I would think the city might be brimming with the destitute and infirm. My understanding is Scottish commoners have suffered more from unfair taxation than their English counterparts."

"I wouldn't say that." John's gut clenched. Did the lass have a clue as to the depth of her assertion?

"Of course not," Evelyn said, looking beyond him. "You are one of the queen's most trusted ministers."

Exactly what did she mean? She had no idea the risks he'd taken to temper some of the most egregious legislation to which he'd ever had the misfortune of being a part. Besides, no gentlewoman bothered to embroil herself in the machinations of politics.

John knit his brows. "Do you mean to ridicule me?"

"In no way would I insult a peer. I was simply stating the facts."

The more they spoke, the more John suspected Her Ladyship must have another courtier in the wings. Well, that wouldn't do. He must speak to her father straightaway or lose his chance.

He followed her gaze to the footpath, where three gentlemen were deep in conversation—two of them allies, though every one a staunch Jacobite—not that any right-minded nobleman heralded his true politics when in London. Truth be told, for obvious reasons, John shared his personal loyalties with no one. But he held the Earl of Seaforth and the Marquis of Tullibardine in high esteem.

Yet Claude Dubois was an enigma. A high-ranking French dignitary, the man had presented letters from Louis XIV avowing that he'd been sent to Britain as an advisor to Queen Anne. His task was to represent France during the ongoing peace negotiations in the Netherlands. But in John's observation, whenever the Frenchman was at court, Dubois appeared to engage in more meddling than advising. Moreover, he was the very man with whom Lady Evelyn had been speaking last eve by the refreshment table.

"Is your father an associate of Mr. Dubois?" John asked. Now that peace with France was practically a foregone conclusion, Kingston-upon-Hull might be moving in early to arrange the transport of imports from France.

"Um…" She snapped her gaze away. "Oh, look! Well done, Phoebe!"

Three years older and a good head taller than John's eldest, Lady Phoebe had taken the lead.

But by Thomas's determined effort, he hadn't given up. "Aye, me hearties, we'll overtake the queen's ship and plunder her gold!"

"No!" Lady Phoebe shrieked, smacking her boat and glancing behind. Thomas was gaining, but poor Oliver had been capsized by a lily pad.

"Now's our chance, me hearties!" Tom gave his boat a thwack as Lady Phoebe caught her toe on a rock. Stumbling, the lass threw out her hands and careened to the ground.

In a blink, John dashed toward her, but she tumbled in the grass, her stick falling into the water, smacking her boat with a forceful prod.

"Phoebe!" Evelyn shouted, close on John's heels.

Just as he reached her, the wee lassie looked up and thrust her finger toward the loch. "Look at the HMS *Thistle*! She's heading out to the depths and will soon be swallowed by the Serpentine's sea monster. Quickly, Evie, you must fetch her."

John kneeled beside the child, who lay on her stomach

beside the bank. "Do not concern yourself with the wee boat—are you all right, lass?"

She looked at each of her palms—dirty but not bloodied. "Um...I think so."

He offered his hand. "Let me help you to your feet."

Once upright, Lady Phoebe winced. "I might have scraped my knee."

John glanced back to beckon Lady Evelyn, but she'd picked up a branch and was already fifty paces away, hastening after the HMS *Thistle*.

"Does it hurt to take a step?" he asked, wishing she were a lad and wearing a kilt so the scrape would be in plain sight.

Her Ladyship walked a few paces. "I'm sure it will be fine if I sit down for a bit."

John waved to Oliver, who had retrieved his boat. "Take Lady Phoebe to the bench and stay there."

"Aye, m'lord."

"I won!" Thomas shouted well beyond the mooring cleat.

"No one is the victor," John growled at the ruffian. "Especially you—now off to the bench with the others."

"Why?"

John was about to tell the whelp he should have stopped to assist Lady Phoebe, but he hadn't time. He broke into a run, watching Lady Evelyn, the daughter of a duke, hold on to a tree limb while she inclined her entire body toward the loch, reaching for the bloody HMS *Thistle*. God's bones, he should have known better than to name the queen's boat after a prickly Scottish symbol.

The bell of her hoopskirt dipped in the water as she reached lower.

Her Ladyship's fingers stretched mere inches from the mast.

If he shouted, would she fall? Bless it, if he didn't shout, she'd fall for certain. "Stop! I'll fetch—"

"Aaack!"

Ker-splash!

John's breath caught in his chest as he bounded into the cold, murky water, shoving lily pads out of his path. He had seconds to wrap his hands around the woman before those heavy skirts pulled her under.

Splashing wildly, Her Ladyship shrieked as her head dipped below the surface.

With one enormous lunge, John broke past a web of water weeds and grabbed a wrist. As he planted his feet into the thick silt, he swept his arms beneath her knees and around her back. Gnashing his teeth, he strained against the weight of woolen skirts, and at least five petticoats weighing upwards of twenty stone.

"I have you," he growled through clenched teeth while he trudged toward the shore.

"Pfth," she sputtered, clutching the damned schooner against her chest. But as the water drained from her clothing, the woman grew considerably lighter. In fact, he rather enjoyed the curve of her hip pressing into his abdomen, the feminine waist cradled against his arm. Truly, Her Ladyship mustn't be as robust beneath all those skirts as he'd envisioned her to be.

By the time he stepped on dry land, she'd grown feather light.

A few steps farther on, Lady Evelyn peered at him over the HMS *Thistle*'s sails. "You may set me down now."

"Are you hurt at all, m'lady?"

Her teeth chattered. "Aside from my pride being badly bruised, I think I am unharmed."

"Perhaps I ought to carry you to the coach. We'll find a dry cloak for you there."

"No, please. I cannot possibly impose on you further."

He did as she asked and took the boat from her grasp. Before he stopped himself, John gawked like an ungentlemanly, adolescent lad. The neckline of Lady Evelyn's gown had shifted, revealing the tips of two very rosy, very erect nipples.

Within a heartbeat, every one of John's male instincts took over. Knees turned boneless while another piece of his anatomy hardened. Lord, the woman had the shapeliest breasts he'd ever seen. Skin like cream. Ample bosoms with enough cleavage in which a man might lose himself.

"Oh, my. You're soaked clean through as well," she said, still completely oblivious to her state of undress.

"Am I?" John cleared his throat, exaggerating the motion of glancing down to her neckline, praying she'd notice, lest he be forced to mention it. "Och...I am."

But she looked at him as if he were mad. "Shall we?"

"Nay." Again he cleared his throat, this time forcing himself to look at her face. "Not until you've adjusted your gown, m'lady." There were the lads, and then the footmen, and then who knew how many randy men would see Her Ladyship before she was safely behind the door of her bedchamber.

A round O formed on her lips as she glanced down. "Oh, heavens!" She whipped around and faced the loch, tugging up the wet cloth. "Curses to this miserable gown. The fabric has stretched."

John extended his hand but snapped it back. What

could he do? He was an expert at removing women's clothing, not at assembling. And his coat was too wet to be of use to her. "Remain here. I'll fetch one of the footmen's doublets and we'll have you covered in no time."

Chapter Four

*W*rapped in a warm robe and drinking a steaming cup of chamomile tea, Evelyn shuddered at the sight of the doublet draped across the foot of her bed.

Lucinda placed a lump of coal on the fire. "Now that you've shooed your sisters away, I'm dying to know exactly what happened, my lady." For the past five years, Lucinda had served as Evelyn's lady's maid and the two had grown close. Though she couldn't share everything with the maid, Evelyn was more comfortable talking to Lucinda than to anyone else.

"'Tis as Lady Phoebe said. She fell, and her toy boat went off course. I tried rescuing it with a stick and only managed to push the tiny schooner into a grove of lily pads, where it wouldn't budge. The earl was busy tending my sister, so I tried to be a hero and dangle from a tree branch while reaching for the silly thing—"

"And the limb snapped?"

"Yes, dunking me in that filthy lake water, mind you."

Evelyn sipped her tea. "If that wasn't horrifying enough, the wool stretched on my gown and left the tips of my bosoms exposed to all of London."

Lucinda turned away and set to dusting—rather vigorously. "Oh, how mortifying."

"Worse, I was so worried about Phoebe and saving the silly HMS *Thistle*, I didn't notice my abominable state of undress until His Lordship bade me to adjust my person."

"It grows worse."

Evelyn set her cup in the saucer. "At least I no longer need to worry about Mar's possible interest in courting me."

"Do you not like him? I would think an influential earl such as he would be an ideal husband. And he's undeniably handsome."

"But he's a queen's man."

"Is that so bad?"

Evelyn feigned indifference while she reached for a book. If Mar were allied with the Earl of Seaforth or the Marquis of Tullibardine, she might think differently, but she didn't want to marry someone who supported her father's politics. And in her estimation, Mar was blameworthy by association. Papa was very particular about his alliances. As a queen's man, it was undeniable that the Earl of Mar's position of influence with the crown impressed the duke. That in itself made Evelyn suspicious of John Erskine's character. A man like Mar possessed the connections to mitigate investigations into the duke's smuggling operations, should they arise.

Was Mar heartless as well? Did he ruin men's lives by turning them out in their advancing years without even a pension as meager as a shilling per month?

Did he pay unlivable wages to the employees of the

coal mine he owned? Did he force children to work in inhuman conditions? Did the earl smuggle his coal into England without paying the queen's duties—duties he and the Duke of Kingston-upon-Hull had voted to impose on the rest of the kingdom's subjects? Evelyn would wager that, just like her father, Mar went to excessive lengths to avoid paying taxes.

If she married someone like the earl, she'd end up fighting him tooth and nail. She'd rather remain a spinster than support tyranny under her own roof.

"Looks fade with time," Evelyn replied.

"Well, I think you ought to consider his suit."

"And what makes you such an expert?" She gave Lucinda a playful smack. "There is no suit whatsoever. Did I not just say there would be no courtship? I bared my breasts, though unknowingly, in a public park. He most likely thinks me a harlot."

"I'm not convinced." Lucinda giggled and scooted beyond Evelyn's reach. "Most men are rather enamored with women's breasts."

"Oh yes? And you have vast experience with such matters?"

"I might be a lady's maid, but I'm not dead. You would be amazed at what goes on in the servants' quarters."

"Ooo, that sounds interesting." As well as a delightful change in subject. Evelyn scooted to the edge of her seat. "Do tell."

"And lose my position?"

"You know you can trust me."

Lucinda drummed her fingers together. "Well, last night the footman was reprimanded for inappropriately groping a scullery maid."

"Who did the reprimanding?"

"Porter, of course."

"Our humorless butler," Evelyn groaned. "My father employs the most pompous, dreary servants in England."

The maid scoffed. "I beg your pardon?"

"Forgive me. I was referring to Porter and the housekeeper...and Mrs. Filch. Thank heavens I no longer need a governess."

Lucinda picked up Evelyn's lake-soiled gown from the floor. "I'd best set to cleaning this."

"I think it is ruined. And if you manage to repair the neckline, please remind me never to wear it anywhere near a body of water."

The maid chuckled. "Will there be anything else, my lady?"

"Please have the footman's doublet cleaned and ask Porter to return it to Mar's residence with my thanks." Evelyn never wanted to set eyes on the garment again. It presently served as an unwanted reminder of the day's humiliation.

Once alone, she took the candelabra from the table and tiptoed to the door. It was Saturday evening—the night when Papa played cards at the gentlemen's club. That meant Saturday night was Evelyn's opportunity to pay a stealthy visit to the library...and the strongbox where her father kept his conspiratorial correspondence.

Quietly, she hurried to the lower floor. When she reached the library, she stopped and listened—with a house full of servants, one could never be too careful.

Still, when the door swung open, her heart nearly burst. Goodness, she hadn't heard a single footstep.

"Lady Evelyn," said Porter, looking as if he'd just swallowed a bitter tonic. "I expected you to be abed after the day's ordeal."

"Can't sleep." She slipped inside. "And I need a new book."

"Then I shall leave you to it."

"Porter," she ventured. "Is something amiss? I didn't expect to see you here."

The butler inclined his head toward the writing table. "A missive arrived for your father."

She offered a warm smile. "I see. Good night."

"Good night, my lady."

As soon as the door closed, she released a long breath. Porter poked his nose into everything in this house. He was the most likely to discover Evelyn spying, and she absolutely could not slip with him nearby. Not ever. She locked the door for good measure, then hastened to the writing table.

Good heavens, the missive was from Mar. Evelyn set her candelabra down and stared at the red seal, her hands perspiring. Papa kept a sharp dagger in the drawer. Should she open it? Did she care enough to risk breaking the seal? After the events of the day, surely the letter was an apology of some sort. And she doubted Mar would ever come calling with a dozen white roses ever again.

She chuckled at the irony, though something inside grew heavy, almost melancholy. To end a courtship before it began was for the best. The earl would soon find a wife—someone who wasn't as opinionated as Evelyn and someone who knew how to manage boys.

She replaced the missive exactly as she'd found it, her fingers itching to hold the seal over the flame just long enough to soften the wax, then run the dagger beneath, quickly read, then reseal it.

Yes. In the name of James Stuart, she'd levered her father's unopened missives before, though doing so was fraught with danger. There was always a chance the wax seal would crack, and then Papa would suspect someone had meddled. Such risks were better left to more important business—things that would help the cause, things she must share with Mr. Dubois.

How much her life had changed the day she met the Frenchman. He'd first approached her at the hospital for wounded soldiers in Nottingham, where she read to the infirm on Tuesdays and Thursdays. Evelyn's eyes had already been opened to her father's pitiless oppression, but Mr. Dubois led her to see the extent of Papa's treachery. Not only did her father dismiss elderly servants without a livable pension, he used children in his mining operations and paid everyone in his employ far less than they deserved. Once Evelyn had learned the truth, it became her civic duty to help the Frenchman when he'd asked. Moreover, Mr. Dubois desperately needed her assistance in his quest to repeal the Act of Succession to enable Prince James to succeed to the throne. Only then would there be a hope for justice to prevail.

Evelyn shared information with the Jacobite emissary on the grounds that he would never incriminate her father or her family. The information was supplied only to help her quest to work toward fairer taxation for all British subjects, as well as better pay and conditions for laborers—which she was convinced would happen once James Stuart succeeded to the throne. Hers was a noble cause, and she would forgo her own happiness to see such positive change occur throughout Britain.

Moving on to more important matters, she opened the drawer and removed the false bottom, exposing the compartment where Papa kept the key to his strongbox. *What have you been up to this past week, Papa dearest?*

The hinges on the box creaked when she opened it. Jolting, she took a panicked look over her shoulder, even though the door was locked. Perhaps on her next visit to the library she ought to bring some oil for the hinges.

But then I would be leaving evidence of tampering. Not a good maneuver for a spy.

Inside she found a mountain of coin and banknotes, none of which she ever touched. What interested Evelyn was the correspondence Papa neatly stacked on the right-hand side.

Here's something new. It was a letter from the captain of the *East Indian*, one of the ships from Holland—a Dutch fluyt Papa had engaged on several occasions.

She pulled out the missive and sat while unfolding it. Evidently the captain had reported the ship wrecked off the Shetland Islands, but in truth it was hidden in a cove near Bettyhill, a remote village in northern Scotland. Among other things, the *East Indian*'s hull contained one hundred barrels of coffee, fifty barrels of rum, and a chest of Spanish gold.

He's nothing short of a pirate.

Reading on, she discovered that the captain intended to refit the ship, rename her the *Flying Robin*, and then sail her to Papa's dockyard in the town of Hull, where the booty would be hidden in hay wagons and smuggled into London. Of course, the captain hadn't used the terms *smuggled* and *booty*, but he may as well have.

Committing the contents to memory, Evelyn re-folded the missive, replaced it in the box, and locked it. As she pulled open the drawer to return the key to its hiding place, heavy footsteps came from the town house stairs. Her heart thrummed. Father never returned this early.

In her haste to return the key, she dropped it. Diving under the writing table, she snatched it from the carpet, slid the key into the drawer, and closed it just as keys jangled. The lock clicked and the door opened.

As footsteps approached, Evelyn gathered the hem of her robe and tucked it under her knees. What would she say if Papa discovered her? Good heavens, why was she hiding? She'd told Porter she was looking for a book. That would have been easy enough to explain.

Papa's square-toed shoes stopped in front of her. "Odd. Porter must have left the candle burning. It's not like him to be careless. And why the blazes did he lock the door, the imbecile?"

Her heart raced. What should she do? Play a trick by untying his garters and telling him it was her candle? Say she'd dropped a hairpin? Good heavens, that might have worked if she was still five years of age.

Please leave!

Parchment rustled while Papa sat, his feet sliding mere inches from Evelyn's legs. Her every breath sounded like a gale-force wind while she pushed herself flush against the wall. Was he reading Mar's missive?

"I'll be damned," Papa said, right before he blew out the candles.

When the door to the library closed, Evelyn released an enormous breath. No matter how much she wanted to run, she waited in the darkness until the sound of his footsteps was long gone. Only then did she climb out from under the writing table. Her fingers brushed Mar's opened missive, though she could scarcely see the contrast of the parchment with the walnut finish. Still, she picked up the letter and inclined it to the window, hoping the moonlight would provide enough light for her to read the contents.

Unfortunately, the only legible word was Mar, signed in a bold hand at the bottom.

Convinced her intuition was right, she replaced the missive and tiptoed back to her chamber.

* * *

As soon as she arose the next morning, Evelyn placed a silk sunflower in her window. It stood as the Jacobite symbol of loyalty because the head of the flower always follows the sun, but no one in her household, including Lucinda, had any clue the sunflower was used as a sign to inform Mr. Dubois that she had information to impart. A day later, she would slip away to the Copper Cauldron in the alley off Bourdon Street, the headquarters where the French emissary would be waiting.

When she went down to break her fast, Evelyn was surprised to find His Grace had already left the house for White's Gentlemen's Club. Papa's absence was both a relief and a disappointment. Surely he would be displeased with Mar's decision but eventually would realize it was for the best. Perhaps Father would brush the matter under the carpet and say nothing. After all, Mar hadn't mentioned the prospect of courting her—he'd merely spoken of courting in more general terms.

While nibbling a slice of toast, Evelyn thoroughly convinced herself the subject had been put to rest with no harm done aside from a tad of injured pride. She turned her attention to her sisters and their appointments for the day while the anticipation of her meeting with Mr. Dubois made her anxious. Tomorrow seemed as if it would never arrive.

But come it did, and promptly at ten o'clock, Evelyn

sneaked away with old Brutus as her chaperone under the guise of taking the waddling Corgi for a stroll. Fortunately, Jacobite headquarters were only a few blocks from the town house, lest she be discovered unchaperoned and Brutus expire from overexertion.

When she turned down the shadowy and narrow alley, she clamped the lead tighter, thankful for the dog. Though not a spry young pup, Brutus could bark. It might be Mayfair in the middle of the day. And the men who comprised the Jacobites in London might be gentlemen whom she trusted implicitly. But a highborn lady without a proper chaperone could never be too careful. If anything happened to her, it would mean the end of her involvement in the cause forever.

From Evelyn's conversations with Mr. Dubois at the soldiers' hospital, she'd learned a great deal about her father's corruption. Time and time again she'd become aware of the poverty of the tenants under Kingston-upon-Hull's care, but through the Frenchman she'd learned so much more, worst of all the extent of Papa's smuggling operations. To her dismay, the duke grew richer while those working in his shadow fell into dire straits.

Those conversations marked a turning point in her life. It was as if she'd been living in a gilded castle and suddenly the walls had crumbled around her. Moreover, when she'd confronted the Duke of Kingston-upon-Hull about his misdeeds, he'd laughed and told her she was naïve and too kindhearted—mainly due to the curse of her sex.

But now she'd found a way to do something about the tyranny. Because she, a mere woman, could be of use in bringing about justice, she stepped into the indistinct coffeehouse as if she belonged. As usual, the Copper

Cauldron's clientele comprised astute men dressed in breeches or kilts, doublets and periwigs. In truth, no respectable woman ought to be seen in a coffeehouse.

Excepting this one.

The heady aroma of ground beans and simmering brew wafted through the smoke-filled air. Evelyn covered her cough with a lacy kerchief.

Two armed guards positioned at the door watched her move inside. Hired by Mr. Dubois, they posed as a deterrent for any patrons who wandered in merely looking for a bowl of strongly brewed Turkish coffee and perhaps a morsel of cake.

Mr. Dubois gave a nod from the back of the room, where he sat against the wall near the steaming cauldron. Beside him, a young man pushed back his chair and stood. The Frenchman followed suit, albeit a fair bit slower.

"*Bonjour.* How fares your day, my lady?" asked the emissary as he gestured to the man. "This is our sea captain, Sir Kennan Cameron. He has put into service a new three-masted barque."

She curtsied. "Captain? Of a tall ship? I am duly impressed."

"Do not let his youthful face fool you, mademoiselle. Sir Kennan sailed under Scotland's Baronet of Sleat and has recently been knighted by James. You'll not find a captain more fit for the perils of the sea or more loyal to *the cause.*"

Sir Kennan skirted around the table and held her chair. "Mr. Dubois tells me you have been an invaluable resource, m'lady."

She tucked under her skirts and sat. "I hope so. I'd like to make a difference."

"*Oui*, and you have." Mr. Dubois signaled for the maid to bring three dishes of coffee. Honestly, Evelyn found the bitter brew muddy and coarse. But she always drank it without complaint. In this coffeehouse she was amongst the only people she considered allies.

The Frenchman smiled. Oddly, for some inexplicable reason, the intensity of his stare always made her stomach agitated. "Now, tell us your news."

She settled herself by taking in a deep breath. "A Dutch fluyt, the *East Indian*, is moored in a cove in the north of Scotland near Bettyhill. She was reported wrecked off Shetland, but in truth she's laden with one hundred barrels of coffee, fifty barrels of rum, and a chest of Spanish gold. They're undertaking a refit, then will sail to Hull, where the cargo will be hidden in hay wagons and shipped to London."

"Rum and coffee, *oui*?" asked Mr. Dubois, giving the maid a nod as she set three dishes of brew on the table.

"And gold," Sir Kennan added. "The coin ought to come in handy as James prepares to sail across the channel."

The emissary drank his brew thoughtfully. "You have a point, though I'm not worried about the contents of her cargo. England appears to have coffee beans aplenty, and a hold full of rum oughtn't affect sales of spirit overmuch."

"Perhaps it might be wise if we ignored this one," Evelyn suggested, "to keep suspicion at bay."

"Och, let us not discount the *East India* so hastily. Not when I've an empty hull and a crew of men ready to set sail." Sir Kennan pushed his untouched dish of coffee aside and eyed the Frenchman. "And we wouldn't want Her Ladyship to be taking risks for naught."

Evelyn stooped and gave Brutus a scratch. "Hmm. I suppose it would be beneficial to sail past. Perhaps just to see what changes they're making to her hull."

"Aye." Sir Kennan snatched a biscuit from a passing maid's tray. "And plunder the gold."

"For James," Mr. Dubois added.

Dipping the treat into his coffee, the captain grinned. "Hear, hear."

Evelyn sat a bit taller, pleased with the reception of her news. "After all, Hull's men stole the chest from the Spanish. Why shouldn't it be used to help *the cause*?"

Sir Kennan grinned. "I knew I'd like you as soon as you stepped inside, m'lady."

"*Oui, oui*," agreed Mr. Dubois. "Now, we've another matter to discuss."

"Oh?" Evelyn took the tiniest of sips.

"You've caught Mar's eye."

Suddenly overwarm, she slipped lower in her chair. "Hardly."

"I saw you in Hyde Park with him just the other day."

"He was there with his sons." Evelyn did her best to sound as if her association with the Secretary of State for Scotland was of no consequence. "And my sister came along as well."

"I know an interested man when I see one—and it didn't slip my notice that you danced with him more than once at the ball. It might be wise to draw yourself into Mar's confidence."

"I am sorry, but I don't think he'll be inviting either Lady Phoebe or me for another outing. Saturday proved an unmitigated disaster."

"*Alors*. We need to know what the queen is up to—and

the best way inside is through her cabinet ministers. The woman grows more reclusive by the day."

Kennan took a long drink of his coffee and then he scowled like a pirate. "Rumor is she's plotting for the ruination of James—and only those on the cabinet are privy to her plans."

"*Ma chérie*, whilst your father is in London, he may entertain Mar or any number of Anne's ministers. Do your best to listen in. I want to know the details of every discussion no matter how trite it may seem." Dubois reached for her dish of coffee and took a drink. "Now to home with you before you're missed."

Chapter Five

*I*t was good of you to come," John said, gesturing to the chair opposite his writing table.

The Duke of Kingston-upon-Hull slid into the seat. "I cannot tell you how delighted I was to receive your missive."

"Good news, indeed." John moved behind his desk and tapped the papers their solicitors had jointly drawn up. "I trust your man is in agreement that all is in order?"

"Most definitely." Hull smiled. "She must have made quite an impression for you to come forward with an offer so quickly."

"Well, if I hadn't, someone might have beat me to it." John started to reach for the quill, but stopped himself and folded his hands. Over the past couple of days he'd thought of little else aside from Evelyn. When he'd first met the lass, she'd seemed standoffish, but after the incident at the lake, she became endearing. In reflection, it was funny how an incident oft drew out the good nature in people.

"Knowing your interest, I would have spoken to you before encouraging anyone else to court her." Hull brushed his signet ring on his lapel. "I want only the best for my daughters—queen's men through and through. Of course, your favor in courtly matters will always be appreciated."

"A-aye." John gulped. He'd been dangling from the queen's marionette strings for too long. And he'd paid his duty by sitting on her cabinet and keeping the royalists from ruining Scotland—but only just. What had he received for his pains? The moniker of "Bobbin' John," a politician who vacillated from one side to the other, unable to make a solid decision. Well, this was his chance to cut those damned strings.

But first he needed to ensure this proposal met with the lady's wishes and not only her father's. "Before we sign, can you please tell me how Lady Evelyn received the news?"

Hull shifted his gaze to his fingernails. "Of course any woman her age would be ecstatic. All young ladies dream of their wedding day."

"Even so soon after we've met? Do you think she'd prefer to wait?"

"Why? Not only are you an earl, I daresay I've heard the whispers from the ladies in the crowd. You are most likely the best catch in London this season."

"I do not ken about other ladies, but Lady Evelyn did make mention of her reluctance to live away from home. I only thought she may desire time to grow accustomed to the idea."

"Hogwash. She will adore you and your sons. I guarantee it."

John plucked the quill from its holder. "Then let us not delay." He signed his name in a bold hand, then watched while Hull did the same. "I must pay Lady Evelyn a visit and properly propose."

"Splendid idea." The duke looked up from the contract. "Why not come for supper this evening?"

"I'd like that—and perhaps I may take a moment with Her Ladyship in the parlor beforehand?"

"Yes, of course, and then we'll feast to our good fortune."

* * *

Standing in the drawing room, suddenly Evelyn couldn't breathe, and it wasn't because Lucinda had tied her stays too tightly. "You've signed a contract agreeing to my marriage with the Earl of Mar without first discussing it with me?"

"Whatever is there to discuss?" asked Papa, as if signing contracts of intent to marry were an everyday occurrence for him. "An offer of marriage has been made by an earl. A quite venerable earl, for whom I have utmost respect. How could you possibly have an objection? You will be a countess."

Evelyn's skin burned as she blinked. "He's seven and thirty."

"Still a young man, perfectly able to sire children."

"That's not what I meant. I'm one and twenty. He's practically twice my age."

"Hardly. And what would you do with a young whippersnapper who has no worldly experience, who possibly hasn't come into his title? Mark me, you will be far better off with Mar."

"And his two sons?"

"Oh, please. With mortality what it is, there are few in the nobility who do not acquire a stepchild now and again."

Or a by-blow. With her sarcasm, Evelyn clenched her fists so tightly her nails bit into her flesh. "But, Papa, I hardly know him."

"I'm told you got on with him quite well at the ball and during your outing to Hyde Park."

"You're told?" She threw her hands out to her sides. "What, did you have spies watching me?"

"Good God, Evelyn, your disrespect is both annoying and ill-fitting for a woman of your station." Her father pounded his fist into his palm. "I have entered into an agreement with the Earl of Mar, and I expect you to honor it."

She moved her hand to her throat and squeezed. Trapped and doomed to spend the rest of her days beneath the roof of yet another royalist. "Do I have no say in the matter?"

"Of course you have a say…as long as you accept him. Bless it, Evelyn, if you waited another seven years I doubt you'd find Mar's equal, and I will hear no whining."

Her head swam. "Please—at least give me some time to grow accustomed to the idea."

"On that I can agree, as long as you don't dawdle. Discuss it with Mar this evening. He'll be here for supper."

Porter's knock came at the door and, to Brutus's ear-piercing barks, Father grinned. "I'll wager the man in question has arrived."

No! Evelyn caught her horrified expression in the mirror. How could Papa do this to her? First tell her about the earl's suit of marriage and then allow her no time to compose herself?

* * *

Before he used the big brass knocker, John paced the footpath in front of Hull's town house. Everything felt rushed. Not that he had a multitude of time. The queen would soon call a recess, and he'd be able to return to Scotland. He needed the dower funds to set his estate to rights on behalf of his sons, and, more importantly, those lads needed a mother—a well-bred woman able to prepare them for their duties as noblemen. Of course, Thomas was the heir, but if anything happened to him, God forbid, Oliver must be groomed as second in line.

Evelyn fit the bill in almost every way. She might be a bit reluctant and nervous, but then so was John. If he were a single man with no children, he'd never marry again. Women were too bloody frail. And losing them brought agony which not only tore out his heart, it ravaged his very soul. Margaret's illness had come on gradually at first. A hundred times he'd asked himself what would have happened if he'd called for the physician sooner. Though the doctor's bleeding her seemed to serve only to make his dear wife weaker.

Clenching his fists, John marched up the stairs, determined to see to his duty and commit to this marriage. He must act in the best interests of Thomas and Oliver. And he would do everything in his power to see to Evelyn's happiness. Many highborn marriages thrived without love between husband and wife, and his would, too.

With his resolution, he grabbed the knocker hanging

from lion's teeth and gave a solid rap, one that announced a man of purpose had come to call.

At once the butler ushered him into the drawing room and closed the door. Evelyn stood alone in the center of the room, twisting a kerchief between her hands while an overweight Corgi growled beside her.

John glanced at the hound, then looked from wall to wall. "I...ah...expected to be greeted by your father and your sisters as well."

"Are you disappointed, my lord?"

"Not at all." Surprised, flummoxed, taken aback? Aye. Tugging down his doublet sleeves, he moved farther inside to the tune of ferocious snarls—not quite the jubilant welcome he'd expected. "Do you ken why I'm here?"

Her lips pursed into a line. "My father spoke to me not but a moment ago."

"But it has been days since I sent a missive to Hull indicating my intent." John's gaze dropped to Evelyn's hands, her knuckles as white as her kerchief. Had the duke acted without discussing the marriage with his daughter? Surely not. John clearly remembered enquiring as to Her Ladyship's feelings on the matter. "I know things are moving a bit hastily."

"Hastily? Things haven't moved, they've jettisoned."

John rubbed his fingers across his clean-shaven chin. "You're not happy with the prospect of marrying me?"

The kerchief twisted. "I...might have grown more accustomed to the idea had there been a courtship, some time to come to know each other."

"Of course, and please let me say here and now, I want to be sensitive to your wishes. Providing..."

"Yes?"

As John took a step, the damned Corgi stood and

barked. "Providing you are willing to agree to this union."

Her Ladyship ignored the dog while a pinch formed between her brows. "You're asking me if *I'm* willing?"

"Aye."

By the expression on Evelyn's face, she was completely at a loss. If only the dog were as well. Fed up with the snarling overtones, John gave the hound a stern eye, which only served to bring on a deafening concert of barking.

Evelyn pointed to a rug in front of the hearth. "Brutus, sit."

The Corgi immediately obeyed, waddling to the mat and turning twice before he lay down with his head between his paws.

With a deep inhalation, John blessed the saints for the silence. "Forgive me, I have made a complete muddle of this. It has been far too long since I played the role of courtier, and I'm afraid it shows." He gave a lopsided grin, stepped before her, and wrenched her left hand from its iron grip on the lacy linen. Then he dropped to his knee. "Lady Evelyn, this humble soul kneels before you not as an earl, but as a man. In the short time of our acquaintance, I have been duly impressed by your kindness and dedication to family..."

He hesitated, trying to come up with a fantastic descriptor for her beauty, but every time he blinked he saw her breasts, gleaming wet from her dip in the loch. Thank God the vase of Great Maiden's Blush roses caught his eye. "You are bonnier than a white rose, and it would be my greatest honor if you would agree to be my wife."

A lovely shade of pink flooded Lady Evelyn's cheeks, though she did not meet John's gaze. In fact, she seemed overcome with fear as her hand perspired between his palms. Was she nervous?

John kissed the back of said sweaty hand. "You have my vow that you will want for nothing."

She stared at her knuckles.

His mouth grew dry. Blast it all, he should have come better prepared. "And do not worry about the lads, they will love and respect you."

"But what about us?" she asked, her face stark and sober. "Surely, you are not in love with me."

"Love?" His neckcloth suddenly grew too tight.

"Am I correct to presume, then, that this is a marriage of convenience?"

To be perfectly honest, the only convenient part of the affair was the lady's dowry. "Ours will be a marriage based on mutual respect, a foundation upon which we can build a lifetime of happiness." In no way would he allow her to force him to say he would come to love her. If those words slipped through his lips, she would expect something he wasn't prepared to give.

"Please," he beseeched, his knee grinding into the hardwood. "What can I say to soothe your concerns?"

Her eyes grew round while she drew in a deep breath as if she had many things to say. "Nothing."

He chanced a smile. "Then you will marry me?"

With a single nod and the resemblance of a smile, Her Ladyship gave her consent.

Satisfied with her cautious agreement, John reverently kissed the back of her hand and stood, but not before Brutus sprang to his feet with a renewed round of grumbles. "I promise you will not regret your decision."

"If only it had been mine to make," she mumbled, but

then offered a warm smile. "Shall we enjoy a long engagement?"

John took a step back. If he hadn't spoken to Hull himself, he would be certain Her Ladyship knew nothing of the terms of the agreement. "Not too long," he ventured. "Parliament will recess soon, and I intend to return to Scotland with my new countess on my arm."

"Countess. It has such a ring." Turning a bit pale, the lass sounded as happy as a death knell.

John's gut twisted. Had he mistaken the perspiration on her palms for nerves? "Are you not well?"

"I…" She drew a hand to her head and swayed.

Before she collapsed, he pulled her into his arms. "You're ill." Ice pulsed through his blood as he picked her up and headed for the settee, accompanied by the snarling dog, now mounting an attack as he sank his bloody teeth into John's heel. "I'll call for a physician at once." He kicked his foot, but that only served to make the dog's teeth gouge a bit farther. "But no bleeding. I swear no one in my care will ever suffer the lance again."

"No," she said, rather abruptly for a woman who had nearly swooned. "There is nothing wrong with me. Nothing in the slightest."

"Oh?" Vicious Corgi or not, John wasn't convinced. Sickness must be dealt with quickly before it had a chance to take root. "That's exactly what Lady Margaret said a sennight before she succumbed to a fever and died."

"I assure you I am not ill in the slightest. I merely felt a tad light-headed given this unexpected news." She jabbed him with her elbow—quite powerfully. What a welcome he'd received—a sharp elbow accompanied by sharper teeth. "Put me down at once."

"Brutus, come behind!" The door to the drawing room swung open and the dog released his hold on John's ankle, ran to his master's side, and wagged his tail as if he expected to be rewarded for mauling their guests.

"Not wasting any time, are you, Mar?" said Hull as he sauntered into the room.

"Forgive me." John swiftly deposited the lass on her feet, noting a bloodstain spreading at the back of his hose. "I feared Her Ladyship had fallen ill and swooned."

"Evelyn?" The duke chuckled. "My daughter might enjoy gardening, but she is no delicate flower. I say, she hasn't been ill a day in her life—have you, dear?"

"No, I have not." Lady Evelyn tucked her kerchief into her sleeve. "I simply had a touch of light-headedness. Perhaps my stays are a bit too tight."

"Youth." Hull chuckled as he gestured to the corridor. "Let us retire to the dining hall and feast to our good fortune."

* * *

By the time the third course finished, Evelyn was still shaking. Why hadn't she put up more resistance? True, Papa had been emphatic that she must perform her duty. He was her father, and she must obey his wishes. An advantageous marriage to a peer was what she'd been bred for, and he would hear no argument.

And Evelyn well knew any objection on her part would fall on deaf ears.

But her resolve had grown weak when the earl had asked if she was willing to marry him. Did such a man care about her opinion? Or was Mar being polite? Of course, Evelyn's thundering heart had betrayed her, nearly beating out of her chest when the drastically attractive earl had dropped to one knee and proposed. How could any woman resist a man who gazed at her with eyes like a winter sky, a face as beautiful as Michelangelo's sculpture of David, and a scent so intoxicating it had taken her breath away?

Deep down, her conversation with Mr. Dubois had silenced her tongue. He'd been very clear when he told her to grow close to any dignitaries who might come to the town house.

But surely he didn't mean marry one of them? Good glory, what have I done?

She signaled the butler to refill her wineglass while Phoebe yammered about sailing toy boats at the park. "When I fell, my schooner was pushed into deep water and I called to Evelyn to rescue it."

"Yes, and His Lordship is well aware of what happened next." Evelyn took a healthy sip of wine, stealing a glance at the earl, who sat beside her. "There is no need to hash through the details."

Phoebe sniffed with a pout. "But I was just coming to the good part."

"It was a fun day out," Mar said. "I'm glad you enjoyed yourself, Lady Phoebe."

"How many glasses of wine have you had?" asked Frances, gaping across the table.

Not enough. Evelyn set her glass down. In truth, it had been two glasses and her head was beginning to swim. But given the day's news, she felt entitled to an extra glass or two even though she was still technically a maid. She gave her sister an evil eye—the one Evelyn used whenever she wanted them to know she was in no mood for jesting.

Lord save her, to her horror, she was engaged to marry someone exactly like her father.

At the head of the table, Papa sat back while the footman placed a bowl of apple tart in front of him. "I've had a word with the vicar at Saint Paul's. Told him you were rather anxious to move ahead with the wedding, and he's already prepared the banns."

"That's so romantic," said Frances. "When will it be?"

Mar turned to Evelyn and arched his eyebrow. "A sennight hence?"

She wrapped her fingers around her dessert spoon. "How can a woman possibly plan for a wedding in a week?"

"A fortnight, then," said Papa. "I'll send for the modiste first thing in the morning."

"New gowns for all of us?" asked Phoebe, clapping her hands—easy for her. She wasn't marrying a man known as Bobbin' John.

Papa sat back while the footman refilled his glass. "Of course, I'll have all my daughters dressed in London's latest fashion."

Evelyn took a gulp of wine. In two weeks she would be the Countess of Mar, married to a man she hardly knew and most likely would never love. At least he was handsome—that might make time in the bedchamber bearable. Shuddering, she nearly drank the entire contents of her glass. Dear Lord, in a fortnight, she would no longer be a virgin.

Frances scooped a bite of tart with her spoon. "You must be over the moon with excitement."

"Quite," Evelyn managed, her head swimming. Either she'd imbibed too much burgundy or she was ill for the first time in her life. *What will Mr. Dubois say about this alliance?* Though he'd advised her to get closer to Mar to garner information for *the cause*, he surely would be appalled that her father had negotiated the union between Kingston-upon-Hull and Mar.

I am doomed.

Mar slid his fingers over the tablecloth, stopping before he reached her bowl of untouched tart. "You look a bit flushed. I imagine all this ado a bit overwhelming."

Overwhelming seemed like an understatement. "I believe you may be right." She slid her chair back and stood. "If you would excuse me, I'd like to adjourn to the courtyard for a bit of air."

Mar immediately rose to his feet. "I'll accompany you."

Good gracious, when would she have a moment to herself? Evelyn ignored his arm as she wove her way through the corridor, the movement making her feel better—or was it the effects of the wine?

"Och, the night's air is much improved over the stuffy dining hall," said the earl as they stepped into the courtyard.

Evelyn opened her arms and let the breeze cool her face as she strolled around the garden of herbs and vegetables—so minuscule compared to the vast acres of manicured gardens at Thoresby Hall.

Walking with his hands clasped behind his back, Mar fell in step beside her. "'Tis pleasant, quiet."

"I miss the country."

"I do as well."

"Surprising. A man like you is required to spend so much time in London, I would think you'd be more inclined to call Town your home."

"Never. And with luck my responsibilities will lessen, enabling me...er...*us* to enjoy Alloa more."

Evelyn paused at his use of "us." "Oh? What will the queen think of your plans?"

Shrugging, he plucked a sprig of rosemary and drew it to his nose. "Mm." Then he held it out to her. "This scent is soothing enough to calm a hairy beast—mayhap even your dog."

She couldn't help but let a giggle slip as she imagined Brutus being tamed by rosemary. But then her breath caught when Mar brushed her cheek with the fragrant herb. The scent not only soothed her, it enlivened her as well, not that she cared to be enlivened in the least.

"Remember when I said you'd enjoy a *ceilidh*?" he asked.

"Yes."

"Highland gatherings are my favorite celebrations as well."

"Not royal balls?"

He tossed the sprig away. "Royal balls are for fops and Whigs."

She smiled. "I never thought I'd hear you say such a thing. Are you not both of those?"

"Mayhap to anyone on the outside looking in." He hummed a few notes, his deep bass resonating between the courtyard walls. "At a *ceilidh* everyone—man, woman, and child, no matter their rank—is welcome to partake. There's always a hog on the spit and singing and dancing well into the wee hours."

He sang a verse of a Gaelic folk song, his voice haunting and beautiful, making gooseflesh rise across Evelyn's skin. "That was very good."

"It is an ancient Celtic tune, passed down at my clan's campfires through the ages."

"It has a lovely but sad overtone. What is it about?"

"The story of a woman sending her man to sea. Only through the depth of her love will he return to her arms." Mar grasped Evelyn's hand and hummed this time. "And the dance to this wee tune is lyrical. My kin have performed it for over a thousand years."

He pulled her around in a circle, showing her by doing. Singing and smiling as he watched her eyes.

For the moment, Evelyn forgot the turmoil surrounding her life and let him lead her in this new, yet ancient, reel. Together they flowed with half turns and glissades. At the far side of the courtyard, he stopped and clasped her hands in his big palms while they swayed to his humming.

"This is why I like a *ceilidh*," he whispered. "Because all the worries of the world are lost on the breeze. And then there is only you…and me."

For the first time since they'd met, Evelyn really looked into his eyes—not the beauty she saw on the surface but what lay in the deep pools. They weren't filled with hate or mal-intent. Mar's eyes were gentle and kind and nothing like her father's. How did he manage it?

Before she asked, he took her face between his palms, his gaze dropping to her lips. The blood in her veins turned molten as he neared, his breath sweet with the overtone of apples.

And then he kissed her.

Evelyn gasped at the sensation of his warm mouth brushing across hers. But he didn't just give her a tiny peck, as she'd expected. He lingered while the effects of the wine swirled in her head. She closed her eyes and grasped his shoulders to steady herself. His tongue slid across the parting of her mouth while tingles fired across her skin.

How should she respond? Was this done?

His tongue teased her again.

Ever so slightly, she opened. Mar eased his hand to the back of her neck while he entered her mouth with unexpected wildness. Evelyn sank her fingers into bands of thick muscle and held on with all her strength as he showed her not just a kiss but a passionate joining of the mouths between man and woman—between lovers.

Except they would never be lovers.

Chapter Six

*J*ohn popped his head through the door to Swenson's rooms. "Please order two dozen dog rose plants to be added to the Alloa gardens."

The butler looked up from his ledger as his sagging jowls grew deeper with his frown. "Dog rose, m'lord?"

"Aye."

Swenson stood a bit slower than usual. "I must caution you on your choice. I've heard reports that rose has some association with the Jacobites."

Yes, John was well aware of the symbolism. The white five-petaled rose had been a prominent feature in the Stuart crest for centuries. But if the daughter of a man like Hull, a staunch royalist, loved dog roses, then so be it. Besides, Tullibardine would enjoy a good laugh when he came to dine at Alloa. "I'm certain I'll not come under Her Majesty's suspicion for adding white roses to my garden."

"Very well. Shall the gardener make a hedgerow out of them?"

"I hadn't thought of that." Dressed for a visit to court, John stretched his neck against his neckcloth's snug knot. "Do you believe that would be best?"

"The flowers of the dog rose are rather plain, but they do sprout ample foliage. And the vines are ideal for hedgerows, if I may say."

"Very well. Tell the gardener to order what he needs for a hedgerow on the south wall."

"Straightaway, m'lord." The butler reached for his quill.

"Oh—and Swenson?"

"Aye?"

"Ensure he's aware they are the favorite flower of the new countess."

Those beetle eyebrows shot up. "I beg your par—"

John shut the door before the man finished. He'd already said enough, and he needed to break the news to the lads before the entire serving staff was spouting gossip about his forthcoming nuptials.

Since taking the evening meal with Evelyn and her family, John was more convinced he'd been correct in his decision to wed the lass. He would give Evelyn a fine home and deny her nothing. She would be a good influence on the boys, and after the kiss they'd shared in the courtyard, he suspected Her Ladyship might provide good sport in the bedchamber. If they were lucky, he would give her bairns tenfold. What would be better than a dozen children running and laughing through Alloa Tower with his sons leading the brood? He chuckled, taking two stairs at a time straight up to the third-floor nursery.

"I don't care about *W*s." Oliver's voice resonated down the corridor. "I'm going to be a knight. Da said so."

"Well, then," Mrs. Kerr replied, "it is doubly important that you learn all your letters. Knights are vital members of the gentry and they oft compose all manner of missives."

"Aye, addressed to earls and even royalty," Thomas added.

"Now then. Fill your page with *W*s, Lord Oliver, else you might have to set your sights on some other vocation."

Clearing his throat, John tapped open the door. "Please tell me I did not hear one of my sons arguing with his governess about the importance of his lessons."

"Da!" Oliver's quill stilled in his black-stained fingers while his eyes bugged wide. "How long have you been there?"

"Long enough and you will be writing *two* pages of *W*s, laddie."

The boy's face fell. "Aye, m'lord."

"Very well, and that's the last I want to hear of any backtalking to your governess. Both of you."

"What did I do?" Tom balked.

John shifted his hands to his hips. "Have I made myself clear?"

Thomas fixated on his parchment. "Aye, m'lord."

Satisfied, John turned to Mrs. Kerr. "Would you mind leaving us for a moment, madam?"

"Of course, m'lord."

Both boys watched him expectantly as John waited for the woman to leave, shutting the door behind her. "Come, let's sit in the embrasure."

"What is it, Da?" asked Oliver.

Thomas dashed across the floor. "Are we going back to Alloa?"

"No, we're not returning to Scotland yet, but I do have hopes the queen will call recess soon." In the little alcove with opposing seat cushions, John sat across from the boys. Funny thing, he was more nervous now than he'd been when he'd dropped to one knee and asked Lady Evelyn to marry him, even with her disagreeable dog's grumbling overture.

In truth, she'd had little choice but to agree.

And John wanted his sons to be happy about his decision. The lads were too young to understand the crippling effects of inherited debt, but they did need to realize that their father was acting in their best interests.

He drew in a deep breath. "I ken things haven't been easy for you these past few months."

Unable to touch the floor, Oliver swung his feet. "If only Mrs. Kerr weren't so hard on us."

Thomas gave his brother a thwack. "Och aye!"

"Your governess is doing exactly what I'm paying her to do. But that's not what I've brought you over here to discuss." Giving the boys a stern eye, John wiped his sweaty palms on his breeches. Bloody oath, this was proving more difficult by the moment. "Men cannot live without women."

"Why the devil not?" asked Thomas as John gaped at his son's outburst. "Pardon me, Da, but why? Lassies are despicable."

Oliver returned his brother's thwack with a shove. "I agree. They're 'aspicable."

"But you..." John looked to the ceiling. As he recalled, Oliver seemed to enjoy playing with Lady Phoebe on their adventure to Hyde Park. However, the youngest always sided with his elder brother. One thing was for certain: The Earl of Mar needed to take charge of the direction of the conversation. There he sat, Secretary of State for Scotland, being sidetracked by a pair of whelps.

He steepled his fingers to his lips and pretended to speak to the Almighty. "Och, do not listen to them, dear Father. I ken my sons loved their mother, no matter what misguided notions slip through their lips."

Thomas picked up a pillow and squeezed it. "We were *no'* talking about Ma."

"You think not?" With a wee scowl, John looked from one lad to the next. "I'll tell you true, lads, every time you speak ill of the fairer sex you disrespect the memory of your mother. And I'll not have it."

Hanging their heads, both lads looked as if they were on the verge of tears. Devil be damned, had he been too hard on them? Blast it all, women were better suited for child nurturing. John's duty was to turn his sons into men, not to mollycoddle them. "Och, I did not come up here to grumble at you. I came bearing good news." Though, given their aversion to females, he wasn't convinced they'd see it as a boon.

Bless it, they need a bloody mother whether they understand it or not.

Oliver slid down from the bench, then climbed up beside his father, leaning against John's arm. "I like it when you come to the nursery and talk to us, Da."

"Thank you." John slipped his arm around the lad. "Both of you have met Lady Evelyn."

"Aye," said Thomas, his arms tightly clutching the pillow.

May as well blurt it out. "She's going to be your stepmother."

Oliver tensed and, across, Thomas stared, saying nothing, his lips quivering.

"But what about Ma?" whispered the youngest. "We cannot forget Ma."

John shifted Oliver onto his lap, then hoisted Thomas across the gap as well. Sitting with his arms around both lads, he let the news sink in before he continued. "I ken Her Ladyship will not replace your mother, but she's the daughter of a duke and she'll help you pair grow into fine noblemen."

"I think we're doing well without a stepmother," whispered Thomas.

Oliver looked up with big, sad eyes. "And Mrs. Kerr has been making us practice our bows, pleases, and thank-yous every day."

John gave a nod. "And I'm very appreciative for Mrs. Kerr. But the root of the matter is you will have a stepmother who is a fine, well-bred woman and we have naught but to show her the utmost respect at all times."

He gave each wee Highlander a kiss on the head. "Now, I've received a summons from the queen and I must leave for court."

"When will you be home?" Thomas asked.

"Knowing Her Majesty, she'll keep the cabinet until the wee hours."

"The queen isn't very nice," said Oliver.

"She has a thankless position, but she perseveres, just as all of us must accept our lot and make the best of it." That was all John would say about the queen. If only his sons were fifteen years older with a bit of hair on their chins, he might offer them a whisky and have a good yarn. Unfortunately, their queen was poorly educated and unprepared to be the supreme leader of Britain, completely ill suited to the throne. But such words were not to be uttered, especially to children who were supposed to believe in the utmost authority of their monarchs.

* * *

Sitting at the back of the Copper Cauldron, Evelyn let out a long breath when Mr. Dubois finally stepped through the door. She'd put the sunflower in the window yesterday, but this afternoon when she hadn't seen him at his table, she had nearly turned and taken Brutus home. She glanced down at the ferocious Corgi asleep at her feet, then looked to the Frenchman approaching with a grimace.

"Two dishes of coffee in the back, *s'il vous plaît*," he said to the maid before he slipped into the chair with his back to the wall—right beside Evelyn. "I hope you do not mind my sitting beside you, m'lady."

"Not at all." Regardless of what she'd said, it was awkward, and Evelyn shifted to her usual seat across the table. "Since I arrived before you, I felt uncomfortable with my back to the door."

"'Tis a good thing—shows you're a natural-born spy."

Choked by the ribbon on her bonnet, she tugged open the bow. "Unfortunately, my spying days are coming to an end."

"*Oui*? Is that why your sunflower graced your window again so soon?"

"Yes. My news is dire, but this time 'tis of a personal nature."

The maid set two dishes on the table. "You're in luck. We cleaned the cauldron this morn and the coffee is freshly brewed."

Evelyn looked to her bowl, doubting the taste would be any more palatable than before.

"You have me addicted." Mr. Dubois acted as if the

woman had just placed a bowl of manna before him. "I cannot go a day without sampling your brew, *ma chérie*."

They both sipped while the woman went on her way. It did taste better—either that or Evelyn was so upset her tongue was playing tricks.

Setting his dish on the board, Mr. Dubois licked his lips. "Now, tell me. What has your *belle visage* looking as if ye've been plundered by an angry Viking?"

Evelyn sputtered in her haste to cover something between a laugh and a cry. "An angry Viking isn't far off the mark—except he's a mad Scot."

The man scowled and rubbed his fingers over the pommel of the dagger at his hip. "Name this miscreant and I'll run my blade across his throat before the night's end."

"He hasn't exactly committed plunder." *Yet.* "He has proposed and entered into a marriage contract with my father."

Mr. Dubois released his hilt. "Your father approves of this scoundrel? Then he must be a man of some substance."

Barely able to bring herself to utter his name, Evelyn bit her lip. Yes, in a moment of inebriation she'd allowed the Scotsman to kiss her, but now she sat in horror of her actions. "'Tis none other than John Erskine, Earl of Mar."

Whistling, the French emissary rocked his chair back against the wall. "Ah, yes."

She pressed her palms to her cheeks. "I am simply devastated. And Papa didn't bother to discuss the alliance with me before the papers were drawn."

"Devastated? Truly? He's an attractive man, is he not?"

"How can you speak of beauty when in a fortnight I'll be taking my vows beside a man with questionable politics. Worse—a man just like my father. Bobbin' John, of all people!"

"Hmm." Mr. Dubois looked the picture of an unruffled

French courtier while he turned his dish with his fingers. How could he be so calm at a moment like this? "Have you forgotten that Mar is an influential man? Perhaps the most influential man in Scotland."

"What on earth does that matter?" Evelyn threw out her hands in exasperation. "How can I ever love anyone who kisses the queen's royal backside?"

"Love?" Dubois laughed from his belly. "*Ma chérie*, I know you are as sharp as the dagger in my scabbard, but you're not thinking with your head. What do you believe? You, the firstborn daughter of a duke, would marry for love?"

"Well, at least I hoped I'd have some say in the matter."

"Let me ask you this, my lady: How deeply are you dedicated to *the cause*?"

After glancing over her shoulder, Evelyn lowered her voice. "You know I have pledged my life to Jacobitism."

"*Oui*, and now you have an opportunity to turn this new alliance to your advantage—our advantage."

A chill snaked down her spine. "Spy on Mar?"

"How different is that from spying on *votre père*?"

"I—" It was a great deal different from skimming her father's correspondence. First of all, having lived all her life under the duke's roof, she knew when and where to find tidbits of information. Things would be completely different with a husband, a new home, new servants, new routines, *children*.

"Think on it, my lady. You could be of more use to me as Mar's wife than Hull's daughter. *Oui*, the information you brought about the *East Indian* was a tasty nugget, and Sir Kennan has set sail for Bettyhill..." The Frenchman licked his lips, his eyes focused and very intent. "Think on what you can uncover from a member of Queen Anne's cabinet."

Chapter Seven

I'm pleased to see you looking so fresh and serene this morn," John said while he helped Lady Evelyn climb into his chaise carriage. He particularly liked this smaller cart made for two. With only one horse to manage, it was easy to drive in the open air while carrying on a conversation. Margaret had enjoyed their rides together very much, and he hoped Evelyn would do the same.

"Did you expect me to appear harrowed and haggard for this outing?" She cast a look toward her father's town house. "Perhaps I ought to go tell my lady's maid to pull out a few hairpins."

For a moment John thought the lass was serious until he caught a glimpse of the sun sparkling in mischievous turquoise eyes. "Why not take off your bonnet and let the breeze remove them at will? Such coiffure might begin a new fashion."

The corners of her mouth turned up in a coy grin. "Indeed? What shall we call it? The windswept maiden?"

He laughed. "I do enjoy a sense of humor, m'lady."

He hastened around to the other side, slipped in beside her, and picked up the reins. "I thought you might need a wee respite from your wedding plans."

She folded her gloved hands. "You weren't wrong. If my modiste stabs me with one more pin I'll...well, I'll tell her where she can put them."

"That does sound unpleasant." He slapped the reins and headed for the embankment along the Thames. "How are the wedding plans coming otherwise?"

"Do you truly want to hear all the sordid details?"

"I've been sequestered in the queen's antechamber for three days, listening to her perseverate on how to settle her grievances with France and getting nowhere, mind you. I think listening to a story about how Lady Phoebe's gown doesn't have enough bows might be diverting."

Evelyn gripped the armrest as they traversed a rough patch in the road. "'Tis Lady Frances who isn't happy with her bows. Lady Phoebe wants more lace, and she thinks she's ready for stays. And both of them would rather be the center of attention."

"They'll have their weddings soon enough."

"Yes, that's what I keep telling them." Evelyn brushed out her skirts. "So, from your tenor, I take it cabinet meetings are rather dull?"

"They're as painful as submitting to a smithy with a pair of tongs."

"Ow. You've had your teeth pulled?"

"One. A molar. 'Twas something I never again wish to endure."

"Surprising."

"The tooth or my aversion to cabinet meetings?"

"Cabinet meetings. Why do you endure them?

There are dozens of noblemen who'd relish taking your place."

John shrugged. "Duty to queen and country, I suppose." And he needed the income to keep the creditors at bay. But the union with Lady Evelyn would allow him to gracefully distance himself from Her Majesty.

"Hmm." The lass folded her gloved hands. "How did Lords Thomas and Oliver take the news?"

"Rather well, I'd say." Aside from their aversion to females—the very thought making him grin. "They'll appreciate having a mother figure as they mature."

"I would think they'd be resistant to the idea."

"Why do you say that?"

"No child who loses a mother wants to see her replaced."

"I suppose it will be an adjustment for the lads. But they will come to adore you in no time. And then..."

"Hmm?"

"Well, you...and I...will have bairns."

Evelyn turned scarlet. "Oh."

John slapped the reins, letting that wee idea hang on the air for a moment. In less than a fortnight this woman would come to his bed for the first time. The better prepared she was, the smoother consummation would be—for the both of them. Though he planned to be as gentle as he had been with Margaret, he didn't need a weeping bride on his hands.

"Oh, look." She pointed as if she'd pushed the idea of their wedding night out of her mind. "There's London Bridge."

"Aye, 'tis a city in itself."

Grinning, she grasped her gold locket and moved it to and fro. "I've never been."

"It is no place for a lady. And during peak times it can take an hour to cross."

"Have you been there before?"

"I have, though if we want to cross the Thames, we'd do well to use the horse ferry."

"But I would truly love to venture across and have a look at the myriad of vendors. Word is many of them are heathens. The day is fine. The sun is high in the sky. What is an hour or two?" Twirling the locket around her finger, she gave him a sidewise glance. "And I have a robust Highland earl as my escort."

Robust? John smiled at the compliment. He'd missed flirting, even though doing so made a chasm stretch in his chest—the same ache which had plagued him ever since Margaret had fallen ill. "Very well, mayhap a ride across and back for my bonny bride."

He nearly choked on the words while Evelyn looked to her tightly folded hands. Clearly she was as apprehensive about their nuptials as he. If only John had an entire season to court the lass, things mightn't be awkward. Pulling on the right rein, he cued the horse onto Bishopsgate, then pointed to the north tower. "There are towers at each end."

Holding her bonnet, she leaned forward, looking up. "And the heads of traitors are impaled on spikes on the south side."

"Aye. Though infrequently since Cromwell met his end."

Her eyes shifted his way, reflecting a bit of defiance this time. "Did you know that a Scot's head was the first to grace an iron spike?"

"William Wallace."

"And King Charles."

John shuddered as they passed beneath the tower's archway. How did they manage to fall on the topic of treason and beheadings? It was not exactly the type of conversation he envisioned having with his betrothed. He cued the horse for a slow walk. Unsteady buildings three and four stories high butted against one another with a narrow causeway between them. The air changed—not just the stench or the chilly wind coming off the Thames, but something made the hair on John's nape prickle. He shifted his gaze from side to side. Now he'd committed there was no turning around.

Lady Evelyn drew a kerchief across her nose. "My, the air is rich."

"It'll improve once we move on a bit, thanks to the wind whipping down the river." Unless the hay wagon in front of them never decided to move. "Walk on!" John hollered.

"Shut your gob," said a disembodied voice.

"Charming."

"I see a break coming. I'll go around." With another slap of the reins, the horse veered into oncoming traffic and trotted forward just as a team of four came barreling through as if they were on a racetrack. John corrected with the reins, veering back to the left.

The chaise tottered on its springs while Evelyn sat like a queen, facing a near collision as if they were taking a ride on a wide-open country lane.

Gritting his teeth, John used a combination of the brake and steady tension on the reins to bring the chaise under control. "Hold on to your bonnet, m'lady!" he growled between his teeth.

As the carriage jolted and careened to one wheel, Lady Evelyn grabbed his arm. "My! I see why you do not always ride in an enclosed coach. You're quite a skilled horseman."

Safely on the left side, the chaise jolted and jerked while John steadied the horse. "Och, I can count on Daisy to pull through." Though even he'd had his doubts for a moment. "I believe all lads should learn to drive a team. That's where the true challenge lies."

The lady released her grip and folded her hands in her lap. "Teams and spirited young horses."

"You're not wrong there."

Now traveling at a snail's pace, they encountered vendors out in droves. A man shoved a foul-smelling brown bottle under John's nose. "This tincture will cure a megrim in the blink of an eye, it will."

He batted the tinker's hand away. "Remove that stench from my face at once."

"Oh, look," Evelyn said, taking a posy of silk flowers from a wench. "Here's a dog rose."

The woman's eyes lit up. "Do you like dog roses, my lady?"

"I do."

"I can make you a grand posy if you'd like."

Clapping, Evelyn turned to John. "It would be ever so fitting to carry a bouquet of dog roses during the wedding."

She couldn't be serious. His bride deserved the most expensive, elaborate bouquet of flowers in London, not some street vendor's moth-eaten silk roses. "Would you not prefer Great Maiden's Blush?"

The wench grinned—one tooth missing in the front. "I can add Maiden's Blush if you'd like, sir."

John glanced at the shop. The shingle hung on one chain, the door weathered, windows cracked—no wonder the woman was incapable of discerning a nobleman from a commoner. "I think fresh flowers would suit my bride best."

"Oh, please, Mar." Evelyn's eyes looked hopeful. "If I carry silk flowers, I'll have them forever."

Odd comment coming from a horticulturist. Not to mention her ladyship certainly had an unusual fetish for dog roses. "I do not—"

"I'll tend your rig, sir." A boy wrapped his fingers around Daisy's bridle and pointed to a pullover. "I'll be just up there."

"Come, miss." The woman tugged Evelyn's arm, coaxing her out of the chaise. "My, that's a rich brocade you're wearing. You must be of quality."

John grumbled under his breath—now he had no choice but to follow. "All right then. We won't be but a moment." He tossed the lad a coin and hastened after Her Ladyship.

The inside of the shop appeared as shabby as the outside. Bolts of fabric were stacked askew on shelves among pots, pans, and pails all filled with assorted cloth flowers—some encrusted with dust and mold.

The woman pulled Evelyn through a door at the back. "The finest roses are through here."

John hastened after them . . . until a burly man blocked his path.

"Hello, sir."

"Lord Mar, if you will."

"An earl, are you?"

John craned his neck aside, trying to catch sight of Evelyn. "An irritated earl if you do not step out of my way, sir."

"Let the ladies look at flowers." The man grasped John's shoulder, his fingers digging in. "I've some fine snuffboxes to show you right over here."

Wrenching his arm away, John stepped nose to nose

with the lout and thrust his finger in the direction where Her Ladyship had disappeared. "That is the daughter of the Duke of Kingston-upon-Hull and you will move aside this instant."

"Right-o. Thing is, the queen's rules do not apply in my shop."

"Is that so? In light of your lack of hospitality, I will be sure to inform the queen's dragoons of your treasonous assertions."

"I think not." Baring his teeth, the man drew a knife. "Now empty that Scottish purse covering your loins and I might be inclined to let you walk out of here alive."

John crouched, his fingers splayed, ready for a fight. He reached for his dirk.

The man swiped with his knife. "Nay, you'll not be drawing against me. Raise your hands above your head."

A shrill scream came from behind the door.

"You picked the wrong Highlander to cross." Lunging to the side, John grasped the back of the man's knife-wielding hand. With a brutal twist, he snapped the cur's wrist, making the blade drop to the floorboards. Howling in pain, the bastard bent forward. John drove his knee into the man's face, then slammed his fist on the back of his neck. The cur dropped unconscious to the floor while John grabbed the knife and raced into the next room.

The place was a disheveled mess, as if it had been abandoned. At the rear, a door swung lazily on its hinges. "Lady Evelyn?"

A grunt came from the far corner, behind a torn screen.

John slid the knife into his belt, drawing his dirk as he crept forward. A man stood over Her Ladyship, pulling off her doeskin gloves.

Rage shot through his veins. "You bloody rutting bastard!"

The man turned and lunged, slashing with a dagger. "I'll gut you!"

"Not this day," John growled as he kicked the blade from the man's hand. Using the momentum to drive his dirk across the blackguard's gullet, he killed the fiend in a heartbeat.

As soon as the attacker clutched his neck and dropped, John fell to his knees and gathered Lady Evelyn in his arms, cradling her head in his hand. Christ, they'd stolen her bonnet, her gold locket, and Lord knew what else. "Are you hurt, lass?" he asked, pulling the rag from her mouth.

"I—they . . ." Her eyes rolled back.

Damnation, warm blood seeped through his fingers. With not a moment to lose, he raced for the door and out to the street. He looked south for his rig, then north. "Where's my bloody horse?"

No one said a damned word. Coaches and wagons rolled past as if he didn't exist. Well, John wasn't about to stand idle cradling his injured betrothed in his arms. He balanced Evelyn in his left while thrusting his palm in front of an approaching cart. "Stop in the name of Her Majesty the queen!"

* * *

Evelyn's head throbbed, punishing her while the wagon jounced over the cobblestones.

"I'm sorry," she repeated over and over again. How could she have been so daft? Her finch-brained effort to rankle Mar and insist on carrying a posy of silk dog roses had misfired and nearly seen them both killed.

"The danger has passed now, lass," he whispered into

her hair. "Close your eyes and rest. Another few minutes and we'll arrive at your da's door."

Could things grow worse? There she was, looking like a complete nincompoop in the arms of her future husband as they rode in the rear of a wagon half filled with rum barrels. Mar's carriage and horse were lost, and those horrible people had stolen her gloves and gold locket with a miniature of her mother.

And Mr. Dubois had said she had the makings of a good spy? She had the makings of a good dolt. If only she weren't the firstborn daughter of a duke, things might have been different. She might have stayed in Nottingham and married the vicar's son. Though Father never would have approved. A vicar's son wasn't likely to help Hull gain favor with the queen. Besides, marrying the lad wouldn't have been a love match, either. And married to a country gentleman, she would be of no use to Mr. Dubois or those she hoped to help. True, Mar would be taking her to the Highlands, but once she was there, who knew what she'd face? Would she be cloistered in some godforsaken tower among a plethora of royalist strangers?

Goodness, her husband-to-be was all but a stranger, a man who had behaved gallantly toward her, yet by his reputation he was anything but a knight in shining armor. How could she cast aside everything she'd heard? Regardless of his chivalry, she was entering the lion's den and must remain vigilant—stay true to her beliefs.

Evelyn's eyes flew open when the wagon jolted to a stop.

"We've arrived," Mar said as the driver came around. The earl slipped his fingers into his sporran and pulled out a crown. "You are a good man, and I thank you."

The driver slipped the coin into his purse. "'Tis generous of you, my lord."

Evelyn squeezed her eyes shut. Why was the earl acting so affable? Everyone knew his reputation to be self-absorbed, indecisive, and surly. Perhaps his ability to change character on a whim was why his critics called him Bobbin' John.

He carried her up the steps and pushed in the door. "Call a physician at once!" Mar shouted as Porter came into the entry with Brutus at his heels barking.

The butler silenced the Corgi with a slice of his hand. "Lord Mar? What has happened?"

"We were set upon by outlaws on London Bridge, of all places. Send word to Her Majesty's dragoons and tell them to exterminate the vermin from the chaff." Mar hastened for the stairs. "Lady Phoebe!"

Evelyn's sister peeked around the landing. "Yes, my lord?"

"Lead the way to Her Ladyship's chamber. Where's your father?"

"A-at the gentleman's club."

"Send a messenger for him."

"Is Evelyn going to be all right?"

"I think she will be, but Her Ladyship has suffered a blow to her head."

"I just have a bit of megrim," Evelyn said, wondering how the earl managed the strength to carry her up three flights of stairs after the effort it took to dispatch those vile miscreants. "I think you can put me down."

"Soon." His face was tense and filled with concern as Phoebe opened the door to her chamber. "Tell the maid to bring water and cloths."

"Straightaway, my lord—should I send for Papa first or the maid?"

"Send up the maid forthwith—and Her Ladyship will

need a tincture of willow bark tea. Then as quickly as you can, send for your da." Mar hastened toward the bed and set Evelyn down ever so gently. "Allow me to fluff the pillows behind you."

She leaned forward. "Truly, I'm feeling much better. There's no need for you to fuss."

"There is every need for me to fuss." He grasped her shoulders and helped her lie back as if she was unable to do so under her own power. Then he gazed at her with those shocking blue eyes, so intense they pinned her to the headboard. "You are *my* family now. We may not have exchanged vows, but we have signed a contract to do so soon. Do you know what family and kin mean to me?"

She shook her head.

"I will protect you with my life. No matter what, I will not let anyone harm you. And if they dare, I will show them no mercy."

A shudder coursed from her belly to her chest. "Dispatch them like you did those men today?"

"If I must." He kissed her forehead, then stood beside her. "Never forget clan and kin come first for any Scot. Only then comes king and country."

Her stomach squeezed. "King?"

Those steely eyes narrowed. "Queen, as it were."

Before Evelyn asked another question, Lucinda rushed inside, her arms laden with cloths. "I came as fast as I could, my lady."

Mar beckoned the maid to the bedside. "I think the bleeding has stopped, but Her Ladyship needs her wound cleaned."

The maid dashed to the washstand and poured a bowl of water. "What happened?"

Evelyn sat forward while Mar explained the whole

debacle and Lucinda doused a cloth and set to cleansing. "At least the gash isn't but a half inch."

"Och, she bled plenty."

"But how did you hit your head, my lady?"

"Someone must have struck me from behind." Reaching back, she swirled her fingers around the sore spot. "I'll be fine. 'Twas just one blow."

"She'll need bedrest until the wedding, for certain," said Mar.

"You must be jesting." Evelyn dropped back against the pillows. "I'll be up and about in the morning."

"I caution you not to push yourself overmuch." His Lordship looked to Lucinda. "Where's the willow bark tea I ordered?"

"Cook's sending it up as soon as it brews."

"Very well." Mar reached back and fluffed the pillows again. "Well then, Lady Evelyn, you've naught but to lie back and rest until the physician arrives."

Sighing, Evelyn did as he said, casting a forlorn look to her lady's maid. It seemed Mar had placed himself in charge and there was no getting around it. The physician was announced about three quarters of an hour later, and the earl stood over the man throughout his examination, on several occasions insisting he would tolerate no bleeding whatsoever.

Papa appeared midway and the three of them discussed Evelyn's condition while she continued to lie on the bed with her hands folded, unable to manage a word edgewise.

The earl won out in the end. Evelyn was restricted to no less than a week of bedrest while being tended by a maid around the clock, which would allow her no privacy and only three days to ready herself for her wedding. How on earth was she to manage?

Chapter Eight

*C*arrying a vase with two dozen tulips, John stopped outside Evelyn's chamber door when Her Ladyship's voice came through the cracked opening.

"It has been six days. I am perfectly able to run a footrace if need be. I absolutely insist you allow me out of this bed this instant!"

"But Mar said—"

"The earl? You are my father. John Erskine has no right to dictate what I can and cannot do until we are wed. You heard the physician. He initially said I'd only need two to three days of rest, but, at Mar's insistence, I have endured twice that."

"But look at all these flowers. The earl has doted on you so. I think it is lovely. Why not humor him for one more day?"

"Because I will die of boredom."

John bit the inside of his cheek. He may have been a tad overzealous when he'd insisted she must rest for an entire week, but then he'd been the one responsible for Evelyn's attack. He should have been more assertive with her from the outset. She was but an inexperienced maid of one and twenty. What did she know of the ruthlessness of men? Furthermore, he should have recognized the gravity of the danger by the hair prickling the back of his neck. And there was another reason he'd acted with undue caution and insisted upon ample bedrest.

If Evelyn were to die because of his neglect, he would never forgive himself. Margaret had died because of him—he hadn't been vigilant enough. He hadn't been firm enough with the physician.

He opened the door wider with his toe and moved inside the chamber filled with vases of blooms he'd brought each day. "Run a footrace, did I hear?"

Evelyn's eyes popped wide as she looked his way. "My Lord? How long have you been listening?"

"Long enough to realize I may have overreacted a wee bit—though I'll nay apologize. At the time I felt every precaution needed to be taken to ensure Your Ladyship's full recovery."

"And you were right to be cautious." Hull turned, rubbing his signet ring on his lapel. "I say, Mar, why do we not allow Lady Evelyn at least a stroll in the courtyard?"

As Evelyn's eyes grew hopeful, John stopped himself from expounding upon his fears—telling them how the physician had bled Margaret, how the fever had grown worse, how the woman he'd loved grew weaker by the day. For heaven's sake, Lady Evelyn had been in good health before she'd been hit in the head.

He forced a smile, hoping it was a playful one. "Of course. I wouldn't want you to perish from boredom before we take our vows."

"There, you see, Evelyn? Mar isn't such an old curmudgeon."

John winced. At the age of seven and thirty he in no way considered himself old and had never referred to himself as a curmudgeon. He'd tried to make Evelyn's convalescence tolerable by bringing flowers every day, by reading to her.

John turned. "Hull, would you mind giving us a moment?"

The duke frowned, glancing between the pair. "Of course, my lord."

John bowed. "Thank you, Your Grace."

Once Evelyn's father left the chamber, closing the door behind him, John held up the vase of tulips. "These are for you."

"They are lovely, thank you." She glanced from one table laden with flowers to the next. "Though I have no idea where you'll put them."

"How about on the windowsill?"

"No—" she gasped, drawing her fingers to her lips. "Ah...silly me, I'm sure they will look very nice there."

He set the flowers on the sill and picked up a silk sunflower, twirling it between his fingers. "I wish I'd known you were partial to sunflowers. They're one of my favorite blooms."

A bit of color sprang to Lady Evelyn's cheeks. "I think they represent happiness."

"Aye, and loyalty."

"Yes," she whispered.

John replaced the sunflower and slipped to Her Ladyship's bedside. "Do you mind if I sit?"

She gestured with an upturned palm. "'Tis because of her, is it not?"

"I beg your pardon?" he asked, sitting so he faced her with one knee up. Yes, he knew exactly what Lady Evelyn meant, but he'd never own to it.

"When you told me you would protect clan and kin with your life, I believed you. But the real reason behind your obsessive worry and all these flowers, albeit glorious, is because of the former countess. Am I right?"

John took her hand between his palms. It was small and soft like Margaret's had been, but different all the same. So many things were different. When he'd married Margaret ten years past, Lady Evelyn would have only been eleven years of age. The wee lassie was proving headstrong where Margaret was affable. Evelyn was opinionated and overly confident...though she had the most diverting turquoise eyes. And the pout of her lips had begun to endear him. Though one thing he needed to be wary of from this day forward was that Her Ladyship was far too perceptive for her own good.

He sighed, owing the lass a response. "I would be lying if I told you Margaret's death hadn't affected me. I mourned her. But all widows and widowers who remain behind holding the torch must go on and live their lives— cherish the good memories and put the bad behind."

She brushed an errant lock of hair away from his brow. "Are you able to put all that you've endured behind you, Mar?"

Whether he was ready or not, he would proceed with the wedding. There was too much riding on this union, and it had everything to do with clan and kin and nothing to do with his bleeding heart.

Placing his hands either side of the lady, he leaned in and stole a wee kiss. "As long as you promise not to follow toothless wenches into derelict buildings, I think things will be pleasurable and engaging between us. I know I will do everything in my power to see to your comfort."

She tapped her finger on his lips. "Do you want to know what I think?"

Watching her gaze, he took that very finger, drew it into his mouth, and licked it. "Aye."

"There's more lying under the surface with you, whether you realize it or not. I saw it in your eyes the first time we met."

"But you're who I desire now," he whispered. Indeed, this woman was too perceptive. But two could play her game. He slid his hand around the back of her neck and captured her lips. And this time he didn't toy about. Taking command, he devoured her mouth and showed her exactly how passionate a kiss could be. When she whimpered, his cock shot ramrod straight as he kissed until she was breathless. Down her neck he licked her with swirls of his tongue.

He stole kisses along the neckline of her shift, watching the heave of her breast below the linen. Full, ripe, and waiting to be fondled.

How long had it been since he'd had a woman?

Too long.

God, if he tarried he might take her right there under her father's roof.

"See, lass?" he growled, forcing himself to ease away.

Her lips parted as she leaned toward him as if asking for more.

He raised her fingers upward. Watching her, he kissed each knuckle, slowly, seductively, showing her how much he looked forward to their wedding night. "Dream of me kissing you, lass. For come Saturday I intend to kiss every inch of your bonny flesh."

Chapter Nine

*G*ripping the bedpost, Evelyn exhaled every bit of air from her lungs and gave a nod.

"Do not breathe in," Lucinda said, her voice straining as she tugged on the ribbons.

Unable to speak, Evelyn held her breath.

"I think you need a larger set of stays," said Frances, ever the not-so-helpful sister. "You're as pale as bed linens."

"These stays are exactly what the modiste—" With Lucinda's words, the ribbon snapped and the accursed contraption released.

Evelyn inhaled a reviving breath while her breasts slid to their normal position. "Will nothing go right this day?"

"See?" said Frances. "I don't even think Phoebe could wear those stays."

"Of course I could." Already dressed in her yellow gown, Phoebe hopped up from her seat and tugged away the broken laces. Then she held the corset against her chest and twirled across the floor. "Look at me. I'm a grown woman with sumptuous bosoms."

Lucinda found a new ribbon and held out her hand. "You ought to appreciate your freedom whilst you have it, Lady Phoebe. You'll be wrapped and bound with boning soon enough."

"I keep telling you stays are horrible, but you won't listen," said Frances. "That's why I said Evelyn needs a larger size."

And the stays were only the half of the disasters on her wedding day. After Lucinda took the rags out of Evelyn's hair, not one curl would sit properly. "I look like Medusa!"

Brush in hand, Lucinda stood back with hairpins hanging from the side of her mouth. "Give me a few minutes and I'll have your locks neat and tidy."

"I think that will take a miracle," said Phoebe.

Evelyn buried her face in her lace veil—which was the wrong shade. It was ivory instead of the pink she'd ordered to match the lace on her gown, bless it. Now she would be walking down the aisle looking as if she were in French mourning.

She bunched the accursed veil in her fists. "I can't do this. Everything is all wrong."

"It will be fine, my lady. All brides are nervous on the morn of their wedding."

"I'd be nervous." Frances drew the veil from Evelyn's fingers, slung it about her shoulders, and admired herself in the mirror. "Behind closed doors with a man."

"You say that as if men are vile creatures," said Phoebe. "I think Mar is very handsome and pleasant, isn't he, Evelyn?"

Her mouth suddenly dry, Evelyn had no quick reply.

Yes, the earl was attractive—and being in the same room with him made her very self-aware. He certainly was quite adept at kissing. She touched her lips. *Quite adept.*

"Isn't he?" Phoebe repeated.

"Yes. He's..." Beautiful, arresting, stately, and oh, so very brawny. "He's pleasant to look upon."

Phoebe shoved Frances away from the mirror and affected a regal pose. "I think weddings are the most important day for any woman. And I want mine to be stupendous. In fact, I think I'll marry a Russian prince."

"Do you have one in mind?" asked Frances.

"Not yet, but I have time."

Evelyn tuned them out. This afternoon she was marrying the Earl of Mar. She would be a countess in a few hours' time. But that wasn't what made her tingle all over. That wasn't what made her feel as if she were floating. And wasn't what terrified her to her very core. This very night she would do more than kiss Mar, and, to her horror, she wanted him—more of him. More touching. More kissing. More of that insatiable desire swirling through her body.

Was her soul betraying her?

She didn't know. She had no idea what being the Countess of Mar would be like. On one hand she expected, almost wanted, her married life to be horrible. But thus far the earl had behaved so differently than she'd expected. Had he been acting like a player would do in one of Shakespeare's tragedies to trick her into liking him? What about Mr. Dubois's expectations? Evelyn had never been more confused in all her days, yet she must not turn her back on everything she had worked for. She would be John Erskine's wife. She would use her position to strive to help the oppressed and work to see that the only true heir to the throne took his rightful place.

Papa came to the door. "Will you ladies please excuse us? I'd like to have a word with my daughter."

Evelyn looked in the mirror. Only half of her hair had been brought under control. "Now?"

"I won't be but a moment." He gave her a once-over. "Good God, Lucinda, what have you done with my daughter's hair?"

"It will be lovely when I'm finished. Mark me."

"I truly hope so, else you'll have to start again."

While the others slipped away, Papa pulled a chair beside Evelyn and crossed both his arms and his legs. Even his face pinched as if he'd just swallowed a bitter tonic. "This is a time when I wish your mother were still alive. She deserved to see her eldest daughter grow up to be so lovely and marrying an earl."

"Even if my hair looks like Medusa?"

"Only one side is a bit unruly. And I've no doubt Lucinda will turn it into a work of art. She always has in the past." Papa grasped Evelyn's hand and gave it a pat. "But that's not why I'm here."

She had a fair idea she didn't want to hear the reason for this visit.

"A mother is duty bound to speak to her daughter before she takes her marriage vows, but today I must do so in her place."

"There's no need to worry, Papa. I'm certain—"

"You understand the need for a nobleman to produce an heir?"

"Yes, though Mar already has an heir."

"Ah…" Papa ran a hand down his mouth, looking somewhat dumbfounded. "Notwithstanding, it is a wife's duty to submit…ah…to her husband's…er…needs."

"I see."

"In the boudoir," Papa continued as if she hadn't spoken. "Do you understand?"

"I am duty bound to submit?"

"Indeed. Well, I'm glad we've had this little chat."

Evelyn dared to ask, "So, even if a wife doesn't agree with her husband's"—she couldn't say politics—"*rules*, she would still be duty bound to sub...submit?"

"You have always been such a bright young lady. I'm sure you will enjoy many years of happiness with Lord Mar." Papa stood and kissed her cheek. "I'll send Lucinda right in. We haven't much time."

Evelyn hardly heard him. She was still fixated on the "years of happiness." Though she knew marriage was for a lifetime, somehow the words struck a chord. By this time tomorrow, her entire life would be changed.

And returning to the old would not be an option.

As Papa had predicted, Lucinda managed to tame Medusa into lovely rows of ringlets topped by a coif and veil. As soon as Evelyn was dressed, Father insisted the family immediately file into the coach rather than enjoy a glass of sherry and a turn around the drawing room, or anything other than departing for the church. During the ride she felt numb, her stomach queasy. Worse, the horses traveled far too quickly.

Once they rolled to a stop outside the enormous cathedral, everyone alighted from the carriage except Evelyn. She sat gripping a bouquet of lilies, scarcely able to breathe.

"Evelyn?" her father called from outside.

She didn't respond.

"Evelyn." The door opened and Papa popped his head inside. "'Tis time. Come."

"Must I?"

"Indeed you must." He offered his palm. "Not to worry, my dear. All young women are nervous on their wedding day. Now take my hand. We shan't keep the earl waiting."

How she managed to move from the carriage into the nave passed in a complete blur, but Evelyn wouldn't have been surprised if later her father told her he'd ordered a pair of footmen to each take an arm and carry her to the door.

Once she and Papa began to process down the aisle of the nave with rows of people standing and staring, Evelyn realized she wasn't in the midst of a dream even though she felt as if she were floating. It all seemed so surreal with the two-story pipe organ playing Bach's great fugue, swirling and building with her every step. And with each footfall, so grew her confidence.

Dressed as a Highlander, Mar stood beneath the enormous dome. Sunbeams radiating downward from the rotunda of windows all shone on the earl, making him appear like a Scottish knight of old—one hand resting on the hilt of his sword, the other fisted by his side.

"Ye are a vision," he whispered as she stepped beside him.

She peered up at him from beneath the shroud of her veil. "Might I say the groom is as well."

He gave her a wink while the priest began the ceremony. A new sensation of courage coursed through her blood as Evelyn recited her vows. And when Mar lifted her veil, she met his gaze, determined to be strong and stand by her principles no matter what may come.

With an arch to his eyebrow, he leaned forward and kissed her forehead. "You will never have anything to fear from me, dear one."

She prayed he spoke the truth.

Chapter Ten

*W*hy did Lady Evelyn not come in to kiss us good night?" asked Oliver, tucked in bed with his floppy Scotsman doll.

John tweaked the lad's nose. "She's in her chamber preparing for bed. I'll ask her to come up with me and kiss you good night on the morrow, how will that be?"

Oliver pulled aside his bedclothes. "I could go kiss her now. That might make her feel more welcome."

John urged him back down and straightened the quilt. At the moment, Evelyn was being readied for her wedding night by her lady's maid. Having an affectionate five-year-old lad wander into her chamber at the moment might unhinge the poor lass. "'Tis best to move slowly for a time. I'm certain your stepmother will want your affection on the morrow."

"Well, I don't want her to kiss me," said Thomas from the adjoining bed.

John glanced to his eldest. The lads oft disagreed, but

when it came to Evelyn, he'd prefer Oliver's exuberance to Thomas's grumbling. "That's no way to speak of your stepmother."

Tom folded his arms and rolled onto his side with his back to John. "She'll never replace Ma. I'm just telling ye now."

"And we've discussed that she will not. I wish things had stayed the same, but they didn't, and we've naught but to accept our lot and be thankful for our gifts."

"Is Lady Evelyn a gift?" asked Oliver, bless him.

"Aye, a gift from God and you mustn't ever forget it." John placed his hand on Tom's shoulder. "You as well."

Again, Oliver pushed away the bedclothes. "Will we always have to call her Lady Evelyn?"

"I think we ought to discuss that with Her Ladyship. Once you have brothers and sisters..."

Thomas glanced over his shoulder. "Brothers and sisters?"

"Eventually, aye. And they will call Lady Evelyn 'Mother.'"

"Och."

Mrs. Kerr came in with a book under her arm. "'Tis time to bid your father good night. And I have the story of Pocahontas from the Americas to tell you."

"That sounds riveting." John kissed his sons good night, thankful for Mrs. Kerr's timing. No matter how much he'd rather spend the rest of the evening with the lads, he had a duty to perform, and hiding in the nursery was no place for a groom on his wedding night.

But he didn't head straight for the countess's chamber. MacVie had the tray prepared as John had requested. He first stopped and removed his periwig. The damned thing was hot and ridiculous, but fashionable and expected. He pulled the ribbon tying his hair back and gave it a quick comb. That was better.

He picked up the tray and tapped on the adjoining door with his toe. When there came no reply, he tapped again.

"Yes?" Lady Evelyn's voice warbled a bit.

"May I come in?"

"Ah…" She sounded terribly nervous. "I am ready."

"Excellent." Opening the door, he smiled and held up the tray, almost disappointed with his plan for a slow seduction—if they got that far. Evelyn reclined in bed with chestnut locks arranged across the pillows like a nymph—except she had the bedclothes pulled up to her chin.

He held up the tray. "I thought we might enjoy a libation with grapes and cheese."

She clutched the coverlet under her chin as she peered over it. "You brought food?"

"Aye. Are you hungry?"

"I…ah." Her eyebrows arched as if surprised he hadn't stormed into the room and set to carrying out the imminent consummation. "Famished," she finally said. "I was too nervous to eat."

He thought about asking permission to sit beside her on the bed but decided being direct might serve at the moment. He sauntered over and placed the tray on the bed. "Move over, please."

"I-I beg your pardon?"

"You do not intend for me to pull up a chair, aye? Now scoot over a wee bit so I may join you."

"We're going to eat on the bed?" she asked while popping a grape in her mouth.

"Why should we not?" He gestured to the tray. "I've brought wine and whisky. Which would you prefer?"

"A lady mustn't drink whisky."

"Nay? Within the confines of her bedchamber, I reckon a lady can enjoy that which she pleases." John wrapped fingers around the wine bottle and pulled out the cork. "But I guessed you'd prefer wine."

A hint of mischief danced in her eyes. "I've never tasted whisky before."

He uprighted the bottle before he started to pour. "Och, lassie. That is a situation we must remedy straightaway."

Evelyn looked from side to side as if there might be peepholes where dragoons were watching in wait to take into custody any whisky-swilling brides who had not yet been deflowered. "Are you sure?"

John gave her a wink and poured a dram. "It has a wee bite, but there's nothing better to take the edge off one's nerves."

She took the glass, her fingers trembling. "W-who said I am nervous?"

"Och, mayhap I'm the anxious one." He guided the dram to his lips and watched his new bride's curious stare while coaxing her to pour a sip into his mouth. Grinning, he licked his lips and took the glass from her grasp. "Now you."

"Perhaps a small taste." Did she have any idea how sensual she looked, her ruby lips parted, her gaze innocent, yet sultry? Everything about this woman was as sultry as a hot summer's day.

Slowly, she directed John's hand to her lips until the smallest of sips spilled into her mouth. Her eyes flashed wide as she fanned her face and coughed. "Oh my, that is potent."

He took a healthy swig and savored the fire as it trickled down his gullet. "Would you prefer wine?"

White teeth scraped over a delicate bottom lip. "Perhaps a bit of cheese and bread first."

"Your wish is my command." He put a slice of cheese on some bread, but when Evelyn reached for it, he drew his hand away from her grasp. He'd planned this seduction and he would damn well follow through with it. "Allow me the honor of feeding you, m'lady."

With a nervous giggle, she opened her mouth wider this time and John slipped the morsel inside. "Mm." The woman's eyes rolled back as she chewed. Holy Moses, she embodied temptation. "Delicious."

"'Tis Scottish cheese."

"Why is it different?"

He served himself and chewed. "Highland coos."

"Coos?"

"Bovine animals that say moo." John poured another tot of whisky, but this time Evelyn plucked the glass before he picked it up.

"Cows." She sipped with hardly a cough this time. "I imagine there are many new words I'll need to learn."

"Most everyone in Alloa speaks English."

"Are your lands in the Highlands or the Lowlands?"

"A bit of both, really. I like to say the tower is at the gateway to the Highlands."

She gave him a curious look, as if his answer didn't sit terribly well. And then she drank down the entire dram.

"Ho, lassie, there's a fire in that spirit, and the first rule is to respect it, else you'll be burned and end up with a megrim the size of Bass Rock come morn."

"I think I like the way it warms my insides." She set the glass on the tray. "Besides, you said it calms one's nerves."

John stoppered the whisky bottle. "A wee tot takes the

edge off your nerves, guzzling it only serves to turn the guzzler into a drunken fool."

As she tossed her locks over her shoulder, Evelyn's smile seemed easier than when he'd first arrived. "I do not think I'm inebriated."

"Nor would I want you to be, else come the morrow you'd never forgive me."

She plucked another grape from the bunch. "So, Mar...am I to continue to call you Mar?"

"If it pleases you, though when in private, I prefer John."

Her teeth grazed her bottom lip. "John when you're visiting my bedchamber?"

"Aye, for starters." He took the grape from her fingertips and popped it into her mouth. "And you? What endearment shall I use for you?"

"Evelyn is fine."

"Hmm." He captured a lock of her hair and let it slide across his finger, the texture far silkier than he'd imagined. Drawing the end of the curl to his lips, he kissed it, again watching her eyes. Oh, yes, they grew dark.

"Eve," he whispered, leaning forward and nuzzling her neck. "Eve is for moments like this when you're seducing me."

A bit of juice moistened her lips. Absently, she licked it away. "How can I be seducing you when you're the one kissing me?"

"Do you think your eyes have no effect on me? Or your lips when they're moist with grapes and whisky?" He slid his finger along her shift's scooped neckline. "Or knowing your unbound breasts are waiting to be suckled beneath this thin bit of linen."

She gasped ever so subtly—the cue John wanted before his lips trailed lower. "You see," he whispered, untying the bow and sliding his hand inside until he cupped her breast. Large, soft, and pliable, he'd never held a breast so exquisite. "I want to kiss you here."

"W-w-what?"

With his next exhale, he blew warm breath over her nipple. "You heard me, lass." He lapped his tongue over the erect pebble, the taste making him instantly hard. As she moaned and slipped lower, he took her breast into his mouth, kneading both with his hands.

Eve's breath grew faster. "What are you doing to me? Heat is swirling through my insides...like...like an insatiable hunger."

John chuckled. "'Tis only the prelude to passion." He looked up. "But before I can go farther I need you bare."

She crossed her arms. "You mean *naked*?"

"Aye." He could pull up her shift and plunge in like an inexperienced lad, but he'd rather return to his chamber and take himself in hand than act the callous buffoon.

Expecting her reluctance, John stood, set the tray aside, and unfastened the brooch at his shoulder.

Evelyn watched him, her eyes wide. "A-are you disrobing as well?"

"It is only fair if I go first, aye, lass?"

Her gaze meandered down to his sporran, exactly where he wanted her to look. It took only a flick of his fingers to remove his belt, and with that, dirk, sporran, and his kilt all dropped to the floorboards. "Undressing a Highlander takes no time whatsoever," he said as he shrugged out of his doublet.

"I see."

He spread his arms to his sides and turned full circle. "This shirt is all that's covering me now."

Evelyn gripped the coverlet. "All?"

"Have you ever seen a naked man before?"

Eyes as round as guineas, she shook her head very slowly.

He untied his neckcloth and let it cascade atop his pile of clothes. "Men are different, and when a man desires a woman, he grows hard."

"Hard?"

"As hard as marble." He tugged the shirt off and stood still for a moment, letting her eyes drink in their fill.

Until a pink tongue slipped to the corner of her mouth. "I-I, I am to submit to that?"

He stroked himself, knowing exactly what the overt display of audaciousness did to a woman's insides. "Not until you are pleading for it."

"But I would never—"

"We shall see." He gently tugged back the bedclothes. "'Tis your turn."

* * *

Within the blink of an eye, John slipped her shift over her head and moved under the coverlet beside her. Evelyn froze, trying not to think about what she'd just seen. But his naked body warmed her—more than warmed—made her intimate parts stir, shocking her half to death. How could a man she didn't love bring about such wanton desire?

His chest moved over her as a gentle push with his hand coaxed Evelyn onto her back. His gaze dipped to her lips right before he kissed her—hot, searing kisses demanding a response. His hands caressed her breast, his thumb and forefinger teasing her burning peak. "I never want to see these bound, for they are too bonny to cover up."

"But—"

Before she uttered an objection, he devoured her mouth, his knee nudging her legs apart.

And as he kissed, his hand trailed down, down, down to where the heat coiled tightly in her belly. A heat that had simmered for days.

Evelyn gasped as his finger slid over skin so sensitive it made her arch her back. Everything around her faded into oblivion as his finger explored recesses as if he'd opened a window of raw desire that had always lurked dormant inside her.

"Do you want more?" he growled, his lips moving down the center of her belly. He seemed to know more about her body than she.

"No," she said—almost sighed. With the single word, his finger stilled. She nearly burst. He couldn't stop. Not now. "Yes. I-I don't know."

"More," he whispered. In the next moment, he licked her. Without warning, his tongue slid over the sensitive private place that craved more—and he knew it.

"*Mon Dieu*," she cried, running his hair through her fingers as his mouth relentlessly sucked. Tossing her head from side to side, Evelyn held on while his mouth did ungodly, delightful, sinful, glorious things to her.

Taking in an enormous gasp, she arched up from the bed as if her entire body was about to shatter. And then it did. Unable to help herself, she dropped to the pillows while her insides convulsed in rapture. "Am I dying?"

John laughed—at a moment like this he chuckled and swept his thumb over her quivering flesh. "But we are not finished. Not by half."

"There's more?" How could there be?

"It may hurt at first, but once this night is over, it will never be painful again."

She bit her lip. She'd seen the size of him. How could that fit inside her?

He rose to his knees, letting the bedclothes slip away, revealing his shaft once more. "I promise I'll be as gentle as possible."

Unable to say no, Evelyn stared at his manhood while he lowered himself over her. "But first I want to bring you undone again."

"Again?" she whispered. The shattering could happen again?

And then slowly, methodically, patiently, he started anew—the kisses, the breasts, his hand between her legs. Only when she was writhing and clinging to him did he lever his member toward her.

"Are you ready?"

Evelyn nodded, too filled with desire to fear.

Taking his weight on his arms, he stroked himself along her channel—back and forth, back and forth.

Hurt? Good gracious, his rubbing drove her to the brink of insanity.

"Please!" she cried, needing more—craving him, all of him.

"More?"

"Yes!"

"Now?"

"Oh God, yes, now! Please!"

As his mouth covered hers, he slid inside, then held himself very still. All the while he kissed her as he inched deeper. Evelyn's body stretched but when the pain came, she sank her fingers into his buttocks and pulled him the length of her.

Hot, searing pain shot to the back of her spine as she struggled to breathe.

"'Tis the worst of it," he whispered, looking her in the eyes. "I'll not make a move until you're ready."

Her husband might be her adversary by day, but right there in her bed, he'd bewitched her soul. Evelyn placed her palms either side of his face and drew him to her lips. And as their tongues entwined, her hips began to rock.

Gradually, Mar matched her rhythm, until together their breathing sped. As she shifted her hands to his backside, his tempo sped. Thrusting, grinding and taking her over the shocking new heights of ecstasy. As she cried out with her peak, he thrust into her as if out of control. Then with one roaring bellow, his seed surged inside her.

* * *

John lay beside his wife, cradling her in his arms until she fell asleep. Only then did he slip out of bed, collect his clothes, and head to his chamber, taking the whisky with him.

Never again would he fall in love, but there was no reason not to enjoy the act of copulation. Besides, his new wife didn't need to know he couldn't love her. Telling her his innermost feelings would only serve to alienate the woman when he needed her to assimilate into the family.

His sons needed her.

John drank from the bottle as he slid between his cold bed linens. Most aristocratic couples slept apart. In truth, Margaret oft slept in her chamber, especially when she was with child.

It was better this way. Evelyn would have her freedoms and he'd have his with the door between their chambers always unlocked.

Chapter Eleven

*E*velyn rolled over, her hand sliding across the bed linens. Somewhere in the myriad of her dreams, she knew John had returned to his chamber in the wee hours, though she hadn't yet come fully awake. Neither had she slept soundly. The countess's chamber was strange—the bed larger, the mantel clock ticking at a lower tone than her own. Perhaps she'd ask Lucinda to replace Mar's.

Her body ached from days of stress leading up to the wedding. As Evelyn's mind drifted through the chasm between sleep and awake, she wondered if the events of last eve had been a dream. But even half asleep, she knew the truth. The dull ache between her legs served to remind her as well.

She opened her eyes for a moment. A ray of light shone through a gap in the curtains. Not ready to wake, she rolled over, the motion making cool bed linens slide across her skin.

Scandalous.

She still wore not a stitch of clothing. Never in her life had she been abed naked.

I'll rise in a moment.

"Wait!" a deep voice boomed from beyond the door to the earl's chamber.

As Evelyn's eyes flashed open, Oliver burst into the chamber, ran across the floor, took a flying leap, and landed, straddling her stomach.

Grasping the bedclothes, she clutched them beneath her chin. "Ahhhh—"

With a smile nearly as wide as his freckled face, the boy grabbed her shoulders and gave her a sloppy kiss on the mouth. "Da said I had to wait until morn to kiss you good night."

"Can you not see Her Ladyship doesn't want us in here?" Thomas said from the doorway.

Stunned, Evelyn looked from one boy to the next. "I-I am—"

Tying a plaid around his waist, John hastened inside, hair mussed as if he'd only just risen. "Oliver, remove yourself from your stepmother's bed this instant!"

Stepmother? The moniker sounded alien.

"But you said I could kiss her come morn." Looking like a dejected puppy, the youngest slid off the mattress. "I only wanted to make Her Ladyship feel welcome."

"Aye, well you mustn't ever enter a lady's chamber without first knocking and being invited inside." John beckoned his youngest. "Now apologize."

The lad scooted toward his brother. "I'm sorry."

"There's no need to feel bad," Evelyn said, slipping lower and ensuring she was completely covered from her chin down. "But your father is right. I might have been dressing or bathing or—" *naked beneath the bedclothes.*

Thomas grabbed Oliver by the wrist. "Come, we'd best go break our fast."

"I'll join you shortly," John said, remaining behind. He leaned against the doorjamb, crossing his arms over a sculpted chest. How could someone rise from his bed and look like a Greek Adonis, mussed hair and all? "I'll have a word with the lads and ensure there are no more uninvited visits to your chamber."

She glanced at her shift still in a heap on the floor— definitely not something she wanted her stepsons to see. They might be too young to understand everything, but crumpled ladies' undergarments should never be on display with the boys present. "Thank you."

His gaze drifted to the shift and back to Evelyn's face. "Unfortunately, the queen is expecting me for her cabinet meeting. I imagine I'll be away afore you're dressed."

"Your presence is expected the day after your wedding?"

"Her Majesty feels she was most generous by allowing me yesterday's holiday." He grasped the latch and stepped back. "But I'll try to slip away early if possible."

"Before you go." Evelyn started to sit up, but as soon as the coverlet slid a bit, she stopped. "'Stepmother' sounds so…so unwarm. And 'my lady' seems inordinately formal for young children. Is there something else they might call me?"

"Believe it or not, the lads asked the same." He tapped a finger to his lips. "Your name wouldn't suit. That would be far too disrespectful. Why don't you ask them? I'll wager they'll appreciate being consulted."

"Very well."

He started to close the door but stopped and popped

his head back through. "How are you feeling this morn, Eve?"

The timbre of his voice reignited the flame deep in her belly while the dark glint in his eyes made her breath catch. "Well, thank you," she croaked. For the love of Moses, there was yet another side to the Earl of Mar. And this version of the man made her very nervous indeed.

* * *

Thank heavens Lucinda suggested ordering a breakfast tray. With Mar away, Evelyn had no idea how she should approach the boys—not after this morning's assault. On one hand, Oliver was endearing and instantly likeable, while Thomas was brooding and standoffish. And, yes, Evelyn had sisters, but boys were completely different— Highland boys who obviously hadn't been taught English manners by the way they barged into her bedchamber.

They were still young and malleable. And naturally, they would soon be accepted into Eton, where most boys from noble families attended school. The vicar's son in Nottingham had gone from being a hellion to a fine gentleman during his years as a student.

Lucinda sat on the ottoman while Evelyn ate her porridge. "You haven't said a word about your wedding night."

The spoon slipped while her cheeks burned. "I suppose it was what a bride ought to expect. And I'll not entertain any further discussion on the subject."

The lady's maid clasped her hands while she looked about the room. "'Tis different here than in Hull's household."

"Oh? Goodness, I've been so immersed in my own

affairs, I haven't thought to ask you how you fared in your new quarters."

"Everyone has been pleasant thus far." Lucinda cupped a hand at the side of her mouth. "At least they all seem to like him."

"Like who?"

"The earl, of course."

"Interesting."

"And he's increased my wages...or Mr. Swenson has—he's the butler."

"Yes." The servants had all been assembled and introduced when Evelyn arrived last eve, but that's not what caught her attention. "He gave you an increase? My stars, that was generous, and unexpected, yes?"

"He said my wages should be commensurate with the last lady's maid to the countess—makes me realize what a miser your father truly is."

Taking a sip of cider, Evelyn eyed the maid over the top of her glass. She was painfully aware that her father prided himself on keeping wages low, and she was working to help bring about reform. Regardless, the topic wasn't proper for Lucinda to discuss. "I pray you will keep your opinions mum around the others."

"Of course, you know I will. I always do." Lucinda stood and ran her fingers along the mantel, then checked them for dust. "It must be difficult for you, moving into a new home and marrying a man you do not love."

"I'm still trying to come to grips with it all." Evelyn took her last bite of porridge and rested the spoon beside her bowl. "I've only moved a few blocks away from Papa's town house, yet I feel as if I'm in another country."

"Mayhap because Mar's a Scot and most of the staff is

Scottish. I think this house is like a tiny Scottish island in the midst of London."

"I believe you might be right." Evelyn chuckled, glancing back to the plaid covering her bed. "So, overnight I've been spirited away to the Highlands?"

"Aye, as Mr. Swenson would put it." Lucinda picked up the tray. "Since Mar is away, why not do some exploring? You'll feel more at home once the house becomes familiar."

"I think I'll do just that."

"The nursery is one floor up."

"Hmm. Perhaps I'm not quite ready to assume a motherly role." Biting the corner of her mouth, Evelyn glanced away. She needed to do some exploring of another nature, no matter how tightly her stomach twisted. "Have you seen the library, perchance?"

"One floor down."

"Brilliant. I shall start there."

* * *

Mar's library was not unlike her father's. Bookshelves lined the walls, with comfortable chairs and couches arranged for games and reading. Two window embrasures were lined with seat cushions and on one end stood Mar's writing table with at least a dozen drawers. It looked as though a few missives awaited the earl. At one side of the table was a portrait—most likely an ancestor—and if Evelyn guessed right there might be a hidden strongbox behind that brooding visage. At first, she strolled around the room, reading spines and listening to the sounds of the house. In the distance, a muffled clatter from the kitchens echoed now and again.

No noises came from the nursery, though it was two floors up.

Her stomach churned as she ran her fingers along the shelves, aware of every breath, every heartbeat. If she looked through Mar's writing table, would she be able to hide her snooping before someone came in?

But then she was his wife…and she was new to the town house, and Mar had left her alone for the day. How else would she come to know her husband with him away on their very first day as man and wife? What better excuse did she have to snoop? And the letters on the desk were so very, very tempting.

Suddenly she found herself across the library, staring down at a missive addressed to the Right Honorable, the Earl of Mar. It bore the broken seal of a barrister's office. She quickly scanned the contents. *Interesting.* Mar had recently come into a fortune and had settled his father's debts.

So, he married me for my dowry. And how he'd avowed the importance of finding a mother for his sons.

It was hardly surprising Mar had needed her money. Though her father hadn't mentioned the fact, all parties involved were well aware theirs was a marriage of convenience. Mar received coin and a suitable stepmother. Papa purchased a family member who sat on the queen's cabinet. And Evelyn had received a title and protection under the House of Mar for the rest of her days whether she wanted it or not.

As she shifted through the correspondence she realized nothing of import would be sitting in plain view. Slipping over to the portrait, she peeked behind and found only a wall.

She opened drawers of the writing table, one after

another, finding coins, seals, wax wafers, snuffboxes, timepieces, broken quills, and all manner of odds and ends. And after opening all the drawers, she stood back and examined the enormous piece of furniture. Either Mar kept sensitive documents elsewhere, or she'd missed something. She walked around the enormous walnut table, giving a globe a spin. With clawed lion's feet, the table truly was a work of art. And such workmanship did not come without secret compartments.

But where are they?

The bookcase behind caught her eye. Just above the fourth row of books was a strip of mahogany carved in a filigree. Evelyn's pulse quickened. It looked decorative, but a spy never ignored her intuition. In three steps she stood before the exquisite piece and ran her fingers over the polished wood. Underneath, she felt a latch and squeezed her fingers. A wide drawer slid open, along with a layer of books.

Evelyn removed the top document. It listed the queen's expectations for the resolution of the war on the Continent along with the location of Britain's military forces during negotiations for peace in the Netherlands. At the bottom of the document were three names: Hawk, Sharpe, and Richards—the queen's spies attending negotiations in Utrecht. Though the extent of their assignment was not mentioned, they were under explicit orders to use whatever means necessary to ensure the queen's objectives were met.

Another document contained the location and home-port of every ship in Her Majesty's fleet. As Evelyn read on, her heartbeat began to thunder. *"Should the Old Pretender, James Stuart, cross the channel and attempt an insurrection, he will be met with the brute force of Britain's navy."* The letter went on to report that the queen's half brother was being watched, but gave no details beyond saying, *"If James sets foot on a warship in France, British vessels along the eastern seaboard will meet him before he reaches our shores."*

Quickly, Evelyn replaced the parchment and shut the drawer. Drawing her hand over her mouth, she paced. She needed to inform Mr. Dubois at once. She wished at least one of the documents had given hint at the queen's objectives in negotiating peace with France. Everyone knew James was exiled and living at the Château de Saint-Germain-en-Laye. Louis XIV acknowledged James as the only monarch of Britain and had refused to recognize Anne or William and Mary before her.

Surely, the queen meant to force France to abandon its support of James.

When the library door swung open, Evelyn practically jumped out of her skin.

"What are you doing?" asked Thomas, looking very self-righteous.

Still shocked, Evelyn stammered while she glanced to the bookshelf.

Calm yourself. How could this child have any clue what I've just uncovered?

Taking in a deep breath, she forced a smile. "I'm exploring my new home. Do you want to come with me?"

The boy drew his finger across the spines on a row of books. "Nay. I think not."

"Do you like to read?" she asked.

"On occasion."

"Well then, what sorts of things do you like to do?"

"Ride my pony mostly. Though I do enjoy shooting a bow and arrow ... and at home I play shinty with the other lads."

"And sail toy boats?"

Thomas snorted, pulling out a book from the shelf and thumbing through it. "Da wanted to do that."

"I see." Evelyn took a few steps toward the door. "Speaking of your father, he thought I should speak to you and Oliver about what you might like to call me."

He shoved the book back into place, rather forcefully. "Well, I'm not going to call you Mother. Not ever."

"I didn't expect you'd want that. But I don't care for Stepmother, either." Evelyn gripped the latch. "I think the decision might be something to put some thought into. After all, Lady Mar is ever so formal."

"What about Countess?"

"Possibly." Countess wouldn't be horrible. "Perhaps you can talk it over with Oliver."

"Perhaps."

Evelyn opened the door and started out, but something about the boy's dismissiveness made her turn around. "Did you know I lost my mother when I was your age?"

He shook his head, a frown furrowing a brow far too young to appear so distraught.

"I did, and I was angry with everyone. I even blamed God." She reached out to smooth her hand over his shoulder, but stopped, realizing he wasn't ready for her to be motherly. And she most certainly wasn't ready to assume the role. "But do you know who I blamed the most?"

Staring at the floor, Thomas said nothing.

"I blamed myself. I thought I didn't do enough to try to save her. I blamed myself for not praying enough, for laughing when I should have been crying, and for falling asleep when I should have been beside Mama's bed trying to make her better."

A tear streamed down his cheek and dripped onto the carpet.

Evelyn's heart twisted. "No one will ever be able to replace your mother. The hole in your heart that hurts because she's gone will always be there, because when she left you, she took that bit of you with her to heaven. But I promise it won't hurt quite as much one day."

Two more tears dropped.

She stepped nearer. "Know what else?"

"What?" The boy's haunting whisper made shivers course down Evelyn's arms.

"More than anything, your mother would have wanted you to be happy. Whenever you're happy, it makes her smile in heaven."

Before she started crying herself, Evelyn shut the door, ran to her room, and put the sunflower in the window to signal Mr. Dubois. He'd know what to do with the information she had uncovered.

Chapter Twelve

*F*or the next two nights the queen kept the cabinet behind closed doors well into the wee hours. In addition
to her failing health, Anne seemed to be growing more
obsessive and disturbed. Due to her inability to make decisions, John feared she'd never adjourn parliament and
he'd be stuck in London for the duration of her reign.

Each night with the house dark, John had stopped by
the library to review his correspondence. And it didn't escape his notice that on both occasions letters had shifted
on his writing table.

He'd also cracked open the door between their chambers and checked on Evelyn. She didn't wait up for him
as Margaret used to, which was probably for the best. In
the mornings he left before she ventured below stairs to
break her fast. The lads, too.

On the third day when the queen complained of a
megrim, every man on her cabinet encouraged her to take
to her bed, and today it was early afternoon when John

handed Swenson his hat and gloves. "Where might I find Her Ladyship?"

"She's out. Took the dog for a walk."

"Dog?"

"Indeed." The butler grimaced. "She sent for her beloved Corgi yesterday. A geriatric mongrel that looks like an overstuffed haggis. The house is already overrun by fur."

"Brutus." How could John forget? The mutt might be a bit long in the tooth, but he knew how to use those teeth.

"That's the one."

"I suppose if the dog makes her happy, we ought to make amends."

"And feed the damned beast?"

"Aye, that, too." John started for the stairs but stopped before he reached for the first step. "Who is accompanying Lady Mar on this walk?"

Swenson's face blanched. "Beg your pardon, m'lord, but she said Brutus was deterrent enough and she wanted to spend some time in quiet reflection."

Though John had firsthand experience with the Corgi's bite, the dog would be no match for a musket ball or the blade of a man's dagger. She was the bloody Countess of Mar, and as the wife of a cabinet minister, she needed a more reliable escort than an old hound. The back of his neck burned. He'd have a word with Evelyn in her chamber. "Thank you. Will you please have Cook prepare luncheon?"

"Straightaway, m'lord."

"Da!" Both lads barreled down the stairs.

"We saw the carriage from the window," said Oliver.

John grasped each of his sons by the shoulder and headed for the dining hall. "'Tis good to be home.

Come, tell me what you've been up to whilst I've been at court."

"Countess has a dog," said Oliver.

Thomas ran his fingers along the wall. "But he growls a lot."

"Perhaps we can remedy that. I'll wager Cook has some scraps of meat and if we hand-feed him, he'll come around." John made a mental note to ensure that happened as soon as Evelyn returned.

"By the way, I've noticed the missives on my writing table have shifted. Do either of you lads ken about that?"

Thomas dashed from beneath John's arm and climbed onto a chair. "I saw Countess in the library. I think I startled her."

"But you know not to touch any of my correspondence? Aye?"

"I didn't touch anything."

"I wasn't even in there," said Oliver.

"Good." John took his seat at the head of the table while two footmen delivered a pitcher of water, three glasses, and a tray of assorted sliced breads and cheeses. "Now, why are you referring to Her Ladyship as Countess?"

Thomas reached for the pitcher, which was immediately relieved from his hand by a footman. "She asked us to think about what we'd like to call her since she's not our real mother—remember, we men discussed it as well?"

John sat back while the footman filled his glass. "Did she give you any suggestions?"

Thomas shoved a slice of cheese into his mouth. "She just told me she thought it sounded too stuffy for us to call her m'lady all the time."

"I see."

"I asked, 'What about Countess?' and she said that was a possibility, so I told Oliver that's what we were going to call her from now on."

"Aye." Oliver snatched a slice of cheddar. "But I'd rather call her Tessie. That's even more friendlier than Countess."

"The proper form is simply *friendlier*," John corrected.

The youngest looked up, his face incredibly sober. "But I wanted my idea to sound bestest."

"Of course you did." To keep from bursting out with a belly laugh, John frowned and stuffed a large bite of bread into his mouth.

* * *

Seated at his place at the rear of the coffeehouse, Mr. Dubois scrawled on a slip of parchment. "Hawk, Sharpe, and Richards, did you say?"

"Yes. They're the queen's spies in the Netherlands— but Anne's representatives are Bishop Robinson and Lord Stafford. Neither the courtiers nor the papers have mentioned these other men. I'm convinced they are embroiled in a plot to ensure King Louis recognizes Anne as queen once and for all."

"If he does, then our *cause* will be all the more difficult when the time of the succession comes." The Frenchman scribbled, sweat beading above his lips. "And the ships? But first, I must know the most critical ports."

"Well, the majority of the fleet are in ports along the eastern seaboard—Hull, Newcastle upon Tyne, and Port Chatham, of course. Portsmouth is well guarded. The west has fewer, but aside from Edinburgh, there are hardly any ships patrolling Scotland."

"I need more. Can you bring me that document?"

"Mar might suspect—"

"Copy it, then," Mr. Dubois clipped. "This information will be invaluable."

"I think I can do that."

"You must."

Evelyn gripped her fingers around Brutus's lead. She'd never seen Mr. Dubois so keenly agitated, but if her efforts would help the Jacobites come to a peaceful resolution as to the succession, then she would do whatever she could to assist them.

She stood. "I'd best hasten away, then."

The table leg screeched against the floor while the Frenchman lumbered to his feet. "When will you have my information?"

Clutching the lead over her heart, she blinked. "*Your* information?"

"I'm certain you understand what I meant, my lady."

Though she did, this entire meeting didn't sit well. This was the first time Evelyn suspected Mr. Dubois might be withholding important information from her, and she didn't like it.

With a rustle of skirts, she curtsied and said her good-byes, pulling Brutus along behind. Perhaps she was just being overly sensitive. It had been easy to do a bit of snooping in her father's house. She knew his comings and goings as well as the servants' routines. But everything was foreign in Mar's town house—as foreign as Scotland.

Chapter Thirteen

It was late afternoon when, from the library window, John had watched Evelyn return home with her dog. At the evening meal she mentioned neither her outing nor Brutus. With the lads present, John kept mum. He didn't want to appear to chide her in front of the boys. Besides, it was best to discuss their differences behind closed doors. Nonetheless, Her Ladyship was not only a countess, she was now the wife of one of the most influential men in Britain. If she enjoyed walking the Corgi, she needed to do so with an escort, no question.

"Do you have a moment?" John asked, popping his head through the door to her chamber.

She looked up from reading a book on the settee in front of the fire. "Of course, my lord."

At her feet, Brutus growled.

John moved inside and gave the dog a morsel—which stopped the growling for three ticks of the clock. "I must apologize for being away so soon after our wedding."

Grrrrr.

Evelyn ignored the rudeness of her canine. "It couldn't be helped."

"No, but it still doesn't make it right." John grabbed the growling mutt by the collar, escorted him into his chamber, and pointed to a meaty bone. "See if that keeps you entertained, ye flea-bitten mongrel."

Evelyn gave John a half-amused, half-questioning look when he returned.

"Och." He shrugged. "There cannot be two masters of the castle. 'Tis best early on to show Brutus his place in the scheme of things."

"Oh?" she asked, setting the book aside. At first she met his gaze, but slowly her attention meandered lower...then stopped at his sporran.

Except he wasn't wearing his sporran.

John glanced downward as well. The minx looked directly at his loins. "Aye, well, 'tis a fair bit easier to talk when the wee hound isn't growling in the background." John moved in front of the hearth and rested his fists on his hips. He wasn't about to let his wife flummox him. "Speaking of the dog, you took him for quite a long stroll this afternoon."

"I did." Again, Her Ladyship's stare traveled from John's head, to his chest, and this time there was no question, her gaze bloody well stopped and gaped at his loins. Even her tongue slipped to the corner of her mouth. "Brutus needed to be exercised," she said like an innocent nymph.

"Hmm..." John rubbed his neck and looked away—she'd moved the sunflower from the window to the seat in the embrasure. Damnation, it was difficult to concentrate on what needed to be said when the lass was distracting him. "I ken the dog is your beloved pet and he needs to be walked, but I must ask that in the future you take along an escort whenever you step out."

In a blink, Evelyn's gaze shot to his face. "Escort?" she asked as if his request were ludicrous.

"Och aye. You're not only a countess, you are the wife of one of the queen's cabinet members. I do not care to own to it, but I have my enemies, and if any one of them realized you were out and about with that wee beastie, you might be kidnapped or worse."

"Good gracious, I hadn't thought about that."

"I'm surprised your father let you wander about Town with only the dog in tow. And you, a highborn lassie."

Evelyn looked away.

"Your da didn't ken you went out alone, did he?"

Nodding, she smoothed her palm over the book at her side. He sensed she had a hundred things to say but chose to hold them all in.

John stepped up and raised her chin with the crook of his finger. "Promise me you'll be more careful in the future."

"I will." Her gaze dipped again.

Holy hellfire!

Cupping her cheek with his palm, John grinned, unable to remember the second matter he'd come in to discuss. "Is there something beneath my kilt that has captured your interest, lass?"

"Um." She turned as red as the wool of his plaid. "I was wondering…"

"Aye?"

"Never mind. I-I cannot utter it."

"Look at me," he said, needing those vibrant eyes on him again. But this time he wanted to acknowledge her not-so-subtle interest. As she looked up, the heat swirling in his loins made him lengthen with the tug of desire.

Gently, he dipped his chin and plied her delicate lips with a kiss. "Behind closed doors is the only place you are free to ask me anything."

"I may?"

"Aye." He waited for a moment, but when she remained silent he added, "I like it when your gaze rakes along my body."

"You do?"

"It makes me feel like a man—as if you desire me." He took a seat beside her and twirled a lock of her hair around his finger. "Tell me now, wife, what were you thinking when your eyes meandered to my kilt?"

"Well, if you promise not to be cross with me." If a scarlet blush could deepen, Evelyn just grew redder. "Ah…I-I was wondering if it, that, um, your…" Her gaze dipped. "Ah…was stiff as an iron rod *all* the time?"

Unable to help himself, he threw back his head and laughed from his belly. "Most of the time my cock, if you will, is more like a sausage, as is every other man's. Though when a woman shows her interest—as you just did—it lengthens like a stallion near a mare in heat. Would you like to watch it grow even more?"

She smiled. "Now?"

"The hour is late. There's no one here but us." He spread open his plaid, revealing himself, already well on the way to being fully erect. "There should be no secrets between husband and wife."

Her wee gasp went straight to his balls. "I think it…ah…your…yes, no question, that is quite amazing."

Who knew Evelyn would take to lovemaking with such curiosity? "Do you want to touch me?"

"May I?"

"It would send me to the stars if you did. Grip it firm but do not squeeze—'tis the most sensitive place on a man."

His thighs quivered as she wrapped her fingers around his shaft, her lips parted as if she were discovering the secret of wisdom and truth.

John watched her examine and toy with him, being ever so gentle. *Mayhap the secret of passion.*

"Like this?" she asked.

He gripped his hand over hers and showed her how to pleasure him. "Like this. All the way up and all the way down."

John dropped his head to the back of the couch and moaned.

Evelyn's hand stilled. "Am I hurting you?"

He studied her through half-cast eyes. "Nay, just driving me to the ragged edge of madness."

She grinned. "Am I?"

"Come here." He pulled her to straddle his lap and pushed up her skirts. "I sense you like being in control, do you now, lassie?"

Those turquoise eyes grew dark as he bared her sex. "I do," she whispered breathlessly.

"Then ride me," he said, brushing himself across her sensitive flesh.

"Here?"

He slid a finger into her hot, wet core. She was ready, and on the verge of panting. "Aye," John growled, coaxing her over his cock.

Her wee gasps and mewls made heat swirl in his balls, made him thrust like a wild man. Grasping his shoulders, Eve held on and rode him like an untamed lioness. John gritted his teeth and made himself wait until her eyes opened wide with lust and she cried his name. Only then did he let loose his ravenous desire, throwing his head back and plunging deep into her core. As he bellowed with his release, she claimed his mouth with a deep, frantic kiss.

For the first time in his life, John stayed hard and pleasured her again and again until finally, soaked with sweat, Eve curled into his arms and slept.

He kissed her temple. She mightn't be his Margaret, but the lass was gifted in the bedchamber beyond his wildest imaginings.

The mantel clock chimed one in the morning when John carried Evelyn to her bed, tucked her in, and kissed her cheek. "I think we will be happy, wife," he whispered as she rolled to her side.

Tiredness weighed in his bones, so much so, he considered climbing in and sleeping beside her. But no, he mustn't. That was where he'd always slept with Margaret—in the countess's chamber. Making love with Evelyn was one thing—after all, John wanted more children and they may as well have fun creating them—but he drew the line at emotional entanglements. He'd already fallen in love once in his life, and once had been quite enough.

Chapter Fourteen

*J*ohn looked up from his writing table as Swenson opened the door. "The Duke of Kingston-upon-Hull is here to see you, m'lord."

"'Tis unusual for him to come without sending advance notice." John rested his quill in its holder. "Did he state the nature of his visit?"

"Only that he needed a word forthwith. Shall I show him in?"

"Please do."

By the time John rose, straightened his cuffs, and squared the plaid across his shoulder, Hull boldly strode through the door with a scowl. "This Scottish piracy had best stop, else I'll be ruined for the rest of my days."

"Piracy, Your Grace?" John asked, looking beyond the duke. Evelyn stood in the corridor with her mouth agape. Frowning, he gave her a subtle shake of his head. This obviously was no social call. "Swenson, leave us and close the door, please."

Once they were alone, he turned to the duke and gestured to a chair. "If you will have a seat."

"Sit? Who can sit at a time such as this?"

"Of course." John leaned against a bookcase, crossing his arms and ankles. He'd lost count of the number of nobles who'd barged into his home and blamed him for all manner of Scottish anarchy. "Tell me, exactly what have my countrymen done now?"

"Bloody thieves, the lot of them." Hull paced while John considered slipping his toe out and tripping the man. The duke might be the father of his wife, but he had no patience with any fellow who waltzed into his house spewing barbed accusations about Scotland. "They've plundered one of my ships—laden with Spanish gold, mind you."

"*Spanish* gold?" asked John. "Exactly who was pirating whom?"

"Hold your tongue. You know as well as I of the peril my ships face on the high seas."

"Very well, let us report your losses as a chest of gold and omit 'Spanish' to avoid suspicion." John moved to his writing table and reached for a sheet of parchment. "What would you say the cargo is worth?"

"Priceless."

"I need a number."

"Upwards of five hundred thousand pounds."

"Good Lord," John said as he wrote. "Who knew you had a king's ransom of gold aboard…which ship?"

"The…ah…*Flying Robin*. No one in Britain knew the value of its cargo aside from the captain of the ship and my factor."

John stilled his quill. "And the Spanish."

"Spain will never catch wind of what really happened."

Hull paced, rapidly rubbing his signet ring on his lapel. "Their plundered ship is at the bottom of the Caribbean Sea—not a soul survived."

"Let us keep that bit of information between us." John looked up, frowning. He dipped his quill in the ink. "What else did you say was in the *Flying Robin*'s hold?"

"Rum and coffee, but the goods are all accounted for."

"Then someone knew." And John doubted it was a Scot. "Do you have possession of a manifest or any document mentioning the gold?"

"I received a letter from Captain Henry advising of the shipment and requesting finder's terms."

"To which you agreed?"

"Of course I agreed." With all the pomp of a duke, Hull strode to the window and peered out. "Henry has never and would never cross me. If he did, he wouldn't have bothered to report the incident so timely."

"And where is this document now?"

"In my strongbox under lock and key, where I keep all such sensitive correspondence."

"And no one other than yourself has the key?"

"Absolutely not."

"Interesting," John mumbled under his breath.

Hull whipped around and jammed his fists into his hips. "Good God, man. I have been robbed of a fortune and you're asking questions as if I staged the incident myself."

"Not at all. I'm only trying to gather the facts." John made a few notes before he continued, "Where did this crime take place?"

"In a cove off the coast of Bettyhill."

"MacKay territory?" He replaced the quill in the holder. "There's no place in the mainland of Scotland more remote."

"That's why Captain Henry moored there for needed repairs."

John tilted his head back and rubbed his eyes. "That makes no sense at all. Why not call in to Edinburgh or Aberdeen—even Sutherland would have helped, but sail her into a cove where you were *likely* to be set upon by pirates? With a chest filled with gold? In my opinion, your captain ought to be held accountable—led to the gallows upon suspicion of collusion."

"I shall handle my man. But you need to do something to stop these thieves and find my gold."

"Of course. I'll dispatch missives to the corners of Scotland straightaway. But I daresay, the thieves could have gone anywhere—Holland, France, the Netherlands."

Hull snorted like an arrogant fop. "I would expect such an answer from you, Mar."

Unfortunately, drawing his sword and threatening the duke was no way to alter his father-in-law's priorities. "How would you prefer I respond? I'll inform the admiral of the fleet of the incident immediately. But it would take an act of God to sail our warships away from the fighting in the Americas, or divert the ships patrolling the channel during these precarious peace negotiations with France."

"Do not patronize me."

"Forgive me. I did not intend to come across as condescending. I simply find this state of affairs unbelievable. And the *Flying Robin*? Never in my life have I heard of a ship named thus and, having been a member of the queen's cabinet for eleven years, I have committed to memory a great many allied ships both merchant and naval."

Waving a dismissive hand, Hull pursed his lips while his eyes slanted sideways. "Her name is of no consequence compared to the fortune lost." Sniffing, he flicked a bit of lint from his silk doublet. "Should your efforts result substantially in recovering my gold, I shall see to it you are rewarded."

John said nothing.

"Handsomely."

In truth, the twice-stolen gold was most likely melted by now, hidden in a pirate's den on some godforsaken island inhabited by man-eating heathens. "I shall use every source at my avail to track down your thieves. But before you take your leave, I have one more question for you."

"Which is?"

John again reached for his quill. "Did Captain Henry identify the criminals as Scottish? And how many losses did he incur in the battle? What damages were sustained by the *Flying Robin*?"

Hull examined his fingernails. "There was no battle. The thieves spirited aboard in the dead of night."

"Was anyone killed?" John persisted. "Surely, the master didn't leave five hundred thousand pounds in gold unguarded."

"The guards were bludgeoned. Neither man saw nor heard a thing."

"Mercenaries," John whispered to himself. *It is sounding more like MacKays all the time—or any trained Highlanders, for that matter. Sutherland might have a hand in it—or MacKenzie. Perhaps I should have a word with the Earl of Seaforth...*

"What is it?" asked Hull.

"Just thinking of possibilities. Leave this with me. I'll dispatch letters and make a few inquiries about Town."

"I think it best if you do not implicate me." *So now the duke asks for anonymity*. John should have guessed.

Spanish gold was obviously pirated by the duke's trading company. No wonder Hull had offered such a generous dowry to ally himself with a cabinet member.

"I wouldn't dream of doing so," John replied—naturally he'd never implicate his wife's father. "This matter must be handled with utmost delicacy. I need not speak of the penalty of importing gold, as well as rum and coffee, without paying duties. It might be considered smuggling and such a malfeasance would create a scandal no man could afford."

"Indeed."

* * *

Her heart still hammered like hummingbird wings when Evelyn peered from around the corner of the ingress to the dining hall and watched Mar shake hands with her father. "Tell my daughter I've sent Frances and Phoebe back to Nottingham. I'll be following as soon as parliament goes into recess."

"I'll let her know," John's deep voice rumbled. "We'll be heading north as well."

"Soon, I hope?"

"The queen will call a recess by the end of June for certain."

"It cannot come soon enough for me."

Once Papa left with Swenson, Mar turned. "Evelyn?"

She stepped out. "How did you know I was still here?"

"What woman can resist a scandal?"

She ran her finger along the wainscoting in the corridor. "Usually Papa insures his shipments."

"Aye, though no bank in all of Christendom would honor an insurance claim on plundered gold."

She nodded.

He ushered her into the library, shut the door, and turned the lock. "What do you ken about this debacle?"

"The gold?"

"That and the *Flying Robin*."

What should she say? The ship is really the *East Indian*, reported lost at sea? Explain the pains her father took to avoid paying taxes? What if she went on to speak of how she'd shared the information with Mr. Dubois while Sir Kennan Cameron, captain of the *Highland Reel*, happened to be present?

Lord save me.

Sir Kennan was no pirate. *Well, he might be.*

She looked her husband square in the eye. "My father rarely ever shared a word of his affairs with me." At least she spoke the truth. Everything Evelyn knew she'd discovered through her own efforts.

Mar's features softened with his smile. And then his gaze meandered to the plunging scoop of her neckline. "Well, you needn't concern yourself."

She traced her finger along the length of tartan wool crossing his chest. "What will you do to help him?"

Grasping her waist, he tugged her nearer and gave her a kiss. "Chances are he'll never see another coin from that shipment. I'll write a few letters and make some enquiries of my allies."

Evelyn dropped her head back as his lips trailed down to the exposed tops of her breasts. "Who are your allies, my lord?"

"Many."

She shuddered as his finger pulled away the damask and he lapped her nipple. "Earls?"

"Aye."

"Powerful clans?"

He lifted her onto his writing desk and hiked up her skirts. "The most powerful in all of Scotland."

If only she could will him to name one. But as his big hands moved up the insides of her thighs, he rendered her powerless to think. "Seaforth?"

"Mm-hmm," his deep voice rumbled against her flesh.

"MacKay?"

He chuckled, paying far more attention to . . .

"Oh, yes," she sighed while her head swooned to the delight of his magical tongue.

"Aye, lassie." He chuckled, licking the inside of her thigh. "This is what you were made for, Eve. Your skin is like satin. And you . . . dear God, with every breath your sweet perfume makes me ravenous. Damn the gold, I've a mind to plunder you."

Chapter Fifteen

*T*here you are, my lady. You'll be the most radiant woman at the theater this night," Lucinda said, standing back and admiring her work.

Evelyn did as well. Her lady's maid had outdone herself, using curls and tufts of saved hair to make a tall coiffure, held together by a diamond-studded tiara that had belonged to the Duchess of Kingston-upon-Hull. "You are an enchantress born of the fairies, is what you are. I have no idea how you turned my withered locks into a work of art."

"Your locks aren't withered, but Lord Mar will not be able to take his eyes off you."

Evelyn's stomach fluttered. Every time His Lordship looked her way it had led straight to the bed. "Truly?" she asked all the same. Theirs was such an odd relationship. They had nothing in common, they hardly knew each other, and she was quite certain Mar harbored no love for her. How could he? She didn't love him. *Right?*

"He hasn't taken his eyes off you for weeks. Why would he do so when you are undeniably ravishing?"

"Stop."

"Beg your pardon, Your Ladyship. Of course, servants never notice things like the state of your bed linens in the morning."

"Lucinda!"

The maid handed Evelyn her fan. "I'm ever so thrilled to see you happy. Remember how you fretted over this union?"

She snatched the fan and shook it under Lucinda's nose. She was definitely not about to have a conversation with anyone regarding the morning linens, even if the maid had been with her forever. "Enough. I want you to do something to enjoy yourself this evening. You've been working much too hard as of late."

Waltzing past with an impish glance, Lucinda opened the door. "Mr. MacVie has invited me to a game of cards."

"Mar's valet?"

"Yes, he's a braw Scotsman, too, you know."

"All the servants in this house are Scottish." Evelyn slipped on her gloves as she headed out. "But have a lovely time, my pet."

"You as well, my lady."

At the landing Evelyn stopped with a sudden catch of her breath. John waited in the entry, his face turned up with a smile. Over the past few weeks it had become increasingly difficult to resist him. Not that she resisted Mar when it came to performing her wifely duties. In truth, it surprised Evelyn how well she'd taken to that part of being married. But since the earl was away at court most days, they were like strangers who met in the boudoir every night and spoke of nothing but passion. And of late, she expected his nightly visits—waited and wondered what new passion their next interlude would bring.

"You are stunning," he said, holding out his hands. "Are you ready for our first public appearance as earl and countess?"

Evelyn proceeded down the final flight. "I hope so. Lucinda performed magic with my hair."

"You did not tell me your lady's maid was a sorceress."

"Sh. 'Tis a well-kept secret."

He offered his elbow. "Well then. Perhaps I should increase her wages so she never feels the need to leave us."

Warmth spread through Evelyn's breast as she placed her fingers in the crook of his arm. "You would do that for her?"

"Why would I not? There is nothing more motivating for a servant than to be rewarded for a job well done."

Swenson opened the door with a bow.

Passing, Evelyn gave the butler a nod. "I cannot tell you how refreshing it is to hear you say it, my lord."

"Why? Is your father not of the same mind?"

"Not at all. His philosophy is that serving staff is there to serve the lord of the house and they should be retained at the lowest possible wages."

"Hmm. Hull's opinion is not unusual among the nobility." John lowered his arm as the footman helped Evelyn up the coach steps. "Perhaps that's why his coffers are full."

She climbed inside and scooted across the velvet bench. "I daresay the few pounds spent if he paid fair wages would do little to reduce the coin in his purse."

John took the seat alongside. "You are surprisingly well versed in your father's affairs."

"One would hope the eldest child of a duke would take

special interest in the estate, especially when Papa sired no male heir."

As the coach headed off, John took Evelyn's hand and kissed it. Then he pushed her sleeve up to her elbow and ran feathery kisses along her arm. "What else does my Eve take special interest in?"

"Please, John. How am I to think when you're doing that?"

"Who needs to think?" His lips moved to her neck while his hand slid down her thigh. "What, exactly, is addling your mind?" he managed to ask while continuing to seduce her.

Arching her back, Evelyn sighed. "You are scandalous."

"Scandalous," he repeated in a deep Highland brogue while his fingers slipped beneath her skirts. "Let us be scandalous together, m'lady."

"But what will the coachman say? Or the footmen?"

"Are there any within?" John peered about through the dim light. Then he faced her and waggled his brows. "Nay. Not a one."

By the time the carriage rolled to a stop, Evelyn's garters were exposed with her skirts hiked up all the way to her hips.

Grinning like a sly rogue, he helped her smooth her gown.

"We've arrived, m'lord," said the footman, opening the door.

Evelyn patted her hair, certain Lucinda's work had turned into a lopsided bird's nest. "Do I look a fright?" she whispered as John helped her alight.

"Thoroughly ravished...I mean ravishing."

She smacked his arm with her fan. "You're horrible."

"Incorrigible, perhaps. When the opera is over, remind me where we left off."

For a moment, Evelyn wanted to climb back into the carriage and return to the town house. But as they proceeded into the vestibule, Mar's demeanor completely changed. It was as if an invisible wall had been erected around him. His mannerisms grew practiced and distant.

"Are you the statesman now?" she asked in a whisper.

He glanced at her out of the corner of his eye. "Hmm?"

"As soon as we stepped away from the carriage you became a different person."

An usher led them up the stairs to their box, and John didn't reply until they were behind closed doors. "When in the public eye, a man in my station cannot afford to feed the gossips. My personal affairs are no one's concern."

"But people call you..." She looked out over the parterre—Sir Kennan had returned, and, farther on, Mr. Dubois was looking straight at them.

"What?" John asked.

Evelyn pursed her lips. Now was definitely not the time to discuss rumors.

John held a chair for her, then leaned down and pressed his lips to her ear. "Bobbin' John?"

Heat flooded her face. He knew of this mockery? "If you are aware of what people have said, then why haven't you defended yourself?"

"Defend myself to whom? Had I not been a member of the cabinet, I assure you, the queen would have squashed Scotland with the scrolling of her quill." The only sign of Mar's ire was a twitch at the corner of his eye. "'Tis easy to pass judgment when one is not embroiled in the midst of the adders at court."

"I see. So am I correct in saying you are not overly fond of being Secretary of State for Scotland?"

He shot her a subtle but heated look—one that undeniably said he would entertain no more conversation on the matter. "The orchestra has taken their places. Let us enjoy *Agrippina* and Handel's brilliance."

* * *

The music was riveting, but Evelyn was too riled to follow the plot. There she sat, beside a man who showed her passion beyond her wildest imaginings at night, yet his opinions and his public life were as foreign to her as the Orient. Was he Jacobite, Tory, or Whig? Or did he follow the beat of a mystical Highland drum? What truly mattered to the Earl of Mar? Family, he'd avowed to. But what else? What in the grander scheme of things? What else beyond the walls of the Scottish island he'd created in his town home?

With each passing day, Evelyn grew more and more confused. She needed to know why John had made some of the decisions of which he was accused. No matter what he thought, a one-sentence answer did not address even a smattering of her doubts. Yet he'd opened the smallest of windows. Clearly, Mar felt himself lord-high protector in defense of the queen's quill. But on what issues? If only she could pry just a little more.

During intermission, John led her to the vestibule, where he was promptly pulled aside by the Duke of Argyll. And no sooner had she accepted a glass of wine from a footman than Sir Kennan grasped her elbow and tugged her in the other direction. "I hear congratulations are in order, m'lady."

"Thank you." She sipped her wine, looking out over the crowd and ensuring no eavesdroppers were about. "I'm surprised to see you, sir."

"Moored the *Highland Reel* at Blackwall. From the port there's easy access to London, as well as easy escape to the sea if need be."

"Escape? That sounds intriguing." When John looked her way, Evelyn smiled and raised her glass in acknowledgment. "You'd best watch what you say. My father is livid."

The corner of Sir Kennan's mouth turned up in a devious grin. "The coin wasn't Hull's to begin with, and now it can be put to use to help James when the time comes."

Evelyn tapped a finger to her mouth. "My lips are forever sealed."

Sir Kennan lowered his head as if he didn't care to be seen. "I'd best make myself scarce." He bowed. "If ever you should need assistance, I trust you will call on me."

"Why should I—"

"Good evening, m'lady," Kennan said, casting a heated glare beyond her shoulder before he turned on his heel.

"Lady Mar."

She recognized Mr. Dubois's voice as he stepped around her, grasped her hand, and plied it with a peck. "It seems marriage becomes you."

Astonished at what she'd just witnessed, Evelyn ignored the compliment. "Is Sir Kennan at odds with you?"

The Frenchman smirked. "Someone is always at odds with me."

"But—"

"I haven't much time and I need your assistance now more than ever."

"Oh?"

"The information you've provided has been invaluable, but James has asked for more."

"You've received a communication from Château de Saint-Germain-en-Laye? So soon?"

The man's thin-lipped grin was a bit unsettling. Why was it everyone was behaving strangely this evening? Grasping her elbow, Dubois urged her to turn toward the wall. "I need you to leave a dining hall window unlocked. Will you do that for me on the morrow?"

"Why the dining hall?"

"'Tis at the side of the house and in the dark. My man will not be seen."

She leaned closer and hissed, "I do not want someone slipping into my house like a thief."

"*Your house*, is it now?"

When Evelyn threw back her shoulders, Mr. Dubois's expression softened. "*Ma chérie*, I needn't tell you your assistance is critical for *the cause*. If it is Mar you are worried about, I can attest no harm will come to your husband. I assure you his identity will be protected just as I protected your father."

"Dubois," John's voice came from behind. His tone was deep and menacing and made a shiver course up Evelyn's spine. "With what contemptible bile are you filling my wife's head this night?"

"My lord." As he turned with a false smile, a bead of sweat streamed from beneath the Frenchman's periwig. "I assure you I was merely congratulating Her Ladyship on her fortuitous alliance."

"Aye?" John pulled Evelyn behind him. "In the future I expect you to speak to Lady Mar only when in my presence."

She inclined her head around her husband's shoulder. "But Mr. Dubois and I have been acquainted for ages."

"That is exactly what I am concerned about." John turned his back on the Frenchman, grasped her wrist, and started for the stairs. "That man is under suspicion by the crown."

"Suspicion for what?"

"Wheesht. You ought to ken by now, I'm not at liberty to discuss such matters. Friend or nay, I forbid you from consorting with that man from here on out."

Evelyn jerked her arm away. How dare Mar tell her whom she could and could not befriend? John might blow with the wind when it came to his principles, but she did not. She stood by what she felt in her bones to be the most forthright and honorable values, and she would be loyal to her convictions.

She stopped on the landing. "Forgive me, my lord, but I have a megrim. I'm afraid I will be unable to endure the remainder of the opera."

* * *

John's blood boiled, but he withheld his ire until he deposited Evelyn into her chamber. "I would think the daughter of a duke would be better versed in how to conduct herself when under public scrutiny."

"I beg your pardon?" The woman faced him with fury in her eyes, while her disagreeable dog growled from his place in front of the hearth. "You stepped away from me! What do you expect me to do—spit upon a man I've known and trusted for years and tell him I must ask my husband's permission before he can congratulate me on my fortunate nuptials?"

"Och, you are not ignorant, lass. You ken exactly what I mean. Dubois had you turned toward the wall with his arm about your shoulders, whispering in your ear as if he were conspiring—"

"How dare you?" Evelyn turned and paced. "He and I spoke for less than two minutes and you're accusing me of colluding with him?"

"Aye, and I've seen you speaking to Dubois before."

"And you don't like him. Why? Because he actually stands for something?"

A hot flame burst through John's chest. "Stands for something? The man is a threat to Britain."

"And there you have it. You are so worried about how you appear in the public eye, you side with the queen and her obsessive fear of her brother. The man who should be king. I knew it all along!" As Her Ladyship raised her voice, Brutus barked.

"You have no idea to what you are referring." John kicked the stool in front of the toilette and watched it clatter to the floor while the damned dog launched into a snarling cacophony, acting as if John were the evil interloper in all this. Well, he wasn't going to take a chiding from a Corgi. He glared at the hound, who then whimpered, tucked his tail, and scampered back to his rug.

Once fully in control, John focused on his misinformed wife. "If that is what you think, madam, then you are a fool. Do you believe it is easy to pick a side and run across the land proclaiming one's desires, no matter how poorly conceived, meanwhile thwarting over half the noblemen in the kingdom?"

Clenching her fists, she stood her ground like a cornered badger. "At least Mr. Dubois has chosen a side. Something of which you seem to be incapable. In fact, you have so many faces I hardly know who I might see whenever we're together."

"So now you reveal what you think of me? You're just like everyone else with their misplaced Bobbin' John rubbish." John thrust his finger at Brutus, commanding him to stay as he sauntered toward Her Ladyship. "My God, you have looked upon me with your haughty English ideals as if you were judge and jury. Well, I'll tell you here and now, there has been a solid reason for my decisions and I will stand behind each and every one. Though I never thought I'd have to defend myself against my bloody wife!"

Without another word, John stormed out, slamming the door behind.

Chapter Sixteen

*A*fter she unlocked a window in the dining hall, Evelyn spent the remainder of the next morning in her chamber pretending she was unaffected by John's tirade, yet under the surface she burned at his arrogance. How dare he accuse her of conspiring with Mr. Dubois? Even though he'd been too close to the mark. Evelyn crossed her arms and paced. She'd given her husband no cause to suspect her. And she'd only gathered information that might be of use to Prince James. Besides, Mar admittedly knew nothing of Dubois and their plans for the succession...to improve the lot of all Britons. Heavens, Mar accused the Frenchman of being under suspicion.

Claude Dubois? Under suspicion? Perhaps the queen has learned of his bent toward her brother?

And even if Evelyn didn't feel quite right about leaving a window unlocked, John had certainly allayed any apprehension on her part.

Curses!

She pounded her fist on the back of the settee. Her husband had no idea how deeply she had allied herself with the French emissary, but she had conspired for the right reasons—at least when living in her father's home. Here in Mar's London island of Scotland, the line between right and wrong seemed to shift with each passing day. Or did it fade?

I am losing my mind.

"Couuuuntessssss?" Oliver hollered from the corridor right before there came a fierce knocking at the door.

Springing to his feet from his place in front of the hearth, Brutus launched into an onslaught of barking.

With a slice of her hand, Evelyn signaled to the dog to stop. "Come in."

Brutus immediately lowered his head, baring his teeth and growling.

The door burst open and Oliver darted straight toward the Corgi, holding out a piece of sausage. "Can we take Brutus to the park?"

Bribed, Evelyn's fierce protector swallowed the meat whole, then rubbed against the boy's leg, begging for more.

Thomas sauntered inside, looking like a miniature form of his father. He tossed up a leather ball and caught it. "Does the old hound play catch?"

"He does, though you boys might be able to outrun him."

"That's okay."

Huffing as if she'd just run a footrace, Mrs. Kerr stepped into the doorway. "Lads, I told you not to bother Her Ladyship."

"Och, someone needs to exercise Brutus," said Oliver. "He's our dog now, too, isn't he, Countess?"

"He is." Evelyn glanced out the window. There wasn't a cloud in the sky. Why not step out with the boys? A bit of air might do her some good, might take her mind off last night's disaster as well.

"A jaunt to the park is a delightful idea." Evelyn turned to the governess. "Mrs. Kerr, why not take a little time to yourself? In my estimation, you have earned it ten times over."

The woman's face first brightened with elation—right before a pinch formed between her brows. "Are you certain, m'lady? The lads can be a handful."

"I'm sure I can manage for a few hours—as long as Thomas and Oliver promise to be on their best behavior."

The boys emphatically agreed, and Mrs. Kerr left them, looking as if she'd been given plum pudding with cream, which she planned to enjoy thoroughly. Brutus was all too happy to waddle to the park while Thomas and Oliver took turns at trying to coax him faster.

"I want a hunting dog," said Thomas. "Corgis are useless."

Though it was hard for Evelyn to argue, there was something endearing about her old hound, even if he was a grumbler. "I don't know. Brutus is a good watchdog, not to mention a fine companion."

"Aye," Tom agreed. "If you do not mind having your hand bit off."

She chuckled to herself. "He never bites my hand, only yours."

Oliver tugged on the lead. "I think he likes me now. I sure have fed him enough sausages."

"Perhaps that's why he looks like a sausage."

"Swensen calls him a haggis." Elbowing his brother aside, Thomas took a turn. "I reckon the dog will soon grow so fat his legs will give out and then we'll be forced to roll him everywhere."

Once they rounded the corner and the park came into view, Oliver dashed into the street. "Come, Brutus. Fetch the ball!"

"Watch for horses and carts!" Evelyn raised her voice, grabbing Thomas by the collar before he stepped off the curb with Brutus. Her heart stopped as, ahead, Oliver dashed in front of a hay wagon.

The driver pulled on his horse's reins, his cart teetering almost to the point of overturning. "Watch yerself, ye young whelp!" the man shouted, cracking his whip at Oliver. The boy threw his hands over his head and ducked behind the wagon.

"Cease your barbarism this instant!" Evelyn took Thomas by the hand and, after looking both ways, they marched directly toward the idiot. "Oliver, hasten to the footpath and wait for us there."

Wide-eyed, the boy ran. "Aye, m'lady."

The driver stood dumbfounded as his Adam's apple bobbed. "Your Ladyship?"

"Indeed," Evelyn snapped. "I might have pardoned you because my son shouldn't have blindly dashed across the street, but then to see you lash out at a defenseless boy of five with a whip? Your actions are deplorable and un-forgiveable!"

"I dodged him, Countess," Oliver yelled from the curb. "I am unharmed."

Evelyn shook her fan at the driver. "It is a very good thing, else I would have no recourse but to have you rep-rimanded. Let me tell you here and now, the Countess of Mar will stand for no man whilst he raises his hand against one of my sons."

The cart driver cowered, looking terrified. "'Pologies, milady. He scared me was all."

"Apology accepted." She squeezed Thomas's hand. "Now go on your way and be mindful of children in the future."

"Yes, milady." The man tipped his hat. "Good day to you."

"Holy Moses, you showed him," Oliver said as Evelyn and Thomas joined him on the footpath.

Evelyn tweaked the child's ear. "Let this be a lesson, young man. Even if you grow as large as your father, you still could be killed if you are struck by a horse and cart! From here on out, I expect you to show me the good sense God gave you to look before you cross any street. Am I understood?"

Hanging his head, Oliver kicked a stone. "Aye, m'lady."

She took charge of the dog's lead. "Promise me?"

"Cross my heart."

"Very well then, since you promised, you can manage Brutus's lead and take him all the way to the park." She arched her eyebrow at the lad's elder brother. "Understood?"

Thomas gave a nod.

But Oliver's face brightened as if she'd just given him a present. "Thank you!"

They managed to proceed the half block to the park without another incident. Thomas threw first and Oliver second. Brutus lumbered to the ball and eventually brought it back. But on the third throw, the dog sat and refused to budge.

Oliver planted his fists on his hips and gaped up at his brother. "You threw it too far."

"Did not. The old hound is just too lazy. We need a better dog."

"I think we must learn to accept that which we have," Evelyn said.

"I'll go fetch it myself." Oliver clipped the lead to Brutus's collar. "But you're going with me, ye huge haggis."

Evelyn clapped a hand over her mouth to stifle her laugh. But Thomas looked anything rather than amused. "How have you been faring of late?" she asked. "Is your heart mending? I've been worried about you ever since our chat in the library."

The boy's lips thinned as he glanced her way. "I do not ken. Mrs. Kerr never gives us a moment's rest. I wish I could go home. There's so much more to do at Alloa."

"Oh? Have you grown bored with tossing the ball for Brutus already?"

"The silly mutt only went after it twice. He's not much fun if you ask me."

"But he's a good companion. And he's always good for a listen."

Thomas shrugged.

Evelyn tried another tack. "So, what keeps you busy at Alloa?"

"My pony, mostly."

"Do you like the stables? Do you clean her stall, brush her, and feed her?"

"Nay, the grooms do all that."

"I think it would be good for you to learn. Hard work gives a young man a sense of accomplishment."

Tom didn't look convinced. "Mrs. Kerr has me working all the time."

"True, but working in the stables is different. It exercises the body and feeds the soul. And I'd wager if you asked, one of the grooms would be willing to let you help, providing you're open to taking direction."

"Help with what?" asked Oliver, skidding to a stop with the dog dragging behind.

As the boy held out the ball, Evelyn took it. "I was just suggesting that Thomas master the art of caring for his pony by learning how things work in the mews here in London."

"Can I do it, too?"

"You must first ask the stable master. I set to gardening when I was about Thomas's age. The master gardener at Thoresby Hall took me under his wing and now I know almost as much as he."

"You could be a master gardener?" asked Oliver.

Evelyn brushed the golden hair away from the boy's face. "I think not. Ladies do not take up such posts."

"But you could if you wanted to," said Thomas.

Taking charge of Brutus, Evelyn started back to the town house. "I am a countess and already have a great deal of responsibility. The two of you will become important men. To prepare, a bit of hard work and sweat will do you good—give you a solid foundation upon which to build strong character."

"Da says I'm already a character," said Oliver.

Thomas cuffed his brother on the arm. "Not that kind of character, ye nut."

"I'm not a nut. You're a nut—you're a hard-shelled walnut."

"Enough!" Reaching the curb, Evelyn stopped and stretched out her hands to stop the lads from stepping into the street. "Oliver—watch the traffic and tell me when it is safe to cross."

* * *

As John headed away from the queen's antechamber at Kensington Palace, the Duke of Argyll pulled him aside. "May I have a word?"

"A word with me?" Everyone at court knew that though they were both Scottish peers, Mar and Argyll stood at odds on nearly every issue. "Something grave must be afoot," he said, unable to keep his sarcasm from showing.

The duke's eyebrows disappeared beneath his periwig. "Treason, if my sources are sound."

John checked over his shoulder. "Treason?"

"I've had a report that Louis of France is scheming—he wants the throne of Britain and will stop at nothing to turn the lot of us into French subjects."

"Interesting, given the peace negotiations underway in the Netherlands."

"What better time to stage an invasion than when your enemy thinks you are beaten?"

"Let us say your suspicions are founded." John crossed his arms. "Who is your traitor? What proof have you?"

Argyll stroked his fingers along his chin, his gaze piercing. "The information I've received is enough to implicate any man on Anne's cabinet. Even you."

Och, another one of the duke's schemes. John threw up his palms. "That is preposterous, and I resent the implication."

"Do not be so quick to anger, Mar. My guess is the leak may not be coming from you directly, but from your house."

"I beg your pardon?" John's hand slipped to the hilt of his dirk. "Surely you do not wish a duel, for everyone kens you'd be no match for me, Your Grace."

"Stop thinking with your brawn and reason." Argyll cupped a hand to his mouth and lowered his voice. "You've recently married, have you not?"

"Aye, ye ken I have."

"And I'm certain it is not news that your bonny wife has been seen in the company of Mr. Dubois."

Hot ire twisted in John's gut. Damnation, he knew Evelyn's alliance with the Frenchman would start the gossip mongers. "Her Ladyship is acquainted with the man—though it goes no further." He held his tongue from commenting more. Surely the man wasn't hugely dangerous. Rumor was Dubois had Jacobite leanings and, since 1707, Jacobite sentiment had grown quiet. In fact, John's allies, the Marquis of Tullibardine and the Earl of Seaforth, who were firm supporters of James Stuart, had confided that the exiled royal intended to wait out his sister's reign before he considered the pursuit of his rightful place as king, which he hoped to achieve peaceably and with parliament's blessing, God willing.

John released his grip from his hilt. "I think you're digging, Your Grace, and I would thank you to stop."

"I assure you, I am as upset by this news as you, m'lord." Argyll pushed a missive into John's midriff. "Take this."

John snatched the letter and read. It was a simple note from Argyll to Mar stating that the queen's officer in the Netherlands had exposed the name of a traitor in her court and that Argyll's man would meet an informant at Black's Tavern at one o'clock on the twenty-third of May.

John tried to hand the letter back, but the duke held up a palm. "What are you on about?"

"'Tis a diversionary tactic and is only meant to bait the scoundrel," said Argyll. "Leave my missive in a conspicuous place. If no one shows up at Black's, then you've nothing to worry about."

Reluctantly, John stuffed the missive inside his doublet. If he refused, Argyll would be accusing him next. "I assure you Lady Mar is innocent."

"We shall find out, shall we not?"

As he headed home, he couldn't help his own suspicions. Before Evelyn had arrived, the correspondence on his writing table had never shifted. And he'd warned her to stay away from Dubois. What truly was her association with the Frenchman? Did Dubois have Jacobite leanings, as he'd led John's allies to believe, or was there something more sinister brewing beneath? From the day the French diplomat had been introduced in court, John hadn't trusted the man. He'd presented Her Majesty his letters from King Louis with undue arrogance. There he'd stood in the presence of the Queen of England with a damned smirk on his face. And though he had come as an advisor, he'd provided little help to Anne. In fact, every time John saw Dubois at court, he was off in some corner whispering in someone's ear. Just as he'd done with Evelyn at the opera.

By the time he arrived home, nothing made sense. Argyll was a meddler of the worst sort, and never ceased to pose as a thorn in John's side. On the other hand, John had never spoken in detail of politics to Evelyn, and he didn't intend to start now. Hell, he was only beginning to know his wife, although their argument had been unsettling—had shown him what little she knew of him. Moreover, Evelyn had quite clearly expressed the passion of her leanings toward Jacobitism. If John had to guess, a bit less than half of England, and possibly three-fifths of Scotland, supported and recognized James Stuart as the rightful heir. Nonetheless, Lady Mar's opinion had absolutely no effect on the outcome of the succession. Hell, if the Old Pretender outlived his sister, John would accept his right to rule with open arms. It was the queen who had insisted on excluding Catholics from inheriting the throne. Once she died, sentiment might very well change.

As he climbed the stairs to the town house, Swenson opened the door but looked to the footpath beyond. Oliver and Thomas approached, dragging Brutus behind them with Lady Evelyn in their wake. All three of them were laughing as if they hadn't a care in the world. Hell, even the dog looked in better spirits, if that was possible.

If Evelyn was engaging in traitorous activity, she certainly had learned how to act as if nothing were amiss.

"Da!" Oliver hollered.

Evelyn glanced up, her pace immediately slowing while her smile faded. Aye, she knew she'd been caught.

John planted his fists on his hips.

"We took Brutus to the park," said Thomas.

He stared at his wife. "Did you, now?"

Oliver climbed the steps. "Aye, though the Corgi isn't much for playing fetch."

"Most likely exercise is good for the dog, though I cannot say I am happy to see the three of you return without an escort."

Evelyn cringed. "We only walked to the park—all three of us together. I didn't think—"

Thomas stepped in front of her. "You should have seen Countess scold a cart driver for nearly running over the top of Oliver."

"Aye—he nearly struck me with his whip, but I dodged him." The youngest sidled to his brother. "And then Brutus almost bit the man's foot right off."

Groaning, Evelyn looked skyward. "The dog did not bite the man at all."

"But you told him, did you not, Countess?" asked Thomas.

"I simply informed the driver he needed to keep a more watchful eye."

"Wonderful." On top of everything, all John needed was to have his wife berating cart drivers on the street. "Lads, go up to the nursery and report to Mrs. Kerr."

"But, Da," said Oliver, looking to his stepmother. "Countess said we could give Brutus a bath."

"Perhaps later." She gave the boy's shoulder a pat. "I'll come up to see you."

"Promise?" asked Thomas before he turned to his father. "Da, you mustn't be angry with Countess. We asked her to take us."

What the hell had happened with his eldest son? At breakfast this morning, he was still acting standoffish toward Her Ladyship. Now they venture to the park, where Oliver is nearly killed, and there the pair of them stood defending the woman? "Off with you, and take that grumpy hound," John barked, grasping Evelyn by the wrist and leading her to the drawing room.

"I didn't see anything wrong with a quick jaunt to the park," she said as he closed the door. "And Mrs. Kerr sorely needed a half-holiday."

"The governess should have accompanied you. Why you didn't consider that, I am without a clue. I know you are an intelligent woman, but to take my sons to the park by yourself is nothing short of irresponsible."

"Irre—" Heaving in a gasp, Evelyn threw out her hands. "I vehemently disagree. For years I have taken my sisters on walks just the three of us and never once were we set upon."

"Och aye? And today, my youngest nearly met with a cart driver's lash. Because he wasn't harmed you continued on and enjoyed a merry day out. Is that it?"

"I reprimanded Oliver for racing out into the street without a care. I then reprimanded the whip-wielding driver for his barbarism. And then, yes, we proceeded to the park, where we enjoyed some time together—time that allowed me to come to know my stepsons better."

"You should have returned home after the incident. I cannot—"

"Stop this instant!" Evelyn thrust her fists down to her sides. "How can you tell me what I should have done when you were not there to observe? I am not your child to reprimand."

"Nay, you are my wife, and with such responsibility comes the promise to obey me."

"Oh, so now I am Your Lordship's disobedient servant. Shall I move my things to the servants' quarters so you can continue to misappropriate my dowry?"

As Evelyn started for the door, John caught her by the wrists. "Where on earth did you get the notion that I have done anything with your dower funds?"

Struggling, she tried to tug away. "Unhand me!"

"Are you conspiring against me?" he asked, restraining himself from saying more.

The color drained from her face as she stilled but did not meet his gaze. "I have no idea why you would ask such a thing."

If only he could tell her about his conversation with Argyll. But not yet. Not while the element of doubt still lurked. "I should have assigned a footman to accompany you on your outings. I will do so today." He almost released her wrists, but Argyll's damned missive was burning beneath his doublet. "In the interim, I have critical correspondence I must attend for the queen." Uttering this lie nearly cut him to the quick. He hated deviousness.

Evelyn wrenched her hands away, giving him a look of contempt—one so filled with anger John rued every spiteful word he'd said. "Then you'd best see to it."

Chapter Seventeen

"You seem bothered, my lady," Lucinda said, removing Evelyn's hairpins for the night.

"'Tis nothing."

"Forgive me for prying, but we all think His Lordship was rather harsh with you this afternoon."

"I'd prefer not to discuss the incident, nor should you be gossiping with the other servants." Evelyn glanced up. She didn't oft admonish her lady's maid, but she needed the speculation to stop immediately. "It is not a servant's place to observe or to express her opinion."

Pursing her lips, Lucinda reached for the brush. "Forgive my impertinence."

Evelyn pushed the hair away from her face. "I'm upset is all. Upset with myself as well as His Lordship."

"Why yourself?"

"I thought I knew all the answers, but now I'm not so sure."

"Is the earl making you doubt yourself?"

"I'm confused beyond all measure. And I'm not certain if the problem is Mar or living away from my father's house. There the difference between right and wrong was entirely clear. Now I fear I've come under the same affliction as—"

"As?"

Evelyn was about to say "Bobbin' John," but that would have been entirely inappropriate to admit to a servant even if Lucinda had been with her for eons. "I just need some time to think. Mar was right. I shouldn't have taken the boys to the park without asking a footman to accompany us. Papa should have insisted on it when I was with him as well."

Lucinda moved around and started plaiting Evelyn's hair. "I think I prefer Nottingham to London. It seems there are unsavory characters lurking in every dark corner."

"It seems there are unsavory characters lurking in plain sight. But you're right about London. When everyone's dressed in court attire 'tis difficult to determine the riffraff from the moral."

"Well, for the most part, everyone in Mar's employ believes him to be an honorable man."

Evelyn twisted her robe's sash. At least earning the affection of one's servants meant something. Everyone in Papa's employ believed him to be a miser, even Lucinda.

Perhaps she had relied too much on hearsay. Perhaps she needed to give him time—to come to know him better. In truth, after a mere month of marriage, they were still little more than strangers who happened to meet in the dark, strip bare, and take their pleasure. Undeniably delectable pleasure.

What an odd state of affairs.

Evelyn regarded herself in the looking glass, not liking what she saw. She'd entered this marriage with preconceived ideas, which now muddled about in her mind. Nothing seemed as unequivocally certain as it had before she'd taken her vows. She shifted her gaze to Lucinda—the only person in Mar's household with whom she had any history whatsoever. "What do you do when you want to know someone better?"

"Hmm." The maid knit her brows while her hands stilled. "I suppose asking questions is a good place to start."

Mar had asked Evelyn a great many questions and, as a result, he probably knew more about her than she did of him. Did he like to fish or hunt? Why did he wear a kilt most of the time, but always dressed as an Englishman at court? What was his favorite food, book, pastime? She didn't know the answer to a single one of those questions.

Moreover, what did he want from her? Naturally, she'd taken over the management of the housekeeping staff and she discussed the daily menus with their London cook since the woman who filled the position at Alloa remained in Scotland to prepare meals for the serving staff up there. Evelyn had been reluctant to fulfill her role as stepmother—not that Mar had noticed. In fact, before this morning and excepting mealtimes, Evelyn had all but ignored the boys—especially since Thomas had clearly not wanted her affection.

Surprisingly, today the boy had stood beside her with his shoulders square while he defended her to his father. Why? Because she'd taken charge of the cart driver? Because she'd shown concern for Oliver? Or was it because her stepson realized she truly cared about his heartache and the need for him to overcome the painful loss of his mother?

All three, John, Oliver, and Thomas, had been through a horrible ordeal. And now they had brought Evelyn into their house to fill a missing hole, each one trying to deal with her presence in his own way, knowing she would never be Margaret, yet not knowing what they truly wanted or needed from a stepmother... or from a second wife.

True, Mar required money to settle his debts—that might be reason enough for marriage. But it wasn't reason enough for Evelyn. Whether Mar knew it or not, he had married a woman, not a purse, and, henceforth, she refused to rest until he saw it.

Lucinda set the brush on the toilette. "Shall I stir the coals, my lady?"

"Not tonight, thank you. Go on and have a good rest."

After the lady's maid took her leave, Evelyn moved to the settee and stared at the fire, mulling over her thoughts. The Earl of Mar mightn't have been her choice for a husband, but she was married to the Highlander now. It was time to learn more about the man with whom she planned to spend the rest of her life, like him or not.

Do I like him?

She had no idea how much time had passed when assured footsteps marched down the corridor. For a moment, Evelyn thought Mar might pop into her chamber, until the steps continued down the hall. The door to the earl's chamber opened with a muffled creak.

Hushed voices came through the timbers. Doubtless, Mar's valet had come in.

Evelyn clutched her arms across her midriff. What if she visited him? Would the earl grouse at her? Or might he be willing to talk?

If she dared to cross the threshold, what should she say? Could she ask him why people called him Bobbin' John? Could she ask him why he allowed such a slight?

She bit her knuckle. *I cannot go in there as if I am judge and jury. He already thinks I'm a highbrow.*

By the time she heard the valet take his leave, Evelyn had convinced herself that to approach John this night was a bad idea.

Which is why, when her wayward hand opened the door, she stood there shaking like a forlorn puppy, her eyes wide, her tongue feeling as if it had swollen twice the size of her mouth.

Standing in front of the hearth with his arms crossed, Mar whipped around. "What are you doing in here?" he barked, the angles of his face sharp with ire.

Evelyn took a step back, her hand gripping the latch. "I wanted…" She considered slamming the door, fleeing to her bed, and hiding beneath the coverlet for the rest of her days.

"Aye?" he pressed impatiently, looking like a Highland king—or a Viking—whichever was more menacing and barbaric.

"I-I said some harsh words last eve for which I am not proud, and I owe you an apology."

Mar dropped his arms to his sides. "Oh?"

"Before we were wed, I prejudged you and I now realize I may have been wrong. I just wanted to say that going forward, I will try to form my opinions without bias."

"I thank you." Rubbing his neck, he looked toward his bed, but it wasn't a smoldering glance as she might have thought with bed involved. His expression was tortured and pained. "I trust you will accept my apology as well. I did not manage our disagreement well."

Saying nothing, Evelyn gave a nod, half expecting John to approach. But as silence swelled in the air, she, too, glanced to the bed—a gargantuan contraption with mahogany posts as big around as her thigh. By the charge in the air, she intuitively stayed put.

Her intuition also told her something was amiss and if she didn't take the situation in hand, the rift between them may not heal. Slowly, deliberately, she untied her sash. Mar watched. He said nothing, his eyes growing dark as she pushed the robe from her shoulders and let it drop to the floor. Wearing only a chemise of holland cloth, she smoothed her hands from her shoulders to her breasts and down to her hips.

Mar's lips parted while his gaze followed her fingers. She gripped her skirt and exposed her ankles. "What do you want?" she asked, her voice husky.

Not answering her question, he sauntered toward her, looking like a man starved—a hunter, a warrior, a plunderer, and a pirate.

"Does my body please you?" she whispered without fear, inching the hem up farther and throwing back her shoulders.

After two more steps, Evelyn shuddered as Mar grasped her waist and backed her into the countess's chamber, kicking the door closed behind. "Your body reminds me I am a man. The way your full lips form a bow, the way your breasts rise and fall with each breath, sends me wild with need," he growled, claiming her lips with a coarse and demanding kiss. Everything about John was raw and rough and nothing like the gentle man who had introduced her to the sport of the boudoir only a month ago. Licking her neck, he lifted her into his arms.

"W-what is your favorite color?" she asked breathlessly, her head swimming as his mouth covered her breast through her shift.

"Turquoise," he mumbled, lifting her onto the bed. He stood back and disrobed in the blink of an eye, his member as hard as a steel rod. "I'm a wee bit partial to turquoise as of late."

Evelyn sank into the pillows as the naked Highlander climbed over her. "What is your favorite f-food?"

"Pork. Cooked on a spit." He kissed her—hot, wet, and ravenous. "No more questions."

In three tugs, he yanked the shift over her head. With his knees, he spread her legs and rubbed himself along her slick channel. "Ye're ready for me, wife."

"I'm hungry for you, John."

Evelyn didn't want to wait. Yes, tonight was unlike any lovemaking they'd ever shared. His wicked assault took her to the precipice of madness with the speed of a shooting star. She opened her knees wider and grasped his member, angling it toward her core. "You're making my blood run hot."

She drew him toward her, but he didn't enter. Teasing her with a low chuckle, he traced the curve of her breast with his tongue while she writhed, wanting, needing, craving him. His mouth was everywhere, making love to her body—everywhere except the one place she wanted him most.

"Please! Are you torturing me?"

"Aye." He pushed up to his knees and stroked himself slowly, drawing out his seduction. "Is this what you want?"

Her thighs quivered. "Yes. Now!"

He hovered above her. "Then you'll have it right now, no holds barred."

God save her, with his every shocking word, her need ratcheted higher. Her body arched, her thighs spread wider. Unable to wait a moment longer, she sank her fingers into his bottom and demanded he enter her.

Fiercely he plunged inside, so deep, the last vestiges of her control exploded into pure passion as together they bucked and rode the wave like never before. As she reached her peak, John threw his head back and roared like a savage.

In each other's arms, they collapsed together, panting. It had never been like this before—rough, fast, and passionate. Every time she made love to this man it was different than the last.

Still trembling, Evelyn gazed into John's eyes. A hundred emotions passed through those silvery blues, still guarded. The same man hovered above her, yet his lovemaking had been different in every way.

She twirled a lock of hair around her finger. "You took me like a Highland barbarian."

The corner of his mouth turned up. "Did I?"

"What happened at court today?"

Before he looked away, the aggressive slash to his brows deepened. "I suppose it was just another day like all the rest." He kissed her forehead, then slid to her side. "'Tis late. You must sleep."

* * *

As Evelyn reached out for John and met with cold bed linens, her eyes flew open. She bolted upright, wiping the sweat from her brow.

The window!

Good gracious, Mr. Dubois never should have asked

her to unlock it. The very idea was treachery. She needed to inform him at once that she in no way would ever be used like that again. What if someone came into the house for more sinister reasons?

She darted out of bed, pulled on her shift and her robe, and lit a candle. The mantel clock read seven minutes past four. Thank heavens there was still time to lock the window before the servants began to stir. She tiptoed to the dining hall, dashed across the floor, and turned the latch.

But her trepidation didn't ease. Had Mr. Dubois's spy already come and gone? What about the urgent correspondence Mar had to take care of on the queen's behalf? Is that what had made him so distant, so savage?

Taking her candle, she tiptoed to the library and hastened to Mar's writing table. Odd, a missive from the Duke of Argyll sat atop, the seal broken. Tempted, Evelyn rubbed the tips of her fingers together. Should she read it?

Why not? What if it contained something critical for *the cause*? Besides, she'd read Mar's correspondence before. Why should this be any different?

She chewed her bottom lip. But things were different now. She had committed to give her husband a chance to prove himself. Further, she must distance herself from Mr. Dubois—at least until she understood why John disliked the French emissary so vehemently.

Perhaps there is an answer in Argyll's missive.

She snatched the letter from the table and unfolded it. *A traitor?*

Evelyn clutched the letter to her chest. *Who?*

Worse, May twenty-third was on the morrow. Regardless of whether she agreed to allow Mr. Dubois's spy into the house, he most certainly needed to know about the meeting at Black's.

She refolded the missive, hastened up to her chamber, and put the sunflower in the window. But there was not enough time to wait. Dashing to her writing table, she scribed a missive, rang for Lucinda, and instructed her to hire a coach and deliver it to Mr. Dubois's residence immediately. No matter how much Evelyn wanted to obey Mar's wishes, this information was too important to ignore. She absolutely must meet with the French emissary once again—but this would be the last time.

Chapter Eighteen

*J*ohn looked twice at Argyll's missive. He had placed it with one end barely touching the inkpot. During the night the letter moved a quarter inch south. His gut squeezed.

Evelyn was no traitor. He knew it in the depths of his soul.

But was she the conduit for information, as Argyll suspected?

If she was innocent, then why did she snoop through his missives?

When they'd argued, she'd made it clear she scorned his reputation as Bobbin' John. Evelyn also accused him of being indecisive. Oh, how little his wife knew of what truly went on behind closed doors in the queen's antechamber. If it weren't for John, Scotland's people would be oppressed to the point of starvation. Anne didn't care about Highlanders. They were merely minions in the distant north whose only purpose was to fill out the numbers of Britain's army.

But there was no time to wonder how or why Evelyn had been misled. John intended to uncover the truth when he confronted her. And if he had to tie the woman to a chair and wait two days for her confession, he would do so. Clenching his teeth, he climbed the stairs, strode down the third-floor corridor, and stood outside her chamber with his fist ready to knock.

Forget pleasantries.

Making his decision, he burst through the door. "We need to talk about that bloody letter from Ar—" John stopped beside the bed and turned full circle. "Evelyn?"

Where the devil has she gone?

His gaze rested on the sunflower, now displayed in the window. Damn, he ought to burn the bloody Jacobite symbol.

"Evelyn?" he shouted, running for the stairs.

He stopped at the drawing room on his way down. She wasn't there, either.

"Swenson, where's the dog!"

The butler looked up from the bottom of the servants' steps. "Brutus is in the kitchens."

John hastened toward the man. "Have you seen Her Ladyship?"

Shaking his head, the butler ran a hand over his hair while Lucinda crossed through the corridor beyond.

"Wait!" John hastened after her. "Where is Lady Mar?"

The lady's maid looked up clutching a feather duster in front of her chest, her face turning red. "I beg your pardon?"

John held up his palms. "You're in no trouble, lass, but I believe your lady is in grave danger."

"W-what kind of trouble, my lord?"

"I'm not at liberty to say, but I can disclose that if I do not find her within the next five minutes, she may end up locked away in the Tower. Am I clear?"

Lucinda nodded.

"Did she tell you where she was off to?"

"No. I had no clue she was stepping out th-this morning." Something about the maid's stutter gave John pause. What was she hiding?

"Haven't you been accompanying her when she walks Brutus?"

"I have. Often, anyway."

John glanced back to Swenson. "And she didn't take the dog?"

"No, m'lord."

What the devil? How could Evelyn disobey him and slip out of the house as if she were a spy?

God's bones. She cannot possibly be…

He grasped the maid by the shoulders. "Lassie, I need you to tell me where Her Ladyship usually goes when she walks her dog—and if you wish to remain in my employ, you'd best not say the park."

"To be honest, most of the time we do go to the park, b-but occasionally she makes me wait on Bourdon Street while…"

"Och, lass. I haven't all day." John squeezed his fingers. "What does Her Ladyship do whilst you're waiting?"

Cringing, Lucinda looked to Swenson.

"Tell him," said the butler.

"She has never explained why, but she takes Brutus down the alley and visits a coffeehouse called the Copper Cauldron." Stepping back, the lady's maid brandished her duster. "'Tis a tottering hidey-hole if you ask me, but Her Ladyship rarely spends more than a few minutes inside."

John pounded his fist against the wall. "She frequents a bloody coffeehouse in an alley?"

"Yes, well, that's why she takes the dog."

"Och aye, an overweight, aged Corgi is guard enough against a mob of miscreants in an alley?" John asked, starting for the mews. "Holy everlasting hell, I should have put a stop to her jaunts the day she brought that flea-bitten hound into this house."

Swenson kept pace beside him. "Shall I reprimand the lady's maid, m'lord?"

"Of course not. Tell her I appreciated her candidness and give her a half-holiday—just not today. Perhaps in a month after I'm finished murdering my wife."

"Very well, m'lord."

John stopped and glanced to his dirk—the only weapon he wore when at leisure. "Go fetch my sword and pistol. Haste!"

"Straightaway, m'lord."

Pushing outside, John raced to the mews and headed for the tack room.

"Shall I saddle your mount, m'lord?" asked the stableboy.

"No time." John grabbed his bridle. "I'll ride bare-back."

By the time John mounted, Swenson appeared, huffing and wheezing, weapons in hand.

"Good man," John said, taking the sword belt and buckling it, then arming himself with his damned dueling pistols.

As he cantered over the cobbled streets, the tightness in his chest crushed him. What had she been thinking by going out alone? Hell, she hadn't even taken her dog. She might be hurt. Worse, the woman was meddling in things she couldn't possibly understand.

* * *

Evelyn glanced over her shoulder before she continued to relay her news. "Argyll's note said the officer was to meet with the duke's man at Black's Tavern at one o'clock this very day."

"One?" Mr. Dubois removed his pocket watch and tapped it. "I must make haste. I only have two hours to intervene."

"But I thought James had decided to wait until the queen—" She cringed, not wanting to hex the woman by saying *died*. "You know—and then he'd take the throne peaceably, Lord willing."

Dubois's eyes slanted aside while he pushed his chair back. "*Alors*, I must go," he said, not answering her question.

The door swung open so violently, it nearly came unhinged. "I should have kent you were behind this treachery!"

As Evelyn turned, ice coursed through her veins. How could she ever explain?

But Mar wasn't looking at her as he strode forward, murder in his eyes and sword in his hand. His gaze honed on the Frenchman. "I always suspected your motives were sinister."

Beads of sweat trickled from Dubois's temples. "You are sorely mistaken. I—"

"I ken the truth now. You're funneling information to King Louis—setting the stage for his plot to invade Britain and claim the throne for himself."

"What?" Evelyn sprang to her feet. "That's a lie! Mr. Dubois is a Jacobite."

John looked at her as if she'd just flung hot coffee in

his face. "You cannot be serious. Dubois has no love for James. In fact, the only reason the queen hasn't booted his arse out of London is because he'd like to see the Old Pretender exiled from France as well as Britain."

The Frenchman scooted around the table, sliding a hand inside his doublet, his eyes shifting from side to side. "I-I do not recall ever having said that."

"No?" Evelyn flattened her hands on the table to steady her trembling legs. By the holy cross, she'd been fooled. Clear to her bones, she knew John spoke true. She gulped against the bile burning her throat. "What about the others you've tricked?" she demanded, looking the traitor in the eye. Dear God, she'd trusted him more than her own family. "What about Seaforth, Cameron, and Tullibardine, to name a few? Do they realize you support Louis's plot to invade Britain?"

Just as Dubois drew a dagger from his coat, John pushed Evelyn toward the wall, away from danger. "Get back!"

Stumbling, she tripped over a chair. With a swing of John's sword, he knocked the knife from Dubois's hand, sending it clattering to the floorboards. Lunging in, he struck the Frenchman in the temple with the weapon's pommel.

His head bloodied, Dubois stumbled but grabbed a chair, using it like a shield. John's sword hissed through the air as the two men circled.

Slashing a quick strike, Mar hacked off a wooden leg. "I will see you hung for your deceit."

Mr. Dubois scurried around a table as he squealed. "My deceit? Look in the mirror. You only care about yourself—you bend with the wind."

Rage blazed in his eyes as John smashed the table into smithereens. "You have no idea, ye traitorous bastard."

Evelyn gasped aloud when the door clattered and the Duke of Argyll stormed inside with a dozen dragoons. "I always kent you were a traitor, Mar. And now you've embroiled your wife in your crooked dealings." Argyll thrust out his finger. "Arrest them!"

"Stay back." Lunging for her, John grabbed Evelyn's arm and tugged her behind him, drew a pistol, and pushed the muzzle flush against Argyll's head. "That foul-smelling Frenchman is the traitor you're looking for. Not me. And not my wife. But if you insist on pursuing me, you'll not live another day to tell tale about it."

Argyll raised his hands, a bead of sweat dribbling from the steel point of Mar's pistol. "Throw down, men."

"Wise call." His finger on the trigger, John skirted around the duke, taking Evelyn with him. "I am the one wronged here, and if you do not see it, you are a greater fool than Dubois."

With a snarl, he pushed the duke to the floorboards and hoisted Evelyn under his arm.

"I can run!" she shouted as he dashed outside.

He set her down, took a flying leap, and landed on the back of a saddleless horse. Taking up the reins, he offered his hand. "I'll pull you up."

As Evelyn grasped his palm, he hoisted her off her feet and deposited her across the horse's withers. "Get down!"

"After him!" the duke shouted, holding his sword aloft.

John cued the horse to a gallop, taking the corner to the racket of musket fire behind.

Clutching the horse's mane in her fists, Evelyn fought to keep from falling to her death while the cobbles passed in a blur beneath. John steadied her with his forearms as he leaned forward, keeping a loose rein to allow the horse more speed.

She chanced a backward glance. "I don't see them."

"They'll follow soon enough," he growled.

Quickly, they turned down the close behind the town house.

"What are you planning?" she asked.

The horse skidded to stop outside the mews.

"Stay here. I'll fetch the lads." John jumped down and helped her dismount. "Tell the grooms to rig the coach. Say there's no time to spare."

She squeezed his hands before he pulled away. "Hurry!"

Chapter Nineteen

*S*wenson!" John bellowed as he raced for the stairs. "Where are my sons?"

The door to the butler's rooms opened and the man stepped out. "They're in the nursery with Mrs. Kerr."

"Shutter the house. Ready the servants." John ascended two steps at a time while Swenson followed. "Take everyone to Alloa via merchant ship. I'll meet you there."

"What the devil has happened?"

"There's no time to explain. Gather our cloaks and meet me at the mews."

"Straightaway, m'lord."

It took less than a minute to race to the nursery.

"Da!" the boys shouted in unison, running for him.

"Quickly fetch your traveling gear." John looked to the governess. "Mrs. Kerr, I entrust you with packing my sons' effects. Swenson will be taking the serving staff to Alloa forthwith."

"My heavens," she said, drawing her palm to her chest. "This is abrupt. Has something happened?"

"It will if I do not spirit my family out of London directly." As the lads returned, he took them by the hands and continued, "Do not worry. Swenson kens what needs to be done."

"Where are we going, Da?" asked Oliver.

"Home." To the tune of their shouts of joy, John lifted the youngest onto his hip and hastened back to the mews. "Climb into the coach with your stepmother."

"Countess," Thomas corrected.

John ignored the lad as Evelyn approached. "Everything is ready," she said.

A tic twitched at the corner of his eye. The woman had no idea as to the extent of his anger. "You'd best alight."

She took Oliver by the hand. "Aren't you coming?"

"Do as I say." John didn't offer assistance. If the lady was capable of taking herself to a dingy coffeehouse in a London alley, she could bloody well climb inside a coach without his help.

"The team is ready, m'lord. Where to?" asked the driver.

John ushered the man aside. "Take us to the Pool of London. Use the byways. Keep an eye out for redcoats."

"The queen's dragoons?"

"Aye."

Huffing, one of the housemaids dashed up. "M'lord—Redcoats are pounding on the door! Swenson said he'd stall as long as possible, but you must go."

"Thank you." John motioned to the coachman to alight. "Quickly now…turn left in the close instead of right."

John followed his damned wife into the coach. God save her when he finally got an opportunity to speak to the woman alone. What had she been thinking? How long had she been meeting with Dubois? And who else knew the Frenchman was part of a plot for King Louis to invade Britain, assume the throne, and make the kingdom a French colony?

John sat across from Evelyn and the boys and glared.

She fixated on her hands. Aye, the woman knew she had crossed the line.

"What is wrong?" Thomas asked while the coach rattled along at a steady trot.

John shifted his gaze to his eldest. "Nothing."

Oliver peeked from beneath his woolen cap, the band almost covering his eyes. "Then why do I feel like I'm in trouble?"

"You're not in trouble," John barked.

Evelyn pulled the youngest onto her lap. "I'm the one who's in trouble."

"What did you do?" asked Thomas.

"I trusted someone I shouldn't have." She looked John in the eye. "And I'm very sorry for it."

Snorting, he crossed his ankles as well as his arms. *Now she understands the gravity of her errors? She should have thought about the effect of her actions afore she went to the Copper Cauldron.*

John's blood simmered near boiling while they moved along, the coach teetering as they took the corners. The wheels creaked and groaned, the horses' shod hooves clattering on the cobbles to the tune of the coachman's cracking whip.

"Ho!" the coachman hollered, bringing the team to an abrupt halt.

They all jolted toward the front quarter.

John slammed his fist against the wall to admonish the driver, though he didn't dare shout.

"The Pool of London is swarming with redcoats," the man's muffled voice filtered throughout.

John parted the curtains only wide enough to peer out. "Shite."

"Da!"

Evelyn covered Oliver's mouth. "Sh."

"Where to, m'lord?" asked the driver.

Her Ladyship pushed the lad's bonnet away from his eyes. "Tell him to go to my father's town house. There we will be able to hide the carriage behind the mews."

"Och aye? And once your father learns we're being pursued by Argyll and his band of misled dragoons, your da will throw us to the wolves."

Evelyn eyed him. "Not if you tell him you're pursuing his gold."

"Damnation, woman, I have had enough!"

Gaping at him with defiance, she pounded on the carriage wall. "Head for Kingston-upon-Hull's mews!"

John gaped. Was there no end to the wench's audacity? "Have you ever in your life obeyed anyone?"

"I beg your pardon? Where else can we flee?"

"And you think you have all the answers? You have pushed me too far. Because of you I am risking the lives of my children, and my reputation, not to mention putting my lands at risk—because you *trusted* someone? How deep does this misplaced trust go, Evelyn?"

The woman lowered her damned gaze. "We'll talk about it later."

"Right. Fob me off. That's convenient."

She slid Oliver off her lap. "Do you know Sir Kennan Cameron?"

"Why in God's name—?"

"Because his ship is moored at Blackwall. Further-more, he also has firsthand information on what happened to the Spanish gold."

"What?" he shouted so loudly, his voice cracked. John clenched his fists, wishing his fingers were wrapped around Evelyn's neck. "Ye kent this and yet withheld it from me?"

"I didn't think you'd give a damn—until now."

"Stop your cursing," John snapped.

Thomas leaned over and laced his hands around Evelyn's arm. "But you cursed as well, Da."

"Wheesht."

"Anyway…" Evelyn drew her arm around the lad's shoulders. "My father might be willing to provide us with a safe haven if he knew you had information as to the whereabouts of his gold."

John sat back and groaned. He needed to think and Hull's town house was possibly the best option they had—though he would never admit it to Her Ladyship. "Very well, but I shall speak to His Grace and the rest of you will remain silent."

* * *

Keeping her lips tightly closed, Evelyn strengthened her hold on the boys' hands, terrified of what John might say while they met with her father in the drawing room. What if Papa discovered how much she knew about his affairs?

"I received anonymous information about your gold, which led me to a rather squalid coffeehouse," John said with a most sober expression. "No sooner had I stepped inside when Argyll and his dragoons barged in and ac-cused me of treason."

"Argyll?" Papa thumped the leather-bound Bible atop his writing table. "I knew that man was a backstabber."

Evelyn could hold her tongue no longer. "We need a place to hide."

John shot her an angry glare, slicing his hand through the air. "Only until I have a moment to explain the situation to Her Majesty."

Evelyn was puzzled. John hadn't mentioned anything about speaking to the queen.

"Tell the queen about the gold? No, no, no. Such an admission would ruin me." Papa strode to the sideboard and poured two drams of brandy. "And Argyll is too powerful to subvert by a mere conversation. Moreover, you cannot hide here. As Lady Evelyn's father, my house is the first place they'll look. You'll fare better pleading your case from Scotland—whilst leaving my name out of the matter altogether."

John accepted the brandy but he didn't drink. "Perhaps you're right. In fact, my servants are shuttering my town house as we speak."

Releasing a pent-up breath, Evelyn pulled the boys forward and gave John a very pointed stare, praying he understood her meaning. "If we make haste to Blackwall, I am certain Sir Kennan will—"

John shook his head vehemently. "There are probably a hundred dragoons scouring the streets between here and the port."

Papa tossed back his dram and coughed. "Good heavens, there's no time to waste."

"Send a maid to Phoebe's chamber." Still holding the children by their hands, Evelyn started for the door. "I'll change into Frances's mourning gown and put a veil over my head, and then we'll use Phoebe's clothes to disguise the boys."

Thomas stopped and wrenched away. "I'm not dressing like a lass."

Oliver did the same. "Me neither."

Evelyn planted her fists on her hips. "Do you know the alternative?"

Thomas hung his head. "Nay."

"Your father will be convicted of a crime he did not commit. He could endure a heinous trial, his lands and title stripped, he could be sent to the colonies or worse. Why? Do not let it be because you refused to don a disguise."

"It will only take a short while to traverse the city, lads." John clapped each boy on the shoulder. "Now go along with your stepmother."

The boys reluctantly followed her to Phoebe's room and, after Evelyn opened her sister's cedar chest, one of the housemaids entered. "Do you need assistance, my lady?"

"Yes." Evelyn shook out two old dresses from last season that would work nicely. "Help the lads into these. And find a couple of straw bonnets. The gowns ought to fit over their clothing." She tossed the dresses at the maid. "I'll be in Frances's chamber if you should need me."

"I cannot believe we have to wear girls' clothes," Thomas mumbled.

"Aye, whatever happened must be terribly grave," said Oliver as Evelyn crossed the corridor and opened the door to the other bedchamber.

Frances's mourning dress was stowed at the bottom of the chest and needed a good pressing. But it couldn't be helped. Besides, if she looked a bit disheveled, that would further draw away suspicion. Evelyn tied the skirt over her clothes and shrugged into the top piece. Thank goodness Frances was a tad larger.

After she found a veil, she dashed back across the corridor and joined the boys. "How is it coming?"

Thomas turned and stared out from under a straw bonnet with a yellow bow. "I look like a fool."

Evelyn clapped a hand over her mouth and forced herself not to laugh. Though it was too small for Phoebe, the gown was easily two inches too long and the hat nearly swallowed him whole.

"I cannot walk in this," said Oliver, the bonnet falling into his face while he bent to look at his feet.

"Goodness, these dresses won't do." Evelyn dashed to the toilette, pulled open a drawer, and found a ribbon. "Tie this around Oliver's waist and cinch up the hem."

Shaking her head, the maid took it. "Yes, my lady."

"And give me your apron, please. It'll hide all these hideous wrinkles."

By the time they all ventured out to the mews, John had changed into a pair of rough-hewn breeches and an old leather doublet—both of which were a tad small. The only thing that fit was the borrowed tricorn atop his head. He tugged a satchel over his shoulder. "We'll be taking your father's coach. It will draw less attention."

"Why not hire one?" she asked.

"Because the only driver in London I trust is mine." John opened the door, gestured inside and, though he offered his hand, he did so with an air of reluctance. "We must haste—and you'd best not be wrong about Cameron."

Evelyn sat on the velvet bench while John helped the boys negotiate their skirts. Sir Kennan had offered his assistance at the theater. But why was her throat so tight she couldn't swallow? Had the sea captain turned pirate?

Chapter Twenty

When the odors from the port wafted through the coach, the driver slowed the team to a walk. John peered through the curtain as they ambled along the Thames. The bustle on the wharf was frenzied with men rolling barrels down long gangways. Lads shouted and ran. Laborers toiled, loading wagons. And all along the footpath, merchants peddled their wares.

Evelyn leaned under him and craned her neck to see out. She pointed downriver. "There it is, the *Highland Reel.*"

"She's moored off the shore," said Thomas as the boys wrestled for a chance for a peek.

Two soldiers carrying muskets strode past. Dropping the curtain, John nudged everyone away from the window.

A thump came from the driver's seat above. "The place is teeming with redcoats, too."

"Turn down a side street. We'll alight there," John said loudly enough to be heard.

As the coach started away, he focused on his sons. "It is very important for you to keep your heads down and pretend you are lassies."

"But I hate being a girl," said Thomas.

"'Tisn't for long. And you may as well learn now that we must make compromises. This is a grave matter. One that may see us all killed if we do not play our parts. Do you understand?"

Squaring his shoulders, Thomas straightened. "Aye, m'lord. But what did you do?"

"Nothing I cannot set to rights once we reach home." He turned to the youngest. "Can you pretend to be a lass, Oliver?"

The boy scratched beneath his hat. "Yes. But this bonnet itches."

Evelyn gave him a pat. "You'll have it off soon enough."

The carriage came to a halt. "I'll do the talking." John pointedly stared at his wife. "I mean it, Eve."

"Of course. I don't know why you think I would speak out of turn."

He snorted. "You did at Hull's."

Her jaw dropped, and then she coughed as if she always portrayed the epitome of acquiescence. "That's because he's my father."

"Enough talk."

The coachman opened the door and, after they alighted, John gathered his family on the footpath. "A bedraggled lot of tinkers we are."

"'Tis a good thing, is it not?" Evelyn asked.

He pointed his finger at her lips. "Wheesht. And I'll not be reminding you again."

Ignoring her exasperated expression, he led them toward the wharf, keeping his eyes on the cobblestones. Disguised, John looked like a common laborer, but if anyone who knew him came close, he risked being arrested on the spot. Ahead, three soldiers blocked the entrance to the port stairs leading to the river.

John's back arched against the pressure of the dirk hidden up his spine. At Hull's he'd hidden daggers in his sleeves and his socks, though his flintlock was in plain view, tucked in his belt.

When a mob of redcoats approached, he picked up Oliver and coaxed the lad's head against his shoulder. "Pretend you're sleepy," he whispered.

The boy whimpered, playing his part like a champion.

While the dragoons marched past, John turned his attention to a fish merchant. "What's the price of herring today?" he asked, in a practiced English accent, watching out of the corner of his eye.

"A ha'penny a pound, sir." The man held up a sample by the gills. "This here's a beauty—she'd sell for a shilling in Town, but I'll give her to you for five pence."

"Thank you, but I'm just browsing. Perhaps on the morrow."

When only three sentries remained at the post, he straightened one arm and coaxed a dagger to slide into his palm. Balancing his son on his forearm, beneath Oliver's skirts he gripped the handle of his pistol.

John glanced back to Evelyn and Thomas. "Now's the time to act your parts," he growled out of the side of his mouth.

A corporal removed his musket from his shoulder and held it across his body, blocking the entrance. "State your purpose."

"Just looking to hire a skiff to take us across the

Thames, governor," John said, sounding like a local—at least his years in London weren't for naught. "Taking the family to see my mother afore the minister reads her last rites, we are."

"Is that so?" The corporal pinched Oliver's sleeve between his fingers and rubbed the fabric.

Jesu, there was enough taffeta to outfit the wee lad with two gowns.

"This is awfully fine cloth for a—"

"We put on our best, we did." Bless it, Evelyn had to bloody open her mouth—and she sounded like a Cockney hen.

The corporal eyed her. "Mourning clothes already?"

John took a step in—idle chat would be their end. "If you'll excuse us—"

Raising his weapon, the soldier stopped him. "Just a moment."

"It's Dubois!" a dragoon shouted from down the street.

The corporal grinned and licked his lips. "I want that bastard." Shouldering his musket, he beckoned his men and started off. "I'll be the first to applaud when the Frenchman swings from the gallows."

John let out a long breath and hastened for the stairs. "Stay on my heels. We're not out of this yet."

"The *Highland Reel*'s sails are unfurling," Evelyn whispered.

Holy everlasting hell, what else might go wrong this day?

John found a man tying his skiff to a mooring cleat. "How much to take us across the river?"

"Sorry. I'm heading home for the day."

"But we're—" Evelyn silenced Thomas with a nudge.

John set Oliver down. "I'll give you a guinea and you do not even need to take us clear across."

"A guinea? That's more than I earn in a week."

"Will you take us?"

The man held out his palm. "Payment first."

John fished a coin out of the satchel and waved it under the sailor's nose. "Once we're aboard."

The man untied the rope while John helped everyone onto the benches. "We must haste."

The sailor sat between the oars and held out his palm. "Why's that?"

Slapping the guinea into his hand, John inclined his head toward the *Highland Reel*. "Because we need to board that ship."

The man glanced over his shoulder. "The *Reel*? But they're hoisting her anchor."

"Row fast, my friend. If you ferry us to that ship afore she sails, there'll be another guinea in it for you."

Chapter Twenty-One

Crack!

Before she could stop herself, Evelyn shrieked while ducking over the top of Thomas and shielding him from the musket shot with her body.

"They're firing at us!" shouted the oarsman.

"'Tis but a warning. It missed by three lengths." Seemingly undaunted, John removed his tricorn and waved it. "Hold the ship!" he hollered. But his efforts were met by another volley from the shore.

The man pulled an oar, making the skiff veer off course. "That does it. I'm turning back."

"Wait," Evelyn said, removing her veil and standing. "Sir Kennan! We need safe passage."

"Bloody Christmas, you'll capsize the boat," John growled.

Evelyn didn't stop. Sailors darted across the deck waving their arms and shouting. A kilted man moved to the rail and held up a spyglass—good heavens, it was Sir Kennan himself.

"Please!" she shouted, frantically waving her veil, trying not to rock the boat.

Muskets cracked behind, but John's confidence had given her strength. The shots weren't even coming close.

Sir Kennan lowered his spyglass and circled his arm over his head.

"He's waving at us," shouted Oliver.

John thumped the oarsman on the shoulder. "Keep on, else I'll toss you over the side."

A boom swung out over the hull and the men lowered a seat that looked like the swing hanging from the big oak tree at Thoresby Hall.

Once Mar convinced the oarsman to continue, it took no time to reach the *Highland Reel*. He grabbed for the swing as it sailed past. "Evelyn, you go up first with Thomas on your lap. I'll follow with Oliver."

"But I want to go up by myself," said Thomas.

"There's no time. Do as I say."

"Thomas and Oliver?" asked the oarsman. "Those are peculiar names for a pair of girls."

Evelyn cringed as she slid onto the seat. They hadn't thought to use aliases.

"What are you on about?" John asked the man as if he'd been affronted. "I said Thomasa and Olive. Are you deaf?"

"Beg your pardon."

Once Thomas was on her lap, Evelyn exhaled. "Thank you for remaining silent about your name."

"I did it for Da," the boy whispered. "He said we had to play our parts."

"And you were splendid," Evelyn said, swearing to herself never to mention the names Thomasa or Olive again in her life.

Three pairs of hands reached to pull them aboard as Sir Kennan's confused expression came into view. "What the devil has happened, m'lady?"

"Dubois is a double spy—he's behind a plot for the French invasion of England."

"Aye, we've just heard the news as well. 'Tis why I'm setting sail." He looked to Thomas. "Who's this?"

Evelyn removed the frilly hat from the child's head. "We disguised the boys in my sister Phoebe's clothing."

"Mar kens about Dubois?"

"Aye!" the earl's voice resounded from below. "And I need some bloody answers."

Sir Kennan pulled Evelyn away from the rail and cupped a hand to the side of his mouth. "I do not trust him."

She patted the captain's arm reassuringly. "I didn't initially, either. But I was wrong. Please, I ask you to give Mar a chance."

The Cameron heir looked to the skies and hesitated before the men pulled the boom with Mar and Oliver over the side. John immediately stepped forward. "Exactly what dealings have you with my wife?"

"Beg your pardon, m'lord, but presently I've a ship to sail." Sir Kennan gave a curt bow before he bounded up to the quarterdeck. "Weigh anchor!"

"Captain," Mar prefaced, following. "To where are we sailing?"

Evelyn took the boys by the hands and climbed the steps as well. "Please, Sir Kennan, might we have a word? There is a great deal to tell you."

"A bloody great deal," said John, his tone sharp, clearly expressing his annoyance.

Ignoring them both, the captain extended his spyglass. "Mr. Tailor, set a course for Edinburgh."

"Aye, aye, Edinburgh, sir."

Sir Kennan gestured to a sailor standing beside the helmsman. "Mr. MacNeil is our boatswain. He'll show you to your quarters. I'll send for you once the *Highland Reel* is under way."

* * *

John was ready to spit darts. He'd just been usurped by a sea captain—a knighted sea captain and heir to a laird-ship, but the man wasn't a peer. Cameron could have taken a few moments to explain why he happened to be setting sail at the same time the whole mess with Dubois's treachery had been revealed. Why did Sir Kennan possess information about the missing Spanish gold? On top of it all, the bastard seemed to have an affinity for Evelyn—something John intended to address forthwith.

Fortunately, once the crew discovered Oliver and Thomas were lads, they discarded Lady Phoebe's dresses and a cabin boy took them under his wing to explore the ship. John allowed it, praying to God the pair would survive their escapades without adding too many new curse words to their vocabulary.

But John needed answers from Evelyn—and in private where they wouldn't be overheard by a crew of probable miscreants. Once they were alone in a crude cabin with a narrow bed and a meager writing table, he gestured to a wooden chair. "Please sit." Surprisingly, she did as he requested without posing a quarrel. "I need the truth from you before meeting with Sir Kennan."

She gave a nod.

"How long have you been meeting with Dubois?"

"Are you not going to ask me why first?"

"I ken why. The bloody letter on my writing table from Argyll was the duke's damned idea—and you fell right into his trap. He suspected you and I told him he was full of rubbish, even though I've known you've been reading my correspondence since the day we took our vows."

"You knew?"

"Aye, and I should have put an end to it posthaste."

"Oh dear," she mumbled, her brow furrowed as she clutched her arms across her midriff. "But after what happened, I'm certain Argyll suspected you to be casting lots with Dubois as well."

"Obviously. I should have refused his request and torn the missive in front of His Grace's face." John raked his fingers through his hair. "Now answer me. How long have you been passing information to Dubois?"

"A bit over a year."

"A year?" John threw out his hands. "My word, woman, you haven't been in London that long."

"I met Mr. Dubois when I was reading to the soldiers at the hospital in Nottingham."

"A soldiers' hospital? That's an odd place for him to be."

"Yes, now that I think on it, you're right. But after a dear servant died because of my father's callousness, the things Mr. Dubois said about supporting Prince James and fighting for better lives for all Britons struck a chord with me."

"Wait." John slashed both hands through the air. "That's right, at the Copper Cauldron, you were adamant that Dubois was sympathetic with the Jacobites."

"Everyone thought so—Seaforth, Tullibardine, and Sir Kennan, just to name a few. When Mr. Dubois first approached me, he asked me to provide information about my father's business dealings to further the cause for James."

"And you spied on your father?"

Evelyn drew a hand across her furrowed brow. "I thought I was helping improve conditions for common laborers and the like. My father is not the man you are. He pays a pittance to his servants and he has them whipped for the slightest insubordination. Moreover, he goes to shocking lengths to avoid paying taxes."

"Hardly things for which a daughter should be disloyal to her kin."

"In my mind, I was acting with honor and loyalty to my country. Papa is a smuggler—the goods he brings in illegally subvert English and especially Scottish producers, making poverty rife within our country. He imposes duties on those beneath him, though he goes to great lengths to not pay them himself, profiting every way he can. I do love him, but I do not approve of or condone his politics."

John folded his arms while a lead ball dropped in his gut. "Nor mine, I presume."

"You are different altogether."

"Yet you brought your deceit into my house."

"I knew you would never understand." Hiding her face in her hands, she shook her head. "I thought you were just like my father. But now I realize I was wrong to do so."

"What's this? You do not believe you should spy on your husband, but have no issues with spying on your father?"

"I don't know." Evelyn's shoulders curled over as if she were on the verge of tears. "You make it sound as if my every action was wrong. And I'll admit it didn't feel right when Dubois asked me to keep snooping once we were wed. Even though at first I thought you were..."

"What?"

"I initially judged you by your reputation. I was mortified when my father agreed to our union. I believed I was marrying a hideous beast."

John dropped his hands to his sides. "And then look who turned out to be the beast."

"I'm no beast! Please, John." Evelyn straightened, looking like a Viking princess. "Dubois has betrayed me—he has betrayed us all. Please believe me when I say I thought I was working for right—for good."

"But you were working for a traitor."

John hovered over her, his hands gripping the chair's armrests. "What is your relationship with Cameron? Is he your lover?"

She gaped, clearly taken aback by the notion. "Good heavens *no*!"

"Och aye?" But John wasn't about to let his suspicions lie. Not yet. "Well, he seems unduly fond of you."

"I assure you Sir Kennan has never even hinted at such a thing."

"How did you come to know him?"

"Through Mr. Dubois, of course. Just like all the others."

"*All* the others?"

"I mentioned them. Most Jacobite loyalists have visited the Copper Cauldron at one time or another."

"Jesu, this is a cocked-up mess."

"It is a calamitous disaster."

"I may never be able to trust you again. What in God's name were you thinking, Evelyn? You have not only deceived me, you have smeared my good name." He thrust his finger westward. "Back there you risked Oliver and Thomas's lives, spiriting them through London in girls' clothing as if we all were common criminals."

She hid her face again. "I'm ever so sorry."

"Being sorry will solve nothing!" Unable to abide remaining in the same berth, John stormed out, slamming the door behind.

Chapter Twenty-Two

*H*er insides shredding into a thousand bits, Evelyn had no idea how long she'd been doubled over, sobbing into her palms. Until today, she had been unequivocally convinced she was supporting the right cause. How had she become an evil person?

She never intended to hurt anyone. And all along, her efforts were supposed to be helping *the cause*, not helping King Louis annex England to France. How could she have been so naïve?

And now John would never trust her again. What would he do with her? Lock her in the hold? When the ship moored in Edinburgh, would he send her to a convent on the Continent? Dear God, he might go so far as to put her on trial. She could be shipped to the Americas on a convict ship—or, worse, shipped back to London and hanged for treason.

When a knock came at the door, she chose to ignore it. Mar wouldn't have knocked—he would have barged in with an army of musketeers to take her to the bilges and tie her to a barrel for the duration of the voyage.

All this time she'd thought John was the deceitful one, and in the blink of an eye the tables turned and now she felt like the most despicable person in all of Christendom.

The door cracked open. "May I enter, m'lady?" asked Sir Kennan.

Evelyn's shoulders curled over farther. "Please do not. It wouldn't be proper."

"I only need a moment." The captain slipped inside. "Good Lord, your eyes are swollen and red."

"That's because I've been deceived." Evelyn sat straight. "And now I'm the one who is a traitor to the country I love. Worse, I doubt my husband will ever see fit to speak to me again."

"If he doesn't, he's a fool." Sir Kennan leaned against the wall. "Dubois deceived us all, and it sounds as if you were embroiled in the thick of it. Tell me what happened with Argyll."

Wiping her eyes and nose with a kerchief, she straightened and drew in a deep breath. "I may as well start from the night I saw you at the theater. Mr. Dubois indicated he'd received a communication from James and said it was imperative for me to leave a window unlocked."

"Bloody bastard," the captain swore under his breath. "Did you ask why he wanted access to Mar's town house?"

"I should have. But after all this time, I saw no reason to doubt him, although..." Evelyn clenched her fists beneath her chin and gasped.

"What is it?"

"That was the first time I sensed Mr. Dubois's motives might be sinister. In fact, I awoke in the dead of night and resecured the latch."

"Good Lord, you could have been in grave danger had you encountered his spy."

"Thank heavens I didn't." Evelyn went on to explain the missive Argyll had given to Mar, which was meant to trick her but ended up implicating them both for treason. By the time she finished, she was a weeping mess.

Sir Kennan pulled her up into a gentle hug. "There, there, m'lady. If anyone can sort through this mire, 'tis the Earl of Mar."

"B-but I thought you haaaaaaated him."

The captain patted a kind hand on her back. "I'm none too fond—though I'll admit I ken him from a distance only. But I'll tell ye true, if anyone in Scotland can bend the ear of the queen, it is your husband."

She drew in a stuttered breath. "He is a good man. If you would only give him a chance."

The door burst open. Mar stood in the doorway, disbelief etching the hard lines of his face. Clutching a dirk and a sword, he strode inside. "I kent the pair of you were too familiar to be mere acquaintances. Unhand my wife this instant!"

Kennan stepped away and held up his palms. "'Tisn't what you think, m'lord. I was just consoling a weeping woman."

Evelyn pushed between them. "Please, John. He speaks true. I—"

"And how am I to believe anything you say?" He glared at Sir Kennan over her head. "I'm calling you out, Cameron. A duel is the only way to settle this."

"No!" Evelyn shrieked. "He has done nothing ungentlemanly."

John pointed his dirk over her shoulder. "He is in this chamber, is he not?"

Grasping Evelyn's wrist, Sir Kennan ushered her aside. "I have no qualms dueling with you, Mar. But first I ask you to hear me out."

She pressed her fingers to her lips. "Please, John, listen to him."

Mar narrowed his eyes and glanced between them. "You'd best speak quickly."

The captain's Adam's apple bobbed. "Revealing my hand might send me to hell's fire, but I cannot sit idle whilst you drag this wee woman through the mire. Aye, ye ken Dubois fooled us all."

Mar lowered his dirk. "Who is all?"

"Every Jacobite from London to the Outer Hebrides." Kennan moved to the door and clamped his fingers around the latch as if he might be planning to make a hasty escape. "At first, the Frenchman came to us with letters from James—though only recently I've discovered they were forged."

"So you were planning a rising. I kent it all along."

"You're wrong. Thank God the forgeries didn't ask us to stage a revolt."

"What did they say?" asked Evelyn.

"One asked us to organize our forces and be patient. Another said with Her Majesty's failing health, the prince would see us soon and reward all those who remained loyal."

"Nothing new, then?" asked Mar. "No imminent call to arms?"

Sir Kennan's grip on the latch eased. "We all ken that is not his plan. Since James failed to step ashore at Edinburgh in '07, he asked us to remain idle but vigilant throughout the remainder of his sister's reign."

John sheathed his sword but not his dirk. "I've heard

that as well, but what about after? You ken James cannot take the throne unless he converts to Protestantism."

"Because of the Act of Union that you signed, mind you."

"Signed because if I did not, a civil war would have ensued."

Sir Kennan pulled out a small compass and slid it from its leather sheath. "As we've established, 'tis not news to you that James intends on taking the throne after Anne's reign."

"He wants to do so peaceably," Evelyn added.

"Agreed." Kennan tapped the compass and frowned, looking to what seemed to be northward. "*The cause* has been working to earn coin should it become necessary to use force."

John's face remained impassive.

"You are aware of this, are you not?" Evelyn asked.

"I am, though I still do not ken where Dubois plays into the Jacobite cause. The queen and her ministers initially believed him to be an emissary of King Louis to assist with peace negotiations."

"Yes, I understand that was his ploy," Evelyn agreed. "And it seemed plausible to me—after all, Louis has harbored James since his exile."

John finally sheathed his dirk. "Dubois was sent by Louis under the guise of advising the queen on peace talks in the Netherlands. Meanwhile, he began recruiting those loyal to James to raise funds for the eventual succession. Yet in truth, he was deceiving everyone by spying for the king of France, who has plans to invade Britain and annex her as a province of France."

"Aye." Replacing his compass, Sir Kennan smirked. "And that's not the worst of it."

When the ship rolled with a wave, John braced himself against the wall. "Let me guess—the bastard's taken the Spanish gold and James hasn't seen a farthing."

As she gasped, Evelyn's stomach turned sour. "The gold?" she squeaked.

Kennan grimaced. "Gone."

"Fie," John growled. "God's bones, can the two of you dig your graves any deeper?"

Neither of them had a word to say. Evelyn staggered for the chair. The Spanish gold would have been better in her father's hands than in those of that deceitful scoundrel.

"Now, Cameron, this story has been most entertaining, but my challenge still stands. Why the devil did I find you behind closed doors with my wife?"

The captain's fingers slipped to the pommel of his dirk. "I wished to speak to Lady Mar privately."

"Why?"

"To ask about what had happened this day."

"And why not ask me? I was present as well as Her Ladyship."

The captain's chin inched up. "I found it difficult to trust you." At least Sir Kennan didn't attempt to lie.

A tic twitched aside John's eye—the bloody spasm was becoming a permanent annoyance. "But you trust Lady Mar, a woman who has been spying on her husband and her father for over a year? Tell me, how did you come to be acquainted with my wife?"

"At the Copper Cauldron," Evelyn said. "Sir Kennan was with Mr. Dubois when I brought news of the *East India*'s cargo."

John knit his brows. "*East India*?"

Evelyn fanned her face with her kerchief. "That was

the name of the Dutch fluyt reported wrecked off the coast of Shetland. But you know the ship as the *Flying Robin*—not sunk but hidden in a cove near Bettyhill for an overhaul. The *Flying Robin* was the name Papa used when he reported the gold missing."

Sir Kennan nodded. "Aye, after His Grace had the boat refitted so as not to draw suspicion when he smuggled its booty into England."

"Damnation." John shook his head. "The depths of these misdeeds boggle the mind. And you pair, your association is only on account of Dubois?"

"Aye, m'lord." Kennan's brow arched as his gaze shifted to Mar's sword. "I would swear the same on my life."

John gave the captain a dead-eyed glare. "I'll remember you said that—after this is over your life still may be forfeit."

Sir Kennan opened the door, eyes growing dark like a man ready to draw his weapons. "Shall I plan on our duel, m'lord?"

John gave a clipped bow. "At the moment you may leave us."

As soon as Sir Kennan slipped away, Evelyn dropped to her knees. "Please believe me, I came to our marriage bed a virgin."

"Those may be the first truthful words you've ever uttered in my presence." He pulled her up by the arm. "Do not grovel. It doesn't become you."

"Please John, I promise I did not act out of malice. What can I do to earn your forgiveness?"

He released his grasp, his face looking older and tired, but no less handsome. "I wish I knew."

Chapter Twenty-Three

*U*sing the writing table in the captain's cabin, John reread the letter he'd written to the queen. Though it was likely that Argyll had inflicted enough damage to ruin him, John had acted as Her Majesty's faithful servant for more than a decade, and that must account for something. He knew her well enough not to try to deny Argyll's allegations. Instead, he'd explained the situation truthfully, though stretching the facts a bit by saying that Lady Mar had been blackmailed by Mr. Dubois, who had led Her Ladyship to believe that Mar's life was in danger if she didn't comply.

Of course, he added all the proper apologies and stridently vowed that Evelyn would never again fall victim to such treachery and that the circumstances were a painful lesson for such a young, newly married noblewoman.

When confident his plea would be accepted and he would be forgiven, John folded and sealed the parchment with a dollop of red wax, using the stamp from his signet ring.

Sir Kennan entered. "Ah, my dueling partner."

"I must ask your forgiveness on that count." John pushed his chair away from the writing table and stood. "It seems my life has been shattered for the second time within a year." He hadn't thought of Margaret as much in the past several weeks, but in this moment, he missed her terribly. Margaret never would have deceived him. Goodness, merely the thought of sneaking into the library to read John's correspondence would have mortified his first wife.

"Things cannot have been easy for you, I'll say that for certain." Sir Kennan offered his hand. "When my sister Janet cries, I always give her my shoulder. I'm sorry if I led you to believe something more was afoot."

John shook the captain's hand. He needed allies, and if Cameron was extending an olive branch, he'd take it. "Honestly, when I saw you I didn't ken what to believe." He'd been hot with anger and ready to bring the man to blows. How could Evelyn have managed an affair? John was certain he'd kept her satisfied in the bedchamber, if nowhere else.

"Well, I'm no saint, but I've never bedded another man's wife. On that I will swear on penalty of death."

"Fair enough." John held up the missive. "I need to dispatch this forthwith. When will we arrive in Edinburgh?"

"That depends on the wind and the seas, but if everything proceeds as planned, I hope to moor alongside Leith by sundown on the morrow."

"Very well."

"I trust your letter will put an end to Argyll's allegations."

"It ought to. The queen might not be the most beloved monarch Britain has ever seen, but she assesses people well. She kens Argyll to be a power-hungry buffoon."

"And I take it she thinks you to be a good man."

"I believe she does." John rubbed the back of his neck and looked Sir Kennan in the eye. "Unlike so many of my countrymen."

Wisely, the captain held his gaze. "Lady Mar told me to give you a chance."

"I'm heartened to hear it."

Sir Kennan placed his spyglass on the table. "Your lads have made up pallets alongside my cabin boy's on the lower deck."

"Thank you. I'd best find them." John bowed and started for the door. "Lord save us, two days asea and they'll be cursing like seasoned tars."

Chuckling, the captain cleared his throat. "May I ask you a question, m'lord?"

"You may."

"You seem to ken a great deal about James's plans."

"It has been my duty to ken all I can about the queen's brother."

"I see, but when the time comes, whose side will you be on?"

John opened the door then looked back, affecting a serious mien. "The right side."

Without another word, he made his way down the ladders and found his sons using their fingers to eat from bowls containing some ghastly-looking concoction. "What is that?"

"Fish stew," said Oliver, licking his thumb.

Thomas inclined his head to a dirty-faced older lad. "Did you meet Runner? He's two years older than Lady

Phoebe and works on the ship—earns his own coin and everything."

"Runner?" John asked. "I had no idea that was a Christian name."

The lad was quite sturdy even for fourteen. "My real name is Baltazar, but the shipmates call me Runner on account of I do most of the running across decks—I run with missives when we're ashore as well."

"You have a great deal of responsibility, then." He also had the strangest name John had ever heard. Baltazar? No wonder the sailors gave him a moniker.

"He does, and he's an orphan—no parents at all," said Oliver, holding the foul-smelling stew under John's nose. "Would you like some, Da?"

He'd rather eat straw. "You finish it."

Thomas held up a bit of rope. "This is a lark's-head knot."

Oliver did the same. "And mine's a double overhand."

John admired them both. "Fine work, men."

"I showed 'em how." Runner pushed his bowl aside. "I've never met a real earl afore."

"I don't suppose you've had many opportunities to do so."

"You seem kinda stiff to me."

"I'd rather think of it as composed."

"You need to be polite and say 'm'lord' when you address my father," said Thomas.

John mussed the lad's hair. "We ought to be able to dispense with such formalities when we're eating fish stew with our fingers." He spotted an open bale and started in spreading it beside the boys.

"What are you doing?" asked Runner.

"I'm fashioning a pallet alongside my lads."

"But aren't you going to sleep with Countess?" asked Thomas.

"I thought I'd sleep with you tonight—this being the first time you lads have camped below decks."

"I like it down here," said Oliver.

Thomas stood and nudged the straw with his toe. "Did you do something to upset her?"

Bloody hell, my own sons have become mutineers.

Oliver looked up, pulling two fingers out of his mouth. "If you did, you ought to apologize."

"I agree," said Tom. "We do not want Countess to be mad at us."

John spread his cloak over the straw. "I assure you she isn't mad at anyone." *Aside from herself—and she bloody well ought to be.*

When the stew had been eaten and the lads had fallen asleep, John stared up at the timbers above. The ship creaked and swayed, tacking its way northward. Aside from Margaret's death, this had been the worst day of his life. Clan and kin meant everything to him—more than his country, more than his duties to the crown. That his own wife would betray him stretched the limits of his tolerance.

Damnation, he'd entered into the marriage with Evelyn because she was the daughter of a duke. *A bloody English duke.* As such, John had assumed she would be properly schooled and fit to be his wife.

After all these years at court, I'm still too trusting.

Aye, he'd witnessed enough deception and skullduggery to turn any man sour. He'd been propositioned with bribes. He'd been betrayed. And for some godforsaken reason, his own countrymen had labeled him with the name Bobbin' John.

Worse, if what Evelyn had said was true, he'd misjudged Hull. No wonder the man was wealthier than the queen.

Sighing, John draped his arm over his eyes.

What am I to do with her now?

To that question, he had no answer.

Chapter Twenty-Four

*E*velyn gripped the back of the chair and stared at the locked door while Lucinda tied her stays. A sennight had passed since they'd arrived at Alloa Tower and she'd barely seen her husband. After depositing her in her chamber, Mar had walked through their adjoining door, shut it, and then the bolt had creaked as if it hadn't been used in a century.

Worse, the door continued to remain locked. The only time Evelyn saw John was at evening meals with the children. And while he seemed content to engage the boys in conversation, he responded to her in monosyllables.

Thank heavens the servants from London had arrived yesterday with Brutus in tow. "Don't you think, my lady?" Lucinda asked. Ever since the lady's maid had arrived, she'd prattled on about her adventure.

"Think about what?" Evelyn asked, grunting with the maid's next tug on the strings.

"I was saying that everyone ought to travel by ship—it is ever so fast."

"I suppose that depends on whether the sea is nearby. And you must not forget a great many ships are lost—along with their cargo and passengers."

"Mr. MacVie says the earl always takes them to London on a transport and there's never been a mishap."

"MacVie?" Evelyn glanced over her shoulder. "Are you still interested in His Lordship's valet?"

"I'd be lying if I said I wasn't…and I know 'tis not proper to speak of such things—but he kissed me on the deck at sunset." Lucinda sighed, her hands stilling while the stays slackened.

Evelyn stole a deep breath. "Might I suggest you maintain your focus whilst you're swooning about your kiss. Now you'll have to retighten the laces."

"Forgive me."

"Not to worry." Though her heart was twisted in a knot, Evelyn smiled. "I'm happy for you, my dear."

Lucinda tugged, making Evelyn's breath whoosh. "Is something amiss, my lady?"

Groaning, she tightened her grip on the chair. She'd endured the past week without anyone to talk to. In fact, it felt as if her lady's maid might be Evelyn's only ally between Alloa and Nottingham. "Mar is angry with me."

"Angry? Who could remain angry with you for long? You are the kindest gentlewoman I know."

"Believe me, I've given him cause."

Lucinda tied the strings and gave her work a pat. "There was a great deal of talk among the servants."

Evelyn straightened and arched her back to gain some breathing room. "I suppose they all hate me."

"I don't think so, but everyone's gossiping about what they think happened."

"What are they saying?"

Lucinda collected a maroon overskirt, pulled it over Evelyn's head, and tied it in place. "That we were forced to leave London because of something you did—and everyone has their ideas on what that might be."

"I can only imagine."

"And now we've arrived, come to find Mar's army patrolling the grounds around the clock with lookouts posted at the four corners atop the tower."

"I know."

"What is this about?" Lucinda asked, holding up the matching bodice. "Are we in danger?"

Evelyn slid her arms into the sleeves, then turned her back for lacing. "I know one thing: We're far safer here than we were in London."

"But what happened?"

"I trusted someone I shouldn't. Remember my walks with Brutus?"

"Of course I do." Lucinda tucked the bodice's laces into the skirt. "Did it have something to do with the coffeehouse?"

"Not the Copper Cauldron itself, but a person who'd lured me into his traitorous scheme. I thought I was taking action to support the Jacobite cause and help fight for better lives for our countrymen and women, but I was playing into the hands of a tyrant planning France's invasion of England."

"No."

"Yes. And it is all my fault."

"Oh, how awful. But surely you cannot be blamed when your actions were meant to be good."

"If only that were the case." Sighing, Evelyn dropped to the settee. "But Mar refuses to talk to me. I know he's written to the queen requesting clemency, but my husband will never trust me again. My marriage is over."

"Oh dear, surely his anger will pass, my lady." Lucinda kneeled alongside her. "Once he gains the queen's pardon, you'll be able to put all this behind you and I'll wager he will do so, too."

Evelyn took the maid's hand and gave it a pat.

But Lucinda chuckled—quite unfeeling of her.

"My life has fallen to pieces and you laugh?"

"I just remember how reluctant you were to marry His Lordship."

Glancing away, Evelyn scraped her teeth over her lip. "True, and now I would do most anything to win him back."

"Have you thought of what that might be?"

An idea suddenly popped into Evelyn's head. For the first time since she and John fled the Copper Cauldron, the weight crushing her chest eased. Standing, she pulled Lucinda to her feet and squeezed her hands. "Now I know why you're so dear to me, my pet. I think you may have touched on something brilliant."

* * *

Seated at his writing table in his private library where family records were kept dating back seventeen generations, John sorted through his most recent correspondence, irritated to see a plethora of bills and invitations to weddings, balls, recitals, and Lord knew what else. But there wasn't a single missive from any of his friends in London. Even Hull hadn't written.

Though it had only been eight days, he expected someone to write. And there he sat like a medieval knight in a tower waiting for his enemy to make the first move.

Blast Argyll and blast Evelyn. It drove John insane to have her living in the chamber beside his. Perfume wafted from beneath her door. Soft, feminine voices carried though the timbers when Her Ladyship was conversing with her maid—her voice oft strained and higher in pitch than usual. He could hear the water trickle when she was in the bath, imagining her fair skin exposed and glistening with droplets reflecting the firelight. He fought his urges to go to her—to gather her in his arms and tell her all would be well. Damn it, everything he'd worked his entire life to preserve was under threat because of her. But sleeping just beyond her door proved enough to drive him to the brink of madness.

The door to the servants' entrance opened. "I brought your tea service, my lord."

John didn't bother looking up from his reading. "Set it on the table."

"Straightaway." Light footsteps brushed the woolen carpet. "Shall I pour for you?"

With a jolt of his heart, John paused his reading. The maid clearly had an English accent, and furthermore, she sounded...He looked up. "Why in all of Jehovah are you bringing in the tea service?"

Evelyn's smile reflected a bit of insecurity. "Would you like it on your writing table or on the pedestal table by the fire?"

John slapped the invitation he'd been reading on the table. "If you were a servant, you would ken where I take my tea."

"Forgive me." The cup and saucer rattled as she set the tray beside him, nearly knocking over a stack of correspondence ready to be dispatched.

As she bent over and poured, John caught himself staring at her neckline. Good God, he'd missed those creamy breasts.

She straightened and spooned in a bit of sugar—a half of a teaspoon, just how he liked it. "I've arranged to have the lads measured for new suits of clothes."

He opened his ledger and feigned interest in his factor's entries. "Do as you will."

Moving beside him, Evelyn placed the cup at his elbow along with two oatcakes. Must she smell like a vat of simmering lilacs in summer? "Thank you, my lord." She shook out a serviette and placed it on his lap, her breasts practically spilling out of her bodice.

John shifted in his seat and growled for good measure. "You are not a bloody serving maid, and I will not have you acting as one."

"But I pour the tea all the time."

"Pouring tea and bringing in the service are two entirely different things." John grabbed the serviette from his lap and threw it onto the table. "Furthermore, you are a matron and ought to be wearing a privacy panel over your bosom. Those breasts are too distracting for any man to ignore."

A hint of a smile flashed across her lips, but it disappeared before John could be sure. "Interesting, I'd never thought of my chest as a distraction."

Glowering, John jammed the spoon into the sugar bowl and added a heaping serving to his tea, just to spite her.

"Have you thought about Eton?" she asked, moving

a bowl of jam beside the oatcakes. "Thomas is at an age—"

Ah ha! Now there was something with which John could spar. "Are you suggesting I send my sons away when Mrs. Kerr is doing a fine job managing their education?"

Evelyn took a step back and folded her hands. "I said no such thing. I'm simply posing the question since so many well-born boys near Nottingham spoke fondly of the alliances they made at the school."

"I did not attend Eton. I was educated at home—learned to manage the estate as Thomas will do."

She curtsied. "Of course, my lord."

"Is there anything else about the rearing of my sons you feel you need to discuss?"

"Oliver wants a pony like his older brother."

"Aye, he does. He wants everything his older brother has, and he will receive his pony on his next birthday—Thomas was the same age. I will not favor one lad over the other." He picked up an oatcake and pointed it at her. "They are my sons and I will decide upon every facet of their education, including when they will learn to ride a pony, when they will receive their first full-sized horse, and when they will learn to drive a team. Is that clear?"

Evelyn stared at him for a long pause, her head held high, her turquoise eyes glistening and sharp as an eagle's. Composed as a queen, she'd affected a façade of indifference, clearly hiding the hurt from his callous berating. "Perfectly," she finally said, dropping into a deep curtsy before she hastened out the door.

John threw the crusty oatcake onto the plate. Fie, he'd handled his wife's inquiries like a sore-headed beast. But blast her for coming into his private rooms when he was tending to correspondence. The last place he wanted her was anywhere near his writings. And why had she brought the tea, anyway? Did she not realize being in her presence was nothing short of torture?

Chapter Twenty-Five

*E*velyn found her straw gardening bonnet in her withdrawing room and moved to the full-length mirror to put it on.

"Oh, I didn't expect to see you here, my lady," said Lucinda as she came in, her arms laden with bed linens. "Do you need some help with that?"

Tying the ribbons beneath her chin, Evelyn glanced at her lady's maid in the mirror. "I can manage, thank you."

The maid pulled back the bed's coverlet and tugged away the linens. "How did His Lordship react to his tea service this morning?"

"I'd say the encounter was just shy of a calamitous disaster. I almost dropped the tray, it was so heavy. I think I'll need to build up the strength in my arms before I try it again."

"Almost dropping is nowhere near as awful as completely dropping. I have firsthand experience with the latter." After shaking out a clean sheet, Lucinda let it slowly drift to the mattress. "What happened next? Did he turn into an ogre and order you out of his rooms as you predicted?"

"He may as well have." Evelyn moved to the opposite side of the bed to help. "My husband certainly wasn't amenable to anything I said aside from having the boys measured for new suits of clothes."

"So, he engaged you in conversation?"

"Somewhat." As she tucked in the corners, Evelyn's bonnet fell over her eyes. She shoved it back into place. "He spoke a bit more than his usual monosyllables, though there was a great deal of rancor."

"I'm sorry, though I suppose grumpiness is better than silence, wouldn't you say?"

"Only slightly better." Truly, Evelyn had been hurt by Mar's boorishness, though not surprised. Regardless of her feelings, it was a step in the right direction for him to engage in any conversation whatsoever. "But the most confounding thing of all was the mention of my bosom."

Holding the top sheet in her hands, Lucinda stopped moving and gaped across the bed. "Your *bosom*, my lady?"

Though she'd known the lady's maid most of her life, heat rushed to Evelyn's face as she slid her palm over her cleavage. "Evidently since I am a matron, I should be wearing a privacy panel because my breasts are far too distracting."

"Ha, ha!" The sheet sailed through the air and landed on the bed in a heap while Lucinda applauded. "Distracting? Oh, my, oh my, oh my, you have just found the magical elixir!"

Looking down, Evelyn examined one breast and then

the other. "I suppose the neckline of this gown is a tad low—mayhap Mar's right. I should—"

"Absolutely not." Lucinda headed for the withdrawing room. "In fact, I shall find every low-cut gown in your wardrobe and ensure they are pressed, and I might just enhance the neckline on a few."

"Oh, please." Evelyn followed. "You'll make him angrier than he already is."

"Perhaps at first, but do you not see? He said your bosom distracted him. That means he's having difficulty keeping himself from staring at his heart's desire."

"I'm not certain about that. He was very clear in stating he doesn't *want* to stare at it."

"He only thinks he doesn't want to. All red-blooded men adore breasts, and if you don't mind my saying, yours are unusually appealing—which is why you should never remotely consider wearing a privacy panel."

Wringing her hands, Evelyn drew in a hiss through her teeth. "Are you certain?"

"I'm more than certain. If you do not believe me, ask Mr. MacVie. He will attest to the same."

"Wonderful, my lady's maid and my husband's valet are helping me dig my grave deeper than it was before."

Lucinda held up a sky-blue frock, one Mar had admired. "Were you not going somewhere, my lady? I wouldn't want you to be late."

"I have an appointment to meet with the master gardener." Evelyn retied her bonnet's ribbons. "And leave my blue gown alone. The bodice is plenty low, and I'll not have Mar shouting at me because he can see my nipples, heaven forbid."

Hastening toward the door, visions of her maid insanely wielding a pair of shears came to mind. "I mean it,

Lucinda. Do not alter anything unless it is pinned at the throat."

There. After giving explicit direction, Evelyn marched out to the glorious gardens, complete with a manicured maze. She found the gardener in the caretaker's shop.

"Good day, Mr. Morten. Thank you for setting aside some time to visit with me."

Sporting a feathered cap atop what looked to be a full head of gray hair, the gardener stood about five feet tall and was as thin as a fire poker. He took her hand in his gnarled fingers, bowed over it, and planted a kiss, his wiry beard scratching her knuckles. "I always like to please m'lady. Shall we start in the herb garden?"

"Yes, that will do nicely, thank you."

"I figured you might want to supplement your medicine bundle. The last countess was quite fond of yarrow."

"Yarrow is very useful." Evelyn drummed her fingers together. "With two young boys, we'll also need a ready supply of avens, Saint-John's-wort, mallow, common valerian, feverfew, and comfrey for starters."

"Agreed—though we may need to cultivate more avens." His fingers tremored a bit as he gestured to a large, well-maintained plot. "Elsewise, I think you'll find everything in order. You do ken your herbs, m'lady."

"I spent a great deal of time with the gardener at Thoresby Hall, though I have more of an affinity for flowers."

"We have plenty in bloom at the moment as well— peony, irises, roses, lilacs. Och, and I've planted your dog rose hedgerow, but I'm afraid it will be a few years before it begins to take shape."

Evelyn looked in the direction of the man's pointed finger. "*My* hedgerow?"

"Aye, ordered by His Lordship on the announcement of your nuptials."

Evelyn's insides grew hollow, which had been happening far too often of late. A hedgerow of dog rose would only serve to remind her of exactly how horribly she'd behaved toward Mar at first. Perhaps she needed such a reminder of the earl's thoughtfulness—which she'd taken for granted. "Gazing upon them shall be my eternal penance," she mumbled under her breath.

"I beg your pardon?"

"Lord Mar's kindness is quite touching." She forced a smile, though inside she felt wretched. "Now tell me, what are His Lordship's favorite flowers?"

"Oh, that would be peonies and roses for certain. We have an entire section of the garden dedicated to those blooms."

"Lovely, then I'd like a vase of peonies or roses on the table during the evening meal every day whilst they're in bloom."

"Splendid idea."

"And Mar's favorite fruits and vegetables?"

"He's very fond of berries of any sort, and he has an unusual affinity for neeps."

Evelyn leaned in. "Neeps?"

The weathered lines around Mr. Morten's eyes crinkled with his wink. "Sassenachs call them turnips."

"Right." She straightened. "Then why have they not been on the table, not once in the entire sennight since we've come to Alloa?"

"You'll have to ask Mrs. Troup, but I'd reckon 'tis on account that there aren't any. Last season's neep and berry supply is gone, and this season's will not be ready for harvest for another two months yet."

"I see." Evelyn bowed her head. "Thank you, sir. I must hasten to the kitchens."

"My pleasure, m'lady. I…er…" The gardener scratched his beard. "Ah…"

"What is it?"

"Well, the last countess used to accompany me to the village on market day. I load the barrow with fruits and vegetables and anything Mrs. Troup has to spare."

"For the market?"

"Nay. We visit the widows and infirm and the like." He clasped his hands, his eyes unsure. "Would you perchance—"

"Like to join you?" Evelyn nodded emphatically. "Oh, yes, I would dearly love to. And 'tis nigh time I met the villagers."

"Splendid," he said, turning and starting off.

For the first time since she'd arrived at Alloa, Evelyn's heart soared. "Thank you!"

* * *

"It isn't easy to run the kitchens for an estate the size of Mar's," said Mrs. Troup, holding forth like a Scottish warrioress in battle armor. Another of the servants who didn't travel to London, the cook was a stout woman who, though she would have been at home in a coat of arms, wore a linen apron over a plaid kirtle and a coif atop her head. "And I do not like to have people underfoot, no matter who they are."

For the past ten minutes, Evelyn had listened while the woman detailed the magnitude of her duties with iconic Scottish bravado. But at the suggestion that the lady of the house might be an inconvenience, she held up her palm.

"I am quite impressed with your efficiency, madam. I see now why the meals are always on time and so well presented. However, now that I am settled at Alloa, I will definitely want to discuss menus and the ordering of supplies."

Mrs. Troup sliced off a chicken wing with a swing of a cleaver. "I can assure you I do not need anyone meddling with my orders—I run a tight ship here and—"

"And..." Hoping to placate the woman, Evelyn offered a sincere smile. "I do not doubt your abilities for one minute. But I would not be upholding my duty as countess if I did not provide you with the support you need."

The cook rested her cleaver on the board and wiped her hands on her apron. "What kind of support?"

"Agreeing on dishes of the earl's fancy—especially turnips... ah, *neeps*."

"Och nay. Out of season neeps exceed my budget for certain. You'll have to talk to Mr. Swenson if you intend to spend the earl's coin."

"I assure you Swenson's purse strings have been lengthened considerably and, as such, I give you all the approval you need to acquire the delicacy." Evelyn took in a deep breath and patted her chest, positive none of the servants had any clue her dowry had saved Mar from financial ruin. "Now, I didn't come to the kitchens to talk about menus. Today I rather need your help."

The woman's face brightened. "My help, m'lady?"

Encouraged by Mrs. Troup's change in demeanor, Evelyn leaned nearer. "Can you keep a secret?"

"Of course I can." The woman thumped her robust chest. "Nearly everyone comes to Mrs. Troup to discuss their worries. I say there isn't a more sympathetic ear in all of Alloa than mine."

"I'm incredibly happy to hear it."

"Shall I pour us a cup of tea?" The cook used a cloth to remove the cast-iron kettle from the hob. "The water's hot."

Evelyn pulled a stool from beneath the big wooden table standing in the center of the kitchen and sat. "Tea would be lovely, thank you."

It didn't take long to prepare a pot of tea and slice two pieces of cake. "Now," the cook began, holding a dainty cup, her stout pinky turned upward. "You had a secret you wanted to share, did you, m'lady?"

"Indeed. You see, I did something that made the earl very angry with me."

"You?" Mrs. Troup asked in disbelief.

"Unfortunately, the recent turn of events was an enormous misunderstanding, but I now realize I was incredibly wrong." Evelyn bit into a piece of cake. "And I personally want to make something special for Mar, but I have no idea what that might be."

"Och, you've come to the right place, m'lady." Mrs. Troup cut another slice of cake and put it on Evelyn's plate. "You ken I've known the earl since he was a lad."

"I did not. How fortunate. What is his favorite last course for the evening meal?"

"Plum tart with warm cream—and when there are no plums in season, he's fond of sweetmeats as well."

Evelyn stared into her cup. Curses, sweetmeats were for the holidays. "And plums won't be ripe until August, will they?"

"Nay." The cook swiped the remainder of the cake from the plate and took an enormous bite. "But the Alloa vines are filled with raspberries at the moment."

"Raspberries? I thought you said Mar preferred sweet-meats?"

"That's only in winter. He adores raspberries this time of year."

"More than plums?"

"As much as plums, I'd reckon." Goodness, why didn't the woman say so earlier?

Evelyn sipped her tea. "Well then, here's what I'd like to do…"

Chapter Twenty-Six

Seated on the back of his favorite gelding, John relished the breeze in his face. Daily of late he'd ridden the boundaries of his estate with the Erskine men.

"Shall we stop at the mine?" asked Callan, the man-at-arms.

"Aye, after I've had a look at the progress on the canal." Last summer the excavation had begun to dig a canal from the Firth of Forth to the coal mine. John's ancestor had discovered the coal when he was tunneling to the firth to create a secret passageway. Needless to say, the tunnel had never been finished, but the Erskines had advanced through the peerage ranks as a result of the discovery.

After years of neglect during his father's tenure as earl, running the mine without investing in improvements, it had almost fallen to ruin. John had kept the business afloat, but now with the improvements he'd already made with money from Evelyn's dowry, production had taken a turn for the better.

"Da!" Oliver hollered from the gardens, and not the well-manicured maze where he and Thomas usually played. They were in the raspberry patch, and Evelyn was right there with them wearing an enormous straw bonnet.

What is she up to now? He shifted the reins to the left, cuing his horse to canter over by his sons.

Thomas ran to the end of the row, his face smeared with red juice. "Countess says we can eat as many raspberries as we like."

As John reined the horse to a stop, he gave the woman a frown. "Och, if you gorge yourselves, ye'll end up with a bellyache for certain."

"I think raspberries are my favorite food ever," said Oliver, his face even redder with berries. Stepping near the horse, he held up a wooden pail. "We're picking them, too."

A few berries rolled around the bottom. When John glanced beyond, Evelyn peered up from where she was stooped over a vine. She held her full pail aloft. "We have quite the harvest, my lord."

He clenched his reins in his fist. Blast it all, since she'd blatantly ignored his request to wear a privacy panel, he'd have a word with her lady's maid.

"Carry on then," he said, unable to help his frown. "But I expect you to come to the table with clean faces for the evening meal."

As he continued the ride to the canal, Callan rode beside him. "'Tis nice to see Her Ladyship out with the lads."

"They seem to be warming to her." John kicked his heels and demanded a canter to avoid any further talk about his damned wife.

Work on the canal had made significant progress since

he'd been in London, and they'd already started testing by taking small loads of coal down to the pier.

"I am overjoyed," John said to the overseer while he strode down a line of laborers with sooty faces.

"And the men are happy with the new tools. Production is up by half."

"Half?" John stopped and gave the man an appreciative once-over. "Already?"

"Aye, m'lord. And I have plans to increase by another half within a year's time."

"Excellent." Smiling, John addressed the men. "I am impressed. I do believe we ought to celebrate your achievements with a midsummer's holiday."

Mumbles of approval rose among the ranks.

"A day well deserved," said the overseer.

"Will there be a ceilidh, m'lord?" asked one of the men.

Callan stepped toward the outspoken laborer. "It is not fitting for you to ask."

But the whites of every pair of eyes brightened with anticipation. They'd all mourned Margaret's loss with him. John ought to celebrate their achievements with them as well.

"Forgive me for speaking out of turn, m'lord, but everyone's eager to meet the new countess."

"Aye." He gulped while a lead weight sank to his toes. "'Tis agreed. We shall have a ceilidh with your holiday Friday next!"

John shook the hands of every single man until all that remained was the overseer and the retinue of Erskine soldiers. "I'd like to sail down the new canal before I return to the tower. 'Tis a notable day indeed. Good news has not been plentiful enough as of late. Thank you for raising my spirits."

* * *

John stepped lighter as he walked from the stables to the tower's rear entrance. An overpoweringly delicious smell came from the kitchens, reminding him he'd missed his nooning. His stomach growled. Perhaps he'd stop in and sample whatever Mrs. Troup had baked.

"I want to forgo the first courses and only have the third course for the evening meal." Thomas's voice came from the open window.

"I think I only want to eat sweets from this day forward," echoed his little brother.

John grinned, moving toward the door. But the sound of Evelyn's voice stopped him.

"I'm not certain your father would approve of such a diet."

"But you'd let us, wouldn't you, Countess?" asked Thomas.

John's muscles tensed. Was the woman plotting against him?

"No, it isn't healthful to eat only sweets. One must exercise self-control and moderation."

"But why?" asked Oliver.

"Because the healthiest of men are like your father—those who eat meat, vegetables, bread, cheese, all manner of food."

"Including sweets," said Thomas.

"Yes," Evelyn replied. "In moderation."

Unable to argue with her logic, John changed course and headed above stairs for a bath. Regardless if his stomach was growling, if he went into the kitchens with Her Ladyship inside, it would be awkward.

* * *

After Lucinda helped brush the flour from Evelyn's hair, the countess dressed for the evening meal and paced the floor. Perhaps if she thought of all the horrible things Mar might say, it wouldn't hurt so much to hear them. And if he missed half of the horrible things she dreamed up, perhaps her spirits wouldn't drop to the dungeon of her soul.

He might say he didn't like the tart. Or that the boys should have been tending to their studies. But most likely, he'd focus any hostility on her.

Mar might tell her she was irresponsible, finch-minded, and her behavior was ill-fitting of a countess. Those things shouldn't hurt overmuch. She'd already heard them.

When the gong sounded, Brutus lumbered to his feet and yelped. Looking at the dog, Evelyn threw up her hands. "Why are you complaining? I think the earl is fonder of you than he is of me. And I tell you true, he'll have some barbed remark I've never dreamed of, and I simply must be prepared for it."

She stooped to give the Corgi a scratch behind the ears.

When she arrived in the dining hall, the boys were standing behind their chairs, waiting. "Where's your father?" she asked, admiring the crystal vase of violet peonies adorning the table.

Thomas rattled the back of his chair impatiently. "Da hasn't come down as of yet."

Evelyn took her place and stood behind her chair as was customary until the lord of the manor entered. "I'm certain he's on his way." She prayed. After working the whole day, the boys were as excited as she to present John with the fruits of their labor. Leave it to him to come up with an excuse not to make an appearance.

The mantel clock ticked a rhythm, which reminded Evelyn of a drum on a Roman prison ship. Of course she'd never experienced the sound of such a drum, but she'd read about them. And at this moment, she felt like a prisoner of this tower, tried and convicted of treachery.

She was about to tell the boys to sit and the footmen to start serving when the door opened.

"Forgive my tardiness," Mar said, strolling inside. "I received a missive that required a reply straightaway."

Evelyn looked at him expectantly. Was it a communication from the queen? From anyone else in London? From her father? From Sir Kennan?

When His Lordship volunteered nothing, she slipped into her chair and sat back while one of the footmen placed a serviette in her lap. "How was your ride?" she asked—she had no idea where he'd gone but assumed he'd ridden the boundary, which seemed likely given he'd been in the company of his retinue.

Swenson poured a splash of wine, which John swirled in his glass, tasted, then gave a nod of approval. "'Twas a fine day."

"I agree," said Thomas while the soup was being served. "Did you visit the mine?"

Evelyn listened intently. The only time she garnered any information was when her husband conversed with his sons.

"I did," John replied. "They have increased their output by a half and—"

She picked up her spoon. "A half? My, that is impressive."

John didn't bother glancing at her. He took a dollop of

butter and spread it on a slice of bread. "As a result I gave the men a midsummer's holiday."

"Will we have a ceilidh, Da?" asked Oliver. "We always have ceilidhs when the laborers have holidays."

Evelyn didn't miss John's eyes shift in her direction, along with his dour frown. But when he focused his attention on the boys, he smiled as if she weren't at the table. "Aye. Bonfire and all."

"I recall your telling me about them not long after we met." She dipped her spoon into her soup. "There's country dancing."

"Aye, and reels," said Oliver while Evelyn watched John's reaction, yet there was none. Doubtless, the Earl and Countess of Mar would not be dancing.

Thomas waved his knife through the air. "I like the sword dance."

John reached over and stilled the boy's hand. "Do not play with the cutlery, son."

Evelyn sat quietly through the remainder of the meal, since that was what her husband expected of late. And though he didn't say a word about the peonies, she didn't miss John asking the footman for a second helping of buttery mashed neeps. When the third course was placed on the sideboard, she motioned to the boys. "Are you ready?"

"Past ready," said Thomas.

Oliver slipped off his chair and spun in a circle. "I've been ready all afternoon."

"'Tis time," she said, beckoning them to the sideboard.

For once, John looked at her expectantly without malice narrowing his eyes. Evelyn's heartbeat sped so fast it nearly pounded out of her chest. She couldn't help but smile along with the infectious grins on the boys' faces.

"We made your favorite!" said Oliver, kicking his feet like he was dancing a reel.

"Well." Evelyn picked up the bowl with the largest portion from the tray. "Mrs. Troup said your favorite is plum tart, but since plums aren't in season, she suggested you might enjoy raspberry tart with warm cream."

John actually licked his lips. "It does sound delicious. Hats off to Mrs. Troup."

Evelyn's breath stilled in her chest. There it was, the first gibe—but a trifle, really. Forcing a deep inhalation, she smiled. "The boys and I picked the berries, as you saw, then we spent most of the day baking."

"Most of the day?" A crease furrowed in his brow. "What about their lessons?"

"We didn't miss anything, Da." Thomas walked at her side as they approached the table. "Mrs. Kerr taught us reading and letters in the morning."

"And maths in the late afternoon," Oliver finished.

"Och aye?" John sat back and rubbed his belly. "I'm surprised Mrs. Troup allowed you in the kitchen. She's very territorial, that woman."

Evelyn smiled as she placed the confection in front of her husband. Mrs. Troup certainly was territorial, but she'd never be again where the Countess of Mar was concerned. The cook could shoo everyone else in the household out of her kitchens, but not Evelyn. That had been their agreement.

John picked up his dessert spoon. "Aren't the rest of you eating?"

"We want you to taste it first," said Thomas.

Evelyn held her breath as she watched Mar take a bite. His eyes closed while a smile played on his lips. "Mm.

This must be the best raspberry tart I've ever sampled in all my days."

Oliver's dance resumed with ten times the vigor. "I kent you'd like it."

"Excellent work, lads. Your labors have paid dividends." The footmen brought three more bowls to the table. "Now sit and enjoy the fruits of your labor."

As Evelyn joined them, she chanced a smile at her husband, but the gesture was lost. Focused on his tart, John continued to make idle chat with the boys.

She stirred the cream, making the raspberry juice swirl from pink to red. To unlock the door and win Mar's favor would take a great deal more than beautiful flowers and fine food.

The challenge is to find the right key.

Chapter Twenty-Seven

*A*re you sure that barrow isn't too much for you to push all the way to town?" Evelyn asked. "It wouldn't take but a moment to ask a groom to hitch up a cart and pony."

Stooped and looking more weathered than he had a few days prior, Mr. Morten shook his head as he trudged forward. "'Twould be far too much trouble. Besides, the Widow Boyd's cottage is only a quarter-mile yonder. We'll rest there."

Evelyn didn't believe him until they crossed under the arch of the mammoth stone wall and walked around a bend. "Oh my." She stopped at the picturesque village before her. "I didn't realize Alloa was so nearby."

"Once you traverse the mile-long drive, everything changes."

"How so?"

Mr. Morten inclined his head toward the tower. "On the earl's estate, the world seems as if it exists in a fairy story. But beyond her gates exist all the foibles of man. Life is not so easy out here."

"It is much like Thoresby Hall, I would imagine. Within the confines of my father's walls, I knew nothing of poverty and despair. It wasn't until I began traveling to Nottingham and read to the soldiers of the wars that my eyes were opened to the oppression of the common man."

Mr. Morten turned down an overgrown drive leading to a cottage with a tottering roof. "Frightful thing, hardship."

Evelyn selected one of the baskets she'd prepared with Mrs. Troup and stood behind the gardener as he knocked.

"A moment," said a reedy voice from inside. After a bit of a wait an elderly woman opened the door. Leaning on a cane, she grinned at Mr. Morten, one tooth missing and the others brown. "Thank the stars for market day."

"Mrs. Boyd, please meet the new Lady Mar, come to pay her respects."

Evelyn curtsied. "It is ever so lovely to meet you."

"Oh, aye?" The widow looked her over from head to toe. "They said His Lordship married a Sassenach."

Though Evelyn hadn't expected to be welcomed with open arms, she was surprised not to receive the slightest of curtsies. "Indeed he did."

Mr. Morten gestured to the basket. "We've a parcel for you."

"Lamb shanks, oatcakes, a chicken, and plenty of raspberries." Evelyn held out the offering. "I hope there is something inside that will be of use."

Mrs. Boyd pulled a moth-eaten shawl around her shoulders and peeked inside. "My thanks, m'lady. Won't you come in for a spot of peppermint tea?"

Evelyn smiled. "We'd be delighted."

Inside, the air was musty and the furniture worn. Mrs. Boyd hobbled about using her cane. "We were all surprised to see the earl marry so soon."

"To be honest, I was as well." When Mr. Morten took a seat at the rough wooden table, Evelyn moved to the hob. "May I assist?"

"Nay, just make yourself comfortable and I'll have the tea made in no time."

"Very well." Evelyn perched on a stool. "Your home is cozy. Do you have anyone to help you with repairs and the like?"

"Just the townsfolk."

Evelyn learned that Mrs. Boyd's husband had died fifteen years prior, and that her two sons were killed in the wars. The woman complained of rheumatism and relied on the assistance of others to make ends meet and had thought the world of the former countess—a Scottish woman from East Lothian. The tea was watery, which may have been why Mr. Morten added a tot from his flask. Evelyn finished every last drop, leaving a guinea under her saucer for the widow to find later.

Before they stepped outside, she grasped the woman's gnarled hands. "Thank you ever so much for your hospitality. I am looking forward to seeing you again."

Mrs. Boyd bowed her head and managed a curtsy. "It has been lovely to meet you, m'lady."

"You made quite an impression," whispered Mr. Morten as he picked up the barrow's handles.

"Why do you say that?"

"Because I think by the time Mrs. Boyd served the tea, she'd forgotten how much she hates the English."

They continued on, meeting Mrs. Hardie and her son, Graham, who was off work due to a broken leg. There were other widows, widowers, and a single mother with a newborn babe who had been turned out by her family. All were in sore want, and all were living near the tower.

And Evelyn didn't care for what she'd seen. "Does Mar know of this poverty within his midst?"

"The earl does what he can—a great deal, truth be told. He employs over half the town at the mine, and more on the estate." Gripping the barrow handles, Mr. Morten trudged back up the slope and around the bend. "Though things are improving of late, 'tis why we take the baskets out on market day. And why you slip coins beneath your cups."

Evelyn cringed. "You saw that?"

The gardener stopped and wiped his brow, then dug in his sporran and took a sip from his flask. "I may be old, but I'm nay blind."

By the time they reached the gates, the old man was breathing heavily, his brow streaming with sweat.

"Perhaps we should stop and rest."

"I'll be fine. Not far to go now."

Evelyn pursed her lips and followed. At least they'd given away all but one basket and the barrow was much lighter now. "I think the boys should come along next—"

The gardener stumbled and fell, collapsing in a heap.

"Mr. Morten!" Evelyn dropped to her knees beside him, fanning his face. "What happened?"

His tongue slipped across chapped lips. "It seems I'm not feeling too terribly well after all, m'lady."

"Clearly." She took his hand. "You're trembling."

"Perhaps I need a tot of whisky."

Evelyn didn't like that idea. She'd seen him take a few tots already that day. "You need water—or cider."

He fumbled for his sporran.

"Oh, blast it all, I'll find it." She fished out the flask and found it empty. "Was this full when we set out?"

The man's eyes rolled back. "Only half."

She tossed it in the barrow, found the remaining basket, and pulled out a pair of dates. "Can you eat these?"

He shook his head, seeming disoriented.

She pushed one into his lips. "Chew it."

Slowly Mr. Morten did as she commanded. And as soon as he gulped down one, she made him eat the next. By the time he finished that, his eyes weren't quite as dazed. "You need to be seen by a physician."

"N-not me," he slurred. "I'll be right as rain—just give me a good meal and a bit o' rest."

"Has this happened before?"

"Once or twice. But do not tell His Lordship."

"Why? Do you think he'll be unkind?"

His eyes glazing, Mr. Morten didn't answer.

"Oh dear." She tugged on his arm, convinced Mr. Morten was in fear of being dismissed. "Let me help you into the cart."

He tugged away feebly. "N-nay."

"I'll not take no for an answer, sir." She moved behind him and shoved her hands under his arms. "Now on the count of three you will rise and allow me to deposit you into the barrow."

"But—"

"One...two..." Evelyn bent her knees and braced herself. "Threeeeee!"

By the grace of God, somehow she managed to help the man to his feet, turn him, and deposit his behind in the scoop of the cart. And by the pallid color of Mr. Morten's complexion, the effort had sapped him of every last bit of strength.

Evelyn heaved up on the handles. "Hold on. I'll have you to the tower in no time."

* * *

"Help!" Evelyn shouted, the weight of the barrow straining her every muscle as she trudged toward the tower. "Swenson! Somebody. Please!"

The butler burst out the door, a cloth in hand. "Good heavens, Your Ladyship, what has happened?"

Mr. Morten's head lolled. "I'm…"

"He collapsed near the gate. Quickly." Evelyn kept pushing all the way to the stairs. "Have the footmen carry him to a guest chamber and call for the physician."

"A guest chamber? Why not his quarters?"

With no time to argue she gave the butler a stern look. "Do it now, please." All Evelyn knew about Mr. Morten's quarters was that they were situated at the rear of the estate adjoining the caretaker's shop. The man was in sore need of care, and he'd be best tended in the tower, not off alone in what might be a hovel.

"Straightaway, m'lady."

Evelyn removed her kerchief and wiped Mr. Morten's brow. "We must inform the earl at once."

"He's still out on his ride." The butler motioned to the footmen. "Hurry. Take him to the blue bedchamber."

"Thank you." Evelyn found the housekeeper as soon as she stepped inside. "I'll need water and food—cider. Definitely no whisky."

While the men took the gardener to his chamber she collected her medicine bundle, and by the time she reached the guest chamber, Mr. Morten was tucked under the bedclothes and propped up against pillows. His eyes were closed, his face drawn and still very pale.

Evelyn moistened a cloth and ran it over his forehead. "Swenson has sent for the physician. He'll be here shortly."

The gardener opened one eye and scowled. "The charlatan will most likely bleed me to death."

"I'll not allow it." She drew the cloth over his cheeks. "Now tell me, I noticed your tremors earlier. How long have you had them?"

"I'm older than most men—seven and sixty. My hands shake."

"Does anything make it better?"

"Food helps. Eating those dates gave me a wee bit of strength."

A maid brought in a tray with a cup of cider and a plate of cheese slices with oatcakes.

Evelyn gestured to the table beside the bed. "Please put it here. Thank you for coming so quickly."

"Of course, m'lady." After setting the tray down, the maid wrung her hands. "Is Mr. Morten going to be all right?"

"I hope he will be. But make no bones about it, he is gravely ill."

The maid glanced at the bed. "What's wrong with him?"

"I'll be right." Mr. Morten still slurred his words. "Just bring me a tot of whisky to steel my nerves."

"Cider first." Evelyn took the cup and helped him drink. "Good?"

He coughed, wiping his mouth with the back of his hand. He gave a nod.

"Do you think you can manage a bit of cheese?"

"I'll try." Mr. Morten nibbled at first and it wasn't long before he finished the cider and ate a few more slices of cheese. When the physician came, Evelyn stood in the corridor with the door slightly ajar and listened until the man came out.

"What is your diagnosis, sir?" she asked.

Wearing a black coif, the doctor was about as gaunt as Mr. Morten, but his eyes shone, reflecting kindness. "He's suffering from a bout of dropsy for certain. Also, without a urine taster I cannot be certain, but by the odor in the chamber pot, I suspect he has sweet urine."

Evelyn had suspected as much. "His hands shake, and he seems to improve with food."

"Aye, he mentioned that. He'll need at least three days' bedrest, and he'd best not skip any meals. Let's see if we can pack a wee bit of fat on those old bones."

"I'll tend to it." Evelyn led the man down the corridor and lowered her voice. "And what of his work?"

"I'm nay about to retire!" Mr. Morten's reedy voice came through quite clearly for a man who'd appeared to be at death's door not but an hour or two ago.

But those words struck a chilly chord. Evelyn would see to this man's care, no matter what.

* * *

After spending the entire day at the mine, John returned home late.

Swenson immediately approached with a furrow in his brow. "Thank goodness you've returned, m'lord."

His gaze shot to the stairs. "Is something wrong with Her Ladyship? One of the lads?"

"'Tis Mr. Morten. He collapsed returning from his trip to town with Lady Mar."

"Collapsed? Where is he now?"

Swenson turned a bit red. "The blue guest chamber. Her Ladyship insisted."

"And she was right to do so." Mar started up. "Did you call for the physician?"

"We did. It seems the master gardener is suffering from dropsy and sweet urine. But..."

"There's more?"

"The countess hasn't left his side all day. Further, somehow she managed to lift the gardener into the barrow and then she wheeled him all the way up the drive by herself."

"Och, why did someone not rush to her aid?" Mar stopped and jammed his fists into his hips. "You let Her Ladyship struggle to push a man in a wheelbarrow an entire mile?"

"Forgive me, m'lord." The butler bowed. "I was cleaning the silver. I-I didn't know she was in peril until I heard her shout for help."

"Bloody hell." John ran the distance, burst through the blue-chamber door, and stopped.

Standing beside the sickbed, Evelyn straightened with a cloth in her hands. "My lord," she said as she turned and squared her shoulders almost as if she expected a berating.

John glanced at the butler. "Leave us."

His wife thrust her finger at the sleeping man. "I refuse to stand idle whilst you dismiss him because he is old and infirm," she said in a heated whisper.

John blinked and shook his head. "I arrive home to learn my master gardener has collapsed, and the first thing I hear when I enter his sickroom is nonsense about dismissing him?"

"My father would have done so." Evelyn backed against the bed and spread her arms, acting Morten's supreme protector. "And I'm not about to allow such scorn and disrespect for a servant who has been loyal throughout his lifetime."

"I agree."

"Furthermore," she continued as if he'd said nothing, "he has expressed that he desires to continue his service, though it is my opinion he will not be able to sustain the same pace. He needs help. And I'm not about to stand by and listen to any argument to the contrary."

John crossed his arms. "What do you recommend?"

"An apprentice master gardener. Someone Mr. Morten can groom." She shook her finger. "And the sooner the better. But let there be no question, I will not watch whilst this man is dismissed because there are a few weeds in the flower beds."

Finally unable to tolerate her continual implications that he might turn into a tyrant and immediately toss the gentleman out the window, John grasped his wife by the wrist. "Come. We will continue this conversation elsewhere."

"You're hurting me," she said as he pulled her into the library.

"Forgive me," he said with an edge to his voice. "I suppose I should stand and smile whilst you choose to indicate that I am some sort of barbaric landowner—a man who would turn his back on his servants in their old age."

"Are you not?" She thrust her damned fists to her sides. "Mr. Morten was afraid to have you find out that he was ill—and he's afraid to retire."

John mirrored her stance. "I've given him no cause. If he wants to retire, he may do so, of course."

"With a pension? A-and a cottage?"

"That is standard for his position."

She stared for a moment, her mouth agape. "Truly?"

"I would have it no other way. And it cuts me deeply that you still see me in the same light as your damned father."

Shaking her head, she pressed the heels of her palms against her forehead. "Goodness, forgive me."

"What happened to make you so bitter?"

Releasing a long breath, Evelyn paced. "You may recall in London my father told you that I spent years under the tutelage of the master gardener at Thoresby Hall."

"Aye."

"Whilst Mr. Wilson grew old and I grew up, he taught me everything about soil, flowers, herbs, pruning—a lifetime of knowledge he imparted with care and love. But when he fell ill and the hedges weren't properly trimmed, and a few weeds sprouted in the gardens, Papa dismissed him for dereliction of duty. Worse, he left the poor man without a pension and no place to live out the remainder of his days."

"I find that difficult to believe." John rubbed his fingers over the stubble on his jaw. "There was no real cause other than the man's failing health?"

"None whatsoever. My father pays deplorable wages and his servants grumble and complain behind his back. He uses children in his mine because he can pay them less and they fit into smaller spaces. If a servant grows old, he'll find a reason to dismiss the poor soul without a care."

"Good Lord."

"When Mr. Wilson was discharged from service, I found a widow in Nottingham who took him in. I used my pin money to pay for his board. But the trauma over-burdened him, so he only lived six more months. Then I was forced to borrow from Frances to pay for his funeral." Evelyn had paced to the door and she rested her hand on the latch. "I'll not stand for such disdain in my own home. If you choose to send me away, then so be it."

Before John organized his thoughts with a reasonable response, she left. No wonder she'd oft expressed a fierce loyalty toward the common man. She'd experienced tyranny in her own home, and then Dubois had preyed on her convictions. Good Lord, the woman wasn't a misled conspirator, she was a bloody saint.

In conversation John mightn't be able to convince her of his benevolence for the elderly servants in his employ, but he could do so with his actions. He took a seat at his writing table and dipped the quill into the inkpot.

Dear Mr. Morten,

Please accept my sincere concerns for your health. As you convalesce, I want to be clear that I admire your desire to continue your service as Master Gardener to my estate. I believe it is time to appoint an apprentice to work beneath your tutelage, and once you are able, I will enlist your expertise in finding the right candidate.

Please let it be known that when you do decide to retire, you will receive a pension and a cottage that will enable you to live out the remainder of your days in comfort.

Yours sincerely,
Mar

John opted to end the letter informally. He'd known the master gardener all his life and scribbling *The Rt. Honorable the Earl of Mar* seemed snobbish.

Then he slipped it under the door of the blue guest chamber and headed for his bed.

Chapter Twenty-Eight

*W*here the devil is she?" asked Thomas as Oliver chased him through the entry of Alloa Tower.

"We can do without the expletives," John scolded. "'Where is she' is sufficient."

"But you say 'devil' all the time," squealed Oliver, dashing past.

Thomas leaped up to the third step. "Is 'devil' a curse word?"

"It ought to be." John reached for the eldest's wrist. "Now, would the pair of you stand still for a time?"

Thomas dragged his feet while he took his place beside his father. "But who can stand still when there's a ceilidh to attend?"

Oliver followed suit as he usually did. "I can hear the pipers from here."

"Forgive me if I'm a tad late." Evelyn appeared at the curve in the grand staircase wearing a tartan arisaid and kirtle, of all things. "Mrs. Troup was giving me some instruction in Highland dress."

John hadn't really thought about what Her Ladyship might wear, but now he saw her, it came as a surprise for the Countess of Mar not to be dressed in an evening gown. But Evelyn was covered to the throat with a plaid pinned in the Highland style, though the simple attire did nothing to detract from her allure. In fact, she looked wholesome, except for the sad reflection in her eyes.

John, also dressed in full Highland garb, offered his elbow. "The lads are eager to join the celebration."

Swenson opened the door, making music swirl through the hall.

"Aye, the pipers have been playing for hours," shouted Oliver as the two lads ran for the grounds.

John's skin tingled beneath Her Ladyship's fingertips. "You look lovely."

She glanced up, her gaze unsure, her hands clenching for a moment. "I know it may not mean anything, but I owe you an apology. I misunderstood the reason behind Mr. Morten's concerns, and it seems I've misjudged you once again."

John grimaced. "Thank you." He hadn't slept a wink last night, and the only thing that kept him from unlocking the door between their chambers was the fact that she had been so quick to accuse him of cruelty. Though welcomed, her apology took him off guard, and he stood flummoxed, staring at her for an uncomfortable moment. "The days are so long this time of year, 'tis hard to believe it is already time for the evening meal," he finally said.

Evelyn smiled up at him, her eyes sparkling with the glimmer of the setting sun. "They are. No matter how much I love summer, 'tis difficult to fall asleep when the sky is still bright past ten o'clock."

It was time to call a truce. "I've done some thinking and—"

"M'lord!" hollered Callan. Not only was he Mar's man-at-arms, he always took charge at clan gatherings. "Will you not say a few words and formally introduce Her Ladyship to clan and kin?"

As the music silenced, every man and woman stood and faced them. Offering an apologetic smile to his wife, John spread his arms wide. "Welcome, Clan Erskine!"

As greetings rose from the crowd, he pulled Evelyn beside him. "'Tis past time I introduced my bride, Lady Mar."

Though she smiled, the expression in her eyes reflected her unease. "It is lovely to meet you all," she said. "I simply love Alloa and the warm welcome I have received here. Of course, my husband has gone out of his way to make me feel at home."

John looked to his toes, not recalling one single thing he'd done to make her move to Scotland pleasant. In fact, throughout the duration of his rift with her, he hadn't considered how she might feel being in a new home and surrounded by opinionated Highlanders.

"Callan, is the pork cooked?" he asked.

"Aye, m'lord, ready and waiting for you to give the word."

One of the men gave them each a tankard of ale. John held his aloft. "Then let us make merry and celebrate our good fortune. *Slàinte Mhath*!"

Everyone raised their cups in kind. "*Slàinte Mhath*!"

John took Evelyn by the hand and led her to his plaid. "We sit among the others."

"I like that."

"You do?"

"Why should we always put on airs simply because we're higher born?"

"I'm happy to hear you say it."

She sat with her knees to the side and tucked her skirts under. "But what if it rains?"

He took his place beside her. "Then we'll head for the ballroom."

"Truly?"

"This is Scotland, lass. Believe me, it has happened more than once."

"Will you join the lads in the shinty, m'lord?" asked Callan.

"I think this night I'll remain beside my lady wife and chat among my clansmen." John pointed toward his sons. "But keep an eye on my lads and ensure they remain out of harm's way."

"They'll be safe with me—no broken bones or bloody noses. I'll not be held accountable for bruises and blackened eyes, however."

"Fair enough."

Evelyn seemed to relax when a group of women stopped by and thanked her for the baskets.

"Mrs. Boyd ordered a new dress," said Martha.

Her Ladyship glanced at John and blushed scarlet. "I'm happy to hear it."

"How is Mr. Morten?" another asked.

"He's already grousing about being abed." Evelyn chuckled. "Imagine that? A few days of pampering in the earl's castle and he's champing at the bit to return to his beautifully manicured gardens."

After the women moved on, John stepped beside her. "What's this about a new dress for Mrs. Boyd?"

"Hmm." Evelyn tugged her arisaid tighter about her shoulders and looked away. "Nothing."

"Did you use your pin money to help the widow?"

"What if I did?"

"Then I shall repay you."

"Oh." Looking surprised, she swung her kirtle's skirts. "That is very generous. Thank you."

The boys joined them when food was served—juicy shreds of pork cooked over an open fire. There was nothing better—aside from Eve's raspberry tart.

Once the musicians started playing again, the lads ran off with their friends.

"Are you not worried they'll grow overtired?"

John batted his hand through the air. "Let them play. 'Tis good for the soul."

"Why are you..." Turning away, Evelyn stopped herself from speaking further. She plucked a tiny daisy from the grass and twirled it in her finger. "My sisters and I used to make daisy chains when we attended family outings."

"Do you miss them?" he asked.

"Very much."

"Would you excuse me for a moment?"

While the ale flowed and dancers picked up their heels, John set out to find more daisies. He'd gathered a fistful when Oliver joined him. "What're you doing, Da?"

"I'm making a daisy chain for Countess. Would you like to help?"

With the lad's eager nod, John showed his son how to make a slit with his fingernail and pull the stem through.

"You're quite good."

"But lassies should play with flowers, not men."

"Mr. Morten isn't a lass, and he takes care of all our flowers."

In no time they had two substantial chains. "Come, let us take these to Lady Mar."

John tensed when they returned to find Evelyn missing. It had grown dark and the torches had been lit. Mrs. Troup pointed to the lines of dancers, thank heavens. "She's over there, and so she should be kicking up her heels, a young lass left alone with no kin about."

John looked on. "All of us are her kin."

"Aye, and that's why she's dancing with Swenson. He was kind enough to ask her for a turn."

"Then I must thank him." John motioned to Oliver to sit on the plaid. "Where's your brother?"

"Gave me the slip." Aye, two days aboard the *Highland Reel* and the lad would forever talk like a sailor.

John glanced about, seeing neither Thomas nor Callan. "And he's gone where?"

"Snuck back to the stables to show the other lads his pony."

"Was Callan with them?"

"I saw him follow. He's always following us about."

Releasing a breath, he gave Oliver's bonnet a rap. "That's because his job is to watch your backs and see to it nothing ill befalls you."

"And that we do not end up in mischief."

"That, too, I suppose."

"Suppose?" Oliver snorted. "I ken."

"Thank you for the dance. You are thoroughly light on your feet," Evelyn said while Swenson escorted her back to the plaid.

"I was quite a sought-after dance partner in my time."

"Your time? Why, you speak as if you have one foot in the grave." Stopping at the plaid, she bowed her head. "I would think you have countless more gatherings to attend of which you will be kicking up your heels at every one."

"You are most kind." The old butler bowed over her hand, then gave a respectful nod to John before he headed off to find his next dancing partner.

Oliver held up his daisy chain. "Look what I made for you, Countess."

Evelyn's mouth formed an O and John could have sworn he caught a glimmer of a tear in her eye. "For me? Why that's the most beautiful daisy chain I've ever seen in all my days." She kneeled. "Would you put it on for me?"

Oliver draped it over her head.

John reached in and threaded one end through the other to make a crown. It was right for Oliver to be the one to give it to her, though he couldn't stop the churning in his stomach. He'd intended to make the chain as a peace offering—at least the start of one.

When Evelyn straightened, she glanced to the chain in his fingers. "Perhaps we need the king and queen of the gathering." She pulled the damned flowers from his grasp and pointed to the ground. "Kneel."

It wasn't a request, but an order. Filled with meaning, the single word expressed more emotion than the vicar during Sunday services, saying, *"Bow to me, you overbearing brute, for I have had enough of your churlishness."*

But wear a crown of daisies amidst his kin? "Crowns of flowers are meant for fair maidens."

She thrust another sharp point to the ground. "By law, I am a matron, not a maid. And I bid you kneel."

Oliver stepped beside her, his expression ominous. "You'd best do it, else she might make you go to your chamber and miss the remainder of the gathering."

"Bloody Christmas," John cursed under his breath as he bent his knee.

Evelyn placed the ridiculous daisies atop his head. "There."

He glanced up, expecting some sort of compliment or at least a mocking remark. When none came, he pulled Oliver onto his thigh. "Well?"

"Ye look like the king of the fairies in my picture book."

"Ah, exactly the image I was hoping for." John set the lad on his feet and stood, offering his elbow to Her Ladyship. "Since we are bedecked like royalty, may I have this dance?"

Looking to the merrymakers, Evelyn tugged her arisaid tighter about her shoulders rather than take his arm. "I do not think it necessary for us to put on airs as if we were..." Pursing her lips, she glanced to Oliver. "You know."

"You are my wife and I believe it would be impolite of us not to dance. After all, Eachan and Gilreith are playing the fiddle, there's Lachlan on the drum, Alec is our piper, and that's wee Morag with the flute. 'Twould be very improper, indeed, to disregard their music."

Her Ladyship released an overburdened sigh. "Of course. It was not my intention to imply that I did not appreciate the musicians."

"Can I dance, too?"

Evelyn took Oliver's hand. "What a splendid—"

"You can have a go after I've taken a turn with Countess." Fie, now John was using the silly moniker. He took the lady by the hand. "Come, the dancers are queuing for the next reel."

"But I don't know the steps," she complained as he pulled her toward the floor.

"Just follow—'tis bound to be akin to an English country dance, just a bit livelier."

"Wonderful."

"I'll hear no more complaining."

She gave him a curious look as if she wasn't quite sure what he was on about. He understood why. And though he'd had a change of heart, he was not ready to cast all of his doubts aside and start anew. No. The process of allowing Evelyn back into his good graces would take a great deal of time. He'd married the lass far too hastily. Her behavior had been sneaky and underhanded and had nearly sent them both to the Tower to await trial. And he mustn't overlook the fact that neither his name nor his reputation had been redeemed as of yet.

After escorting Evelyn to the ladies' line, John closed his eyes and drew a hand down his face. He must put doubt behind him and trust in his ability to influence the crown—moreover, tonight was a time for merriment. Clan Erskine deserved to see him at his best. They deserved a ceilidh filled with laughter and song.

Standing in the men's line, he grinned at his wife and bowed as the music began.

Evelyn curtsied, her smile guarded.

Damnation, he was the cause of her misery.

The music began, requiring clapping and skipping, which made talking difficult. Mar twirled Evelyn once and then was forced to serpentine with every woman in the line aside from his wife. When finally they joined hands and sashayed down the tunnel of dancers, he found his chance. "I've thought a great deal about your experiences with your father's ah…unfairness and felt we should discuss clan and kin and what it means to a Highlander."

"I would like that very much."

When she turned away, her skirts swished across his legs. But when she reached to join elbows with the Highlander across, Mar edged in. "Pardon me, friend. Don't mind if I change the steps a wee bit, do you?"

Without waiting for a reply, he took Her Ladyship's elbow firmly in his grasp to prevent her from twirling on to the next man in line. "First of all, Highlanders live by a code of ethics which has nothing to do with rank and everything to do with honor. Every man here would take up arms and defend Clan Erskine, and that is a privilege I must never take for granted. I pay a fair wage, I treat my kin with respect, and I never kick a man when he's down."

She stopped dancing altogether and drew a hand over her heart. "I cannot tell you how happy it makes me to hear it. If only I would have fully understood when we'd met."

"How could you?" John brushed his knuckle over her cheek. "With your father's example and my reputation as Bobbin' John, it is natural for you to have assumed the worst."

"Lord Mar!" An Erskine sentinel rode into the light, holding a letter above his head. "We caught a messenger riding onto your lands. He said this missive is of grave importance."

John hastened to retrieve it:

By the time you read this I'll be shaking your hand—

"Ha, ha!" John glanced through the darkness. "Tullibardine? Where the devil are you?"

"Here." The marquis rode in from the shadows, flanked by his men.

Chapter Twenty-Nine

Aiden Murray, Marquis of Tullibardine, one of Mar's greatest allies and confidants, followed John into the library. "I bring grave news."

John strode to the sideboard and poured two drams of whisky. "How can it grow worse?"

"Ye ken how—and you have not been in London to defend yourself." Tullibardine took a glass and sipped. "As usual, Argyll has been braying louder than a donkey in a castrating pen."

John gestured to a chair beside the hearth and, though the marquis sat, he remained standing. "Tell me the worst of it."

"For starters, Her Majesty has revoked your charter as the Secretary of State for Scotland."

"I was afraid of that—and after eleven years of faithful service. Damn it all! I'll wager she's bloody given my post to Argyll, the asp."

"Aye, she has. But there's more. The bastard has taken

it upon himself to declare you an outlaw suspected of treason."

"Fie!" John threw back his whisky and slammed the glass on the mantel. "My missives have not done a bloody thing."

"They might have at first, but to keep his neck from the noose Claude Dubois confessed that you and Lady Mar were his accomplices in King Louis's plot to invade. And then he bloody escaped."

John marched back to the sideboard and removed the stopper from the decanter. "Holy damnation, I'm as good as hanged." He poured, drank, and poured again. Aside from the brief interaction at the Copper Cauldron, John had never had anything to do with Claude Dubois. He'd stayed away from the conniving, guileful blackguard because, contrary to many of his friends, John had never trusted the Frenchman.

"What more can you do to clear your name?" Tullibardine crossed the floor and topped up his own glass. "Word is the queen has her doubts about the confession, but, nonetheless, she gave the order to have you arrested and taken to the Tower."

John rubbed his hand over his head, his fingers brushing the damned daisy crown—the one he'd made for his wife, blast her. This very night he'd been on the verge of forgiving Evelyn. If not for her, he wouldn't be in this predicament. He'd finally relieved his estate of his father's debts only to be staring utter ruination in the face.

"Once Anne gave her consent," Tullibardine continued, "Argyll set sail at once for Scotland to assemble his regiment of dragoons. From there he plans to march on Alloa."

"I should have known the duke would be champing at the bit to see to my demise, the maggot. Is there time to set my affairs in order, or must I flee with my family this night?"

"I came as fast as I could—set sail the same day as Argyll. By my calculations you have a few days at best, but I'd recommend you leave on the morrow."

"Blast it all, I blame Lady Mar for this."

"Her Ladyship? No!" Tullibardine threw out his hands. "You're blaming her for Dubois's treachery?"

"I followed her to the Copper Cauldron—baited by Argyll, of course. Nonetheless, she'd been spying for Dubois for over a year."

"She's not the only one. The man had us all thinking he was supporting James in the succession, not to annex Britain to France."

"But she's my wife. If what you say is true, her actions led to my ruination."

"I understand your anger. I'd be angry as well if my wife did the same, but think on this: Lady Mar believed her actions to be in support of not only the succession, but in support of the oppressed—the same crofters and laborers for whom you have fought all these years. No, sir. I would not be so hasty to judge your wife."

"In light of my present predicament, I find it near impossible not to do so."

"Och, if it weren't Lady Mar's involvement with *the cause*, Argyll would have come up with some other ruse to bury you." The marquis pulled a porcelain snuffbox from his pocket. "Did you ken your wife is the reason Hull was prevented from flooding the market with two shiploads of stolen wool from the Orient? Had the fleece been smuggled into England, prices would have dropped so low Scottish crofters wouldn't have been able to sell a damned bushel, let alone woven goods. Half the country would have suffered from undue poverty."

"You kent this and you didn't tell me?"

"Forgive me. I didn't realize you had blamed her until this very night." Tullibardine inhaled a pinch of snuff and sneezed. "Had you mentioned it in your missives, I would have provided a testimony in her defense. Good God, Mar, you must understand. I was deceived by Dubois. So were Seaforth and a host of Scottish lairds. He used us, but Lady Mar, and you as a result, caught the brunt of his deceit."

"God on the bloody cross." John fell onto a chair and dropped his head against his palms. He'd behaved like a domineering boar. His wife had more of a backbone than most men he'd met. Evelyn, an Englishwoman, had fought for his countrymen—fought for their livelihoods—simply because it was the right thing to do. Several times she'd tried to explain her motives and he'd stopped her. Never once had she boasted about anything she'd done for the good—though he may not have listened if she had.

"What will you do?" Tullibardine asked.

"Jesu." Running his fingers down his face, John glanced up at his friend. "First I must send my family to my cousin's estate in Ayr. They will be safe there. Then I'll set out to find Dubois."

"Force him to confess the truth?"

"Aye, if I can find the bastard I'll make him kneel before Her Majesty and attest my innocence." But he'd need help—and he knew the perfect man. "Do ye ken where I can find Sir Kennan?"

"Aye. But at long last I must ken where your loyalties lie. There is only one thing on which you and I disagree."

"The succession?"

Tullibardine gave a nod.

"To you and only to you will I reveal my hand." John lowered his voice and scooted to the edge of his chair. "You ken, as Secretary of State for Scotland, I was never at liberty to have such an opinion."

"Thanks to Argyll, those shackles have been released."

"Och aye? I may be free of the queen's whip, but I'm now a wanted man about to go into hiding whilst I run for my very life."

The marquis eyed him. "Ye ken you have my sword and that of my army. But tell me true—are you James's man?"

"Aye. Have been all along." Standing, John grasped his friend's hand. "'Tis why we are allies, brother—now tell me, where can I find Cameron and his ship?"

"He's on the Continent at the moment, though I expect him to moor in the Port of Dundee with a shipment within the fortnight."

John winced. A day or two would have been preferable. "He's bringing communications from James, is he not?"

"You didn't hear such news from me, though I'd be lying if I said he wasn't. But why are you looking for Sir Kennan?"

"First of all, he has as much at risk as I."

"Truly?" Tullibardine asked. "Please tell me more."

"Let us just say, the man has the heart of a pirate and cause to hate Dubois as well." John might be fast allies with Tullibardine, but now was not the time to reveal anything about the missing gold or Sir Kennan's role in the affair. Either the captain was dallying on both sides of the fence, or he'd be as invested in finding Dubois as John.

Either way, locating Cameron was the first step in clearing his name—and Evelyn's as well.

* * *

Pacing the floor of her chamber, Evelyn pressed a hand to her forehead. Every fiber of her being demanded she tiptoe through the corridors, stop outside the library, and listen at the door. Something of grave importance was afoot. And it most likely, unquestionably, concerned her.

As soon as the marquis had arrived, the gathering ended. John had barked orders at everyone, including her. She'd been tasked with taking Oliver and Thomas to the nursery and tucking them in. It was right for her to assume charge of the lads, even though Tullibardine was among her Jacobite confidants. If only the marquis could have taken her aside for a moment to explain the nature of his visit.

A knock came at the door. Evelyn jolted, her heart nearly leaping out of her chest. Was it John? Did she dare hope her husband would see fit to bring her the news?

"Enter," she said, trying to sound composed.

Thank heavens Mar stepped inside and not one of the servants. "Most likely you've guessed Tullibardine's visit was not a social call."

"I gathered." She started to step toward him but stopped herself. If she moved too close, she might do something too intimate, like grasp his hands while pleading for leniency.

Mar's expression grew dark, grave. "Dubois is at large. Worse, before he escaped the Tower, he named the pair of us as conspirators in the plot for France to invade."

She couldn't breathe. "Holy Father. Then the charge of treason stands?"

"Aye."

"No, no, no!" A tear dribbled from her eye. "This is all my fault."

"Nay, lass." Warm fingers gripped her hands. Mar pulled her toward him, but Evelyn resisted. "The blame does not lie with you. I ken now—you tried to work for good but were taken advantage of just like the rest."

Evelyn froze. Had she heard right?

Steeling her nerves, she ventured to look him in the eyes, to stare at those sky-blues, which had been ever so distant and filled with contempt of late. More tears spilled onto her cheeks. Through the blurriness, she saw compassion and something else she didn't dare mistake as love. "Oh, John. What will we do?"

She let him draw her into his embrace. His strong arms surrounded her like a warm cocoon, far away from the danger lurking beyond the walls of Alloa. His hand gently rubbed up and down her back. "We must flee. The only way to clear our names is to find Dubois." He told her about his plans to meet Sir Kennan and his ship in Dundee, a day's ride northeast of Alloa—perhaps more if they encountered roadblocks.

"And the boys? How will we keep them safe?"

"I'm sending you with them to my cousin's estate in Ayr."

"Wait." Evelyn pulled back. "You're sending me?"

"Aye. Seeking out that snake will lead to peril for certain—there will be hardship: nights without sleep, days without food—but I will not rest until I'm holding that man's life in my hands."

"But don't you see? If you send me to Ayr, the boys will not be safe. You said Dubois named me as well as you. If we are not together, the soldiers will find me—possibly use me, or your sons, to ferret you out."

He drew her to his chest, hugging her ever so tightly. "Bless it. I do not want you in harm's way."

"And I do not want you to face this alone." Evelyn squeezed her eyes shut, reveling in the relief of his embrace, yet knowing they were on the precipice of facing unknown hardship. "If you can find it in your heart to forgive me, even just a little, I vow to be steadfast. I vow to help you in any way I can. I am not afraid to take risks. I am not afraid to stand against evil."

"Wheesht. I cannot place your life in danger."

"My life is already in danger. Please—I can help you."

"But you are not equipped to fight."

"In Nottingham I am unsurpassed with a bow and arrow. I can cause a diversion. I'm not completely helpless." Brutus rubbed against her leg as if he agreed. "Please. Let me stand beside you. I want to prove my worth."

"Och, *mo leannan*. It is I who has behaved badly. You are more a victim to Dubois's treachery than any of us."

"Then you'll let me go with you?"

"I do not ken what I'd do if anything happened to you."

"John, I want to find Dubois as much as you do."

"Wheesht." He kissed her lips. "Ring for Lucinda. Have her pack a satchel—something you can tie to the back of your saddle. We'll take a packhorse with food. We'll leave at dawn."

"But what about Thomas and Oliver? Are we not accompanying them to Ayr?"

He cupped her cheek, his features tense. "There's no time. In the morning, dress in something unpretentious. We'll disguise ourselves as commoners once more."

"I hate this." Throwing herself against him, she grasped his face between her hands. "I want you to stay with me tonight."

"Och, I can imagine nothing I would enjoy more." Crystal-blue eyes shifted to her lips while his chin slowly lowered.

Evelyn rose up and met him halfway as John's arms closed around her. This time their kiss was different than ever before. With it came a promise—an unspoken vow expressing the depth of his affection and the power of something ancient—of clan and kin and all the fellowship they'd shared at the ceilidh that night. As the kiss deepened, the force of their beating hearts could only be that of the joining of their souls. Evelyn held on for dear life.

It had taken the deceit of Dubois and the shame of being betrayed to make her realize how much she loved this man.

By God, I will never lose his trust again.

As he straightened, his breath came in gasps, his eyes dark and filled with more desire than she'd ever seen them. "Remember where we left off, lass."

"Must you go?"

"I need to meet with Callan and the guard and send runners to call the clans to arms. There's much to do and only a few hours of night remain." He strode to the door. "Sleep well, my dear, for I shall need you come the dawn."

Chapter Thirty

M'lord!"

John stirred while a fog expanded inside his skull. Surely he'd only been asleep for a few minutes. "A moment longer," he mumbled, his voice sounding as if he'd swallowed a rasp.

"Nay, nay. You must wake." The sadist shook his shoulder. "Argyll and the queen's dragoons are riding from Castle Campbell this very moment!"

Before the mantel clock ticked another second, John leaped out of bed. "Why the bloody hell did you not say something sooner?"

"I—"

"Where were they spotted?"

The valet grabbed a shirt. "Devonside."

"Holy hellfire." John snatched the damned garment from MacVie's hands and tugged it over his head. "I told you to wake me at dawn."

"Aye, but that's half past four this time of year. Swenson thought—"

"I don't give a damn what Swenson thought. Quickly, wake Mrs. Kerr. Tell her we leave anon—there's not a moment to dally. Next, haste to the stables. Have the coachman hitch up a wagon straightaway."

"A wagon?"

"To take us to the mine—but keep that wee bit of information under wraps."

MacVie shook out John's kilt. "Aye, m'lord."

"Leave that. Haste ye above stairs!"

With no time to worry about making pleats, John wrapped his tartan around his waist and belted it. "Evelyn!" he bellowed, kicking open the door between their chambers. "You have two minutes to don your clothes."

She sat up, her hair mussed, her eyes barely open. "Wha...?"

He ran inside and drew down the bedclothes. "Two minutes to dress. Dragoons are in pursuit." He offered his hand. "Put on the kirtle and arisaid you wore last eve."

She slid to her feet. "But I didn't think the soldiers would be here for days."

"Nor did I." He sprinted back to his chamber, grabbed the case with his pistols, strapped his sword to his hip, and shoved a tricorn atop his head, then tossed the satchel he'd packed last night over his shoulder.

"Are you ready?" he asked, moving back into Evelyn's chamber.

She glanced over her shoulder. "I need help with my stays."

"Shove the contraption in your satchel." He grabbed the kirtle from the back of the chair and held it up. "Here."

She ducked her head under and tugged on the front laces. "Did you say we have two minutes?"

"Less. Where are your shoes?"

"The withdrawing room."

John dashed inside, found a pair of stockings and a pair of sturdy riding boots. "Put these on—they're the most practical."

"Where are the garters?"

"There's no time for bloody garters."

"On the dresser." She pointed. "At least we can bring them, else my stockings will be hanging down around the tops of my boots."

John stuffed the garters in the satchel, handed her the arisaid, and took her hand. "Come. We must fetch the lads."

"We're taking Thomas and Oliver with us?"

"I'm not bloody-well leaving them here." John ascended the spiral stairs two steps at a time while a plan formed. "We'll slip out the canal—we have to continue from there."

By the time they stepped into the nursery, both lads were up—John and Evelyn helped them finish dressing, while Mrs. Kerr collected their effects.

"Are we not taking a coach to Ayr?" the governess asked.

John ushered everyone down the servants' stairs leading to the kitchens. "We're all boarding the boat from the mine."

"But what about the horses?" asked Evelyn.

"We'll have to buy some after we've sailed across to Airth."

"Airth?" Evelyn asked. "But isn't that the wrong direction?"

"Any direction not in the path of the queen's dragoons is the right direction." John picked up Oliver and looked from Thomas to Mrs. Kerr. "Can you run to the stables from here?"

"I'll beat everyone," said Tom, shoving out the kitchen door.

Mrs. Kerr gave a stoic nod. "Let us make haste."

As John had asked, the wagon was already waiting, thank God. "Take us to the mine," he said, setting Oliver in the back.

"The mine, m'lord?" asked Callan, armed to the teeth. "Shall I follow with the Erskine regiment?"

"Stay here. Guard the tower." John hoisted Thomas up as well, as he shifted his attention to the coachman. "Can you man a wherry sail?"

"Aye, m'lord."

"Then help the ladies alight and make haste for the canal."

Sitting beside the coachman, John kept his pocket watch open. It had taken fifteen minutes to dress and spirit the family out of the tower, and another five minutes to reach the canal at the mine.

As they filed into the boat, he heard the thunder of horse hooves in the distance. He grabbed the oars while the coachman manned the sail of the shallow-bottomed boat, but it was too wide for one man to reach both oars. Evelyn moved to the rowing bench beside him. "I'll help. It may take some time for the sail to catch the wind."

"Good lass." A breeze whipped at his face. "With God's grace we will soon be across the River Forth."

"If I may make a suggestion." Mrs. Kerr drew the boys back to her side. "You may recall my father is a vicar in Linlithgow. We could take the lads there for safekeeping. 'Tis only across the Firth and a great deal closer than Ayr, not to mention, he keeps workhorses. I'm certain he'll have a pair of geldings that will suit Your Lordship nicely."

"Linlithgow?" John said, mulling it over. The idea was tempting. And if they stepped ashore at Bo'ness, the town was only a few miles inland from there.

"Do you think the boys would be as safe with the vicar as with your cousin?" Evelyn asked him.

"Perhaps more so." The sail picked up the wind and together he and Evelyn drew in their oars. "I'd reckon the only person who kens where Mrs. Kerr hails from is Swenson."

"Then you like the idea?" asked the governess.

"We'll pay a visit to the vicarage. But your father must be amenable." As they sailed into the churning waters of the river not far from where it emptied into the Firth of Forth, John glanced over his shoulder.

Thank the stars the dragoons hadn't found his mode of escape.

Yet.

Argyll had caught Mar unawares, and that wouldn't happen again.

This morn's near miss served as a harsh alarm. Until he cleared his name, his family would not be safe.

* * *

Evelyn had no idea where they were on a map, aside from the fact they'd traveled south when Dundee was northeast. While they were riding on a hay wagon to Linlithgow, John had confided that Sir Kennan wasn't expected to return from France for a fortnight. Such news was as much of an alarm as it was a relief.

But it had purchased time to see to Thomas and

Oliver's safety, and that was worth more than anything. Once Mrs. Kerr's father learned not only that the Earl of Mar was there to request his help, but that he was being pursued by dragoons, the old Jacobite vicar was eager to help.

Two stocky garron ponies stood saddled and tied to a fence post while the boys chased an enormous deerhound around the paddock. Evelyn ran her fingers through the mane of the horse fitted with a weathered sidesaddle. "These fellas look a bit shaggy and ornery to me."

John used a leather thong to tie the satchel to the back of his mount. "There's none better to negotiate the Highlands. They mightn't be as pretty as the horses in my stable, but they're sturdy, and that's what we need."

"Will we be traversing the wilds of the Highlands?"

"I hope it will not be necessary." He gave his horse's hip a pat. "But not to worry, the Highlands are in my blood—I'm as comfortable there as I am in Alloa."

Hundreds of questions played on the tip of Evelyn's tongue, but she dared not utter a one. Though John had realized she'd been tricked by Dubois, this state of affairs was still her fault, and she refused to predict doom or utter a word of complaint.

The vicar tottered out from his stone cottage, carrying a parcel. "You'd best take some bread and cheese along."

"My thanks." John accepted the offering. "But will you have enough?"

"Plenty," said Mrs. Kerr, following. "My da's a hoarder. Besides, with the coin you gave us, we can eat like kings for a month or more."

The boys dashed up and Oliver threw his arms around John's leg. "Don't go."

"Truly, you're welcome to stay," said the vicar. "With a

bit o' prayer the holy Father will send fire and brimstone to smite those dastardly dragoons."

"I wouldn't want to test it." John chuckled while he patted Oliver's back. "Besides, the longer I tarry, the more dangerous things grow for my sons."

Evelyn kneeled and pulled Thomas into her arms. "You'll look after your brother until we return?"

"Aye." He squeezed her tightly while nodding his head. "But we left Brutus behind. What if the redcoats take him?"

John kneeled as well. "Och, the old dog would never let one of those vile beasts near him."

"I can attest to that," Evelyn agreed. "And Swenson will take care of him."

Thomas swiped away a tear. "But he always bites Swenson's heels."

She kissed the boy's cheek. "Perhaps they'll bond a bit whilst we're away."

John gathered both of his sons in his arms. "Now I want you to be mindful of everything Mrs. Kerr asks of you, for disobeying her is akin to disrespecting me. Ye ken?"

"Aye," they echoed in unison, sniffling and wiping their eyes.

"W-when will you be back?" asked Oliver.

"As soon as I possibly can. But in the interim pay a mind to your studies. I'll want to hear all about what you've accomplished—and I'll reckon the vicar has ponies for you to ride."

"Me as well?" asked Oliver.

John tweaked the rascal's nose. "If the Father sees fit, you as well."

Evelyn dabbed her eyes with her kerchief, then gave

each boy a hug of her own. "Neither of you have any idea how much you mean to me. But your father and I will be thinking of you every moment. And when you look up at the stars and the moon, you can rest assured that we're looking at the same and sending you our love."

Thomas dropped his head back and turned in a circle. "What about during the day? What about the clouds and the sun?"

"The clouds and the sun, too." John tugged Evelyn to her feet. "We must away."

Though the good-byes were torturous, once they were mounted, Evelyn settled and used the position of the sun to find her bearings. "Are we not headed west?"

"We must go west before we can turn north. After Falkirk we'll take the road to Stirling."

Evelyn bit her tongue. There was no use asking questions to which she knew very well there were no answers. She simply needed to stop doubting.

They'd been riding at a steady trot for quite a while when John pointed to a fortress atop a mighty hill. "There sits Stirling Castle."

"Oh my, she's magnificent."

"She's seen many a battle over the centuries."

"If only we could lock ourselves behind her doors and keep out the dragoons."

"Unfortunately the place is crawling with them at the moment."

But Evelyn hadn't imagined the worst of it. As they passed beneath the ominous castle walls, the redcoats had set up an inspection point at Stirling Bridge.

Pulling on the reins, John motioned to Evelyn to slow her horse. "Bless it, there's not another crossing for miles."

"But we're in disguise…my darling Mr. Ramsey," she said, fluttering her eyelashes as she spoke the alias John had dreamed up.

"Aye, but we're not far enough away from Alloa. One of them might recognize me." John laid his reins across his horse's neck. "We'll head north. The river branches at Doune. This time of year the water is low and we can ride across there."

"How much further is that?"

"Eight to ten miles."

"Good heavens, the horses will need rest."

"And they'll have it—right after we've crossed the river and found a place to camp."

But the sound of horse hooves thundered behind.

"Ho! Stop in the name of Her Majesty, Queen Anne!" bellowed the lead rider.

"God on the cross." John reined his horse to find a half-dozen dragoons riding straight for them as if they were chasing down a band of outlaws. "Well, lady wife, now's our chance to test our disguises."

Chapter Thirty-One

*J*ohn dipped his shoulder and twisted, turning away from the soldiers while he reached across his midriff and wrapped his fingers around his pistol's handle.

A lieutenant walked his mount forward. "It looks as if you were trying to avoid the queen's barricade."

A hundred retorts came to John's tongue. If uttered aloud, every last one of them would send him to the gallows without a bloody trial. "What gave you that idea?" he asked, quietly thumbing the cock.

The man's chin raised arrogantly. "You were heading for the bridge. I saw you."

"Beg your pardon, sir, but you are mistaken." John squinted. Blast it all, the lieutenant looked like a Campbell with his long, narrow nose. If he were placing wagers, he'd swear the lieutenant was kin to Argyll.

The red-coated varlet hopped from his horse and approached. "Where are you headed?"

"My croft. Up past Doune."

"Stuart lands, aye?" the man asked, setting his trap. He was sly, for certain. Stuart lands bordered Doune, but to agree would be folly.

"Drummond," John corrected, eyeing a copse of trees but fifty paces north. "Now if ye do not mind, me wife and I would like to continue on our way."

The lieutenant rested his hand on John's horse's bridle and looked up, suspicion filling his eyes. "Why such haste?"

"Ye ken Scotland, a Highlander takes advantage of fine weather whilst he can." John cued his horse to back, making the dragoon drop his hand. "Besides, have you not anything better to do than pester a poor crofter and his wife?"

"To be honest, we haven't." The lieutenant's gaze shifted to John's fingers…and his blasted signet ring. "God's stones," the man said as if he'd found a buried treasure.

Before the lieutenant could raise his voice, in one motion John drew his pistol, shot the bastard's hat off, kicked his heels, and grabbed Evelyn's bridle. "Run!"

Together they raced for the trees while John leaned over his horse's withers. "Put your head down!" he shouted.

Just as they dashed into the protection of the forest, the soldiers' muskets fired.

"Do not slow down," he growled, releasing his grip on the bridle.

"This way!" he shouted, finding a path.

John led her up a steep hill. At the top, he chanced a backward glance. Blast, the dragoons were too close. Ahead was open lea all the way to the river—forest and hills to the north, rugged and craggy Highlands to the east.

"Where to?" Evelyn asked.

"We'll outrun them—follow me."

They barreled down the hill at full tilt, but still the sound of thundering hoofbeats rumbled behind them. Once they hit the meadow, John took the lead. "Give your horse its head," he shouted. If Evelyn lightened her grip on the reins, her horse might keep pace with his. She was lighter, but she still had the disadvantage of riding aside.

Out in the open they were an easy mark, but there was little other choice than to try to outrun them. The problem was the garrons were no match for the taller hackneys except in the hills.

Crack! A shot came from the east.

Evelyn ducked, her head almost even with her gelding's neck. "Lord save us."

John's gut sank as reinforcements rode straight toward them.

Crack, crack!

"Are you shot?" he asked, kicking his heels and demanding more speed.

"I'm fine." Evelyn slapped her reins and gained behind him. "Faster!"

Crack, crack, crack!

The riders from the east veered toward the soldiers.

John glanced over his shoulder. Merciful saints, those were Highlanders cutting off the lieutenant and his men. "Ho," he shouted, pulling on his reins.

Evelyn stopped beside him. "The soldiers are running."

Half the Highland retinue continued the chase while their leader turned with a contingent of men. John squinted. "Holy Moses, Tullibardine?"

The marquis's white teeth glinted in the sunlight. "Thought I might find you somewhere nearby."

"Truly?" John asked, leading Evelyn as they fell into step with the man's horse.

"When I learned you'd escaped out through the River Forth, there really was no other way for you to travel other than through Stirling—not with Argyll and the queen's dragoons already blocking the road from Alloa to Dundee."

"Is that what Argyll thinks as well?"

"I reckon he has no idea where you're headed. At the moment the bastard is in the process of establishing blockades at every major road in bloody Scotland." Tullibardine led them into the forest on a narrow path—one John hadn't traveled before. "We must haste. My men will cover our tracks, but those dragoons will send up the alarm soon enough."

John peered through the trees, estimating their direction. "I was planning to cross the river at Doune."

"Callander is better."

"Up the path to the Highlands?"

"Aye. You can change horses there."

"And swap out my plaid." While he was thinking about it, he slid his signet ring off his finger and slipped it into his sporran. "I had been thinking about taking Evelyn to my lodge up near Gordon territory."

"Nay, Argyll kens every estate you own. If I were you, I'd head to the old hunting cottage at Loch Katrine. Do you ken it?"

"All the way up there? Has the winter snow melted as of yet?"

"'Tis the end of June. If it hasn't, 'tis likely to still be there come fall."

John regarded Evelyn over his shoulder. Riding like a champion, she'd kept up so far, but the woman was bred of English nobility. She might soon wither. "I'm not fond of the idea of taking Lady Mar up into the wilds. She's not accustomed to our rugged hills."

"Do not worry about me," she said. "I am far sturdier than I may look."

Tullibardine chuckled. "I like your spirit, m'lady. It reminds me of my lovely wife, Maddie."

John recalled the marquis's bride. The illegitimate daughter of the Earl Marischal, Magdalen Keith had been accused of treason about seven years past, and Tullibardine had been the one to prove her innocence. "It seems you've become quite the Robin Hood for the cause."

"I ken what's right."

"Thank God someone does. I am in your debt, my friend."

"Och, 'tis I who should be thanking you. With your background on Anne's cabinet, I reckon you'll make a fine leader when the time comes to raise the standard for James."

So that's why the marquis had come to their rescue. "Are you not putting the cart afore the horse?"

"I'm planting a seed—one that's long overdue."

John snorted. He and Evelyn had a good long ride ahead of them, which, with luck, would afford him plenty of time to think.

* * *

Tullibardine looked on while John bent forward and laced his fingers to make a step. "My lady."

Evelyn still hadn't come to grips with her husband's change of demeanor, but she liked it—almost hoped this time of danger might never end. "It's already past six.

Do you think we'll make it all the way to the cottage by dark?" Even though sunset wouldn't be until eleven, they had an arduous journey ahead.

"Not afore dark, but I ken the way—and we'll not stop unless you're fond of sleeping in the rain."

Evelyn looked up. The blue skies from earlier in the day had been replaced by ominous clouds—and it had rained a bit while they'd eaten a meager meal of oatcakes and cheese. "I think we'll end up wet no matter what."

"She's right. I reckon the rain will be upon us within an hour, perhaps two," said Tullibardine.

John moved to the packhorse he'd purchased, now laden with supplies acquired from the only shop in Callander. He pulled out two oiled tarpaulins, shook one, and handed it to her. "Drape this over yourself. You'll stay warm and dry, as well as keep the ticks off."

"Ticks?"

"Aye. We're heading into the Highlands, lass. Many of your countrymen cannot manage to follow a Scotsman up there due to the perils. 'Tis why it is the best place to hide."

"Lovely."

"I can take you to Blair Castle," suggested the marquis. "You could pose as Lady Tullibardine's maid."

"I am not about to tuck my tail and hide. Especially not when this mess is my fault." And she wanted to be with John. How could she possibly leave his side when they were only beginning to make amends?

The marquis patted her horse's neck. "Och, Argyll would have found a reason to dirk Mar in the back no matter what."

"Thank you for the offer, my lord. But I will not abandon my husband."

Mounting, John slid into his saddle. "Ye say that as if I'm helpless."

"Hardly." She tapped her riding crop and started off. "Shall we?"

"Aye, but you're headed the wrong direction." As Evelyn groaned and turned her mount, John reached down and shook hands with the marquis. "Thank you, Tullibardine. You will always be shown hospitality at my table."

"Mark me, we'll set up a diversion. No one will have a clue where you've gone."

John kicked his heels and gave a wave. "Too right. I wouldn't even look for myself up there."

"Let us hope Argyll gives up the chase in a sennight or less." The marquis gave a salute. "I'll spread the word you've fled to Ireland."

Evelyn allowed herself to smile for the first time that day. "Brilliant."

It took less than five minutes to start up the steep slope leading to mountains so high their peaks were hidden by the clouds. Under cover of the forest, she had no other thought but to follow John, praying nothing ill would befall them. As they climbed, the pony beneath her proved his worth as a sure-footed shaggy mount.

About an hour on, the rain came as the marquis had predicted. Evelyn hunched over the pony's withers, keeping the tarpaulin clinched tight at her throat as the temperature grew icy cold.

Evelyn had lost all concept of time when John stopped at the acme of a mountain and pointed. "The cottage is at the far side of the loch down below."

Narrow and long, the lake looked more like a great river. "I cannot see the end of it." Shadows from the setting sun, a sliver of a ray peeking through the clouds, made the water look fathomless.

John looked at his pocket watch. "It will be dark in a half hour."

A brown eagle screeched overhead, making Evelyn hunch lower.

"Are there any wild animals I should be wary of?"

"Only the two-legged variety." John looked out over the great expanse. "But I've not seen one of them since we left Callander."

"I doubt we're the only folk silly enough to ride in the rain."

"You'd be surprised." John tapped his heels. "Come, there's another hour or two yet. How's your backside?"

Her bum was stiff and sore and most likely chafed, but she wasn't about to complain. "Fine."

John's shoulders shook with his deep laugh. "Ye must stop telling me tall tales, wife."

A laugh tickled her insides. "Very well. My backside will be quite relieved when it's no longer sitting atop this old saddle."

"Aye, but at least the leathers were broken in afore we set out. A new saddle would have made ye sore afore we reached Stirling."

Evelyn grinned the whole journey down the slope. Aside from last night, he'd hardly said a kind word to her over the past month. Early this morning they'd left his sons with a vicar in Linlithgow, had been shot at by dragoons, run for their lives, and as they rode down to the loch in the midst of the wild Highlands, he saw fit to speak to her as if they were once again allies.

If a crisis was what gave John a change of mind, she'd endure hardship any day. Last night there had been so much to say. Obviously Tullibardine had painted her in a good light—bless him. Still, Evelyn needed to make peace with John. She needed to confess all now he seemed willing to listen.

"John?"

His horse faltered and he lowered his reins. "Ho there, lassie. You'll have to let your horse pick its way from here out. We'll follow the course of the loch." The whites of his eyes flashed as he turned back. "Do not lag behind."

"I haven't yet, have I?" It seemed as if with her next blink, all rays of daylight disappeared and the horses made their way through complete darkness. No, now wasn't the time to talk about the past. But soon.

Chapter Thirty-Two

*E*velyn braced her hands on John's shoulders while he helped her dismount. "Ugh." The groan pealed from her throat as she took her weight on her feet. After riding for countless hours, straightening her knees hurt. Rubbing life back into her thighs, she peered at the cottage through the darkness. It had a thatched roof and squat stone walls. And though the light was dim, she'd seen stables in better repair.

Though she'd expected the cottage to be rough-hewn, she hadn't anticipated staying in accommodations quite so crude even if they were in hiding.

He pushed on the door. It didn't budge. "Not what you expected?"

Evelyn clasped her hands expectantly. "I'm sure it will be quaint inside."

"'Tis a hunting cottage. You're more likely to see the bones of a stag than tea service." Running his hand above the lintel, he found a rope and pulled it. Groaning like a dragon awakening from a hundred-year sleep, the door opened. "I'll go inside first, ensure all the silkies have gone away home for the night."

Evelyn shivered. "The what?"

"Ye ken." She could see the whites of his eyes just enough to catch him wink. "The fairy folk."

"You're jesting."

"Aye." He shoved the door fully open. "But you're out of your element, m'lady."

"I suppose any English duke's daughter would be." She peered around him. It was inky black inside and impossible to see a thing, but something scurried for certain. "What's that?"

He pulled his dirk from its scabbard. "Och, I wish it were fairy folk."

"Rodents?" she ventured.

"Most likely."

"Oh, my goodness." Hopping back, Evelyn wrapped her arms across her midriff. "If we slept outside, rodents oughtn't bother us."

He took a step inside and looked back. "Ye reckon?"

She nodded emphatically.

"Why do you not gather some wood for a fire whilst I make a torch and rid the place of all vermin."

"Wonderful idea." Evelyn picked up a twig and dropped it alongside the door. "I'll just start a stack here...where I ought not be eaten by Scottish silkies."

Evelyn set to task, piling up bits of wood she found around the clearing while a great deal of banging came from inside the...whatever it was. It certainly did not fit her idea of a cottage. *Shelter. I'll call it a shelter—for vermin.*

When finally the door burst open, John headed for the bushes, carrying a parcel of sorts.

Evelyn only imagined the carnage wrapped in the old bit of cloth. "Where are you off to?"

"The hay is musty. It won't take me but a moment to cut some rushes."

"Rushes? Is there no bed?"

John didn't answer as he disappeared into the shadows.

Standing with her muscles tense as iron, Evelyn had never missed Brutus so much in her life. On tiptoes she stepped inside, ready to run if some rat or badger came dashing out the door. John had lit an oil lamp and left it sitting on a wooden table surrounded by four stumps. In the center of the cottage was a fire pit, of all things, with a griddle suspended from the rafters above. And to her horror, there was no bed—just a bit of straw piled in the corner, and she didn't dare go near it.

Crude seemed too pleasant a descriptor for this place. No wonder John had tried to persuade her to go to Blair Castle and pose as the Marchioness of Tullibardine's lady's maid. At least Evelyn would have been able to sleep in a bed. Again, she shuddered.

Do people actually live in such filth?

As the thought passed through her mind, she threw back her shoulders.

My word, I sound like my father.

Hadn't she pledged her life to helping those less fortunate than she?

Appalled with herself, Evelyn checked every corner for rats, even the disgusting pile of straw, and when she found none, she marched outside, gathered an armload of wood, and dropped it beside the pit. Spying a bit of flint and flax tow, she set to lighting a fire—not that she had any practical experience whatsoever at starting fires, but she certainly had seen it done enough.

Unfortunately, fire-starting wasn't as easy as it looked. By the time she ignited a spark by striking the flint to stone, her knuckles were bloodied. Encouraged with her efforts, however, she moved the flax tow beside the stone and struck again. And again. And again.

When a tiny spark leaped from the flint and glowed upon the white fluff, her heart soared. Ever so carefully, she lowered her lips and blew.

Smoke swirled around her—but no flame.

Please, please, please work.

She blew again and, this time, a bit of fire about the size of a candlewick came to life.

"Oh praises be."

Evelyn lowered the bundle to the center of the pit and stacked dry twigs around it. The pop and crackle of burning wood grew like music to her ears and, once the twigs were glowing red, she added bigger sticks.

John stepped through the door, his arms laden with fresh rushes. "Good of you to set the fire. 'Tis cold out."

Evelyn rocked back on her haunches and smiled at the popping blaze. "Thank you." There was no use in boasting that she'd just accomplished the impossible. He'd never understand.

* * *

Had John known the cottage had fallen into such ruin, he wouldn't have brought Evelyn up there. She'd been bred for a life of privilege. That she was capable of starting a fire surprised him.

He spread the rushes over the dirt floor. At least it was dry. And once he placed a woolen blanket over the top, they'd be cozy enough.

Cozy.

Heat spread through his loins. Every night for a month he'd longed to hold Eve in his arms.

He stood and brushed off his hands. "With the fire you built and this wee pallet, we ought to be toasty warm tonight."

Sitting like a queen on one of the stumps, Evelyn wrung her hands. "Only one bed?"

John scratched the stubble on his jaw—itching already. She'd be far more comfortable beside him. "We're married, are we not?"

"Yes but...never mind."

"Are you hungry?" he asked, glancing to the pallet forlornly. God, he was tired. And he wanted her more than he'd ever wanted anything in his life. "If it would make you feel better, I'll sleep by the fire."

She stood and picked up a stick of wood and put it on the flame. "To your first question, yes, I am famished. And to your second, how on earth do you intend to keep the silkies at bay if you're over by the fire?"

He gave her a crooked grin and sauntered toward her. Until his stomach growled. Damn, he should have thought about eating sooner, rather than sleeping...and holding Eve in his arms. "I'll fetch the supplies."

He found a leather parcel, spread it open on the table, and uncorked a bottle of spirit. "I ken it's not what you're accustomed to, but the fare will keep us alive."

"I'm glad to have it."

He offered her the bottle. "Have a swallow of this. It will help you sleep."

She took a tiny sip and coughed. "'Tis awful."

"You'll grow accustomed to the burn." He inched the leather her way. "Go on, take a bit of meat."

She did, her face reflective as if she had a great deal on her mind.

As he bit into a chewy piece, John didn't doubt that she did. A lot had transpired since they'd awakened at dawn this morn—yesterday morn, given it was past the witching hour. "Would you mind..."

She looked up, a bit of dried meat halfway to her mouth. "Hmm?"

Shaking his head, John reached for the whisky. "I'm sure you're not in a mood to recount the past. Perhaps on the morrow."

"But what were you about to ask? Would I mind what?"

"I'd like to ken what led you to become a spy."

There. He'd said what had been on his mind for a bloody age.

"Well, it wasn't as if I opened my eyes one morn and decided to become a Jacobite."

"Nay?"

"I told you about Mr. Wilson and the way Papa dismissed him."

"Aye."

"I also used to read to the soldiers at the hospital, and not long after Mr. Wilson died, Mr. Dubois began speaking to me."

"At the hospital?"

"Yes."

John swirled the salty meat in his mouth and swallowed. "What was that backstabbing Frenchman doing in Nottingham?"

Evelyn bit into a piece of oatcake. "Now that you ask, I have no idea."

"But he knew your father, did he not?"

"He did, and he was well versed in Papa's affairs. Of course it didn't take a great deal of convincing after Mr. Wilson died, but Mr. Dubois made it quite clear that I was living under the roof of a tyrannical, elitist monster and that it was my bounden duty to do something about it."

"I reckon the scoundrel sought you out and played you like a fiddle from the outset." After taking a drink, John corked the bottle. "He's an ill-bred cur."

"I couldn't agree more." Evelyn pulled a comb out of her hair and let the locks cascade down to her waist in waves. "At first he convinced everyone he was working for *the cause* not only to bring James back to England, but to improve the lot of the common man. And the more I learned about my own father's treacherous, underhanded dealings, the more I wanted to do something about it."

Taking a silken wisp, he twisted it around his finger. "Weren't you concerned about hurting your da?"

"I was, of course. Though dukes—and earls—are above the law."

John gestured to himself. "Unless they've committed treason."

"Quite." Evelyn removed the brooch from her arisaid and placed it on the table. "When you boil it right down, I wanted to make a difference for good."

It took only a downward glance to reignite a flame beneath his sporran—but he needed to uncover her full story before he acted on his desire. "And Dubois promised you the moon."

"That and he made me feel as if I were an important part of his work."

"Did you ever suspect him?"

"Not until I married you."

John cracked his knuckles. "I can only imagine."

"Though he was the one who convinced me to accept your suit."

"Dubois?"

She rubbed her palms on her skirts. "He thought I could gain more information for *the cause* through you."

"Of course he did, the lout. I should have known."

"If it weren't for him, I might have refused you. Truly, at the time I was blind as to who was the hero and who was the dastard."

"What are you saying?"

"I knew you through reputation only—and at the time I thought you stood for everything I abhorred."

Any amorous feelings he may have had were quashed by a surge of angry heat flushing through his body. Aye, he knew Evelyn had her doubts, though he'd had no way of knowing why. He'd assumed it was their difference in age and the fact they were practically strangers when he'd proposed.

"Why did you marry me with such haste?" she asked.

As long as they were making confessions, she deserved to know the truth. "I cannot lie and tell you ours was a love match—though I found you lovely and endearing."

Sniffing, she gave a nod and lowered her gaze to her hands.

He chose to omit the part about how much he'd been in love with Margaret and how her passing had cut him to the quick. Besides, his first marriage now seemed like a lifetime away. "To be honest, I desperately needed your dowry. But not to squander the coin, as you accused. My father left the estate riddled with debt, and I didn't want the same for my sons."

Eve gave a nod as if she already knew. "Your decision was governed by necessity."

"I'll nay deny it, though I did find you most agreeable—someone I could see as my countess."

She looked him in the eye and her spine straightened like a valiant soldier. "But you loved your first wife."

He nodded. "I did. And now I've realized the living must continue on."

Her countenance softened and she took another bite of oatcake, sitting thoughtfully while she chewed. "Is your need for coin why you held the post as Secretary of State for Scotland for so long?"

"Aye. The post afforded me an income to keep Da's creditors at bay, though not enough to settle the debts."

"But what about all the vile legislation put into play by the queen? Did you not vote for the Act of Union?"

"I did not, but once it was enacted, it was my duty to support it—and sign my name, of course, just as all cabinet ministers were required to do."

"I never could have done that."

"You are not close to the queen as I. She is insane in her fear of popery, and if left to her own devices, the kingdom would be far worse off. The few of us on her cabinet who support James dare not reveal our positions. When *and if* the time comes, we could attempt to rescind the act, or convince James to convert to Protestantism."

Evelyn's turquoise eyes brightened. "Is there a chance parliament will rescind?"

"Nay. In truth the prince has a far better chance of succeeding to the throne if he converts. The problem is convincing him of it."

Her teeth scraped her bottom lip. "You've tried?"

"Many attempts have been made."

"Oh dear." Evelyn buried her face in her hands. "And here we sit, both of us accused of treason for trying to do the right thing—tied together in an eternal loveless marriage neither of us wanted."

"I beg your pardon?" He brushed a lock of hair away from her forehead. "Och, lass, is that what you think?"

"I doubt you harbor any affection for me after what I've done."

He gently smoothed his hand to her shoulder. "Is that so?"

She splayed her fingers and peered at him. "I hate myself even more. I cannot believe I could have been so entirely gullible."

"Or entirely brave." John pulled her onto his lap. Turning her head, Eve tried to draw away, but he held her fast and inclined his lips to her ear. "Tullibardine told me about your da and the stolen wool you prevented from flooding the market."

She shook her head. "I shouldn't have meddled."

"If you hadn't, many Scottish families would have starved. As the Secretary of State, I personally would have been blamed." He pressed a kiss to her temple. "Ye are a brave woman, Evelyn Erskine, and I am proud to call you my wife."

As she raised her chin, she looked him in the eye, her cheeks wet with tears. "You are?"

"Aye."

She cupped his cheek, while a tear streamed down her face. "I never meant to do anything to harm you or the boys."

"I ken." Lowering his gaze to her lips, he reverently kissed her. "But I reckon afore you go off saving the world from evil ever again, you ought to have a word with me about it first. Agreed?"

She almost smiled. "Yes. Most definitely yes."

He kissed each of her eyes. "Well then, shall we start anew? I'm John."

Wiping a tear from her cheek, she smiled this time—even chuckled. "I'm Evelyn, but I like it when you call me Eve."

"You do?" He gathered her in his arms and stood. "The name quite suits you."

"Because in the Bible she led her husband to sin?"

"Nay." Kneeling, he laid her on the pallet. "I like it because you are full of life. You are voluptuous and sensual and you give me pleasure. Och, lass, when my heart was heavy and black, you shone a light into my soul."

He stretched out beside her and claimed her mouth, his hands exploring her delicious curves, just as he'd longed to do every night while the door between their chambers had remained locked.

In a maelstrom of kissing and touching and frenzied disrobing, hands groped and caressed, setting John's skin afire. Off went his doublet and Evelyn's arisaid. In the midst of nuzzling into her silken throat, his plaid fell away. Shoes dropped. Laces by the dozens sprang apart until John wore only his shirt and Evelyn her shift.

John drew away, pulled off his shirt, and grasped her hem. "I feel as if I have gone a lifetime without you in my arms, Eve."

"Eve," she repeated on a sigh, stilling his hand. "Let me gaze upon you for a moment."

He grinned. Aye, he was harder than steel, and having her eyes rake down his body was like having her take him in hand.

"You're beautiful beyond words," she said, coyly inching the shift to her thighs.

Unable to resist, John grasped the linen and pulled it over her head. "I'm nay half as bonny as you, *mo leanan*."

The soft Holland cloth floated to the pile of discarded clothing as their bare bodies joined together in a frantic tangle of limbs, tongues, gasps, and heat so warm John could swear steam sizzled between them.

Chapter Thirty-Three

Stretching, Evelyn awoke with a satiated sigh. She reached out for John, but he wasn't there. He'd never been beside her in the morning. But somehow, this time emptiness didn't fill her breast, perhaps because she'd been aware of him keeping her warm throughout the night—a delight which had never happened before, either. She rolled over and looked across the cottage. Even the roughness of it didn't bother her. And as sunshine streamed in from around the edges of the door, warmth spilled through her.

At long last she no longer had secrets to harbor from her husband. He'd forgiven her. He'd bared his soul to her. And never in a hundred years would she have believed they had so much in common.

She pushed to her feet and found two oatcakes on the table with a cup of water. Nibbling one, she turned full circle. John had stoked the fire and the coals glowed red hot. Against one wall hung cooking utensils and a broom.

Near the door there was a bow and a quiver of arrows. She finished the oatcake and moved to examine the bow, still strung taut. Beside the arrows were two leather pouches, one filled with lead musket balls and another containing black powder. At least the hunters who frequented this place were serious about hunting.

The door opened and John strode in, his chest bare, his muscles flexing from the weight of a cast-iron pot filled with water. "Sleeping Beauty awakes." Droplets of water streamed from his shoulder-length hair, making his skin glisten all the way down to the kilt belted low across his hips.

Scraping her teeth over her bottom lip, Evelyn homed in on the trail of tawny hair leading from his navel and disappearing beneath the wool. She glanced to the pallet, wishing it were nightfall. Oh, how glorious it would be to smooth her hands over the damp curls on his chest— magnificent and scandalous. She fanned her face as if to fan away her errant thoughts. "Have you been for a swim?"

"A wee dip, aye." He grinned, setting the kettle atop the fire. "'Tis near freezing. But I thought you'd rather bathe with a bit of warm water."

"That's very thoughtful of you."

"But then…" Waggling his brows mischievously, John held his hands to the blaze and rubbed them. "There's a stone beside the loch—hollowed like a bath with enough room for us both."

She chuckled. "You do not mean for us to disrobe out in the open?"

"Why not? There isn't another soul around for miles."

"But we're wanted. We could be set upon by dragoons at any moment."

"Not if I ken Tullibardine."

"And what of hunters? How many people know of this place?"

"Not many, I reckon. These lands belong to the Graham laird, and he's too old to enjoy them."

"But you and the marquis have been here before."

"Years ago. With Graham himself." John moved behind Evelyn and ran his fingers through her hair while his lips touched her ear. "Come bathe with me, *mo leannan*. I will protect you from the silkies of the forest."

Leaning her head back, she melted against him. "I do not believe in silkies."

Warm lips tickled her neck as his hands slipped around her waist. "Then you have nothing to worry yourself about."

Eve rested her head against John's chest as his fingers swirled across her breasts. "'Tis scandalous," she said breathlessly, her resistance holding by a thread.

"Nay, 'tis the way of the Highlands, lassie. And though we cannot stay by Loch Katrine forever, I aim to show you a wee bit o' what it is like to be free from the burden of nobility."

By the time the water was simmering, Evelyn wouldn't have been able to refuse John if it were blizzarding outside. In fact, her flesh was so steamy hot she welcomed stepping outside into the cool breeze wearing only her shift.

Carrying the soap and a drying cloth they'd purchased in Callander, she followed as he gingerly carried the heavy kettle—using his shirt to keep from singeing his fingers. Evelyn's heart skipped a beat while she admired the muscles flexing in his back. They stopped at the shore upon the soft, rounded stones with cool water lapping at their toes. Indeed, atop an enormous stone a hollow had been etched by years of rain and snow.

John grinned—devilish, endearing, irresistible. "'Tis better than a copper pot."

"And big enough for two."

After adding the steaming water, it took only a flick of his fingers for John to release his belt and drop his kilt to the ground.

Evelyn gasped. "I'll never grow tired of seeing you disrobed."

He coaxed her shift over her head and let it fall to the ground. Then he grasped her hands and stood back. "Nor I with you. You are like manna to my soul."

Sweeping her into his arms, he placed her in the water. "Not too hot?"

"Perfect."

John slid in, the water only coming to the tops of his thighs. "I reckon we needed another kettle."

She reached for him. "I think there is ample water for the both of us."

He pulled her onto his lap, coaxing her knees apart until she straddled him. The cool breeze enlivened her as John enveloped her in his powerful arms. She cupped his face and kissed him, their bodies melding in a torrent of passion.

"Let me wash you afore the water grows cold," he growled.

"I like kissing you better," she whispered, breathless.

But who knew how diverting bathing could be— especially when Evelyn's husband was wielding the soap. Torturously, he lathered every inch of her skin, swirling the bar in a rhythmic pattern while the breeze made gooseflesh spring across her flesh. She in turn did the same to him, avoiding his member until the very end. His very hard, very-difficult-to-ignore member.

When at last she wrapped her fingers around his shaft, John threw his head back with a roar. "You will be the death of me."

Encouraged, Evelyn watched the rapture on his face as she moved her hand up and down as he'd shown her. He growled and moved with her rhythm as his passion escalated.

Suddenly, John's eyes flashed wide. "Impale me, wife."

He lifted her by the arms as she coaxed herself to slide over him. Barely joined, Evelyn held very still as they gazed into each other's eyes. No words were spoken as she took him into her body ever so slowly until he was buried to his hilt.

While she watched his face, his blue eyes shining in the sunlight, she rocked her hips in tandem with his powerful thrusts. The forest surrounding them disappeared, and all that was left were Eve and John, making love under the sunlit sky while the breeze took them to the pinnacle of no return.

* * *

John had never felt so alive in his life. "I should have been born a crofter," he said, filling his sporran with a handful of musket balls.

Evelyn slung the bow and quiver of arrows over her shoulder. "Why do you say that?"

"I love the Highlands." He led her outdoors and raised his arms, turning full circle. "I love the freedom, the fresh air, and being shed of endless responsibility."

"But wouldn't you eventually miss London and court?"

"I'd be happy if I never laid eyes on Kensington Palace again in all my days."

"But you're renowned for your political prowess."

"I have no interest in it. I only became involved at court to pay my father's debts. And thanks to you, I am shed of that yoke." He climbed higher up into the hills. "Of the both of us, I reckon you'd make the better statesman."

"Why on earth would you say such a thing?"

"Because you fiercely stand by your convictions."

"Right, and look where my strong-mindedness got us."

"Perhaps, but with the right training, you'd be marvelous. That women aren't allowed is a folly."

"A moment while I stop and fan my face."

"What? Do you believe me to be like the rest of my peers? Gentlemen only. Women must stay home and raise the bairns."

"'Tis just I've never heard you speak so liberally."

"Perhaps it is on account of the mountain air, but believe me, if Anne Stuart can sit on the throne of Britain, you ought to be fully qualified to sit on her cabinet. My oath, you are far more in tune with the issues of our countrymen than most of the nobility."

The Countess of Mar rapidly patted her hands over her heart. "Thank you. Your confidence in me is inspiring—and very forward thinking."

Something ahead moved through the brush. Stopping, John focused and held up his palm.

"What is it?" Evelyn whispered.

Unsure, he crept forward, raising his flintlock. As his foot fell with his next step, a rabbit sprang from the heather. John took aim as the animal jumped in a zigzag pattern and dipped behind a clump of brush.

A hiss filled the air.

"Got it," Evelyn said, standing below with her bow.

John looked from the woman to where she'd been behind him when he'd held up his palm. He hadn't heard a single footstep. "How did you end up down there?"

Her Ladyship grinned and slung her weapon over her shoulder as if she were an archery champion. "When you started forward, I circled around. We hunt in Nottingham, I'll have you know, and it was likely the rabbit would run—just as he did. Thank heavens I went the right direction." She pointed. "But I'm not touching the creature."

John did the honors. "Who kent my wife was a sharpshooter? For that I'll clean the wee beastie as well."

He started off—heading for the top of the peak. "If you see a wild pig, shoot it."

"Now?"

"Why not now?"

"Because we have a rabbit for our supper. We ought to go back to the cottage and cook it."

"We will, but first I want to show you something."

"What would that be?"

"You'll see in a moment."

As he stepped out from the forest and climbed up the rocks, he set the rabbit down and offered Evelyn his hand. "Feast your eyes, lass. We're atop Ben A'an. Not Scotland's highest mountain, but from here you can see the expanse of Loch Katrine."

Her Ladyship's turquoise eyes glistened like never before. "My word—and not another human being in sight."

"These mountains are covered with snow from

October to May, but after the melt there's no place on earth bonnier."

Green hills sloped dramatically to the sparkling blue water.

Evelyn walked forward and stood on the precipice of the mountain, the wind picking up her skirts and hair, making them sail like a bird in flight. She stretched out her arms and closed her eyes, fearless of the height. "I feel like I'm flying!"

John stepped behind her and secured her waist. "Ye are flying, lass. Flying with the eagles."

"Can we stay here forever?"

He slid his hands around her waist. "You'd be happy living in a hovel?"

"Yes." Laughing, she turned her face to the sun. "Perhaps we could make some improvements."

"Now there's an idea. I'll scrap the plans for Alloa and we'll build here—though we may have a bit of difficulty finding laborers."

Leaning against him, she giggled. "It is a grand plan."

"If only."

They stood for a time, Eve wrapped in his embrace while they gazed out over the splendor of the mountain loch. "What plans have you for Alloa?" she asked.

"I sketched some architectural drawings to add a manor on to the tower when I was at university."

"Oh?"

"I've never been able to build my dream because my purse strings were tied."

"But now you are free to do so."

"Aye, if we are able to clear our names."

"Is architecture an interest?"

"It is. Had I not been beholden to the crown, the manor

would have already been built—along with matching stables. And my canal would have been finished years ago."

"The canal was your idea?"

"Mm-hmm, and it is the most important project."

"Because it saves labor?"

"And ferries the coal to the river far more efficiently."

Evelyn turned and cupped his face in her hands. "You are an amazing man."

"I'm no different from any other, I suppose." He kissed her. "But it is you who never cease to surprise me. Do you ken what else?"

She shook her head.

"In this moment there's no place I'd rather be than in your arms."

Chapter Thirty-Four

*N*ine days in the Highlands had passed as if it were but a flicker in the night sky. As he tied the horses to a post outside the cottage, John now sported a full beard, blonder in color than his light-brown hair. The whiskers made him look nothing like an earl, and everything like a rugged Highlander—so entirely different from Evelyn's first impression of him clad in a suit of silk at the royal ball in London.

She watched as he stooped to pick up her sidesaddle. "Wait a moment." Goodness, why hadn't she thought of this sooner?

John glanced up with a pointed stare. "We've been over this time and time again. It will take three days to reach Dundee and—"

"I know, and we must skirt past the towns and villages, which will add time to the journey. But that's not why I stopped you."

He arched an eyebrow, the saddle balanced against his shoulder.

Evelyn unfastened the brooch pinning her arisaid. "The soldiers are looking for a man and a woman, correct?"

"Aye."

"And they've seen my arisaid as well as my saddle."

"'Tis hardly likely anyone will take note of this saddle." He inclined his head toward it. "After all, the leathers are well worn."

"Yes, but what if I wore the arisaid like a kilt? Then I'd be able to ride like a man."

John audaciously rolled his eyes. "You do not have the proper saddle to ride straddling a horse like a lad."

Evelyn turned a toe inward while she batted her eyelashes. "I could use yours."

"Och, I'm glad you didn't suggest you go without."

"That's because I knew you wouldn't stand for it if I had."

John lowered the old saddle to his hip. "Are you certain about this? Your legs are not accustomed to riding astride. I reckon you'll be sore after the first hour."

"I don't know about that." She sniggered, while dancing through her mind came an image of numerous hours in her husband's arms, riding a beast of a different nature. "I've been doing a lot of *riding* since we've been here."

"What a wanton wife you've turned out to be." Laughing, he started for the cottage. "I'll leave your sidesaddle inside, then. Come along. We have some work to do if you intend to impersonate a laddie."

Evelyn followed with ideas brewing for her disguise. Folding the arisaid in pleats and forming a kilt was easy enough. So was binding her breasts. She wore John's spare shirt, her own boots, and among the castoffs in the cottage they found a moth-eaten feathered bonnet. She even shouldered the bow and quiver of arrows for added effect.

John unsheathed his dirk. "I can help you club your hair, but 'tis far too long. We'll have to cut to the shoulder."

"I beg your pardon?" Throwing up her hands, Evelyn scooted away. "Sheathe your weapon this instant!"

"But—"

"No. You are not hacking off my tresses with that monstrous dagger. Do you know how long it will take to grow them back?" She dashed to the satchel and retrieved a drying cloth. "We can tie it back, fold it under, and wrap it up in this rag."

He stood agape, the dirk still firm in his fist. "What if a bit comes out? You'll have mile-long strands whipping everywhere—a sure clue of your true sex."

"Hardly." Evelyn shook the cloth a safe distance from the accursed knife. "Lesson one in being a lady's maid. Take a thong and tie my tresses taut, braid the tail, fold it half the length, then wrap a strip of cloth down and up—very, very tightly. Trust me, it will look just like a club."

"A thick one."

"Some people have thicker hair than others."

John sheathed his dirk and dug in his sporran for a leather thong. "I'll give it a go, but if you end up looking like a lass trying to impersonate a lad, I'm cutting your blasted mane off at the shoulders."

Turning Evelyn into a man took a good hour longer than she'd anticipated, but when she went outside and studied her reflection in the lake, she thought she looked like a Highland chieftain with a cape draped around her shoulders. "See? It was well worth the effort."

John's towering reflection moved in behind her. "Ye

might pass if no one looks too closely. But no red-blooded man will be fooled for long."

"Let us just pray we fool them for long enough."

John inclined his head toward the horses. "Then let's away afore nightfall."

Evelyn tsked her tongue. By the angle of the sun, it was still morning. "My disguise didn't take all that long. And now we ought to be able to travel via a more direct route, mayhap even stay at an inn."

The first test to her disguise came when they approached the bridge to Dunblane, where a whole contingent of soldiers barricaded the road. Suddenly the leathers slipped in Evelyn's palms. And though her legs ached, she threw back her shoulders and affected a masculine sneer.

"Should we turn back?" she asked after the reins slipped again.

"Nay. The last time we tried to avoid them, we would have ended up with our necks in a noose if it hadn't been for Tullibardine's diversion." John motioned for her to ride alongside him. "Keep your head down and utter not a sound."

As they neared the soldiers, the silly reins started shaking of their own volition, and tensing her muscles only made the problem worse. She lowered her fists to the horse's withers, trying to keep her head down exactly as John instructed. No matter how much she wanted to look up and take note of what the soldiers were up to, she kept her gaze fixated on her horse's ears.

"Ho," boomed a dragoon, moving beside them and grasping Evelyn's bridle.

"Is there a wee problem with the bridge?" asked His Lordship. Normally he spoke with a Scottish brogue,

but now he poured it on thicker than she had ever
heard.

"State your name and where you're from," said the soldier, ignoring John's question.

"I'm Jimmy MacDonald and this is my son Lachlan."

Evelyn forced a frown against her urge to smile.
Lachlan, was it? She'd have to commit the name to memory. Jimmy, too.

John stroked his hand along his horse's mane and tilted
up his chin. "We hail from the Coe."

Suspicion filling his eyes, the soldier inspected their
horses while he moved over to John's side. "You mean to
say you survived the bloody massacre?"

"'Twas but a lad of twelve." John watched as the man
stroked his hand down the horse's nose. "Me, I was lucky,
but my parents didna make it."

Goodness, he sounded convincing, but was a tale about
being from Glencoe the right choice?

The soldier took a step back. "Where are you headed?"

"Up to Crieff," John explained. "I aim to buy a milking
cow."

"Or cause trouble," said another dragoon.

Evelyn bit her lip. She and her husband looked like
a pair of poor crofters, not a pair of mercenaries. Why
couldn't these mutton-heads leave them alone?

"Nay, sir." John pointed across the bridge. "We aim to
stop at an inn, have a warm meal and find a cozy loft, and
bed down for the night, then we'll be on our way."

Squinting his eyes, the redcoat studied their faces.
"We're looking for a pair of renegades. A man and a
woman." He held up a slip of parchment. Evelyn leaned
in and shifted her gaze enough for a glimpse of the worst
rendering of the Earl of Mar she'd ever imagined. The

sketch looked like the Angel of Death wearing a periwig. "Have you seen this man?"

"I canna say I have," John replied with a straight face. "In truth I havena seen many Sassenach fops crossing the Highlands."

"Hmm. If these miscreants ever come down from the hills they will be tried and hung for treason." The man backed away from their horses. "I'll grant you leave to stop for a meal, but then you'd best be on your way. And we'll be watching. Your kind are not welcome in these parts."

John's fist tightened around his reins, making his knuckles white. "My kind?" he growled. "It sounds as if Scots are no' welcome on their own lands."

Before the soldier responded, John kicked his heels. Evelyn did as well, urging her horse to keep pace as they crossed the bridge. "Do you think your last comment was wise?" she asked once they were out of earshot.

"Mayhap not wise, but necessary."

She glanced over her shoulder. "Two dragoons are following."

* * *

John opted to stop in Dunblane for two reasons. First, the horses were spent and wouldn't make it much farther. Second, they hadn't eaten since the morning meal, a good seven or eight hours past. If two soldiers opted to follow, then God save them.

After they stabled the horses, John almost made the mistake of taking Evelyn by the hand. "Och," he growled, speaking for the benefit of any eavesdroppers. "Come, son. We'll eat whilst the horses are resting."

She fell in step beside him. Damn. No matter how hard she tried, the woman would never look like a lad. Her feet were too small. Her gait was too—too bloody feminine. And no matter how long they'd been staying in the Highlands, she still smelled like fragrant blooms.

As they stepped inside the alehouse, John grabbed Evelyn's shoulder and stopped her while he took in the scene. Only a half-day's ride from Alloa, even with his ragged clothes and a scruffy beard, someone might recognize him.

The place was thick with pipe smoke and smelled of stale beer. A boisterous group of men filled the south wall, toying with a barmaid. But there was an empty table at the back near the bar.

John nodded at the bristly barman and pointed to the table. "Two ales, bread, and pottage for a pair of weary travelers."

Using a cloth to dry a tankard, the man stared back through beady eyes, his thick black beard hiding his mouth. One thing for certain, he looked none too happy.

It nearly cut John to the quick not to hold the chair for Evelyn, but it mustn't be done. She started for the seat with its back to the stone wall. "Not that one," John groused with a bit more bile in his tone than he'd normally use with her.

The lass's lips parted with a silent gasp and then she gave a knowing nod. "I should have thought," she whispered.

"Oh?" John slipped into the spot where he had a view of the door, the bar, and the miscreants slapping the barmaid's behind.

Evelyn didn't take the chair across but the one around

the corner, and once she sat, she cupped a hand over her mouth. "Dubois never sat with his back to the door."

That bloody figured, the lout. The Frenchman had cause to be worried about being dirked in the back—and John wouldn't mind being the one to wield the blade.

The door opened and in sauntered the two dragoons who'd obviously been assigned to ensure John and Evelyn didn't linger about town.

She turned her head away and spoke over her shoulder. "They're looking straight at us."

"Pay them no mind."

But his hackles stood on end when the bastards moved to the bar and were served ale first. *Bloody hell.* He might be an earl in disguise, but he expected common courtesy from the damned Scotsman behind the bar.

Rather than rescue the barmaid and have her bring the ale, the barman stepped from behind the board with two frothy tankards.

"I'll wager he's a royalist dyed in the queen's red," Evelyn mumbled.

"Wheesht."

The man set the drinks on the table, then glanced over his shoulder. "Those yellow dogs appear to have quite an interest in you pair—even asked me if I kent who ye were."

"They've no cause to suspect us of any wrongdoing." John casually took a drink, his fingers brushing the hilt of his dirk. "What did you tell them?"

"I said I'd never seen the likes of you afore and hope I never again do." The man wrapped his meaty fingers around the back of an empty chair as he leaned very near. "But I *do* ken who ye are. Recognized you as soon as ye opened the door, I did."

"Ye reckon?" As his fingers gripped his dirk's handle, the familiar tic twitched beside John's eye as he imagined all manner of blackmail brewing in the barman's piddling mind. "Who might that be?"

The big man's gaze intensified. "Listen well, m'lord. Those underhanded dragoons have the road to Crieff and the road to Stirling blocked."

John's heart nearly stopped. *Shite.*

There were two main roads out of Dunblane, one leading north and one south. Only the locals knew about the third, and it was little more than a path. "What about the road to Sheriffmuir?" he asked.

"That's what I recommend." The barman threw a thumb over his shoulder. "But those pair aim to follow whichever road you choose—and just when you think you've lost them—"

"Can you help us?" Evelyn whispered.

"Stay for a bit. Nurse your ale and eat your pottage."

The barman pulled a vial from his apron and held it up. "A few drops of this and they ought to be in their cups within an hour."

"What the blazes are you yammering about?" hollered one of the dragoons. "Bring us some bloody food, ye flea-bitten wastrel."

A tempest passed through those beady eyes. "See what I mean? Everyone in town is hankering to dirk the lot of them." The barman turned. "A moment, sirs."

John grabbed the man's arm. "Thank you, friend."

The big fellow leaned over the back of the chair and lowered his voice. "Rumor is you're raising the standard for James. If that is true, every man in this town will take up arms and join ye."

"Your news is a wee bit premature. But the queen's

health is failing and mind you, when the time comes, I'll remember you, friend." John inclined his head in the direction of the stables. "Our horses are spent. Is there any chance—"

"I'll arrange for two of Dunblane's finest to be waiting out the back."

"Without anyone knowing?"

The barman winked. "Ye can count on me."

"Are you going to flap your bloody mouth all day?" bellowed one of the soldiers.

John flicked his hand toward the dragoons. "Go on then. Tame the angry beasts."

Evelyn stared while the black-bearded Highlander left to tend to the dragoons. "Mercy."

John's gut twisted. He wasn't about to raise the standard for anyone until he cleared his name. "I reckon the townspeople are a bit tired of being browbeaten by those sniveling maggots."

"Clearly." She placed her hand atop his. "But the time to take a stand is anon."

"I'll be the one to decide if, when, and where." John snapped his fingers away. "And it will serve you well to remember that you are parading about as a lad."

Chapter Thirty-Five

They might have made it through Dunblane without being caught, but after seeing the concentration of red-coated dragoons amassed on the Dundee pier, Evelyn feared their luck may have run its course. Worse, a three-masted barque appeared to be at the center of the turmoil.

"Is that Sir Kennan's ship?" she asked as a lead weight dropped in her stomach.

John reined his horse to a stop and groaned. "Fie, can something not be immersed in complication for once?"

"Should we find a place to weather the storm—come back after things have settled?"

"Nay. It looks as if the men on deck are unfurling the sails yet again. If we wait, Cameron will not be here when we return." John reached for her nearest rein and tugged Evelyn's horse alongside his. "Stay beside me and stop for no one. I aim to ride straight up to the gangway."

But that was where the dragoons congregated, shouting, waving their arms. Evelyn spotted a familiar face. Oh dear, in the middle of the mayhem stood Sir Kennan himself. Not to mention the myriad of barrels stacked on the pier as well as on deck. Riding for the gangway now was insanity.

Nonetheless, the Earl of Mar, disguised as a crofter, led her toward anarchy.

And as they neared, the shouting escalated. "You're robbing me of my livelihood!" Sir Kennan bellowed. "With your inflated duties I cannot pay my men, let alone feed them."

A dragoon dressed in an officer's coat stood holding a musket across his chest. "I don't give a rat's arse if you starve. You're not offloading another barrel without payment."

"You're thieves, the lot of you," yelled a man from the pier.

"Hang the bastards by the cods!" another yelled while Evelyn's horse stutter-stepped in the midst of growing unease.

"The queen doesn't give a lick about her Scottish subjects."

"Aye, all she cares about is to use our sons to man her armies."

"And pay her bloody taxes!" Kennan bellowed, throwing up his arms to encourage the hecklers.

Evelyn ducked as something soft and sloppy sailed overhead. "I fear the men will riot."

As she spoke, a skirmish broke out on the gangway. Men pushed and shoved. Fists flew. Her horse whinnied and reared. Leaning forward, Evelyn brought the pony under control as a snarling man grabbed her arm and tugged.

"No!" she shrieked, clenching her knees, fighting to

maintain her seat while the horse snorted, growing more and more agitated.

"Unhand my—" John grunted as, in one move, he latched his arm around her waist and leaned across, smashing his fist across the rioter's temple.

With a tumultuous uproar, the entire pier broke out into the very insurrection Evelyn had predicted. John dragged her across his lap while her horse was pulled away. Kicking his heels, he forced open a gap. His mount managed to surge ahead, only to have their momentum stopped by a stack of barrels.

"Hide in between the casks!" John hollered, sliding off his mount and depositing her in the only spot on the entire pier where she might be safe.

Evelyn crouched low, removing the bow from her shoulder and reaching for an arrow.

Sword in hand, John leaped onto the barrels and hopped across them, fending off rioters until he landed in a crouch on the gangway beside Kennan.

Peeking over the tops of casks, Evelyn gulped, her pulse quickening. *How on earth did I ever believe him to be anything other than a brawny Highland warrior?*

Kennan addressed John with his sword, but as soon as the captain recognized him, they stood back to back and took charge of the fight. Looters began smashing the barrels and stealing the booty inside. Before she was exposed, Evelyn spun and let an arrow fly, hitting a dragoon with a musket aimed straight at John. The weapon fired as the soldier fell. Thank God the bullet went astray.

Crouching, she skittered nearer the *Highland Reel*, its sails slowly winching higher above.

The sound of clanging swords resounded from the gangway. With the pommel of his sword, a dragoon bashed Sir Kennan in the shoulder and sent him falling over the ropes and down to the pier.

"No!" Evelyn screamed above the mayhem with no time to spare.

Five dragoons attacked John—two in back and three in front. He swung his sword so fast it blurred, but no man could maintain such a pace. Evelyn took aim and shot one, then another.

"There's the archer!" someone shouted.

God, no! Dragoons surrounded her from three sides. Heart pounding, she backed until her heels hung over the edge of the pier. "I'll jump!"

She panned the bow across the scowling men as they crept toward her, their swords at the ready. Evelyn's fingers perspired and slipped on the string.

Suddenly a deafening screech came from above.

In the blink of an eye, a firm arm wrapped around her waist and hoisted her into the air.

"Aaaaah!" Her shrill scream resounded across the expanse of the pier. As she flew out over the sea, her arrow dropped while her arms flailed, grasping at nothing.

"Heeeelp!" she howled, kicking her feet.

"God blind me, ye're a bloody lass," growled a youthful voice behind her. "I kent ye were too light to be a lad."

"Aaaaack!" she shrieked, unable to provide a coherent reply while her stomach flew to her throat.

"Brace yerself."

Evelyn caught a glimpse of her savior right before he released the rope. Good heavens, it was Baltazar, Sir Kennan's cabin boy.

"Ayeeee!" she yelled again as they crashed onto the deck and rolled into a heap. Any other time, she would have given the young man a firm talking to about handling women, but she was neither wearing a dress nor had she a spare minute. "Quickly! Mar and Sir Kennan!"

"My lady?" the adolescent squawked.

"No time," she snapped, dashing across the deck and reaching for an arrow. As she arrived at the rail and lined up her sights, Sir Kennan and John leaped onto the ship's deck.

"Cast off now!" bellowed the captain, sprinting for the helm.

Stopping, John searched from bow to stern. "Evelyn!"

"Here," she shouted, waving a hand.

"Shove off the gangway!" hollered Mr. MacNeil.

With a thunderous and rumbling groan, the ship listed away while Evelyn watched the plank drop to the pier with a half-dozen dragoons still atop her timbers.

Crack, crack!

"Get down, m'lady," shouted the cabin boy, coaxing her to the deck. "They're shooting at us."

John dove behind the wall, sliding beside them. "Are you hurt?"

"Never better." She clasped his hands and squeezed, gasping at the blood on his sleeve. "You're bleeding."

He grinned with a saucy wink. "'Tisn't my blood, lass."

"Oh, thank the good Lord."

Muskets blasted from the shore, the bullets stopped by the thick wooden hull. Her heart still hammering, Evelyn hardly believed they'd escaped unharmed. She turned and kissed the cabin boy on the cheek. "Baltazar, I owe you a world of thanks."

The boy blushed. "Och, m'lady, no one calls me by my real name."

"Well they ought to. It is a very stately name, indeed."

John leaned around her and shook the lad's hand. "Runner, there will be a reward for your heroism, this day."

As the sails billowed with the wind, the musket fire faded into the sounds of the wind and the rushing sea. And Evelyn had never felt so alive. "Did you see him?" she asked. "If it weren't for this young man, I would have had to jump off the pier and swim for my life."

John slid his arm around her shoulders. "Aye, but not before you took care of a parcel of dragoons. Good shooting, wife—better yet, no one in Dundee has any idea it was the Countess of Mar who fired those arrows."

* * *

"It seems we are destined to voyage on Sir Kennan's ship," said John, feeling refreshed after a quick wash with bowl and ewer. With Evelyn on his arm, together they proceeded aft to the captain's cabin, where they'd been summoned.

Now clad in her arisaid and kirtle like a proper lady, she sighed. "I just thank the stars we managed to make it aboard alive."

"I wish I could have stopped fighting just to watch Runner swing past and snatch you from the pier." John chuckled. "If it is any consolation, Mr. MacNeil reported that Runner was mortified when he realized you were Lady Mar."

"And so he should have been—he's awfully brash for a boy of fourteen."

"I'd expect no less from a youth who spends all his time with a crew of Scottish sailors. I'll wager he kens words even I haven't heard."

She gave John's arm a pat. "Though I'll always thank the stars for that young man's heroism."

"Och aye."

Once they were introduced, Sir Kennan welcomed them into his cabin. "Please, come share a meal—that is if you've found your sea legs."

"The waters do not seem to be too rough this evening," Evelyn said as a steward held a chair for her.

John moved to the table alongside Kennan. "What happened on the pier today? I've heard bits and pieces, though it would be nice to ken exactly what I was fighting for aside from a berth on your ship, sir."

The captain gestured to a chair and sat as well. "The usual skullduggery Highlanders have come to expect from the queen's soldiers. Dragoons are forever padding their purses by inflating import duties."

"Inflating? Are present taxes not high enough?"

"They are abominable without the soldiers' sticky fingers. And if I had paid them what they asked, I would have forgone my profits."

John arched an eyebrow. "Not very lucrative."

Evelyn sat back as the steward placed a napkin in her lap. "Perhaps that's why my father does everything he can to avoid paying duties."

"Aye," Kennan agreed, "and I need not tell you the Scots are taxed higher than the swindlers south of the border."

Evelyn looked on while the steward poured the wine. "That's hardly fair."

"It is not. The very thought makes my hackles stand on end. 'Tis something I've been fighting for years." John picked up his butter knife and reached for the bread. "But things grew a tad out of hand in Dundee—there'll be a formal complaint, mark me."

Sir Kennan swirled his wine, then took a healthy swig. "'Tisn't the first skirmish and will not be the last."

John let it pass. If he ever cleared his name, he'd do everything in his power to ensure Sir Kennan received a pardon as well as a commendation. "Aside from taxes and what happened on the pier, Lady Mar and I were actually seeking you out."

"Oh?"

After taking a bite of bread, John frowned. "It seems my plea to Queen Anne has been tainted by the Duke of Argyll."

"The cur." Sir Kennan scowled. "I've never met a more heinous snake."

"Agreed," John said, explaining about how Claude Dubois had perjured himself against Mar to save his own neck, after which Argyll attacked Alloa. And then he continued with the story of how they'd escaped with their lives and had been on the run ever since. "I need your help, Cameron. The only way to clear my name is to find Dubois and strangle a confession from his corrupt lips."

Kennan raised his glass in toast. "And take back the bloody gold."

Evelyn followed suit. "Amen to that."

John drank thoughtfully as the stewards brought in a meal of haddock. "Have you heard anything of Dubois's whereabouts?"

Knife and fork in hand, the captain's face grew dark. "Word on the Continent is the fiend is under King Louis's protection at Versailles."

"Fie!" John cursed. "We'll never be able to reach him there."

Sir Kennan leaned forward and shifted his gaze between his two guests. "I wouldn't be so certain. I for one would relish a chance to slit his throat."

"After he leads us to the gold and attests to our innocence." Evelyn sliced into her fish. "But Versailles? It would take an army to lure him away from the palace."

Chewing, Sir Kennan reached for the salt cellar. "Aye, but you forget one very important fact, m'lady."

"What is that?" asked John.

"Prince James is well acquainted with Louis—and he oft is a welcome visitor to Versailles."

For the first time since they'd left Loch Katrine, the heavy weight bearing down on John's shoulders eased.

Chapter Thirty-Six

*U*pon their arrival at Château de Saint-Germain-en-Laye, the trio were welcomed by James Francis Edward Stuart. Though the prince had lived in exile since infancy, Evelyn hadn't expected his French accent.

As it turned out, James and his wife, Maria, a Polish princess, had been invited to a feast at Versailles one week hence. The news that Louis had used Claude Dubois to plan an invasion of Great Britain and annex the country had reached James, but he had discarded it as another contrived report to create a rift between him and the king of France, who had harbored his family and treated them like royalty since their exile five and twenty years ago.

Dubois's true motives came as a severe blow to James. In fact, Dubois had been received at Versailles as a hero, though James had heard nothing about the Spanish gold.

Fortunately for Evelyn and John, Louis's underhandedness in the matter was the impetus needed to convince the prince to assist them with their plans to confront the French traitor.

During the week leading up to the feast, John, Evelyn, Kennan, and the prince passed many hours locked in James's antechamber both planning their attack and discussing the future of Great Britain, with James claiming his rightful place as king.

Nights were passed in pure luxury at Saint-Germain-en-Laye, where Evelyn and John enjoyed a suite and servants to rival their own at Alloa. If only Thomas and Oliver had been with them, their time at the château would have been like a grand holiday. Planning the future gave Evelyn a sense of excitement, of power, and importance.

But all too soon came their departure for Versailles, and tension filled the coach. John sat beside Evelyn throughout the twenty-mile carriage ride, his brow furrowed, his arms crossed.

"We went over our strategy time and time again," she finally whispered while James and Maria smiled pleasantly across the coach. "I'm the only one who can do this. No one else."

"That doesn't mean I have to like it," John groused out of the corner of his mouth.

On Evelyn's other side, Sir Kennan leaned forward and looked around her. "If I had to place a wager, I'd bet on Lady Mar every time. She's a natural-born spy."

John glared but didn't respond.

Five minutes later, the carriage rolled to a stop.

"Ah," said Prince James. "We have arrived."

John helped Evelyn alight, then pulled her aside. "There's still time to change your mind."

At first she gave him a stern look, but once she read the

torture in his eyes, she gently squeezed his hand. "I only have the strength to face that vile beast because I know you will be there."

"But anything—"

"No." She tightened her grip. They both knew the risks. Once they stepped inside the palace, anything could happen. Their plans might be thwarted. Their very lives might be forfeit. But they had faced grave danger before, and this was no time to back out. "I trust you, and I need you to believe in me."

"Believe?" His mouth gaped as he blinked. "Believing in you is the one and only reason I am going along with this harebrained scheme."

The prince beckoned her. "Come along, Lady Mar. Unless there has been a change of plan?"

"Absolutely not." Evelyn gave her husband an intense stare, praying she imparted the powerful love in her heart before she fell in step beside James and Maria. She was to be introduced as herself, but John and Kennan were now posing as businessmen from America. Once they passed through the gates, the men would blend into the shadows and disappear.

The entire affair made being introduced at Kensington Palace pale in comparison. A grand walkway carpeted with red rose petals guided them through the vast courtyard while trumpets heralded their arrival. Roman architecture prevailed, eaves clad with gold trim, iridescent in the torchlight.

Men wearing lavishly embroidered silks and voluminous periwigs led stately women as if they were marionettes processing across a grand stage. Everywhere Evelyn looked, gowns with bows and jewels and furs, all crafted in splendorous style, surrounded her. She, herself, wore a gown of rose silk, the skirt embroidered with peacock tails and far more lavish than anything she'd ever owned before.

Inside they were shown to the Hall of Mirrors, a grand gallery of unsurpassed opulence. The walls were inlaid with burgundy marble and white Grecian statues. Above, the ceiling trimmed with gold foil displayed extravagantly ornate Baroque paintings that depicted angels and demons battling in the heavens. Mirrored crystal chandeliers, each lit with countless candles, hung overhead. And throughout the gallery stood six-foot golden pillars supported by cherubs who held high their own crystal candelabras. Though it was night, the room glowed like the interior of a golden carriage.

Still in the company of the prince and princess, Evelyn breathed a sigh of relief and fanned herself when she spotted Mr. Dubois across the hall.

"It appears as though stage one of your plan is a success," whispered James.

"It has indeed, Your Highness. Finding the man is my cue." Evelyn curtsied. "Please excuse me."

Evelyn used the gilt cherub candelabras to conceal herself as she stealthily made her way toward the deceitful Frenchman. Having never visited Versailles before, she would have enjoyed the opportunity to stop and admire every marble statue and ornately carved sideboard, but such indulgence would surely thwart the plan.

Once she arrived at the gilt pillar nearest Dubois, Evelyn waited and turned her ear toward the man's conversation. Speaking in French, he chatted with someone about the weather, of all things. And he seemed to be quite content to do so. For the love of God, who cared about whether it would rain on the morrow?

If only Dubois's companion would move along. If she didn't find a way to speak to the man alone, dinner would be called for soon and they'd have to take their seats. That simply would not do.

Just step out and confront him!

Evelyn tiptoed until she stopped right behind the Frenchman's shoulder. She cleared her throat. "Well, well. If it is not Claude Dubois. Just the man I wanted to see," she said with exalted happiness.

He turned, his movement calculated and slow, as if he'd expected her there. But the surprise reflected in his eyes was unmistakable. "Lady Mar!" he said with far too much exuberance as he took her hand.

When he bent down to apply a kiss, Evelyn gave his friend an evil eye and inclined her head away. The man understood her silent dismissal and moved along.

Stage two of the plan had just begun.

Mr. Dubois looked too merry—drunk on happiness, the swindler. "*Ma chérie*, I cannot tell you how surprised I am to see your lovely face. Whatever has brought you to France?"

Evelyn drew upon years of training as the daughter of a duke and, though a tempest of rage inflamed her breast, her face remained as unmoved as the surface of a glassy pond. "I sought you out, sir."

Beads of sweat dappled the stout man's brow as his gaze swept through the hall. "With Mar?"

"Of course not." She inhaled, standing taller. "Due to certain circumstances occurring in London, of which I believe you are intimately aware, my husband and I have parted ways."

The shameless fop didn't bother to hide his amusement. "Oh, how unfortunate."

She played right along. "Truly, I do not believe so."

"If you are blaming me—"

Evelyn overtly held her fan over her heart, informing him of her interest and that he had won her love, though doing so made her stomach ill. "I assure you, placing blame is the farthest thing from my mind."

Dubois shook out a kerchief and wiped the sweat from his brow. "Then how may I assist you, madam?"

"You have not guessed?" Evelyn pulled the kerchief from his fingers and playfully dashed it across his cheek, managing to smile and bat her eyelashes. Good Lord, she'd need a scalding bath when this charade came to an end. "You ought to."

"My lady, I doubt I'll be traveling back to England."

"Of course you will not and nor will I." She looped her arm through his, wondering if her flirting would ever manage to get through the Frenchman's thick skull. "But surely you're not retired from, from...you know."

"Retired?"

"Does the king no longer require your services?"

"No...ah, *oui*. I am still His Majesty's faithful servant."

"That is as I suspected." Forcing a smile, she gave his cheek a kiss, revolting and further souring her stomach. "Imagine the things we can do together."

"Together? You and me?" he asked, with an air of disbelief.

She playfully smacked his shoulder with the kerchief. "After all the time we spent scheming in London, can you truly tell me you did not entertain a liaison of a more *romantic* nature?" There, she'd blurted it out. Now would he manage to take the bloody bait?

"Well I—"

"Of course you did." She pulled him by the hand. "Come, there is ever so much to discuss."

He glanced over his shoulder. "But what about the feast?"

"Surely we will not be missed..." Bless it, how much more convincing must she be?

Nonetheless, he followed and allowed her to tug him out to the corridor, where he promptly stopped. "My lady. Evelyn. Correct me if I am mistaken, but you never showed any interest in me before—and believe me, I was waiting with bated breath for you to do so."

She faced him and stepped so near, she smelled soured wine on his breath. Giving the performance of her life, she smoothed her fingers along the lapels of his over-stuffed doublet. "Before I was unable to act upon my attraction. But now..."

"Now?"

"I am a fallen woman, you see."

He licked his lips. "I do see. Quite clearly."

"Then let us not tarry. Take me to your rooms and show me the passion that thrums through your blood."

He leaned forward as if about to kiss her. Evelyn stepped back quickly and pulled his hand. "Not here, my darling."

* * *

There were several holes in their plan to corner Claude Dubois, but the one John rued most was that no weapons were allowed inside Versailles—aside from the daggers he had hidden up his sleeves, in his breeches, and in his garters. John's fingers itched to wield a dirk, a pair of dueling pistols, and his bloody sword.

Now, as John and Cameron followed the lecherous cur while he led Evelyn through the labyrinth of opulent passageways, they hid behind corners and columns like common thieves. Playing their part, he and Sir Kennan pretended to be deep in conversation whenever they encountered passersby.

But then a woman opened a door, seemingly ecstatic to find two able-bodied men. She babbled in French, asking them to help her move a harpsichord, of all things.

Cameron started to go inside the woman's rooms until John gripped his shoulder and pulled him back. Feeling like a heel, he looked the woman in the eye, apologized, and suggested she ring for a pair of footmen to assist her.

To the lady's shocked and indignant scolding, which echoed through the corridors like a cathedral bell, John hurried Sir Kennan along. "Since when does a bloody pirate turn gentleman?"

"Some of the most gracious gentlemen in my acquaintance are pirates." Chuckling, the seafaring heir to the Cameron chieftainship jabbed the heel of his hand into John's shoulder. "Besides, the lass was bonny."

"Och aye? You'd leave Lady Mar's fate and a chest of gold in the hands of Dubois whilst you pushed some bit of muslin's harpsichord across the bleeding floor?"

"I kent you would have stopped me," the captain whispered.

"I see," John growled under his breath as they hastened toward a marble set of stairs. "It was your intention to make me look like a pompous prick."

Cameron sniggered. "Aye."

John silently moved to the wall, where he could look up the steps without being noticed. He beckoned Sir Kennan. "'Tis clear."

But when they reached the top, Dubois and Evelyn were nowhere to be seen. John stared down the long corridor lined with doors on either side, at least twenty of them. "Shite!"

Together they hastened through the passageway, only to find yet another long corridor with too many doors.

"Why the bloody hell did you have to stop for the harpsichord woman?"

"That took all of two ticks of the clock." Throwing up his hands, Kennan turned in a circle. "We have to be close."

"I don't like this." John turned his ear but heard nothing. "I'll kick in every door if I must."

"I've a better idea." Cameron grabbed a bouquet of roses off a gilt table adorning the juncture of the two passageways and headed off.

"Where are you going?"

"For help."

"Och, I'd rather start kicking," John growled and followed, though grudgingly.

They hadn't gone but a few paces when one of the doors opened and a maid stepped out, her arms laden with linens.

The pirate held up the flowers. "*Pardonnez-moi, mademoiselle. S'il vous plaît, Monsieur Dubois?*"

She pointed down the corridor. "*Numéro deux cent cinquante-six.*"

"*Merci*," said John, bowing, then hastening after Cameron.

"See?" The man shoved the flowers back into the vase as they passed. "Number two hundred fifty-six."

John ran down the next passageway, reading numbers until they reached the end, and another stairwell. "Fie!" The numbers stopped at two hundred forty-nine.

"Dubois has to be on this floor."

"Unless..." John studied the last door. It was numbered 250, except beneath it in small letters were two words: *et tous*.

"And all," said Kennan, translating as well.

John grabbed the latch and pulled the door wide.

A high-pitched gasp came from midway down the corridor, lined with doors only on one side.

A fire ignited in John's chest as he surged forward. "I'll kill him!"

"Not before we find out about the gold."

John didn't give a rat's arse about the gold. He wanted a confession written in blood and, afterward, Dubois could hang.

"Shall we not enjoy a Bordeaux before—?" Evelyn squealed loudly.

John didn't even try the latch. Using his heel, he kicked the door so hard it burst open with a loud slam.

Dubois had Evelyn bent backward over a settee with one hand on her breast, the beast.

"Unhand her!" he bellowed, surging forward.

But Lady Mar was faster. "You bastard!" she snapped, slapping the Frenchman across the face and kneeing him in the loins.

"Oof," Dubois grunted as he recoiled, reaching to protect his manhood.

John grabbed him by the shoulders and threw him to the floorboards, landing a kick to the man's kidney, and another and another. "You bloody ruined me, you festering pustule."

Covering his head, the Frenchman drew his knees beneath his chin. "I did nothing. Please. Stop!"

Sir Kennan kneeled and tied Dubois's wrists and ankles.

John gestured toward a wooden chair. "Put him there."

"You cannot harm me," Dubois whined. "I am under the protection of the king."

"Not my king," John said, spreading his hands to his sides and turning full circle.

Evelyn stepped in and slapped the man. "You bastard."

The Frenchman licked a trickle of blood at the corner of his mouth and sneered at her. "You're a hellion of the worst sort."

"I am—"

John pulled her aside as he slammed his fist across the lout's chin. "If you want to live through the night, you'll watch your mouth. I need a signed confession admitting I had nothing to do with King Louis's plot to invade England."

The horse's arse had the audacity to smirk. "The Earl of Mar needs me to clear his name?"

Sir Kennan produced a pair of iron pliers and clamped them shut in front of Dubois's nose. "And I need to ken where ye stashed the gold, ye villainous whoreson."

His eyes growing round, the Frenchman leaned away. "I-I-I gave it to Louis, of course."

"I'll believe that when Hell freezes over." Kennan gave John a nod. "Hold his head back."

"My pleasure."

"Where's the gold?" Evelyn demanded. "For once in your life tell the truth!"

The man's eyes shifted to a rectangular Oriental carpet while sweat bled from his temples. "I swear it has been given to the king!"

John grabbed Dubois's head while Kennan moved in with the pliers. "Pull the top front. 'Tis crooked anyway."

Dubois squealed.

John nodded to Evelyn, who drew back the slip of carpet. "What's this?"

Applying the pliers to the tooth, Kennan's hand stilled as all eyes shifted to a door hidden in the floorboards.

"Open it, m'lady," John said, sinking his fingers into the flesh on Dubois's cheeks while the man kicked.

After throwing back the hatch, Evelyn pulled out a bit of black cloth, then clapped her hands over her mouth and gasped.

The sheen of gold coins reflected the firelight.

"Bloody miserable thief." Snarling, Sir Kennan yanked out the tooth. "Ye planned to keep it for yourself all along."

Dubois howled and launched himself from the chair. "It is mine!" His arms and feet tied, the blackguard hopped to the hearth, snatched a poker, and swung it at Evelyn's head.

John caught the Frenchman's arms midstrike. "You've just made your last mistake." Twisting the poker from Dubois's grip, he jabbed it into the bastard's belly. As the man doubled over, John slammed the iron rod across the back of his head.

The Frenchman collapsed onto his face, blood pooling beneath.

"Is he dead?" Evelyn gasped, looking horrified.

Sir Kennan kneeled and held the back of his hand to the cur's nose. "He breathes."

"I should have hit him harder," John said, tossing the poker on the settee. "Though he'll not be signing a damned confession."

Sir Kennan reached into the hiding place and scooped up a handful of coins. "I doubt we'll need it with this."

Evelyn took a Spanish doubloon from his palm and studied it. "This goes to Prince James. All of it."

"Agreed." John found a valise and a satchel. "It will be heavy."

Evelyn removed her wrap and spread it on the floor. "I'll carry my share enfolded in this."

John paused and cupped her cheek. "You've helped quite enough this eve. Without you, we wouldn't have got to Dubois so easily."

Sir Kennan began scooping handfuls of coins into the satchel. "But what about your pardon?"

The familiar tic twitched above John's eye. "I'll have to face the queen and tell her the truth. 'Tis the only way."

Chapter Thirty-Seven

*I*t was nearly dawn when the trio finally made their way back to Château de Saint-Germain-en-Laye. The prince and princess had accepted the hospitality of King Louis, remaining at Versailles, and weren't expected until the feasting was at an end.

After bidding good night to Sir Kennan, Evelyn stood in their lavish French boudoir, her arms wrapped around her husband's neck. "I doubt we'll hear anything further from Dubois. If he complains about the gold, Louis will know the extent of his emissary's double dealings."

John cradled her head against his chest. "I wonder where that man's loyalties lie."

"I'm quite convinced he cares only for himself."

"Then let us speak of him no more."

Evelyn looked up. She'd wanted to discuss his plan and now they were alone, she no longer could hold her tongue. "Perhaps we should send for the boys and stay in France, since he didn't sign a confession."

"Hush." John kissed her lips. "I've been Anne's faithful servant for eleven years. She can very well face me and listen to truth. I have never given her cause to doubt me. Why shouldn't she believe my word over that of a traitor?"

"And Argyll?"

"True, he poses the greatest thorn in my side—but with parliament in recess and the duke in Scotland, this may be my only chance to influence the queen."

"What happens when you set foot on British soil? Do you not fear capture?"

John rubbed his little finger along her lip. "Mark me, I'll have a solid plan by the time we reach London."

He gave her side a tickle. Evelyn giggled and squirmed. "Do you believe so, my lord?"

Scooping her into his arms, he carried her to the bed and climbed in beside her. "What was that, wife? A wee laugh?" He tickled her again. "I like it when you writhe, especially when you're beneath me."

Evelyn raised her arms and drew him over her. "Then stop toying with me and let me watch you disrobe."

Chuckling, he rocked back on his haunches. Buttons sprang open, silk and cambric sailed to the floor. "I cannot abide court clothing," he said, his blue eyes shining with humor.

Evelyn licked her lips, her gaze drinking in his sleek, naked body. "You prefer to wear the garb of a Scotsman?"

"Of a Highlander."

"Indeed. And that's how I like you second best."

His brow furrowed. "Only second?"

"Well." She smoothed her fingers up his muscular thighs, stopping right before she reached his... "Stark naked is my favorite."

"I always wanted to be wed to a daringly scandalous woman." His deft fingers removed her clothing. How he could be more efficient than a lady's maid always boggled Evelyn's mind.

She brushed a strand of hair away from his face. "The first time I saw you, I thought you were the most beautiful man I'd ever seen. I was hardly able to stop myself from staring."

"Truly?" His gaze dipped to her breasts, and his tongue slipped to the corner of his mouth. "I didn't think you cared much for me."

"I suppose I did try to give that impression."

"Because you thought me an arrogant fop?"

"And I was ever so wrong." Drawing his face to hers, she kissed him. "Know what else?"

He grinned like a man who didn't have a care in the world. "You love me?"

Reaching back, Evelyn drew the ribbon from his hair and let his locks fall forward, making him look wild and dangerous. "How did you know that's what I was about to say?"

He cupped her cheek in his palm, his eyes growing dark and serious. "I never thought anyone would ever again capture my heart." He kissed one cheek and then the other. "But in you I have found love so deep it makes me feel like the king of the universe."

Evelyn's heart soared as, in each other's arms, they truly became one.

For three days, she reveled in the adoration of her husband's arms, making love often and taking long strolls through the château gardens. On the fourth day, the sound of the royal carriage approached from the tree-lined drive, and their days of bliss had come to an end.

* * *

"Come in, come in," said the prince, beckoning the trio into his drawing room. "I've been anxious to hear about your escapades."

Sir Kennan motioned to the footmen to place a chest on the table. "And we've been ever so anxious for your return."

James tapped his fingers together. "It appears as if your efforts yielded success. I saw not a glimpse of Dubois during my visit."

"Indeed, I imagine he suffered a nagging megrim, Your Highness," said John.

The prince gestured to a set of velvet upholstered armchairs. "Well then, please do not make me wait a moment longer."

But John wasn't ready to sit. He moved beside Sir Kennan and the chest. "As we suspected, we found the gold."

"And Lady Mar led you straight to the varlet's den," said James, holding the chair for Evelyn.

"Aye." John motioned for Kennan to open the chest and reveal the gold. "And we've recovered a king's fortune—your fortune, sire."

"My heavens." James crossed the floor and plucked a coin. "Where did he hide such treasure? And within the walls of Versailles without the king's knowledge?"

"Beneath the floorboards of his apartments," Kennan explained. "Lord only kens what he planned to do with it."

John grasped his hands behind his back. "He was most likely waiting for his opportunity to smuggle it out once he was assured Hull and the rest of us had given up the chase."

"But he didn't relinquish the gold without a fight," said Evelyn. "Mr. Dubois attacked me, and during the skirmish, Mar knocked him out cold. As a result, the man wasn't merely unwilling, he was unable to sign a confession proving my husband was not guilty of treason."

"I see." James tossed the coin back into the chest, then scooped a handful and watched them slide from his palm. "You are right, there is a king's fortune here—more than enough to raise an army should it become necessary."

John nodded. "And I believe it will. There are too many Whigs at court who fear you."

"Exactly." James closed the chest's lid. "I need allies, especially you, Mar. You know the players at court. You know whom I can trust and who will stab me in the back at their first opportunity."

"I do."

The prince looked him in the eye. "I can ill afford to see you, my Secretary of State for Great Britain, with your head in a noose."

John took in a sharp breath. "Aye, however—"

"I agree," Evelyn interrupted. "There is no other high-ranking peer at court more loyal or more knowledgeable than my husband."

Sir Kennan pounded his fist over his heart. "Hear, hear."

"It is settled," said James. "Mar, you will take one-third of this coin to my half sister to purchase your pardon—that should be quite ample payment to bend her will. One-third of it will then be divided between you two men as a finder's fee, and the last third will be held here to finance my succession."

John's mouth grew dry. He hadn't planned to tell James about rendering Dubois unconscious and his inability to secure a confession. He'd planned to return to

London and face the queen alone—explain what had happened and take his punishment. "Your Highness, your generosity exceeds my wildest imaginings."

Joining the men at the table, Evelyn pressed praying fingers to her lips while her eyes welled. "We are truly grateful."

"I will forever be your most humble servant," said Kennan.

"Then let us toast to our success." James snapped his fingers at a footman, who poured glasses of sherry for all. "To allies and the future of Great Britain. And you, Sir Kennan, you will be my Lord High Admiral."

Bending into a deep bow, Sir Kennan clasped his hands over his heart. "I am honored, Your Majesty."

The prince smiled regally. "I shall never forget those who have been loyal during my exile, my friends."

They spent the remainder of the afternoon discussing plans for the succession. And later, as John and Evelyn retired to their chambers to dress for the evening meal, his wife took him by the arm and whispered, "I wish I could see my father's face when he learns you've given his gold to Queen Anne."

John dipped his chin and nuzzled into her neck. "It wasn't Hull's gold to begin with, and now we've put it to a far greater purpose."

Chapter Thirty-Eight

I'd like you to remain aboard the ship until I send for you," John said, standing on the deck of the transport they'd taken from Calais to the Pool of London under the guise of Mr. and Mrs. Hay.

By the look in Evelyn's eyes, she was less than fond of the idea. Why should he be surprised? The woman attracted trouble like flies to honey. "You wait until we are about to disembark to tell me this?"

"I could never forgive myself if you were arrested and imprisoned." He drew her into his embrace. "And besides, if for some misbegotten reason my plans go awry, I desperately need you to look after the lads."

She pursed her lips. "You would bring them into this."

"Anything to keep you from harm's way, my love. I allowed you to ferret out Dubois, and it tore my heart to shreds to do so. Should the queen cast aside my plea for leniency, I have no doubt she will send me to the Tower directly."

Evelyn gripped his hands. "Then let us send for the boys, return to France, and put this madness behind us."

"You ken I cannot do that. Thomas and Oliver do not deserve a coward for a father. I will set my affairs to rights or die trying."

"God's mercy." Evelyn drew his fingers to her lips, squeezed her eyes closed, and kissed him. "The queen will grant a pardon because I cannot live without you."

If only he could be certain of her safety, it would mean the world to have his bonny lass beside him as he faced the queen. But he must do this alone. John again pulled her into his embrace. "I never believed it possible, but I love you more than life, more than every breath that fills my lungs with precious air. Please, please promise me you will honor my wishes and remain aboard."

"If you wish it, I will await your return, but I will not be happy until I again hold you in my arms."

Gazing into her mesmerizing eyes, he kissed her. Then he beckoned the two footmen he'd hired to carry the gold and hastened down the gangway, where he hailed a rickety old coach to ferry them to Kensington Palace. John proudly wore Highland garb, leaving periwigs and silks behind. He would face the queen as a Scot, tossing his courtly airs to the wind. Such a bold move might be folly, but he was no longer the Secretary of State and no longer a member of Anne's cabinet. She would see him as the Scotsman he was and none other.

When the coach rolled to a stop, he straightened his red-and-black sash and patted the brooch bearing his family crest—one that had been worn by the chiefs of Clan Erskine for countless generations. With a surge of confidence, he boldly strode to the guardhouse and addressed the queen's dragoons. "The Earl of Mar requests an audience with Her Majesty."

"God blind me. 'Tis the traitor himself," said the lieutenant. "Seize him!"

"Nay!" John held up a gold coin. "One of these for each of you. I will have an audience with the queen and clear my name."

The soldier snatched the coin from his fingers. "You'll go in bloody irons."

"Not irons. However, if you'd enjoy a second coin, you may relieve me of my sword."

The man weighed the doubloon in his palm. "And your dirk, my lord."

"If you insist," John said. "But I must see Her Majesty forthwith. I have gone to great lengths to prove my innocence, and I will be called a traitor no longer."

"Payment first." Each man held out a greedy palm. Once paid, the lieutenant's coins disappeared into a purse at the man's hip. "Affix bayonets, men. If he makes one wrong move, run him through."

John gave the officer a droll frown. "Charming." But he'd bought his way through the gates, thank God. The footmen toting the chest followed while the dragoons escorted John through the familiar halls to the queen's withdrawing room.

"The Earl of Mar," announced the steward in a booming voice.

Queen Anne looked up from her throne, her eyes wide. "Mar? You have quite a nerve coming before me."

He boldly strode forward, bowed his head, and kneeled. "I have come to profess my innocence, Your Majesty."

"Oh? Do make it quick." She sniffed. "For I cannot abide the stench of traitors in my midst."

Remaining on his knee, he looked up. "I am no traitor, and I believe you were misled in taking the word of the conspirator, Claude Dubois, as to my guilt."

Anne smoothed her hands along the shiny mahogany armrests. "Your guilt was professed by Argyll."

"A man who has coveted my position for years."

The queen shifted in her seat and waved her hand through the air. "Then what is this proof you have?"

"After I learned of the extent of Dubois's treachery, I found him at Versailles and the gold he stole, which was intended to pay for duties owed by Kingston-upon-Hull. You may consult with the duke himself. He sought me out before my conviction, asking for my assistance." John beckoned the footmen forward. "Dubois and his accomplices stole this gold from one of the duke's vessels when moored in a Scottish port."

"Thief!" shouted the lieutenant. "Seize him!"

Springing to his feet, John lunged for a guard's sword and unsheathed it from the man's scabbard. Turning in place, the weapon hissed through the air as he faced the dragoons. "I am no thief."

"Stand down," snapped the queen. "Allow me to see this gold."

Panning the sword across the soldiers while they stood with their bayonets at the ready, John eyed each one in turn. "Back away. Now." And once the men had moved clear to the wall, he himself opened the chest and again kneeled. "This is for you, my queen. The spoils of Claude Dubois's treachery have returned to England to compensate you for the damages he wrought."

The queen peered inside the chest, then gestured to the Lord Privy Seal, who examined the contents. "'Tis genuine," he said.

The queen's eyes brightened. "You traveled to France to retrieve this coin on my behalf?"

"I did, Your Highness." That wasn't quite the full truth, but it was the story upon which they had agreed. Besides, the coin should be used for the betterment of Great Britain, the country John fiercely loved.

Anne drummed her fingers. "I could take this gold and still have you thrown in the Tower."

"Aye, you could. But what of our history? For eleven years I acted as your loyal subject. I have supported you in your every endeavor. I have never once given you cause to believe me unfaithful. Why would you now take the word of a miscreant Frenchman, sent here to spy on all of us with intent to seize your kingdom for Louis?" John looked to the gold and frowned, then stared Anne in the eye. "Such allegations against me simply do not hold water."

Anne let out a long sigh. "You have no idea how many nights I lay awake wondering the same. You have never given me cause to doubt you, and in light of the risks you bore to secure this fortune for the crown, I hereby grant your pardon."

A hundred doves took flight in John's breast as he bent forward and kissed the royal ring. "Thank you, Your Highness."

"Now leave me. I am overtired and need rest."

He stood. "I will pray for your good health, madam."

"I'm afraid my health declines with each passing day. Soon I will join George in heaven. The good Lord knows I long to be by his side once again."

After bowing, John returned the sword to the soldier and strode toward the door.

"Mar," called the queen.

He stopped and looked back.

"I expect you will want to resume your position as a cabinet minister."

Clearing his throat, he assumed a respectful stance. He knew Anne too well not to accept. If he followed his heart and refused, she'd see it as an act of rebellion. "Serving you, my queen, is the greatest honor to which a man can aspire."

"I am happy to hear you understand where best to place your loyalties. I shall expect to see you when parliament reconvenes in the spring."

John again bowed. "Your Majesty." As he strode through the courtyard a weight as heavy as the chest of gold lifted from his shoulders. There were only three people on this earth he wanted to see, and one was waiting for him aboard the ship in the Pool of London. With God's grace, on the morrow they would sail for Scotland and join with the other two.

Och, to be a family again.

* * *

Evelyn paced the ship's deck for hours. She watched every coach that stopped beside the pier, and her heartbeat sped with anticipation as she waited for each rider to alight. And while the time droned past, her heart squeezed tighter and tighter until she could scarcely breathe.

"Mrs. Hay," someone called behind her as she continued her vigil.

"Good heavens, Mrs. Hay. You ought to come in and eat something, else you'll wear down the timbers on my deck," said the captain, falling into pace beside her.

Evelyn gave him a look, suddenly remembering her alias. "Forgive me, but I'm anxious for Mr. Hay's return."

"Worrying will not make him arrive any faster."

"I know, but I cannot help myself."

A shiny black coach stopped with a royal crest emblazoned on the door. Holding her breath, Evelyn grasped the rail.

Can it be?

Yes! The Earl of Mar stepped to the footpath with a bouquet of roses in his hand.

Tears stung Evelyn's eyes as she drew her hands over her mouth. "John!"

Without a moment's hesitation and throwing all decorum out the window, she ran down the gangway and flung herself into her husband's arms. "Thank Heaven and all the silkies in Scotland you're here." Stretching up onto her toes, she smothered him with dozens of kisses.

"Why, Lady Mar, I do believe you are happy to see me," he said, spinning her in a circle.

"You absolutely must tell me all, and do not omit a single word!"

He stopped but didn't set her down. "Things proceeded much as we'd planned. Her Majesty accepted the gift in lieu of your father's owed duties, mind you, and asked if I wanted my position on her cabinet reinstated."

"And how did you respond?"

John produced the enormous bouquet of Maiden's Blush roses—pink this time. "I had no choice but to politely accept, but it was as difficult as submitting to a pair of smithy's tongs. Bless it, Eve, there is nowhere I'd rather be than at Alloa spending the rest of my days with you and the lads."

Chapter Thirty-Nine

Three months later

I'll race you to the first pile of leaves!" hollered Oliver, gaining a head start on his older brother.

With longer legs, it only took a few strides for Thomas to overtake the little one. "Never. I'm the king of the hill, not you!"

Evelyn looped her arm through her husband's elbow. "Are you intending to allow Tom to act so domineering?"

"Let the lads have their fun. I'll intervene should they come to blows."

Evelyn gave his shoulder a playful thwack. "Growing up with two sisters, boys seem so inordinately rambunctious to me."

John arched a tawny eyebrow, amusement dancing in

his eyes. "Do not tell me as the eldest you never wielded your power over Frances and Phoebe."

She thought back to the many times she'd scoffed at her sisters' antics or scolded them for their juvenile behavior. "I suppose you're right." As they walked beneath the canopy of ancient oaks, she leaned into him. "But I'll tolerate no bullying and no blood."

"Agreed." John gave her a playful nudge. "Speaking of your family, I've received a rather scathing missive from your father."

"Truly? After so much time has passed, I had assumed he'd forgotten that you gave his gold to the queen."

"But it wasn't *his* gold," they both said in unison, laughing.

As they passed beneath a low-hanging branch, she plucked the last remaining leaf and twirled it between her fingers. "I do hope Papa wasn't overly harsh."

John shrugged. "Perhaps that's why we must face bullies from time to time in our lives—so we do not take angry dukes too seriously."

"Oh dear, that doesn't sound good."

"He blamed me for purchasing our pardon and said if you weren't his daughter, he would have preferred to see us hang from the gallows."

"Truly?" Evelyn stopped. "I'm surprised he didn't demand some form of recompense."

"Well, he did mention something about ensuring his grandson receives a good settlement upon my death."

"Lovely. But grandson? Do you know something I do not?"

"I stand corrected…he mentioned future grandson and indicated that in his opinion I have fallen down on my duties because he hadn't received news of any expected additions to the family."

She winked, straightening the tartan across his shoulder. Good heavens, her husband was a deliciously braw Highlander. "I can attest without question your duties are being performed quite satisfactorily, my lord."

John tickled her ribs. "Only satisfactorily?"

Jumping aside, Evelyn giggled. "Pleasingly?"

He picked her up and ran toward a stack of leaves. "What about expertly?"

"Yes!" she hollered, playfully slapping his arm. "Now put me down."

"As you wish," he said, laughing and depositing her in a huge pile.

"Heeelp!" Evelyn cried, brushing leaves away from her face.

"We'll save you, Countess," hollered Thomas as the two boys dashed to the rescue.

John caught each of his sons and hurled them onto the leaves. "She's mine and so are you! I'll have you for me supper!"

In a flurry of legs and arms, they rolled around, spreading the neatly raked leaves everywhere. Evelyn clung to her bonnet and slipped away as the two boys jumped on John's back.

She clapped her hands. "Conquer the towering beast!"

John glanced over his shoulder as he tossed Oliver in the air. "Has everyone turned against me?"

"I'm the king!" shouted Thomas, climbing onto his father's shoulders.

John flung him deep into the pile. "I'm king and you'd best not forget it."

A sudden bout of queasiness hit, burning Evelyn's

throat. She clutched her stomach and stepped away from the game. She'd experienced a few waves of nausea of late and fanned her face, hoping the cool air would help. But the churning grew worse. Trying to gulp down the bile, she pressed her fingers to her lips.

Oh no!

She started for the house.

"Evelyn?" John called.

"I'm fine," she said, right before she gagged. To her horror, she lost her breakfast on the front lawn, of all places.

"You're ill!" The earl raced beside her, panic contorting his features. "Why did you not tell me you were feeling poorly?"

She swallowed, hard. "I didn't know I was sick."

Oliver grasped her hand. "But you were perfectly well a moment ago."

She patted her chest, trying to will the queasiness away. "I was indeed. Perhaps I simply need a spot of peppermint tea."

"Tea?" John swept her into his arms. "You are not going to eat or drink a thing until you are tucked into bed."

"But—"

"Send for the physician! Take Thomas and Oliver to the nursery," John bellowed as he pushed inside the door.

"But, Da," Thomas complained.

"Now is not the time to argue. Go find Mrs. Kerr." As John headed for the stairs, Swenson appeared in the entry. "Have Lucinda bring up a tonic for an upset stomach."

The butler bowed. "Straightaway, m'lord. A footman has already been dispatched to fetch the physician."

"Thank you," John said over his shoulder as he took

two stairs at a time. "We'll have you set to rights in no time, *mo leannan*. I do not want you to worry."

"Safe in your arms?" She rested her head on her husband's chest. "I'm far from worried."

He pushed into her chamber, rested her on the bed. "Under the coverlet with you."

"I'm feeling much better now." She started to rise, but John nudged her back down to the pillows. "I'm sure all I need is a glass of water."

"You've just been violently ill. I'm not about to allow you to rise from this bed until you've been examined by the doctor."

Sighing, Evelyn pursed her lips. She'd seen this side of John before. "Very well. But I think you may be over-reacting."

He gave a disbelieving snort. "I never overreact."

"Right. And insisting I remain abed for an entire week after I bumped my head when we visited London Bridge wasn't a tad excessive."

John kissed her temple. "It most certainly was not."

"I beg your pardon, my lord, my lady," said Lucinda, entering with a mug. "I've brought a tincture of peppermint and dandelion root."

"Lovely." Evelyn drank, then made a sour face. "Goodness, that's awful."

"The worse it tastes, the better it is for you," said John, smoothing his hand over her hair.

After she managed to drink half the horrible mixture, Swenson announced the physician. He removed his tricorn hat. "What seems to be the problem, my lord?"

John stood, gravely shaking his head. "It came on like a rogue wind. One moment Her Ladyship was fine and the next she was on death's door."

Evelyn stifled a guffaw. "Hardly. My breakfast didn't agree with me is all. I am perfectly fine now."

"I see," said the physician, managing a grave expression.

John thrust a stern pointed finger at the doctor's chest. "I'll tolerate no lances and no bleeding."

"Understood, though I must examine the patient before I can make a proper diagnosis." The man set his bag on the bedside table. "I'd like to visit with Lady Mar alone, if I may. Of course, the maid may remain."

John clapped a hand over his heart. "Good God, is it that grave?"

"I have no idea, Your Lordship. But if I am to give Lady Mar a proper examination, it is best done without you present."

"Of course." John took Evelyn's hand. "As long as that meets with Her Ladyship's approval."

She kissed his fingers. "I'm feeling better with every breath."

"'Tis good to hear." He again kissed her forehead. "I shall wait just outside the door should you need me."

Once John had taken his leave, Evelyn apologized. "The earl may have been a bit hasty when he sent for you."

"Not to worry, m'lady. He has cause. If you don't mind me saying, the last countess went downhill very quickly after she contracted the fever."

Evelyn watched as he drew down the bedclothes. "So I've been told. Awful that."

"May I examine you?"

After she nodded, he proceeded to press his ear against her chest and listen to her heart and her breathing. He poked and prodded, repeatedly asking "Does this hurt?"

all the way down to her abdomen, where he promptly did quite a bit of pushing around.

The furrow in the physician's brow grew deeper. "Hmm."

Evelyn clutched her fists beneath her chin. "What is it?"

"Have you missed your courses?"

"Courses?" The question mortified her down to her toes. No man had ever spoken to her about *that*. Still, things had been so chaotic, Evelyn hadn't thought to track her monthly curse.

"Yes," Lucinda said from the foot of the bed. "Her Ladyship hasn't had a show since her return from France."

Fluttering swarmed throughout Evelyn's body as she grinned. "Heavens, I think you're right."

* * *

John pushed away from the bedchamber door when footsteps approached. He'd done his damnedest to listen in, but they'd kept their voices so low, he hadn't heard a thing. Further, a bit of fire shot up the back of his neck as Evelyn emerged with the doctor and they both appeared happier than a pair of larks.

He grasped his wife by the hands. "What are you doing out of bed, my dearest?"

"You were right, m'lord." The physician patted John on the shoulder. "Bleeding out the toxin made no sense at all."

John's jaw dropped as he glanced between the two. "What the devil is going on?"

The doctor tipped his hat and bowed. "You'd best hasten to tell him, m'lady, else His Lordship will be the one needing a tonic."

As the doctor retreated, Evelyn laughed—she bloody laughed!

"What?" John asked, ready to swoop her up and chain her to the bed until he was convinced she had made a full recovery.

"It turns out"—she spun away and into her chamber—"I am with child!"

"Child?" John stumbled inside, managing to close the door behind. "You mean to say you are not gravely ill? What of your sickness outside?"

"Many women succumb to bouts of queasiness when they are expecting." She turned a lovely shade of rose. "I would assume you had experience with... with the whole process."

"I've heard of the morning sickness, but the boys' mother was never afflicted." He grasped her hands and squeezed. "Are you truly well enough to be out of bed?"

She gripped his fingers and danced in a circle. "I've never felt better."

"Better?" The woman was in the family way. Caution was ever so necessary—and she flitted about her chamber like a happy puppy. "Should you be dancing? Should you not at least sit with your feet up?"

"No, no, no!" She stopped and cupped his cheeks. "The doctor says as long as I am feeling well, I need no restrictions, aside from a tad more rest."

Evelyn looked so happy, John couldn't help but grin, though he did so cautiously. "Did he say tad?"

"Not exactly. He said a wee bit."

And then the realization hit him. Dropping to his knees, John took Evelyn's hands and kissed them. "So, we're going to have a bairn, you and I?"

"We are."

"When?"

"In the spring." She cradled his head to her breast. "Oh, John, you cannot believe how happy this makes me. Thomas and Oliver will have a sister."

"Or a brother."

"Yes... or twins."

He pulled back, his head swimming. "Does the doctor believe you are expecting twins?"

"No, it is far too early to tell, but my mother was a twin... and one never knows!"

"Och, lad or lass, twins or triplets, our bairns will be born into a house filled with laughter and love."

"Indeed they will." His bonny wife smiled with all the radiance of the sun and kissed him. "I love you."

John picked her up and cradled her in his arms, cherishing her every breath. "I never thought I'd be able to feel again, but then I met you, Lady Eve. You breathed life into my soul and I will love you for the rest of my days."

Author's Note

Ever since I visited Alloa Tower in Scotland, I have been looking forward to writing John Erskine's story, and it came earlier in my plan due to my editor's enthusiasm. Mar's life was fraught with contradictions. Born in 1675, he was the 23rd Earl of Mar, or the 27th, or the 6th, or the 11th, depending on which record I read, though the general consensus was the 23rd. He did inherit crippling debt from his father. He became a statesman and held many positions, including that of Secretary of State for Scotland.

Mar's first countess, Margaret Hay, bore him a son, Thomas Erskine, and I used literary license to write his brother, Oliver, into the story. John then married Frances Pierrepont (Evelyn in the story), who was the first daughter of the Duke of Kingston-upon-Hull. This union enabled him to clear his father's debts, and in conversation with a historian at Alloa Tower, I discovered he did build a canal for his coal mine, as well as add a grand manor to the tower. Though Lady Mar grew up in Thoresby Hall, the building that exists on the site today was constructed in 1864. The Thoresby lands were acquired by her family in 1633, and the first grand house was built in 1670.

In 1707 John signed his name to the Treaty of Union (also known as the Act of Union) to prevent a civil war between England and Scotland over the succession to the throne. Also, at the time, Scotland was in a critical financial situation, and many politicians saw no alternative but to agree to the union of parliaments. This made the Earl of Mar unpopular with many of his contemporaries. Dubbed Bobbin' John, he led the Jacobite rebellion of 1715, raising the standard for James Francis Edward Stuart, the Old Pretender, who, by the way, granted John the title of Duke of Mar, though the post was never recognized by the British monarch.

He and Evelyn (Frances) endured difficult lives, and I felt they deserved a story with a happy ending. I truly believe he was misunderstood and misrepresented in many historical accounts of his life.

Also, it is important to note that the Serpentine in Hyde Park, often referred to as a river though it is actually a lake, is a man-made body of water and was not constructed until 1730. I considered placing the boat-sailing scene in Saint James Park, but in 1713, Saint James was a dangerous place frequented by thieves and people of unsavory character—definitely not a place for children and ladies. Thus I did, yet again, lean on literary license and created the scene in Hyde Park, Serpentine and all.

Look for Kennan Cameron's story in
The Highland Rogue.

Coming in spring 2020.

About the Author

Multiaward-winning and Amazon All-Star author Amy Jarecki likes to grab life, latch on, and reach for the stars. She's married to a mountain-biking pharmacist and has put four kids through college. She studies karate, ballet, yoga, and often you'll find her hiking Utah's Santa Clara Hills. Reinventing herself a number of times, Amy sang and danced with the Follies, was a ballet dancer, a plant manager, and an accountant for Arnott's Biscuits in Australia. After earning her MBA from Heroit-Watt University in Scotland, she dove into the world of Scottish historical romance and hasn't returned. Become a part of her world and learn more about Amy's books on amyjarecki.com.